ALIEN BROTHER

David Lawrence

First originally published by Page Publishing, Inc. 2017

ISBN 978-1-917736-57-2 (Paperback)
ISBN 978-1-917736-58-9 (Digital)
ISBN 978-1-917736-61-9 (Hardback)

Printed in the United States of America

CONTENTS

PROLOGUE

The heat continued to surge. The humidity was high like a sauna turning hotter and hotter. It was only 10:00 a.m., and the temperature was 89 degrees. The birds had stopped singing. An eerie quiet pervaded the dense woods. Every living thing was taken aback by the stifling heat.

The fluid flow within him was surging with great force. As a balloon expanded to its limit, his heart could not continue to survive the rate of flow. Regardless of any action that might be taken, system failure was inevitable.

Clyde first sensed something was wrong when his feet began to miss the railroad ties.

At first he was amused at his sudden loss of coordination.

It took years of habit to be able to walk the seldom-used spur between West End and Carthage. Long ago this once-popular transportation line had been abandoned. It was now only occasionally used by the railroad maintenance cars carrying personnel or equipment to the main terminal in Southern Pines, North Carolina.

The railroad ties had worn away with little maintenance. They were scheduled to be fixed, but the priority was very low, and they suffered from lack of attention. For Clyde, the spur was the most direct route to his sister's home. He used it when he left the small millhouse where he could make a few dollars doing odd cleanup jobs. Despite the shape the railroad ties were in, Clyde had learned how to walk them without having to constantly look where his feet would land. He took pride in that.

Even with a bottle of Black Aces or some of Jimmy's special white brew, Clyde could walk the ties better than most sober men. Seemingly a small insignificant accomplishment, yet for this sixty-seven-year-old alcoholic, his sanity demanded he feel good about anything he could do well. Born with an Irish man's temper and stubbornness, Clyde didn't do well taking orders. This and his PTSD from Vietnam hampered his ability to stay focused and complete tasks. The Lord knew there were not too many things for Clyde to feel good about.

As soon as he would reach his sister's home, she would wear him down with her complaints about his lifestyle and what a disappointment he had been to Daddy. Muriel didn't mean to be so hard on Clyde. She had her own characteristics of the Irish temper. Physically she followed the Irish line. She was not terribly tall. She had a certain type of chin, often seen in Ireland but hard to describe. Her head was of a "long" shape (longer than wide). It was of a type often characterized as "Mediterranean," after their Roman ancestors. She wore her hair shoulder length in such a way it gave a strange, almost wild look. It gave the impression she was always having a bad hair day. "Unruly" would be an understatement to describe her hair. Her Roman ancestors would often describe this kind of Celtic hair as like that in a horse's mane. Her head gave witness to the expression "my hair has a mind of its own." Yet everything else about her, contrary to Clyde, was absolutely "neat as a pin."

She and Clyde had always been very close as children. It seemed like when he got back from Vietnam, his life spiraled downhill. She tried to get Clyde to counseling. She tried to get the VA to help. Clyde refused any help. He just turned to drugs and alcohol to drive his demons away. Muriel was eventually able to get Clyde off of drugs, thanks to the loving and persistent help of Bill Nicholass, a trained substance counselor with Muriel's church.

Even though Clyde had been drug free for years, he never found the strength to release himself from the grips of alcohol.

In the Army, Clyde was 5'9" tall and 150 lb. Now at sixty-seven, Clyde looked more like 5'4".

He walked with a stoop. He carried his head and shoulders habitually bowed forward. He refused to wear the clothes Muriel would purchase. She did so in hopes she could get Clyde to wear them to church. Try as hard as she could, she could not get Clyde to abandon what she described as a hideous face cover. Clyde wore a semblance of the "Winnfield Wide" sideburns. They extended below the ear combined, but not connected, to a mustache that extended downward from the corners of the mouth to the jawline.

It was a style popularized by the character Jules Winnfield in the movie *Pulp Fiction.*

Although Clyde made attempts to keep it groomed, normally it lay as a shaggy mess that Gave Clyde an unkempt, shaggy look. This feature— combined with his light skin, pale eyes, freckles, and reddish undertones in hair color—gave him a menacing look.

With his drooping coveralls and his brightly colored corduroy shirt, Clyde gave all the appearance of an old prospector plucked from a 1930s stream panning for gold. Only his duck-billed Army hat gave him any indication he was living in the year of 1965.

It had been a warm summer night when the forest first spoke to Clyde. He was slowly waddling back from the West End. Having downed half a bottle of white lightening that he got from Jimmy Crow for two dollars, Clyde was feeling no pain. As he tipped the bottle to enjoy another sip, Clyde's foot missed the railroad tie, and Clyde and his bottle fell off the pitched rise of the railroad track into the ditch below. Clyde began cussing and fuming as he realized not only did he stumble, but in doing so, he had landed on his bottle, which now lay in pieces as the earth drank its remains.

Clyde started to get up when he felt a sharp pain in his left knee. Barely able to raise himself, Clyde was looking at the rise he would have to surmount when the forest first spoke to him.

It scared Clyde at first. He tensed with fear as he waited for some of the local hooligans to jump out of the woods and beat him up. They were known to roam these parts and smoke dope and drink and do whatever. Usually he could hear them long before they could see him. That way he always avoided any confrontation.

Yet no one jumped out. The voice continued. It was gentle and assuring. Clyde shook his head repeatedly as his senses, what little there were left, seemed to spot a tiny holly bush as the source for the sound. Clyde wanted to look closer. He stepped toward the bush, and the pain shot through his leg. He put his hand into the bush even though he throbbed in pain. A tiny glow rippled around his hand. The voice continued. "I am rather weak right now, but if you let me walk with you awhile, I can take away the pain."

"Surely it was either Mudda Nature *herself or someone is playing themselves a fine joke,"* Clyde thought to himself.

Clyde was too full of drink that night to remember it all. Yet he remembered *Mudda Nature* had asked if she could walk within Clyde for a while and that she could take his pain away.

"Sure," he had said not understanding in the least what was happening. Then as an afterthought Clyde muttered "Ya won hurt me?"

"No," *Mudda Nature* replied.

"An ya won try to change me? Everyone always try'n to change me."

"I can do some wonderful things for you."

"I don wan ya to change nothen about me, is that clear?" His question demanded in his Irish red neck brogue. Then in an afterthought he added, "Except for the pain in me leg."

Thus, the simple bargain was made. Clyde did as the presence instructed. Whatever happened next, Clyde didn't remember.

Muriel went into a rage when Clyde talked about his union with *Mudda Nature*. Even when Clyde would demonstrate how healthy his legs were by dancing an old Scottish jig on the living room floor, Muriel would not put up with his talk that *Mudda Nature* had given him new legs. Soon after that he kept the secret to himself.

Even Clyde forgot the bargain he had made until one Friday night so long ago. He had received his small wage. Together with Jimmy's special brew, he had forged his way home. It was dark. Fortunately the moon was ¾ full giving some light to his path. A small rain had started to fall. It didn't hurry Clyde though. The cool rain was soothing and a welcomed relief. Besides, nothing hurried Clyde. His legs felt strong and the white lightening warmed Clyde's belly.

Because of the rain and the rustling of the leaves as they sought out the life blood of the water, he didn't hear the bushes move. Clyde wasn't actually aware of anyone's presence out on the tracks other than his own until he saw the two of them standing on the track ahead blocking his path.

"Hey, ole man, don ya know it's rannen? Ya'll needs ta git yur ass unda cuver." They both laughed. They laughed as if they knew something Clyde didn't know. It was a sinister laugh.

Their cold laugh made Clyde stop. Clyde turned to look behind him for an escape route. There behind him was a third figure walking slowly toward his back.

In deep panic, Clyde, for the first time reached into his past. "Okay Mudda Nature," he said quietly to himself, "now's da time to len a hand."

"The ole man's talken to hisself." From behind Clyde came the voice also slurred from the effects of too much drink.

Suddenly, Clyde was surrounded by the three thugs. The one from the rear grabbed Jimmie's bottle. Clyde lost his balance. As he stumbled from the railroad tie, the larger of the two thugs in front pushed him roughly to the ground. Clyde looked up as the rain made grooves in his face and poured from his beard.

Each of the thugs snickered at the pitiful sight of the old man holding onto the railroad tie as if he were on a bridge about to fall hundreds of feet should he let go.

Suddenly, Max Sumler, the leader of the crew, leaned over and snarled. He was only sixteen, yet he had the body and strength of a grown man.

"Look you ole piece of sheet, we know ya got paid. Now ya give it up now, or we will beat it outa ya and leave ya here cryin' in yur sheet. Ya hear me?"

Clyde tried to get to his feet. The thug standing next to Max let out with a kick. His boot caught Clyde in the side. The blow sent Clyde reeling into the small muddy rain stream running alongside the track. Clyde landed face first into the mud and water. With mud dripping from his face, Clyde turned and looked at Max.

"Now is da time ta help Mudda Nature," Clyde muttered to himself.

Then with brazen contempt for the thugs, Clyde shouted at them, "Ya betta not fuck wid Mudda Nature you bastards."

Max was just looking for an excuse to beat the old man up. His father was an alcoholic who took his life's misery out on him. Max felt he had all the lessons a person needed on how to be a bully. Now he intended to do to Clyde just as his father had done to him.

Max moved swiftly off the track down to where Clyde lay. He picked Clyde up with one hand. Anger burned across his face. His eyes bulged and his mouth became a sinister smirk. His right hand came back. Then at full speed his fist was launched at Clyde's cheek.

Clyde's hand instantly reached out in front of him as if to protect himself from what would be a devastating blow. Max's fist struck Clyde's open hand with full force. Max stiffened as the pain shot through him.

It hurt as much as it had when he punched his father's barn door in anger. Stunned, he and the other two thugs watched Clyde's hand slowly close around Max's fist. The pain and force caused Max to come right up on his toes. His head bent back, and his eyes closed as the pain cascaded through every inch of his body.

In the same motion, and using Max's straightened arm as a counter weight, Clyde came up on his feet. The thug standing behind Clyde, not believing what he had seen raised his right hand to come down on Clyde's neck. Without even acknowledging the threat, Clyde's right arm swung back catching the thug square in the chest. As if hit by a 2x4, the thug expelled a large volume of air. The force not only knocked the breath out of him but threw him back about 5 feet where he lay moaning and groaning in the same stream of mud from which Clyde had just removed himself.

Max's third companion, still on his feet, pulled his switch blade. In an instant he launched the knife into Clyde's side. Shouting and swearing at Clyde, he attempted to pull it out to strike again. Clyde let go of Max who fell backwards. Almost quicker than the eye could see, Clyde's right hand wrapped itself around the thug's wrist. An aura of white, blue and orange came from Clyde's hand and enveloped the young thug. The thug became suddenly very quiet. His face turned blank and he sat down on the railroad tie just staring up at the stars.

Clyde removed the steel blade from his side. In front of Max's unbelieving eyes, he crumbled the knife with his bare hand and threw it aside.

As if throwing a lasso, the aura that had enveloped the knife-wielding thug spun out from Clyde's body and enveloped all four of them.

Clearly heard, by each, was Clyde speaking. Yet it was a voice different than Clyde's voice. It had a different tone. It spoke in an articulate way not with the uneducated Irish red neck drawl of Clyde. *"Boys, there is a better life for you on this planet than the one you have presently chosen to live. Go. Make a better life for you and those around you."*

The mesmeric voice, which was Clyde's and yet it wasn't Clyde's, engrossed the thugs. As the white, blue, orange aura seemed to surround and go thru the thugs, they stood or sat where they were. It was as if they were suddenly suspended in animation. The aura shimmered with phosphorescence. It moved in, around, and through them.

As quickly as it had begun, the aura retreated back into Clyde. The thugs regained their senses. They looked around at each other and then at Clyde.

Max looked at Clyde with serene countenance. "Sorry ole man. We had no right ta do what we set out ta do. We shant botha ya ever again. Come on fellas."

With that, the thugs quietly and quickly disappeared into the woods back the way they came.

As Clyde gained control of his own senses, he couldn't believe what he had just witnessed. He had seen it. He had felt the surges of strength. Yet it was more like an out-of-the-body experience. It was as though he, in fact, had been a spectator.

Suddenly his senses yanked him back to his own self with searing pain coming from the burning knife incision in his side. He pulled up his tattered shirt. He looked at where the knife had penetrated. It was bright red where the blood had already begun to ooze. The actual cut was not more than an inch in width. Clyde had seen men cut like this before. He had seen some men die from a cut like this.

"It don't look like much, but dems the dangerous kind," he thought.

Suddenly something caught his eye. As he looked closer he could see a glow around the edges of the cut. The blood had stopped flowing. He stretched his neck to get closer to the cut. He watched as the skin closed around the rapidly healing cut.

"Damn," he kept repeating to himself in amazement, "Damn."

"Mudda Nature, we make a great team, yup a great team," Clyde muttered to himself as he straightened up his clothes. He walked on down the tracks with a new confidence in his step.

Despite his enthusiasm and excitement, he kept the presence of his companion secret. Everyone already felt he was daft. Surely this would be all the excuse Muriel would need to have him locked up.

For years Clyde and his companion existed this way. The companion kept to the bargain they had made. Despite its occasional pleas to Clyde to let it bring health to Clyde, Clyde rejected any changes or assistance unless requested.

So it was. The companion never interfered or worked any changes to Clyde's benefit except on occasion when Clyde would call upon his guest for some help.

Now many years later, Clyde's body, without warning, was exacting the price for the toil Clyde had put it through.

Now at 10:00 a.m. exactly, on Thursday morning, Clyde's foot slipped on the railroad tie. It would be on this extremely hot day in the middle of July, Clyde was to pay the price for ignoring his health for so long.

Upon losing his coordination, Clyde could have called upon his companion for help. Yet he didn't. He didn't because his mind was not aware of it. He didn't know what had happened. Somewhere in the middle of the second stroke, there may have been some slight awareness. It was all too sudden for Clyde to ask for help. In any case, the shock had quickly closed down Clyde's awareness of anything. His system failure brought his earthly existence to an end.

The companion had waited for Clyde to ask for help. It never came. Such was their bargain. Then something happened just before Clyde's heart stop for the final time. The companion noticed it; a force within Clyde left Clyde's body. The companion had noticed it before and had been unable to identify it. Now just before they were both to expire, the companion sensed Clyde's inner force leave.

It was late that night when Muriel called the Sheriff's office to report Clyde as missing. The sheriff's office was well aware of Clyde and his drinking. "Miss Muriel," they responded, "Clyde has probably laid down some place to sleep off... well, you know what I mean?"

Muriel protested but she knew they were right. No one was going to be concerned about an old drunk not showing up for one night. It would be the next day before railroad personnel would call the Sheriff's office and report they had found Clyde Brewer's body on the side of one of the old railroad spurs between West End and Carthage.

Although grief stricken, Clyde's sister and only relative was relieved in a strange sense. Now this crazy man who had fooled everyone by lasting into his mid-eighties could hopefully find some piece. She would no longer have to worry about Clyde making it home safely each night.

With nothing but a fixed income and expensive medicines prescribed to take each month, Muriel had little money left over for a funeral. She worried about getting a loan to bury poor Clyde. Over that and Clyde's wasted life, Muriel was caught between this frustration turned to anger and her love for the Clyde she knew as a little girl; the little Clyde who existed before his life twisted him so.

Muriel was taken aback when the recently elected chairman of the town council called and said he knew Clyde and that he was a special soul. He had only been twenty years old when he first was elected to the council. Despite his young age of twenty when he was elected, he seemed very wise. That plus his personality had given him the votes he needed to be the youngest ever to be elected to the town council. It was to no one's surprise that eventually he would be voted to chair the council. He asked if she would object to his paying for the funeral and then asked if he could give Clyde's eulogy. Muriel was overcome by such outreach from such a member of the community.

At the funeral, many people attended. Muriel's good friend from church put her arm around her. "Wow Muriel who would have guessed Clyde knew so many people?" Muriel was speechless.

It was a lovely service. Clyde was in the finest of caskets. At the eulogy, she listened to the young council man tell how meeting Clyde had changed his life and given him a sense of purpose.

As people made their way out of the funeral home, Muriel approached the council man. "I was apparently not aware of many of Clyde's friends. Your eulogy was beautiful. Thank you."

"Yes, ma'am, I knew brother Clyde in a very special way. I owe him more than I could tell you. As a matter of fact, he gave me every month a small pittance and asked me to invest it for him. I think you will be very pleased what he has left you."

You could have knocked Muriel over with a feather. "Oh my god," she exclaimed, "I never knew." Of course Clyde had never put anything away for a rainy day but the council man knew Muriel would refuse any more charity.

"Now I have taken care of all the funeral expenses, but none of that comes out of what he left you." The man put his hand on Muriel's shoulder and smiled gently. He excused himself after telling her that if she ever needed anything to let him know. Muriel was speechless. She muttered a "thank you," as he moved away to greet some of the others.

Muriel stood there in shock trying to understand the connection between the man and her dear Clyde.

"Muriel," one of Muriel's church friends called to her as she watched the council man making his way out of the funeral home, "how did you ever get him to give such a beautiful eulogy?" She asked.

Muriel gained her composure and cast an irritated glance at her friend. "Well, Beth, he just volunteered. Said he just felt obliged to do it."

"Maybe," Muriel continued as she turned her eyes toward the exit, "there was a part of Clyde we all just didn't see. To tell you the truth, I myself never knew Max Sumler was a friend of Clyde.

CHAPTER 1

2002
THE CONTACT

It was pitch dark when Jon returned to his home. His mind was having difficulty comprehending what had just happened in the woods. He felt he was insane to have agreed to the strange bargain he had made.

"I have to do this, if there is any hope it might help Lance," he thought to himself.

At the same time as he was trying to rationalize what he had just done, the first tremor struck. From the middle of his back up thru his neck into his head, the pain was so deep, so intense. Surely someone or something had just laid into him with a heavy axe. For a moment his mind took him back to the beating he had survived near the road house.

Yet there was no one there. At least there was no one there he could see. Now the pain began to come in waves. They were excruciating. He began to spin around at the door way. He lurched forward. His subconscious led him to the bedroom wherein Lance had spent some precious time before he had to leave for home. The thought of his son brought a flicker of relief. It was much too brief. Then the relentless pain, now in his buttocks, grasped him as a dog might grab its favorite toy before shaking it in feverous motion.

A slight grasp at consciousness, the thought he was having a brutal heart attack. Before he could linger with rationale thought, he lost consciousness and complete control as his body collapsed on the bed. Now he was no longer able to feel any pain. An observer would have thought otherwise. Surely he must be feeling pain as his face grimaced one minute and then relaxed the next only to go back to another strange distorted grimace. His eyes, wide opened, stared as his body pulsated with the tremors that would be expected of someone in the middle of seizures. Throughout the night his body would react this way.

Within him, Jon's organs, his pathology, the science of the mechanical, physical, and biochemical functions of his tissues and organs was in a state of change. The 1.3 gallons of blood flowing every single minute through almost 100,000 kilometers (62,000 miles) of blood vessels were as if in a raging storm. Every cell was undergoing examination and change as if being remodeled by some outside source that was now inside. Jon's molecular makeup was in the middle of drastic changes.

Likened to a race car being tuned up while in the middle of a Daytona 500 as it was flying down the track, Jon's body heaved up and down, back and forth as his internal and external mechanical, physical, and biochemical make up was changed or adjusted. Every fiber and muscle was examined and reexamined until they were in perfect condition.

From the view point of a molecule within him it was like an explosion of the universe wherein a new planet is created. From the outside to a visitor looking in, it would look like a beautiful multicolor light show with glowing pastels and sharp colors intermingled over and under and through Jon's helpless body as he heaved up and down and back and forth on the bed. The waves of light coming from Jon's body played melodically off the walls and ceiling of the room.

As the night lingered on the intensity of the light storm lessened. Jon's body became more relaxed and soon he was lying quietly. His breathing was deep. A medical examination of him at this time would reveal a body of a much younger man. Imperfections were changed to perfections. The old was changed to new.

Now Jon lay peaceful engaged in a deep resting sleep.

At 6:30 a.m., the alarm clock announced the beginning of a new day.

Jon opened his eyes. As he laid there in the same clothes he had worn the day before, he slowly moved about. He had a sense there was something different. At first He couldn't put his finger on what it was. Perhaps it was an after effect of the beers he had the night before. But as soon as he thought that he dismissed the thought. He began to stretch. As he shrugged his shoulders, he realized the pain he was always waking up to in his injured back was not there. As he sat up to turn and get out of bed, he saw the blood on the pillow.

"What the... ?"

Then he noticed the teeth rolling around in the bed.

Again, he exclaimed "What the... ? He began to feel freaked out. Immediately he jumped out of the bed and ran into the bathroom. As he hesitantly looked into the mirror, he stood there startled by what he saw.

He couldn't believe what he saw. The face looking back at him was not the one he went to bed with. The slight childhood scar he had under his right eye was gone. His skin was absent of the few freckles he had and was clear and vibrant. And his teeth... It was like someone had pulled all his teeth and replaced them with clean, new, white dentures. He reached into his mouth and pulled on his teeth. They were real.

"How can this be?" He said to himself.

Suddenly he was caught up with the thought he had to be at work. Even so, Jon was mesmerized and dumbfounded by this new him.

Looking at his arm where the burn scars had been, they were no longer visible. Instead, his arm was clear. His back, which was sore from a 4x4 which had fallen on it at work, felt strong and without pain.

Quickly pulling of his clothes and getting into the shower to get ready for work, Jon could not help but try to find reality, some explanation as to what was going on. As the water beat down, Jon began to remember the night before. He remembered the deal he had made with the energy source who claimed he could heal Lance who was in a hospital in Massachusetts after being hit by a hit and run driver. He remembered the strange source had asked to be allowed to reside within Jon.

Three days earlier

It was just another gorgeous day in July in the small community of Carthage, NC. A light breeze kept the 92-degree heat from feeling wickedly oppressive. From the vantage of an old Pine, which Jon rested against, he scanned the 7 acres on which his temporary home rested.

He looked up at the old loblolly pine which stood a majestic 60 feet slightly swaying in the breeze. "Sorry, fella," Jon muttered to himself as he scanned the damage done by beetles. Remembering what the county extension agent had told him when he sought out an explanation for the apparent demise of this long time resident, "Loblolly pine is generally the preferred host of the southern pine beetle, which is the most destructive insect for this species," the agent had shared. Jon measured the tree by sight to see how it would fall when he laid it down.

Jon could, but preferred not to have to climb the tree and take it down in sections. Betsy Collingswood, from whom Jon was renting the double wide, had come down to look at the tree which leaned ominously close to the doublewide. She loved trees and would always seek any alternative to taking one down. Reluctantly, she had agreed this one should probably come down. She offered to bring in a crew to do so. Jon had convinced her he could do it, would rather do it, and it would save Betsy some money. In the brief time she had known Jon when he answered her ad for the rental unit, Betsy sensed Jon was a quiet, focused man who with his carpenter skills could probably do just about anything he set his mind on. He had added a back deck, installed new windows and made numerous other improvements to the property. She had smiled at Jon, shrugged her shoulders as if to say okay, and ambled back up to her house which sat on the end of the cul-de-sac known as McCrory Rd. As she thought about the task of taking down the tree, the thought of liability quickly flashed across her mind but she dismissed it as soon as it appeared.

Betsy hadn't known much about Jon except from his rental application. Then of course there was the personal reference from a local resident. The man gave Jon high praises. However, Betsy didn't know the guy. Interestingly she never did check his other references. That was very unusual for her. There was just something about him. Whatever it was, she liked it. "Won't be the first time I have gotten burnt by a misjudging of character," she had thought to herself. "Yet," her mind fast forwarded to the present and other thoughts rushed in, "he has been here for about 3 yrs. and has been nothing but a perfect tenant."

As Betsy climbed the slight incline that led to her home at 447 McCrory Rd, she mused over what she knew of Jon. Jon had been born in a Northern Community in a small town approximately 7 miles from Boston, Massachusetts; a town called Reading. According to what he had shared with Betsy, Jon had completed two degrees in engineering at Boston University, married and eventually found a job with International Telephone and Telegraph before moving to Winston-Salem NC for a job at an ITT facility in the small town of Kernersville, NC. He and his wife divorced in 1986 just after the ITT facility closed down. He had refused to move back to Massachusetts where he had been given a job offer. His wife had taken their son who was now fourteen back to Massachusetts where she had wanted to be in the first place and Jon had signed on with a NC construction firm building residential and commercial buildings. Jon had visitation rights so his son Lance would be able to occasionally visit. She liked Lance. He was pleasant and unlike many his age quite polite.

"Oh well," she thought to herself, "It is too late in life to be listening to my inner self feeling some kind of attraction toward Jon. My god, I am thirty-two." In addition, she had her own bruises to deal with. Yet she instinctively knew that Jon had also felt some chemistry just as she had from day one. She sighed. The front porch door closed behind her.

From the vantage of the diseased Loblolly, Jon scanned the 7 acres on which the doublewide rested.

The property lay at the end of McCrory Rd, not more than 2 miles from downtown Carthage. Even so, the peacefulness and solitude of this homestead could lead anyone to believe they were many more miles from any organized community. Of course Carthage could hardly be called organized. With a population of 3,789, Carthage was the smallest County Seat in North Carolina. Carthage was a poor community, nestled among some of the world's best known golf courses. Those with money lived around the beautiful course in the Southern Pines and Pinehurst areas. Those who worked with their hands usually came from Carthage.

Yet the peacefulness was more than just from the distance from the town. It came primarily from the hundreds of acres that backed up to the property. Taking a panoramic view from where Jon stood there was Betsy's house to the West, and a glimpse of McCrory RD to the right. Continuing to swing Northward approximately a quarter of a mile up McCrory road in the direction of 24-27, which was the State Road leading into downtown Carthage, there was little except a couple of houses, spaced well apart, and pines which flooded all but a glimpse of McCrory Rd. This view of a sea of pines washed across the horizon as one would continue to turn 360 degrees back around to where Betsy's house lay.

Jon surveyed his home. A feeling of contentment swept over him. It was a feeling he had not known for a long, long time. A little over three years ago, after his divorce had finalized, a friend had found the ad for this rental doublewide. With his friend vouching for him, he had been successful into talking Betsy into letting him rent the doublewide.

They had sat inside Betsy's neat three-bedroom ranch that sat back from McCrory Rd. She had been extremely hospitable and in between cookies and coffee had questioned him as expertly as an investigator. Yet she did it in such a non-assuming way, few would have picked up on her way of pulling out all the details she felt she needed to know.

Betsy Collingswood had been, unknown to Jon, reluctant to let him move into the double wide. Even though she had put out the ad at the urging of friends, she didn't care if the double wide stayed empty. She had been through a bitter divorce. There had been significant abuse. It had taken much energy and conviction to end the marriage. It was done primarily with her daughter, Julie, in mind and not herself. She did not have any need for any man to be any closer than absolutely necessary.

With a daughter she was trying to get through college and a minimum paying job with a local attorney, she had reluctantly agreed, the rent money was too enticing to turn down.

Being a very attractive thirty-year-old, Betsy had more than once turned away the advances of men. She did it without a second thought. Yet on several occasions, she found herself more than slightly stirred when, through her kitchen window, she would see Jon, stripped down to the waist, chopping wood or working around the property. At 6' 2" tall with a light brown complexion, and a chiseled waist and sinewy features, Jon could easily be a model for a magazine advertising the latest in men's apparel. Betsy did take note of what appeared to be scars running from his right elbow to his wrist but whenever she would approach Jon he would quickly grab a shirt or jacket and cover his frame. She did not bring the scars up in conversation and Jon never mentioned it.

She was grateful Jon respected her need to remain uninvolved. Even though a bystander could detect some chemistry between them, and rumors for a while did abound, as they will in a small town, nothing surfaced between them.

It was edging toward sunset, on this Friday evening. Jon gave one more look to the Loblolly he would be taking down tomorrow and then went up the stairs on the front porch of the doublewide and slipped inside. "Woops," he cautioned himself as he remembered what he had forgotten to do. Jon opened the front door and called a commanding voice "Pete."

Pete was Jon's three-year-old companion. Pete had been given to him by a friend just before he moved into the doublewide. Pete was a German Shepherd. His friend pointed out that the dog was also known as Alsatian, or

SchÄ¤fer. His official name was German Shepherd Dog, but most just say German Shepherd.

Pete grew up fiercely obedient to Jon. It was like the two of them were one. Pete was a quick learner, and a direct and fearless breed. Bold, obedient and cheerful, German Shepard's are also known for their great loyalty and courage. This breed has as its primary feature a complete willingness to protect its home and its master. Although Pete was a calm dog, if the need should arise, Pete would be eager and alert. Usually the temperament of this breed of dog as an adult, like most animals, is dependent upon proper socialization as a pup.

Jon and Pete had a real close bond. When Jon spoke, Pete obeyed immediately without hesitation. Pete had grown use to the home location and Jon allowed him the freedom to roam the woods at his leisure. Yet when Jon called, Pete would immediately turn from whatever he was occupied with and go to Jon. At supper time, Pete would be waiting to be called for dinner. Pete had also become quite a friend of Betsy and her daughter, when she would visit. Needless to say, Betsy always felt more secure with Pete on the property.

Pete suddenly appeared around the corner. With tail wagging Pete slid in past the open door.

Jon opened the refrigerator and took out a cold beer. He threw Pete a new chewy he had picked up and the two of them ambled out to the deck Jon had built on the backside of the home.

Looking into the darkening forest and stroking Pete's neck, Jon enjoyed the smooth taste of the cold beer as his mind raced about tomorrow. The cold fluid rolled around in his throat. It was like the touch of cool hands massaging his neck. He smiled. Tomorrow, his son Lance would be visiting and they would have the whole weekend together.

After the first beer, Jon indulged himself with one more. Jon sat back down on the back porch. He noticed Pete's ears were standing at alert. Pete began to utter a slow, low tone. "OK Pete relax. We will pick up Lance tomorrow and you can have a great time showing him the woods." Pete looked over at Jon as if he understood. He did know the sound of the word "Lance." It was a sound he loved. Pete had become almost as close to Lance as he had his master. Pete put his nose over his paws which he had crossed in front of him. He closed his eyes and whatever had caused him to be aroused had left his attention.

Jon got up and turned back into the house, leaving Pete to doze away on the back porch. He crossed through the kitchen, glancing at a picture of his fourteen-year-old son. As he entered his office which he would now turn into Lance's room while he visited, his right shoulder brusquely hit the shelving as he entered. A thick folder hit the floor scattering papers across the neat oval rug next to his computer desk. As Jon picked up the papers he couldn't help but sink to the floor in a sitting position. His engineering degrees as well as divorce papers were scattered all about.

As he stared at the papers and began to reassemble them, his mind flooded with the past. Jon's thirty-eight years had taken him through two engineering degrees, and a well-respected position within International Telephone & Telegraph Corporation, one of the largest conglomerates in the world. The demands of company time over family time had been excessive. In turn he had traveled throughout the world managing nuclear and fossil fuel power projects. Yes, there had been rewards; material rewards. He had accumulated considerable wealth and a beautiful home in an exclusive section of Winston-Salem, NC.

However, things were sure to change. With the Three Mile Nuclear accident and Joan Fonda and her "nuclear bogey man theory," over played in the movie "China Syndrome," public sentiment grew against nuclear power. The political drama to curtail all nuclear projects began.

Before long it was announced the North Carolina facility would fold. Jon had been given the opportunity to move back to the Massachusetts facility as an officer of the company or out to California. Neither choice was at all inviting, at least to Jon. When Jon decided to go out on his own and start a new business, the marriage to Dorothy began its decline and eventual nosedive.

Dorothy was basically a good, well-mannered and well-meaning woman. She had defied her parents in agreeing to marry this poor German-Negro. She thought initially that the fact Jon was half black and yet had such a light tone to his skin was a novelty. Even her friends were fooled as to Jon's heritage. Most felt the fact he was German accounted for his bronze skin tones. Throughout history mixing races was a taboo. When Jon and Dorothy first met, Jon shared with her his heritage. But Dorothy, despite her wealthy up-bringing and social prominence, liked living life on the edge. And not the least of the factors she considered was Jon's ability in bed. So despite the pleas from her parents not to marry, Dorothy did.

Besides, Jon's position kept the family in the same financial well-being she had always known. After a while, even

Dorothy's family accepted her bronze German and assumed that even though he came from a poor Massachusetts's family, he obviously was from a line of distinguished Germans. Jon's parents had both died just after his entry into college. His mother was a white woman of German heritage and his dad was a black engineer. They had met, fallen in love and had married in Germany. When Jon was in his freshman year at Boston University's College of Engineering, they were killed in a tragic accident. Dorothy's family never met Jon's family except those on his mother's side so Dorothy was spared the ordeal of confessing to Jon's mixed race. It was never discussed by Dorothy and Jon except when she would get angry.

When Jon would complain at home about the corrupt political life within ITT, Dorothy had little patience. Jon's trying to start a new business and give up the large income, drove Dorothy to distraction. She could be especially cruel when she wanted to. Even during small disagreements, Dorothy would turn on him and yell "If you don't like it nigger, get the hell out."

She could never bring herself to understand or forgive Jon for wanting to leave a well-respected position as vice president of engineering. "The fact the company was guilty of shipping defective product with falsified quality records is not your problem," she would yell. As an argument against Jon's position, she would counter that Jon should stay and correct the problem.

"Jon," she would plead, "you are well liked, you're smart, you are respected. It would not be long before you have your own division where you can do things your way."

Over and over they would have this discussion. Over and over Dorothy would deny any validity to Jon's need to remove himself from the corrupt environment he found himself in at ITT.

"You will find the same problem everywhere," she would counter. "Why do you think you are so pure? You can't think you can change the world! You have an obligation to Lance... you have an obligation to me... to our position in the community. I have worked hard to become the president of the Woman's Club. I have been asked to head up the Heart Association's drive next year. I am expected to dress a certain way. I am expected to live a certain way. Can't you think of anyone else but yourself?"

Dorothy would end every discussion they had on the subject this way. The words would not always be the same. The order of needs might change slightly. Nevertheless that was the essence of her chant. Dorothy tried everything to get Jon to change his mind. Even sex didn't work.

When Dorothy found herself pregnant with a second child, Jon was ecstatic. He was doing okay in odd jobs as a consultant. He had hoped this would help them get closer together. Jon honestly loved Dorothy and he held out that although his income was half of what it had been and expenses were somewhat higher, they could pull together as a family and make it all work.

The first crack in their relationship happened one afternoon. Dorothy was going on and on about not being able to buy what she felt she needed. Jon stood in the middle of the den as Dorothy walked toward the kitchen. "Look honey," he had offered. "If worse comes to worse, we get a mobile home and just keep plugging away as a family."

Dorothy spun around as if she were on a dime. "You might live in a mobile home buster, not I!"

Dorothy soon announced she was going to have an abortion. There was to be no discussion. Dorothy felt she had too many outside obligations. She could not and would not relinquish her role in the community. As far as she was concerned, the family was the right size and no additions were needed.

There was also the issue of Lance having "mixed blood." Even though Lance like his dad showed no evidence of anything other than the same bronze tone his father had, Dorothy would harp on the need to get him counseling.

"Mixed race adolescents don't have a natural peer group. Studies show they develop the need to engage in more risky behaviors. Throughout history racial mixing has been taboo. I mean this was the driving force behind the Jim Crow system in the South and the Black Codes in the North. What will we do if anyone should find out? What will our friends think? People think that children of mixed racial heritage are physically and morally inferior to blacks. What are we going to do?" She would lament this over and over in the evening hours behind the bedroom doors after she had had a drink or two.

Jon tried to assuage her fears. Yet no matter what he said she would turn over and cry herself to sleep.

There ceased to be any intimacy between them after Dorothy decided upon the abortion. Jon's insistence to leave behind a sizable pay check every month for the gamble of being in business for himself was more than she could handle. Soon Dorothy turned very cold. Every attempt at discussion ended with her shouting, "If you don't like the way things are then get the hell out."

Leaving Lance, their only child, had been most difficult. Jon and Lance had been very close. Lance was only eleven when the separation took place. He didn't take it well and a year of counseling was required to help Lance cope with the loss of his family unit as well as deal with Dorothy's concerns about mixed races.

The divorce had initially gone smooth enough. Jon had left all assets uncontested. There were several rental properties, a down town office building and a sizable bank account. Jon wanted to minimize lawyer involvement so Dorothy and Lance would keep everything. Jon was content to start over and just felt like it was the right thing to do.

Dorothy just had to be Dorothy, however. She brought in an expensive lawyer anyway. As a result she and Lance got less and the lawyer took a sizeable chunk.

The anger over this kept Jon from being able to deal with Dorothy over anything anymore. In turn, Jon became quite bitter about women in general.

Soon Dorothy had moved herself and Lance back to Boston. There she had close friends and felt more culturally satisfied. As she put it, "In Boston one feels more a part of the civilized world."

Jon chose to stay in the Winston Salem area where they had lived and gone to church over the last fifteen yrs. After the divorce, Jon left the church and discovered the beauty in the sand hills of North Carolina. He took a liking to the area and decided it would be a good change of scenery to re-locate around the Southern Pines area.

It was in Carthage where he met Betsy Collingswood. He met her through a friend who was a resident and knew of the double wide for rent. He liked Betsy right away, not as a woman but just as someone he felt instantly comfortable with. Initially the feelings scared him. So he worked very hard at keeping his distance and ignored the attractiveness he seemed to sense growing for her.

He had kept his engineering degrees to himself and hired himself out as a carpenter. He did not want any complications in his life including the rat race of the corporate world.

He enjoyed working with his hands and the physical activity kept him in shape. Soon his skills got him the lead foreman job with Trusky Construction. He busied himself with building elegant homes and commercial projects. His management skills could have moved him quickly up the chain of command. Yet he chose to remain a worker and just keep busy with his hands.

The outside work kept his 6'2" frame in good shape. This combined with his own regimen of exercise, kept him in unusually good condition for a man his age.

Putting all the paperwork back into place, Jon got up and began to set up the pull out couch in the room Jon used as an office. Lance would sleep there and they would share the bathroom which had an access door from either side of Jon's bedroom or the bedroom where lance would sleep.

Eventually, Jon would call Pete in and they would go to sleep dreaming of the activities for the next day.

The alarm went off at 6:00 a.m. Jon slung his feet onto the floor. His arm was burning where the scar tissues seemed to be on fire. His mind raced back to the fire he had encountered that one winter day when he was making his way to classes at the University. A house was red with flames. There were cars and fire trucks already on the scene. Curiosity had made him pull over and get out. He walked up to the crowd of onlookers. The fire hoses were pouring water down on the small home but anyone could see it didn't matter. An older woman was screaming for her pet pug who was inside in a cage where it slept at night. Jon couldn't believe no one was trying to get the small dog. In the impulsiveness of a young man of eighteen, Jon went under the yellow tape set up to keep people back. Despite the officers yelling at him, Jon disappeared into the doorway. He could hear the pug whining and quickly located it. He unlatched the cage and grabbed the dog. Turning and trying to frantically escape the inferno, he could hear the roof begin to collapse. He sprinted toward the doorway. Just as he was within feet of the outside, the structure collapsed. He threw the dog thru the door opening before the burning beam dropped him to the ground pinning him by his right arm.

The firefighters pulled Jon out but not before he suffered third degree burns up and down his right arm. Between the officers yelling at him for being so foolish to go in a burning house after a dog, and the older woman praising him, Jon lost consciousness. He awoke in the operating room of Massachusetts General Hospital.

He missed about a month of school. The pain of recovery and tissue transplants had been fiercely painful. He was visited by the Boston Police Department who would have cited him for disobeying an officer if it weren't for the fact he had suffered enough.

The Doctor told him they had done the best they could and he would have a functional arm but it would not be pretty to look at. In addition, the nerve damage might be with him for the rest of his life.

Jon reached over to his night stand where he had last put a bottle of pills. He popped two and swaggered into the kitchen as if to say he would not let the pain affect him. The pain began to yield after a cup of coffee. Jon looked at the clock. Lance's flight would come in to Greensboro airport at 10 a.m. Friday morning. Jon had taken the day off as well as Monday when he would put Lance back on a plane. He jumped into the shower and prepared himself to pick up Lance and enjoy the weekend together with his son.

Lance was overjoyed to see his dad. Jon listened as Lance shared what was going on in school and his accomplishments in basketball and football. Lance was already showing his dad's height and athletic ability. Coaches from several colleges had already shown some interest even though Lance was only in the eighth grade. Having a long weekend was something Lance looked forward to because it usually meant he would see his dad.

As they pulled into the property, Betsy came out to meet them. Jon parked the SUV and Lance jumped from the vehicle. "Pete, Pete," He called. Pete came running around the doublewide and jumped into Lance's arms.

Both Betsy and Jon laughed as Lance fell to the ground from the weight of the dog and the two, boy and dog, rolled around playfully. As Lance and Pete played, Betsy moved closer to Jon.

"Jon I was worried. There had been a bad accident on Rt. 1 this morning. I called you but I didn't get you."

"Sorry," Jon sheepishly replied, wondering why he felt it necessary to give an explanation. "We saw the scene when we were on our way back. The signal is bad through there so I must have missed it."

The sun seemed particularly warm as he found himself awash in Betsy's smile. She in turn took in his tall lean frame, his blond hair and green eyes set against his bronze skin. She almost had to catch her breath. "Well, guys, I have prepared a nice lunch for you, if you are hungry."

"Yes," exclaimed Lance, "I am starved."

Betsy and Jon shared a laugh. "OK then, let's go," she said.

With Lance and Pete leading the way, Jon followed Betsy up to her back patio where she had prepared tuna fish sandwiches, chips and cool aide.

"Oh boy," said Lance, "You knew I love tuna. Thanks Ms. Collingswood."

"Now, Lance," Betsy retorted, "you know I asked you to call me Betsy," she laughed.

"Yes, ma'am," Lance replied. And before Jon and Betsy could get seated, Lance was already into his first sandwich.

"Wow, son," cautioned Jon laughing. "You are supposed to eat the tuna not let the tuna eat you." Betsy laughed. "Oh that's okay, Jon; I bet he is starved after that long flight. Now a days they don't give you much to eat on flights anymore."

"Yes, ma'am," Lance stammered, in between bites. "They sure don't and this is sure good." Lance took a corner of his sandwich and gave it to Pete.

Suddenly after Lance had wolfed down several sandwiches, and they had exhausted all the goings on up at Lance's school, he turned to his dad. "Dad, is your arm still giving you a lot of pain?"

Stillness filled the air for a moment and Betsy thought she had detected a slight blush on Jon's cheeks. "Ahh, no, son, it's fine. Now enjoy the sandwiches for we need to go and cut down a tree."

"I'm sorry Jon, did you hurt your arm."

Before Jon could speak, Lance told Betsy all about how his dad had saved a dog and got severally burned. "Wow, Jon did it leave a lot of scar tissue."

"Yes, ma'am, it left some." Jon looked very uncomfortable and stood up from the table. "Lance we need to thank Betsy and get going so we can start on that tree."

"Thanks Betsy, it was a great lunch," Jon said. He called to Pete and they started down toward the doublewide, leaving Lance to grab another sandwich. "Sorry, ma'am," Lance whispered to Betsy, "I forgot my dad hates to talk about his arm, I shouldn't have brought it up."

"That's okay Lance, don't you worry about it. Everything's fine." Her voice was but a whisper as she watched Jon and Pete slowly walking down the slight incline.

After unpacking Lance's suitcase and telling Lance to change into the dungarees and shirt he kept there for Lance when he came, Jon went out to his out building and prepared his chain saw for the job ahead.

Together with Lance, Jon showed his son the art of cutting down a tree and making it turn. The tall Loblolly fell just as Jon had predicted. The sound it made as it hit the ground was a loud thud.

"Okay, son: That was the easy part. Now we go to work." Jon started up the chain saw he had gotten for Lance some time ago and showed his son how to use it and what precautions to take.

With Jon handling the large chain saw and Lance working the small one on smaller branches, the large Loblolly was soon a stack of logs and a pile of burning debris.

The time was now 4:00 p.m. Jon put his arm around Lance and expressed how proud he was to have him work and be around him. Lance smiled and they both walked into the double wide to get something to drink.

After cooking burgers and chatting for a while, they both agreed they were tuckered out and would retire early.

Saturday was to be a fun day together. They both arose early, had breakfast and went fishing.

After returning home about 5:00 p.m., they dressed the three trout they had caught. After cleaning up, Lance said, "Dad could I play with the play station for a while?"

"Sure Son. Remember we will be cooking out tonight so I hope you have a good appetite for mesquite chicken."

"Oh Dad that will be awesome." As Lance hooked up the play station, his mouth began to water just thinking about his dad's specialty.

Jon took 4 skinless chicken breast halves and began to pound them to ½" thickness. Then he took 2 cast iron pans and put them on the grill outside on the back deck. He then lite up the grill and turned the flames under the pans to low. In one pan he poured drops of cooking oil. He added a quantity of freshly sliced mushrooms and 1 table-spoon of mesquite seasoning.

Walking inside, Jon called to Lance. "Son, I forgot to tell you I had invited Betsy to eat with us, is that okay with you?"

"Sure, Dad," Lance replied trying to concentrate on his race in his Nascar Thunder Bolt game.

As Jon walked back out to the deck, Betsy was walking around the corner of the double wide.

"Hi am I too early?"

"No, just in time to steal all the secrets of the chef's specialty." Jon laughed. Betsy chuckled in return and sat down near the flower pot she had made for Jon containing an elephant ear, a dense selection of mini petunia and a vine to spill over creating a stunning look. Even though it was getting late in the afternoon hours, two Monarch but-terflies played amongst the petunia blossoms.

Jon put the chicken on the grill and they sizzled as they began their transformation. Betsy sat and watched Jon. She marveled at how comfortable she felt in his presence. She also took note of the fact Jon was wearing a long sleeve shirt which covered his right arm. Yet when he turned to face her she was struck by how handsome he was in the teal shirt unbuttoned at the top exposing his chest. The contrast with his beautiful skin tone, his blond hair and his green eyes took her breath away.

"How about some refreshment? He asked.

"Great, what do you have in mind?

"Well, I am going to have a cold beer myself."

"That sounds good, make it two."

Jon turned went into the house and returned with two beers and a frosted glass for Betsy.

"Oh special treatment, thank you kind, sir."

"Nothing is too good for a beautiful woman." Jon couldn't believe he had said that. The words came out before he had a chance to think about it.

Betsy blushed, and they both stood staring warmly at each other.

"Well," Jon said, "here's to ya."

"And to you Jon," Betsy softly replied still staring at him as she felt goose bumps from her toes to her arms.

Jon turned his attention to the meal.

"Can I help?" Betsy inquired.

"Ah well, if you would like, you could make a salad. I have everything inside. And I will finish the chicken."

"Good, I would like to do that." Betsy rose and went inside to prepare the salad.

Jon removed the mushrooms from the first pan with a slotted spoon so he would take no juices and put them into his second pan. Then he put the cooked chicken into the first larger pan, added some mesquite seasoning, put the mushrooms back on top of the chicken and cooked them for another 5 minutes so they were brown on both sides and no longer pink in the center. Once the chicken was done, he removed it from the pan, leaving the juices and mushrooms. He placed slices of mozzarella cheese on three of the halves and put the fourth on the side to cool. Then he stirred a can of ready to serve soup with baked potato, bacon and chives in with the mushrooms.

"Are we about ready?" Jon called out.

Betsy came out with a bountiful bowl of salad trailed by Lance who was devouring the smell from the grill.

Jon put the cooled chicken half into Pete's bowl and brought the soup with the mushrooms to a simmer. Seasoning it with salt and oregano, Jon put each chicken breast on a plate and poured the soup mixture over it.

Lance ran inside to get himself something to drink and they all sat down to feast.

They talked about Lance's school. They talked about the work they did with the Loblolly. They talked about Betsy's daughter, Julie, and her progress at school. They ate and shared and had a wonderful meal enjoying each other's company.

After the meal, Betsy appreciating that Jon and Lance needed time together, excused herself after, despite Jon's protest, cleaning the table and putting the food remnants and plates and things in the kitchen.

As Jon proceeded to clean up, Lance announced he was going to play with Pete.

That was fine with Jon as his mind was filled with the scent of Betsy and how enticing she looked as she sat watching him cook. All he could see were her gorgeous legs. Boy she has beautiful legs he thought to himself. "Ah stop that," he admonished himself.

It was now about 5:30. The sun still burned brightly and the heat still lingered. Jon stepped out on the back deck and a gentle breeze rolling out of the forest snapped Jon out of his thoughts. With his right hand he wiped the perspiration off his forehead. He ran his hair through his youthful looking blond hair which he wore just long enough in the back to touch his shirt collar. The breeze carried the pine scent across the forest floor. This provided some relief to the heat of the day. The smell was delicious. He never tired of the smell. He pulled at his shirt to cool himself off and looked around to locate Lance and Pete.

Without Pete by Lance's side, Jon would never let Lance off to roam the woods alone. Even at fourteen, too many things could happen. Yet with Pete by his side, Jon felt Lance was protected and safe. Jon had trained Pete well. So well in fact Betsy had more than once suggested Jon enter the two of them in an obedience training contest. Upon one occasion Betsy had talked Jon into doing just that. Pete had come away with top honors. So well trained was Pete, Jon could get Pete to respond successfully to just hand signals. The only exception to Pete staying close to Jon was when Lance came to visit. Lance and Pete had hit it off in some mystical way the first time they met. In fact, the last time Lance had come to visit, Pete pouted for hours after Lance left.

Lance loved to prowl the woods with Pete. Today was no exception. However, on this particular visit, this irritated Jon a bit. Lance would be leaving soon. They had only the weekend together as opposed to a week last time Lance came. He looked at his watch. It was 5:30 p.m.

Jon walked around the double wide and looked up at Betsy's home. Betsy had changed into a loosely tied halter top. The sight of her as she bent over tending to her garden, her slim waist and a backside seeming to move so seductively as she caressed and cut some flowers, made Jon realize how hot he was. He pulled at his shirt again as if to cool off. Walking back around, Jon walked into the kitchen. The mobile home was very comfortably furnished. It was a 3 bedroom unit which had two bathrooms and all the conveniences a man could ask for.

He moved to the refrigerator. He opened the door and leaned down to pull out a beer. Quickly removing the cap, he flipped it over his shoulders. It landed in the compactor which Jon always left open for that purpose. Ahh two points he thought to himself. He settled down on the couch. Taking a sip of the cold refreshing brew, he hit the power control on the remote control unit. He scanned the programs running until he got a re-run of The Peoples Court. Jon smiled, settled back and became absorbed in the insanity that was featured as real people dealing with real problems on TV.

Feeling tired, Jon stretched out on the comfortable sectional sofa Betsy had helped him choose for the room. The vision of Betsy leaning over her garden floated back into his mind, He finished the beer, and realizing he had just missed the first court case, got up to get another beer. After scoring another "two points," banking the shot off the lid of the compactor, he settled back down into the couch and immersed himself into the next case. He took a couple of sips and set the bottle down beside the couch. Before the case was over, Jon had closed his eyes.

Suddenly Jon jumped up. He had fallen asleep and lost track of time. His inners senses were telling him something was wrong. He could feel it. He looked at the clock. It was 7:15 p.m. Quickly Jon looked around. This was a feeling he hated. He had lost control of time. Now it was in control not him.

"Lance!" he called out, expecting to hear his son tell him he had let his Dad sleep and was playing with the play station.

"Lance!" he called out a little louder.

He walked out onto the back deck still trying to get his wits about him. "Pete," he called.

The beers had apparently given Jon a bit of a buzz and he was still trying to get his bearings. It was getting close to 8:00 p.m. Darkness was beginning to edge into the summer day.

"Lance?"

"Pete?"

Feeling extremely tired for some reason and increasingly agitated over the situation he had put himself in, Jon went to the edge of the back yard and called for the two repeatedly.

"Goddamn it," he finally retorted.

Looking around he could see the barbecue grill lay still dirty although Lance had said he would clean it.

"Lance!"

"Pete!"

Again he called them repeatedly. The breeze had cooled off the day and the sun was but an inkling on the horizon. Jon kicked at a pine branch in disgust. He had worked hard getting his life back in order. He lived now with a discipline which was also a shield against feelings he tried to keep at bay.

This sort of thing was just not the way Jon would have it. Again he called and called for Lance and Pete. Jon walked around to the front. He looked up at Betsy's house.

He could see no activity there. The lights weren't on. Betsy's car was not in her driveway.

"Goddamn it."

"Goddamn it.", he repeated.

Jon picked up some of the loose twigs and threw them in the burn pile he and Lance had made earlier as if this action would get everything back in sync.

Looking around the property and seeing nothing, Jon went around to the back. The sun was now settling behind the horizon. It was now 7:50 p.m. The woods were turning ominously dark. After calling Lance and Pete once more, he turned and went into the house. He opened the refrigerator and stared ominously at what was left of the beer.

"No dammit," he thought, this is no time to be thinking about beer.

Suddenly the back door swung open.

"Dad, Dad, you won't believe what Pete and I just saw."

Jon looked up first startled, then relieved, then angry.

He composed himself. "Lance," he started out slowly, "Do you know what time it is?"

Lance suddenly realizing his new found discovery was not going to be of interest, looked forlorn as he realized how mad his dad was.

"But Dad, you don't realize what..."

"What I realize, young man," Jon interrupted, is that you have been selfishly doing your own thing oblivious to the fact others might be the least bit worried because you were not even close to the time you should have been back home."

"Yes, Dad."

Lance stood staring down at the floor realizing his dad had been worried and he should have come back sooner.

"But Dad…," Lance resumed with excitement as if it was a prelude to a great story.

"NO BUTS! PERIOD! Where is Pete?"

In a quiet and subdued voice Lance motioned his head to the door. "Pete is outside."

Jon walked slowly to the back door and looked at Pete who was lying by the grill with his head placed sorrowfully over his front paws.

"What's wrong with you?" Jon growled at Pete.

Pete's big black eyes looked up at his master without any head movement. They quickly looked away as if admitting to his part in some terrible crime.

Regaining his composure, Jon turned back to Lance.

"Son could I have some kind of explanation?"

Lance moved to the sofa.

"Dad, Pete and I were just exploring the woods together. Then Pete started barking at this Holly Bush. I couldn't get him to leave. He just lay there moaning. I thought he was sick or something Dad." Lanced paused as if trying to think of how to present his story.

"I sat there with him for a while and then it happened."

Lance again paused.

"What happened, Lance?" Jon said impatiently.

Mustering all the courage he had, Lance went for the goal posts. "The Bush, Dad, the Holly Bush, it lit up."

Lance held his breath awaiting his Dad's response.

Slowly, Jon repeated what his son had said. "The Holly Bush, it lit up," Then with slow measured tones, "Son what does that mean, it lit up? Lance what happened?"

Lance now knew his father was not going to accept his explanation. He was reluctant to continue but it was the only story he had.

"Lance, you and Pete did not come back until it was almost pitched dark. I think you owe me an explanation."

"Dad," Lance continued without much enthusiasm, "I know it sounds crazy." He paused. "Even stupid maybe but the bush lit up… it lit up Dad… like it was on fire… but it wasn't on fire… it just lit up." Lance paused and got ready to release the punch line to his story. He wished he had made something up. Yet he and his Dad had a better relationship than that. He was taught to always be honest to his parents if no one else. He had always been.

Tears were starting to flow from his eyes as he realized how stupid this was all sounding. "Dad the bush lit up… and then… the bush spoke to me Dad." Slowly and quietly he repeated "it spoke to me dad."

"What did the bush say, Lance?" Jon quietly and softly asked in a way which would have clued a more mature person to the trap being laid.

Falsely encouraged, Lance's enthusiasm over what he had experienced took over again and he excitedly continued to share with his dad.

"The bush spoke, Dad. It asked if I could help it. I didn't say much but it seemed to read my mind. And uh… Pete, well he just kept laying there moaning like. The bush said it was a traveler who needed my help and wanted to know if it could walk within me. And… the time got away… uh… before…" Lance suddenly realized his dad was not buying this at all. In fact, Dad was becoming very angry. Lance continued slowly now, realizing he was not going to be believed.

"And before I said… um, anything, the, uh, bush asked me to uh think about it and uh…," Lance's voice trailed off as his dad turned, open the refrigerator, grabbed a beer and sat down on the sofa.

He put the beer down on the table with some force. He got up and turned toward Lance who still stood in the same place looking as forlorn as a person could look.

Jon put his hands on his waist almost as if to keep his anger in check. "Lance, I'm more disappointed with you than I can say. It is bad enough for you to pull this kind of nonsense without spinning such a ridiculous tale. Maybe it is unfair to expect you at fourteen to act mature all the time, I don't know. But to come home and launch into such ridiculous drivel, I just don't understand. I just don't understand."

Jon looked at his son with a look of utter frustration. He sighed deeply and sat back down on the sofa.

"If you want to fix yourself anything before you go to bed, do it now, please. We have to get up early tomorrow to get you to the airport in time for you to catch your flight."

Jon pushed the TV power button and sat back down swigging a beer.

"Dad…" Lance sensed this was not the time to continue and he slowly moved to the bedroom. He closed the door behind him after giving his Dad one look of regret.

The TV danced and flickered. Its images danced intermittently across the now dark room. Jon had fallen back and was now snoring away succumbed by the beer and the frustration of the events.

Pete lay outside on the deck. Suddenly his ears cocked. He looked at the door behind which his masters slept. He got up on his paws. He looked out at the woods. His ears were cocked again. He looked back at his master's home. Pete turned and went into the woods.

CHAPTER 2

THE AGREEMENT

A sharp pain woke Jon up. Such a pain especially in the early morning seemed to be a constant companion. It radiated from the middle of his back right up to his neck. He shrugged his shoulder while turning in the bed as if to get rid of the sharp painful needles he felt in his back. It must be time to get up, he thought. Just then the background was filled with an abusive metallic ring. He tried to move to aim a deadly blow at the source of the penetrating sound. The pain in his back gripped him and with a grimace on his face, Jon tried to reach it. His back betrayed him and he lay in pain as the metallic noise continued. Slowly he worked out the kinks. Then with deliberation, he reached and snuffed the life out of the alarm clock.

It was 5:30 a.m. and Jon fell back on the pillow. Something had to be done. This painful morning re-enactment needed to cease. His mind opened to the awareness of the day and the tasks ahead. As he tried to put the pieces together, events of the night before invaded his consciousness. He grimaced again. His back still hurt from the way he was sleeping. Or was it from the way he had not been sleeping?

It had not been a good night. But then he was use to waking up in pain. His back seemed to stay constantly strained. However, the confrontation with Lance had not helped. He remembered getting up from the couch and stumbling over the coffee table. The lower part of his chin was still sore from where he had stumbled and fallen. His arm bothered him. But it always bothered him. The doctors had said the nerve connections were all messed up but eventually he would get used to it. However, he never did. Eventually though he did became less and less aware of the tingling and the sporadic painful impulses. "My god," he thought. "I am a wreck."

With careful forethought, he swung himself carefully onto the floor.

"Let's see," he thought, as he tried to ignore the distractions and focus on the demands of the day. The flight was at 10 a.m. That meant they had to leave by 8:00 a.m. at the latest. Betsy was making breakfast for them at 7am. Focusing on where he needed to be after Lance left, Jon remembered he needed to get to the Daly jobsite by noon so he could inspect the crew's work before they came over from the Kate's projects. These were two big residential jobs for homes in the $2,500,000 range.

After Jon felt he had some meager orientation on the major goals of the day, he felt ready to get going. First thing was to wake Lance.

After turning on the light in Lance's room, Jon said, "Good morning son, time to rise and shine."

"Hmmmm," Lance managed to respond.

"Good morning son," Jon repeated, "time to get up. We need to be up at Betsy's for breakfast at seven."

"Hmmmm," Lance muttered again as he turned over.

Deciding he would give him a few more minutes, Jon went into the kitchen. He put on the coffee and looked around for Pete. "That's odd he thought," and then upon reflection assumed Pete was in Lance's room and he just didn't see him.

Suddenly, Lance appeared in his sleepy, groggy self. He leaned against the door jamb. "Good morning Dad," he said weakly. Lance had not forgotten about last night and he wasn't sure what reception he would have from his dad this morning.

"Good morning, Son," Jon replied in a cheerful enough voice. "I am going to shave and get ready. You need to also get ready and make sure you have everything packed. Then we will go up to Betsy's and have breakfast."

"Good," thought Lance as he turned to go back to his bathroom and get ready.

Jon scratched the stubble on his face and pushed himself toward the bathroom. He turned the hot water on and opened the door on the other side of the bathroom to the bathroom for Lance's room.

"Lance," Jon called out sharply.

Lance had curled back into bed under a mound of blankets.

"Son, it is time to rise and shine," Jon said sharply.

Lance moaned and turned over. He was definitely not a morning person. He raised his head slowly and aimed it toward the noise. "Lance we need to be up at Betsy's at seven all ready to grab a bite to eat and hit the road."

"Ah-uh," said a sleepy voice as its head flopped down on the pillow.

By the time Jon had shaved and showered, Lance was on his feet and splashing water in his face. Jon went into his bedroom to finish dressing. Lance went into the kitchen to get a glass of juice. Just as he was approaching the kitchen there was a knock on the back door. Lance looked up to see Betsy. With only his briefs on, Lance skirted around the corner and threw his dad's shirt over his shoulders. He returned to the kitchen and opened the door for Betsy.

"Good morning, Lance." She said with a warm smile and a delightful tone in her voice. "I don't mean to bug you guys but I know you will be in a hurry and I want to make sure you can come up. I have fixed a nice spread and my Dad has come over to meet you and see you all off.

By this time, Jon had ambled out of the bedroom dressed in only his slacks. For the first time Betsy could fully see Jon's right arm and the mass of scar tissue. Forgetting about his arm which he would usually shield from view or perhaps because he was there and she was there and there was no hiding it, Jon totally ignored the fact his arm was bare.

Jon greeted Betsy as he walked into the kitchen. "Hi Betsy, you're an early riser this morning,"

"Yes, sorry, didn't mean to get in the way so early. I have fixed a nice spread and I wanted to make sure you all had time to grab a bite." Then as an afterthought she added, "I was telling Lance my Dad will be there. He wanted to meet Lance and see you all off."

"Hmmm," thought Jon. Betsy's Dad, Max Sumler was a former chairman of the Carthage Town Council. His wife of thirty years had passed away and for the last 4 years he had been living in Carthage as a retired widower. He had thought about moving to Florida but his reluctance to leave his daughter kept him in Carthage.

Max stayed pretty much by himself. He was a support system for Betsy and tending after his daughter gave his life purpose. Even though Jon had been living on Betsy's property, Jon only saw Max occasionally. They would wave at each other. They might exchange brief pleasantries. On the other hand they never talked to one another for any length of time. Max felt reassured by Betsy's comments about Jon that Jon was a good neighbor and Betsy felt increased safety in Jon's presence.

"I have never engaged Betsy's Dad in much conversation, I wonder what this is all about," Jon thought to himself.

"Well, Lance, does that sound okay with you?" Jon asked.

"Sounds fine with me, Dad."

Lance didn't show much facial communication. He was still in the wake up stages. There was plenty of communication on Jon's. He beamed at Betsy. She felt it as her cheeks flushed. Suddenly she felt uncomfortable.

"Well, when you all are ready, just come up to the house." With a parting smile at Jon, she turned and left.

"Well, that sure sounds great doesn't it Son?"

"Ya, sure, Dad," Lance replied as he disappeared into the bathroom.

"Hmm," Jon thought to himself, "we sure don't sound too enthusiastic this morning."

Jon turned as was his morning ritual and pulled out the dog food. Grabbing a clean bowl from the dish drainer he filled the bowl and took it outside for Pete.

Normally Pete would be at the back door as soon as life stirred in the place. Jon hadn't realized Pete wasn't there until he opened up the back door and stepped out onto the deck. Slowly he looked around for Pete.

"Pete," he called softly.

Putting the bowl down, Jon went into the kitchen and called to Lance. "Lance, is Pete in there with you?"

"No Dad."

He turned and went back to the deck. "Pete?" he said a bit louder.

Suddenly the events of last night began to play in his head. "Pete," Jon called even louder.

Jon stared out into the forest which was just now beginning to twinkle as the sun bounced off a light layer of moisture that had come from a small amount of rain the previous night.

Jon turned around to see Lance all dressed and ready to go standing in the doorway. "Where's Pete?" Lance asked.

"I don't know Son; it is not like him not to be here in the morning."

"This is a little strange…" Jon was starting to talk to himself. His conversation was ended as he looked back at Lance and saw that look like "I told you so."

Lance turned as if disgusted and retreated to his bedroom.

When they were ready they walked up to the house. As Jon got up to Betsy's, he scanned the area once more hoping to see Pete come running to join them.

As they approached the house the aroma of eggs, bacon and sausage drifted temptingly through their nostrils.

"Yum yum," said Jon to himself. Lance gave his dad a funny look. Lance wasn't going to let on how good it smelled.

It tasted even better. The country table in the kitchen was set with an ironed white table cloth. There were four place settings in the middle of which there were plates with sausage, bacon and toast stacked high. Scrambled eggs mixed with cheese and Texas Pete were ready for their plates. There were four different kinds of preserves. Hot corn meal biscuits were coming out of the oven. A blue onion bowl held tasty looking Southern white gravy. To top off the décor, Betsy had picked and placed an arrangement of flowers for the center of the table.

"Wow," Jon exclaimed. I feel like I have walked into a Southern Living magazine.

Even Lance, who at first wasn't sure he was hungry, beamed as he spotted all the food. He could hardly contain how hungry he suddenly felt.

When they were through, they thanked Betsy and got up to go back and pick up their bags.

"Son why don't you just stay here and say good-bye to Betsy. I'll go load up the car and meet you at the top of the driveway."

"Okay, Dad," Lance said as he put a sausage on a piece of toast and made himself one last sausage biscuit.

Jon turned to Betsy. He reached down and took her left hand in his right hand and squeezed gently. "This has been special, thanks."

At this point a third party looking in on the scene could tell both of them wished they were somewhere else. They wished they were alone with no past, no hang-ups, no past torments, just the two of them—alone.

Betsy broke the quiet. She gently withdrew her hand and then in an excited manner, intended to conceal the real emotional content within, clapped her hands together.

"Well, gentlemen, it has been my honor." Then looking at Lance she said, "You, young man must not be a stranger. We want to see a lot of you around here this summer, OK?"

Lance smiled. "Yes, ma'am."

Suddenly a car pulled into Betsy's driveway.

"Oh, it looks like my dad is here," she said as she bent her head to see through the window who the visitor was. "I was hoping he could have gotten here earlier."

As Betsy's dad came in the front door, Jon went out the back door toward the doublewide. As he walked he scanned the woods for any sign of Pete.

"Pete… Pete," he called out as he walked down the incline.

Inside the house, Betsy was making sure Lance and her Dad renewed acquaintances.

"You met my Dad briefly the last time you were here didn't you Lance?"

"Yes, ma'am," Lance replied. He reached out and shook Mr. Sumler's hand.

"It's good to see you young man. You've grown an inch since the last time you were here."

Lance gave Mr. Sumler an embarrassed look as an almost undetectable to the human eye aura quickly enveloped Lance's hand. As quickly as it appeared, it disappeared, when Mr. Sumler let go.

They could hear Jon's car moving up the driveway from where it was parked near the doublewide. Lance said his good-byes and thanked Betsy again for the breakfast.

"Can I give you a hug good-bye?" Betsy asked, knowing how young men shy away from such affections.

"Well, uh, sure that would be okay." Betsy moved over and gave Lance a big squeeze. She looked him in the eye. "Come back soon. We love having you," Betsy smiled.

"Yes, uh, okay and thanks. Bye." With that Lance went out to the car and jumped in the front passenger seat.

Betsy and her Dad stood at the doorway waving good-bye. Jon returned the wave and the car headed up McCrory Rd to Rt. 24-27.

Through Carthage there was no conversation between the car occupants. The car felt constrained as it kept to the 35 mph speed limit in the township. As the car slowly turned around the town circle and headed toward Rt. 1, Jon spoke.

"You know, this is the first morning since I have had Pete, he hasn't been there in the morning." There was silence.

After they had made it through downtown Carthage and got on Rt. 1 toward the Raleigh Durham airport, Lance broke the silence.

"Dad, I'm sorry about last night."

No one said anything for a while. Traffic was very light and the car moved powerfully along with only the hum of the tires audible.

Lance turned and looked at his Dad, as if measuring his mood. He looked back straight down the road ahead

"Dad... do you remember what I told you last night?" Then after a brief pause he added; "I mean about what happened to Pete and me?"

Jon did not respond. He just kept both hands on the wheel and stared directly ahead.

After a mile or two Lance spoke again. "Well, Dad, telling the truth to you and Mom is something you both taught me to do. I'll admit I'm not perfect and I have told a white lie now and then to others. But I have never lied to you Dad... I have never lied to you."

Again there was silence. Both Jon and his Dad stared at the road ahead.

Quietly Lance added: "Dad, Pete and I saw just what I told you we saw." Lance added.

Jon looked over at Lance with a puzzled hurt look on his face. He made no comment. "What could explain way Pete was not there this morning?" He wondered.

Jon reached over and turned the radio on to 88.5 FM, the NPR station. As he drove, he kept thinking about what Lance had said. It didn't make any sense. However, Jon did not want to spoil this time, a moment before he would be sending his son away, arguing about it.

The traffic seemed busy this morning around the Raleigh Durham International airport. Not being able to find a suitable parking spot anywhere and not wanting to lose time looking for one, Jon slid the car into a front space marked "VIP VEHICLES ONLY."

As the car came to a stop, Lance referenced the sign. "What's that Dad?" Lance asked, pointing at the "VIP VEHICLES ONLY" sign.

"Son, that sign says this space is only for "very important persons.""

"Should we be parking here, Dad?" Lance asked as he stared at the sign and became nervous that they were doing something they shouldn't be doing.

"Well, since I have a very special person aboard, I think we qualify, don't you."

With that Jon gave Lance one of his special smiles. The "goofy" look Lance called it, where his Dad's eyebrows would go way up and his smile went from ear to ear.

"Gosh, it was good seeing his dad return from being so upset," Lance thought to himself. He would make no more mention of the holly bush.

Looking at his watch, Jon said, "Son we better go. You carry one bag. I will get the other. We have to check your bags in and get a boarding pass. Then you will have to go through the security check point. Are you okay?"

"Yes, Dad."

After check-in they both walked to the assigned ramp. Both Father and Son gave each other a warm tight hug. Jon reluctantly let go. Lance slowly walked through the security gate. After he got through, he looked back for his Dad who was standing there watching him. They both waved and Lance slowly walked down to the entrance door for Flight 346.

Jon felt sad and a bit confused as he walked through the terminal and back toward the car. He still could not comprehend what had happened last night. He couldn't get Pete out of his mind and he kept going back to what Lance had said last night… and this morning. It made no sense.

"Dad, telling the truth to you and Mom is something you both taught me to do. I'll admit I'm not perfect and I have told a white lie now and then to others. But I have never lied to you Dad… I have never lied to you." The words went around in Jon's head.

"Dad, Pete and I saw just what I told you we saw." Lance had added.

Jon's thoughts were interrupted by the sight of a large uniformed young man leaning over the windshield of Jon's car.

"Hey!" Jon yelled out. "Can I help you?"

Hearing the shout the young security officer rose off of the car's hood where his large belly had left a small bow in the hood.

Jon began a slow burn as he got closer and he could see the indentation left by the guard's belly.

"This yur car, mister?" the security guard said sarcastically in his Southern drawl.

"Yes, it is Sonny, and before you broadsided it with your belly it didn't have a bow in the hood!" The tone and aggressiveness of Jon's reply sat the guard back on his heels.

The guard looked nervously at the hood and saw the slight indentation. He expected this driver to be as intimidated as most are when they are caught parking illegally. Did he make a mistake? He did a slight internal panic. He looked at the car's bumper again. Then realizing the car had no authorization sticker, he resumed his authoritative tone.

"This parking spot is going to cost you a hundred dollars, mister!" The guard ignored Jon's reference to the hood and stood his ground.

A broad smile lit up on Jon's face. Whether win or lose he loved this type of situation. He had no more to lose other than one hundred dollars and the possibility he could bluff a win. It was like playing Texas Holdem with the great Texas Holdem player Daniel Negraneu, his favorite player and betting into Negraneu's hand while holding a 7/2 unsuited.

"Young man," Jon began with a fatherly tone. "I know you are out here doing the best you can. John... John Parker told me to use his sticker and... what's your name?"

Thinking quickly and, at this point, having nothing more to lose, Jon pulled an old, let me tell you who I know, trick. He actually didn't know John Parker personally. Jon had supervised an addition done for the Parker's multimillion dollar home. He knew basically what Parker did. He also knew what an overbearing, obsessive slave driver he was reported to be to his employees.

"Scott," the guard stammered out. The name Parker had gotten his attention. John Parker is the operations manager of the airport. He rules with an iron hand. He is also known for firing anybody who makes a mistake or does anything that offends him. An associate of Scott's had just been let go last week for just questioning Parker's nephew about parking by the loading dock. The questioning was deemed to be in an unnecessarily rude manner.

Jon looked down at his bumper where the guard had looked. "Well, Scott, the sticker must have become dislodged. Parker himself taped it on the bumper. I guess he didn't do an adequate job, did he Scott?"

"Well, ahh…," there was no way Scott was going to say something he knew could get back to Parker. "Look, sir," he humbly replied to Jon, "ahh, I can see how that might happen, sir."

Jon smiled inside. "Negraneu checked!"

"Sure, sure Scott I am sure Parker would be embarrassed if he knew what a lousy job he did in putting on that sticker. Now… about this hood damage…" Jon let his comment sink in.

"I think," Jon continued, studiously studying the indentation, "I can get it popped out okay… shouldn't cost too much." Jon was making his value bet.

"If you will just tell me how much." Scott was beginning to sweat profusely now. He really couldn't afford to pay for this but if it meant keeping his job, he was inclined to do it.

Scott's ass became so tight you couldn't have shoved a needle up it. He really needed this job and here it was about to go down the tubes.

Jon interrupted again. "Naw. Tell you what we will do. You just give me a special parking sticker and we will call it even, fair and square. That way Parker doesn't have to know what an inadequate job he did taping a sticker on, and we don't have to worry about the damage to the hood. How's that sound Scott?"

Scott had already reached into his pocket to pull out a security sticker. It was the only one he had. "Ah, Mr. . . ?"

"Sullivan," Jon replied, "Jon Sullivan."

"Mr. Sullivan all I have is this security sticker, which will allow you access to any parking area at the airport, I hope that will be okay?"

"Scott, this is great. We'll just let the rest of what happened remain our secret. OK?

"Thank you Mr. Sullivan."

"No need to be formal, Scott. You were just doing your job. Feel free to call me Jon, okay?"

Scott replied, "Yes, sir... ahh, I mean thank you... Jon."

Jon put the sticker on his front bumper, nodded to Scott and backed out into the main traffic stream. With a wave good-bye, Jon was on his way home.

Jon was laughing so hard when he got to the first set of lights; tears were streaming down his face. Down the road about a mile, he pulled off into a convenience store gas station. Popping the hood open, Jon gave the underside of the hood a whack. The contour of the hood returned to normal.

After going inside the store and purchasing a cup of coffee, Jon looked briefly back in the direction of the airport and then got in the car. Thinking about how easy it was to talk his way out of the ticket and ending up with a security sticker, Jon started to snicker again. "We don't stand a chance against terrorists," Jon mumbled to himself as he started up the vehicle and pulled back onto the road.

Arriving back at the house to change for work, Betsy walked down to his car as he got out.

"Jon," she called out to him.

Jon looked up to see Betsy approaching. She wore a flowered skirt which reflected the sun's rays and a peach top with a V shape front lined with delicate lace. Jon breathed her in.

"Jon, have you seen Pete?"

"No, he wasn't here this morning. It is strange because he has never done this before."

Betsy had moved up next to him and Jon could smell a bouquet of something that smelled so enticing, it made him want to scoop her up into his arms.

He felt himself stirring inside. Apparently Betsy felt it also as she stood with her arms down by her sides, squared off at Jon looking directly into his eyes.

It felt surreal. For so long Jon had kept himself barricaded from emotional attachments. Except for his son and Pete, Jon revealed little of himself. To most Jon came across as a bit cold; a bit distant. Now the icebergs in him were melting away. No, they were like an avalanche; like a mountain suddenly falling away. The suddenness was overwhelming. It was almost like a dizziness. Betsy's smell permeated his nostrils and flowed through every ounce of him. A whirling sensation overcame him.

Suddenly his arms encircled her waist and brought her gently forward. As if in slow motion their faces came within inches. Then as if he could not get the smell of her right, he would move ever so closer, than back. He would repeat the movement but each time get slightly closer there was no resistance on her part as she found herself almost mesmerized by his touch, his smell. Her breathing seemed to slow yet her heart began to beat furiously. She found her lips warm and tingly. She also was stirred and feelings long suppressed began to emerge.

Their lips barely touched. They stopped. Their eyes met. Each signaled a yearning; a deep longing which accompanied the tenderness of the moment. Then Jon's lips gently touched hers. Then gently but firmly his lips caressed her as if to taste the sweetness that lingered there. She almost involuntarily opened her mouth to receive the full effect of his lips caressing hers.

It seemed like hours yet was only seconds before the reality of her emotional yielding flooded her consciousness. Quickly she pulled away as Jon's embrace beckoned her back. Her mind was reeling and she fought with everything she had to push back the feelings swelling up from deep inside. She gasped. Looking at Jon with a hurt look as he now had only his hands gently resting on her waist, she pulled away. She turned and ran back up to her house.

"Oh shit, you asshole. You stupid asshole," Jon said quietly to himself in disgust. He couldn't believe he had done that; ruined a great friendship by yielding to his desires. His insides ached to run after her, swing her around, take her in his arms and absorb her into his very being.

Pete ceased to be an issue. Jon went in, took off his clothes and jumped into the shower. Slowly he turned up the cold water until the stream was the temperature of the water roaring down Mt Katahdin, in Baxter State Park, Bangor, Maine in September.

As soon as he felt reality pouring back in, his thoughts went to the jobsite he was to visit and inspect the work done by his crew.

Monday AM

Now attendant to the requirements of his job as site foreman, Jon went through the punch list mentally which he had left with the crew. As he sat down to put on his socks, the nerves began to play painfully under the scars. He jumped up to slip into his dungarees and he felt the twinge in his back which had kept him from a solid night of rest. "Gees," he thought to himself, "if Betsy knew what a physical wreck I am she would avoid any emotional relationship with me." He stopped for a second as he pulled out the black polo shirt. "Why in the hell am I even thinking about some emotional entanglement? As if I don't have enough to worry about."

Tying up his work boots, Jon glanced at his watch. "Good, I still have plenty of time before the crew gets there." Jon wanted to be at the jobsite before the crew arrived from the other job so he would know what was done and how to direct their activities.

As he pulled out of the driveway, he couldn't see Betsy, a pillow clutched to her chest, watching him through the front window, as he turned onto McCrory and sped toward 24-27.

Pulling into the site, he was happy to see he was the first to arrive. Gilbert had given him the okay to take time off to get Lance on a plane. Then the plan was for Jon to meet the crew and discuss what needed to be done to finish up this job. He parked off to the side where normally a Trusky vehicle would be parked. He made his way into the rear of the beautiful gambrel roof colonial which overlooked the sixth fairway of the Oaks Pine golf course in Pinehurst.

He enjoyed being alone to inspect the work done by others. He had a good crew. Gilbert Trusky seemed pleased with Jon's knowledge, his workmanship and his dedication to getting things done. Gilbert Trusky had taken over his father's company many years earlier. Where his dad had been primarily a home improvement man, taking on odd jobs to fix up what others had messed up, Gilbert had bigger dreams. It was uncomfortable for Gilbert Sr., when his son had embarked on such grand schemes. But when he saw how his son used his degree from John Hopkins and his savvy in dealing with people, the elder proudly gave way to Gilbert's way of doing things. When he died Gilbert seemed to be motivated into even greater things as he undertook commercial along with residential projects and even bid successfully on several state construction jobs.

Gilbert was a large man, who at 6'6", was an imposing figure. As a starting forward for John Hopkins State basketball, in 1969 under Jim Valvano, he could see the brilliance of Valvano long before he became the coach at NC State University. In 1983 and 1986 when State won the NCAA championship, Gilbert became a strong supporter of NC State. In 1993 when Valvano passed away from Cancer, Gilbert suffered his first bout with heart disease. Yet after a quadruple by-pass, he was back on the job yearning for bigger and better things.

Gilbert was a fair man, but one who demanded honesty and loyalty. He had made many connections throughout the state at some very influential levels. Yet he never tried to put himself above anyone else. He was humble and meek. Those who tried to take advantage of that soon found out Gilbert was not someone to tangle with. There were numerous times when Gilbert begged Jon to take more control over Trusky Construction. Jon was always appreciative and respectful but he graciously refused anything above his title of foreman. Whereas most men could see the possibilities of a potential partnership in the company what with Gilbert only having a daughter and living alone with her, Jon was content to do his job and be shed of management problems other than those which came with a foreman's position.

Jon continued his inspection of the work done earlier in the week. Pulling out the crowbar from his tool chest, he began to pry off the spotter boards set up to align a wall extension. As the boards squeaked loose, he didn't hear the footsteps coming up behind him.

Suddenly he felt a pair of eyes boring a hole in his back. He turned and jumped as he was surprised to see Judy Trusky standing behind him. Looking up at the ceiling rafters with a disgusted look and then back at Judy, Jon complained. "For crying out loud Judy why dontcha shoot a guy rather than scare him to death."

"Oh Jon," she whimpered in her soft voice, "Do I detect a hint of a guilty conscience?"

Jon had picked Judy out as trouble the first time he saw her. It wasn't just that she was the boss's daughter. It was the way she sashayed around. She flounced around like she owned wherever she was. Combined with her striking looks, Jon saw Judy as a stick of dynamite. Her hair, styled so that it flipped upward slightly at her shoulders, was a natural blond —with no cosmetic enhancements. Her eyes were blue, deep blue, in hue. High cheek bones, a small pixie nose, and a full mouth gave her a coy, mischievous look when she smiled. Though only nineteen, she had the alluring form of a fully mature woman. She filled her blue jeans and the blouse she wore in a way that should have been against the law.

Judy knew all the guys on the crews ogled her. They would get sucked into her flirtatious ways and then she would shut them down with a coldness like that from a winter arctic wind.

Jon had tried to speak around his concerns to Gilbert in an attempt to get her off the work sites. But he would just laugh and say "Well, Jon, if I croak tomorrow, she would be your boss." Then he would walk away just laughing to himself.

"Good morning Jon," Judy resumed her conversation. "Good morning, Judy," Jon politely replied as he turned back to his work.

"I guess we are alone, Jon," Judy said in a seductive whisper as she moved closer to him and began to lightly rub his back.

"Damn," Jon thought to himself, "please don't do this to me now." Jon felt himself saying no, but he felt his body saying yes. It had been so long since he had been with a woman; he was almost beyond the point of trusting himself.

"Please, Judy," he pleaded as he turned around. "I need this job. You are a beautiful, no gorgeous woman, and I am old enough to be your Dad. Don't do this to both of us, OK?"

She pursed her lips together and squinted up her face as she looked into Jon's green piercing eyes. "Age, my sweet, has nothing to do with it. And you and I have good spirit. We could light each other up. I know it." Then she paused as she stepped back still looking seductively at him. "We will find our time. Your mouth says no, your beautiful eyes say maybe, but Jon," she gave a dramatic pause as she moved back closer to him. "Your body says a most definite yes!"

Then while still looking him straight in his eyes with a twinkle in her smile, she gently patted the bulge Jon could not hide in his own tight fitting jeans. She turned around and walked away.

Her "gentle" pat had knocked the wind out of Jon. His nuts ached as they would if he had gotten kneed. He held onto a stud and stood there getting his composure back as he heard Judy's BMW spin away from the job site. He picked up a hammer and as he slammed a #3 finish nail into a loose piece of molding, the hammer slipped and collided just above the nail of his left thumb. He cussed the air blue. Then he started to laugh as he realized his hard-on had disappeared and his nuts were no longer aching. He went back and forth from groaning to laughing for a period of time.

As Jon was checking the square on the corners, Gilbert approached.

"Jon the crew has done a great job. We're ahead of schedule and the owners have made their initial inspection tour and love the work. As I was coming over here, Judy called me and suggested we get the crews together and show our appreciation. What do you think?"

Jon shook his head approvingly knowing Judy was behind the invitation. But he also knew Gilbert was a good man. His wife had died shortly after child birth. Gilbert and his wife had Judy late in life and she had given Gilbert a real handful. Jon was amazed how Gilbert and he had bonded. They had a special relationship, more like brothers than employer and employee. Jon had always been humbled by the graciousness of the man and he knew Gilbert had been hurt in a way, when he offered Jon a partnership which Jon politely refused. Yet the bonding of the two men continued to grow.

Gilbert was also aware of Judy's affection with Jon. Initially it angered him. Then as he saw how Jon handled it, his respect for Jon grew. Despite his urging of Judy to find partners her own age, Judy would dismiss the thought. Despite her flirtatious manner, she seemed to only have eyes for Jon. Now he almost wished that Jon would have some interest in Judy. He had an initial concern about their age difference but these days' people seemed to look at such things differently. It was not a social problem. Gilbert knew he could not ask for a finer son-in-law. In fact, sometimes he would catch himself dreaming of grand kids. So now he just looked on at Judy's pursuit with a lot of humor and got an equal amount of enjoyment in watching Jon resist the temptation.

Finally, after some thought, Jon spoke. "Gilbert, I think the guys would appreciate such a gesture. What were you thinking about doing?"

"Well, I thought we might all get together tonight before I have to go out of town this weekend. We could do a barbecue and down some beers. If the chemistry of everyone together is good, we'll plan a big get together when I get back."

Jon knew some of the crew members were not too friendly with one another. Jon couldn't figure out if it was a kind of professional jealousy or what it was. Gilbert had obviously seen it also although he had never brought it up.

"Sounds okay with me," Jon replied, thinking it might be good to relax and get the teams together. "But we will have to limit the beer consumption. We've got to be back here early. We have received the revised blueprints for the changes the owner wanted, and we will be pressed to make the schedule as it is."

Gilbert laughed. "Never knew a little beer to stop construction. But that will be your job."

Then with a devious chuckle, he said, "It ought to be as much fun as trying to keep Judy in check." Gilbert turned and started to walk away. "You check with the men, and let me know what the headcount is. Otherwise, we'll see you all at 7 p.m."

Gilbert walked off still chuckling to himself.

The comment about Judy shocked Jon. "My god, did Gilbert see what went on earlier?" Jon thought to himself.

Jon moaned and went about some of the punch list corrections. Soon the crews began to show up. Larry the lead carpenter was the first to spot Jon and go over and speak to him. Larry Weaks was a top notch carpenter with a talent for finishing work. Because of his reputation for quality and innovations, many companies in the Sandhill area had tried to get him to go on board. Larry, twenty-eight, had been with Trusky for several years before Jon. Because of that Jon felt there might be some animosity after Jon was named top foreman. Yet Larry was happy with Jon and didn't seem to hold it against him that Jon got the job. Besides he knew he couldn't manage the way Jon had shown he could plan and organize and Jon always had a way with words. Larry was barely 6' tall and a Southern Red Neck through and through. He and his wife and two sons lived in a trailer park on the other side of Carthage, about ten miles from Robbins. Jon and Larry had the most seniority of the Trusky crews and together they kept the reign over the crews where guys seemed to just come and go depending on whether or not it was deer season or there was more money to be paid elsewhere. Some got let go, as both Larry and Jon put up with no slack. You either pulled your own weight or you didn't.

Larry and Jon passed the word around. Although it was late notice, everyone could make it. Jon called Gilbert to give him a headcount. Then Jon spent time briefly reviewing the blue prints for the changes.

It was 5:30 p.m. when Jon returned to the doublewide. Betsy's car was gone. After closing the car door, Jon stood there. There was a gentle cool breeze rolling in from the woods. The pine smell filled his nostrils. He sniffed at the air.

"Pete," he called out.

Slowly Jon walked around the doublewide. Neither Pete's dog bowl nor water bowl had been touched. He stood on the deck and looked out into the woods.

"Pete," he called out. Then he turned and went into the doublewide, stopping briefly before entering and turning once again to peer into the woods. Jon washed his hands. He turned and took off his work clothes. He put his work boots in the kitchen. He walked into the bathroom, turned on the shower. Back in the bedroom, he laid out some casual dress clothes.

After a quick shave, a hot shower and a splash of Obsession, Jon slipped into his clothes and walked back onto the back deck. Several times he called for Pete, before leaving for the Trusky's. Between his son's weird account and insistence it was the truth, Pete's disappearance, his embarrassment with Betsy, the new design changes on the job and Gilbert's cavalier attitude about the schedule impact, tonight's shindig was not a welcomed event. Jon had not felt this mentally worn down since leaving corporate America.

By the time he arrived at the Trusky's everyone was there except for Larry. Lou Wagoner, one of the rough carpenters met him as he walked up the sidewalk with a beer in each hand.

"Man," Lou whispered as he handed Jon a beer. "You won believe the eats Ole Trusky has put out for us. Shore was generous. He's all right. Too bad Weeks can't make it."

"What's up with Weeks?" Jon inquired, after he thanked him for the beer.

"Oh he called the Truskys'. Said something about one of his kids was sick and he felt he needed to stay home. Judy took the call."

At the sound of Judy's name, Jon rolled his eyes. He sighed, blew air from his lungs and took a big long swig.

Jon went out onto the patio and mingled with the crew. As he listened to the guys talk sports, his eyes swept the Trusky's home. Gilbert had built this 5 bedroom gambrel roof French Colonial ranch with his own hands for he and his wife. It was built right on the edge of the course at Pine Needles. Four years previously, when Jon had applied for a job with Trusky Construction, Gilbert interviewed Jon at his home. They sat on the deck where they were tonight overlooking the fifteenth hole at the Pine needles Resort. In 1996, Gilbert had invited Jon to sit with him on the same deck during the Open when Annika Sorenstam from Sweden shot an 8 under score for a repeat of the championship she had won the previous year. It was obvious then that Gilbert loved golf and retiring here one day was his goal.

Gilbert had built his home on the fifteenth fairway of Pine Needles Golf Course where he had 125 feet of the golf course accessible to his golf cart. And whenever the mood struck him he would amble out and play.

His home has a great floor plan with the master bedroom on the main level and a long corridor off of which were 4 Bedrooms; one for Judy and two guest rooms. Jon found the space of the home reminiscent to the home he and Dorothy had when they lived in Winston Salem. There was lots of storage space and right off the sun room that faced the golf course was an indoor exercise room featuring an enclosed exercise pool. The master bedroom was at the left side of the house, if you faced the house from the back deck. The bedroom overlooked a long spacious driveway, fitted with security cameras to monitor any traffic coming up to the house toward the three car garage and two utility sheds accessed by the gardener who was responsible for the homes beautiful landscape.

Passing through the kitchen by the hallway leading to the master bedroom was a large 12' x 20" living room, which opened into a den with a gas log fireplace overlooking the fairway. Then there was the playroom accessible from the back deck. There one could play pool, cards or anything else in the 20'x20' room. Off the playroom was a guest bathroom and a corridor that lead down to the bedrooms where Judy and any guests could sleep. Where the rooms did not have marbled floors, they were covered with a beautiful Patagonian rosewood solid prefinished hardwood. The maid who came in every other day made the floors shine and together with the beautiful crown moldings, the home looked like something out of "Southern Living."

The men were all mingling and a number were talking about the MBNA Platinum 400 held in June at Dover International Speedway where Rusty Wallace won the pole but the race was won by Tony Stewart. Some were arguing as to why Kyle Petty didn't qualify and some were surprised Dale Earnhardt wasn't in contention. The beer flowed and finally at 9:30 p.m., Jon and Gilbert started to herd the group out to their cars so they would at least have a semblance of a crew to start the next workday.

As the last of the crew left, Gilbert asked Jon to join him in his den and have a night cap. Jon came in and sat in one of the oversized leather recliners. Gilbert poured them each a small brandy. He gave one to Jon and ambled over to his own recliner.

"Jon, I can't thank you enough for the quality work you have been able to produce."

"Thank you Gilbert, but the majority of the credit goes to the crew. You have some fine craftsmen working for you."

Gilbert breathed in heavily and thought for a moment. "Yes, you are right Jon." Then after a brief hesitation he added, "But an orchestra without a leader doesn't produce fine music."

"Thank you Gilbert, thank you," Jon replied as he listened to the tune of "To Catch a Falling Star," being sung by Perry Como and softly coming across through the overhead speakers. Jon breathed in deeply and turned his glass upside down as he inhaled the last of the Beaujolais Noveau, the rich red wine made from gamay grapes produced in the Beaujolais region of France. Jon smiled a whimsical smile as he remembered how he had to learn the basics of wine knowledge so he could impress his corporate counterparts in previous lifetime. "Ah yes," he mumbled," A most popular vin de primeur, fermented for just a few weeks until officially released for sale on the third Thursday of November."

"Ahh," Gilbert laughed, "a wine connoisseur. Jon you are a man with many talents" Gilbert raised his glass to toast Jon and drank the remnants of his glass. They both laughed.

Jon was staring off in space seemingly lost in thought. "Jon? You okay?"

"Ya, I guess Gilbert. I have had a lot on my mind lately and to be honest I have just had one too many drinks tonight."

Gilbert stared at Jon who was smiling weakly but looked suddenly overly tired.

"No problem Jon. Look, why don't you take one of the guest rooms and lie down for a few minutes. I'll come and get you in a half an hour or Judy will if she is back by then. Then if you need us to, one of us will run you home. Watcha say?"

"Thanks Gilbert, I think I will take you up on your suggestion. Thanks."

Slowly Jon got himself up. He walked over and shook Gilbert's hand. "Thanks for a great evening. I think if I just close my eyes for a few I'll be okay. Then I'll make my way home."

"Jon that will be fine."

Jon turned and went through the living room and kitchen and down the bedroom corridor. He went in and flopped on the bed. Almost instantly he was in a deep sleep.

Everyone had left except for Jon. Gilbert went into the kitchen and put a few things away. Then he wrote a note on a pad attached to the refrigerator he and Judy used to communicate with. He was also pretty tired and he took himself to the master bedroom and began to get himself ready to go to sleep.

Suddenly Jon began to dream of someone rubbing his chest, kissing him around his face. His dream had Betsy kneeling at the bed gently waking him to get up for work. He felt his body being caressed with a soft moist touch. He began to wake up still a bit sleepy. He looked down toward his feet and got the shock of his life.

His slacks were unzipped and pulled down. His privates were out in the fresh air and Judy was caressing him with her tongue, while her hand caressed his chest. Her mouth was upon him and she moved her eyes up from where her head lay to see Jon's look.

"Judy." He exclaimed as he attempted to get up while still in a sleepy, tired daze.

Judy pushed him back down. "Shut up love. You're in my bedroom now so anything goes."

It was now about Midnight. Judy had come back to the house and seen the note her dad had written before retiring for the night. "Sweetheart, Jon Sullivan is taking a short nap in one of the bedrooms. Please gently wake him up no later than 1:00 a.m. I am bushed. Call me if there is any problem. Love Dad."

Feeling too weak to resist, and fighting the waves of pleasure rolling through him, Jon gasped.

"Dammit Judy, your Dad is going to be coming to get me up."

"Shhh," she said gently as she pulled away from her activity only briefly. "I am the messenger, darling and he asked me to be gentle. Now lay back until I'm through being gentle." It was hard for her to concentrate as she was tickled at her reply and started to giggle.

Again Jon tried to get up. She pushed him back down on the bed again and wrapped her tongue around the hard organ that strained for release.

"Dam," he thought. "Have I no control?"

Jon gave in and grasped the bed with one hand in a furious hold while reluctantly but unable to stop using the other to gently touch Judy and stroke her back. Her head moved in strokes each one of which brought an immeasurable pain as well as intense pleasure both at the same time.

At the time of his eruption, Judy groaned and purred deep inside, as if she also had had an orgasmic release. She moved from the flaccid wet organ and came to his face thrusting her tongue deep inside of him. He returned the kiss and could feel the hardness return,

"Judy?" A deep voice, Gilbert's voice called out from the kitchen area.

Jon froze. "Oh my god, I knew it!" he thought.

"Judy." He exclaimed as he again attempted to get up this time in a twisting panic still feeling like he was in a surreal event.

"Shh." Judy said softly in his ear as she felt his body tense. She pushed him back down; jumped up from her bed and quickly got to the door. Opening it up slightly, she said, "Dad, I got Jon up. He has gone out the back patio doors to get some cool air and clear his head. He will be back in a minute."

"OK sugar, would you mind making sure he is okay to drive and seeing to it he gets home all right? Everyone else has left and I have hit the sack."

"OK Dad, I'll take care of it."

Judy slowly closed and locked her door. With an impish look on her face, she slithered over to the bed where Jon was hastily trying to get his pants up and zipped.

"No sweetheart," Judy cooed as she again pushed him back down on the bed. "This is our time, it's perfect and I'm not through with you yet."

"Listen Judy," Jon stammered as he tried to appear in control. "This is not perfect, and we are through."

Judy roughly jumped on Jon and sat on him as he lay almost in shook at her brazenness. She was mad now, but it was more than being mad, she was intense and had purpose.

"Look you son of a bitch, I have wanted you since I first saw you. I am in love with you. You have spurned my every move I have made on you and you are not leaving here without fucking my brains out."

Jon was stunned. "Judy," he tried to say harshly, as he still struggled under her weight and tried to get up from the bed.

"Judy... my ass," she replied, as she pulled him back down and jumped up off the bed. She suddenly ripped her top off. Jon stared at the most perfectly shaped breasts he had seen in a long time. Beautiful white skin and nipples that stood at attention, they heaved up and down as she breathed.

She Spoke to him in a soft but harsh manner. "You either make love to me tonight or I swear to God I will yell rape for all I'm worth and let you and dad sort it all out."

Jon lay there stunned. Yes, he needed a woman. And... this was one hell of a woman. But this was not right. He knew that. He also knew Judy was capable of doing exactly as she threatened.

"Now," Judy purred "you don't worry about a thing. You let me take control. I am going to let you put me to sleep okay?"

Jon lay there stunned as Judy removed her bottoms and began to remove Jon's clothes. As much as he wanted to resist, the pleasure was almost too much to bear.

The two of them together did the things people do in the room where they would never confess what they had done to others.

⊥ ⊥ ⊥

As Jon looked at Judy sleeping, he glanced at his watch. Reality jumped back into focus.

"Oh great, 1:30 a.m."

Jon quickly got dressed and left through the patio door. He walked around to where his vehicle was parked. He started the engine and proceeded home.

As the car pulled down the driveway, Gilbert turned over and looked at the clock. "Hmmm," he said to himself and fell back into a sound sleep.

As he pulled into his and Betsy's driveway, he noticed Betsy's car was still not there. That was strange. She never went out late during the week never mind staying overnight someplace.

"Boy, first Pete disappears than Betsy," Jon said to himself.

Parking, he clamored out, feeling dozy from the night's events.

"Pete," he called as he turned onto his back deck, not really expecting Pete at this point to respond. He stopped in his tracks. A muffled sound came out of the woods. Jon turned toward the sound.

"Pete?" He yelled.

Then there was a bark. It was Pete's bark.

"Pete, come her Pete, come here boy," Jon yelled. His head spinning from the drinking, what had happened with Betsy and then the fiasco with Judy, and now with Pete somewhere in the woods refusing to come when called, He felt like he was in the middle of a twilight zone episode. He couldn't imagine at this point how close that would become a reality.

Jon would call several times. Pete would return a bark or two in response but would not appear. It didn't sound like Pete was that far away. Fearing Pete might be caught; Jon turned and went into the house. He browsed through drawers in the kitchen trying to locate the flashlight he got for Christmas. "Ahh," he said to himself as he found it. Then as he turn to leave he clicked the flash light on, but there was no light. Cussing under his breath Jon went back to find some replacement batteries. Finally locating some, Jon installed the batteries, checked the light and headed out the door.

Using Pete's barks as a guide, Jon made his way through the woods which were now, with no moon light, as dark as the other side of the moon. Vines and pickers snared Jon as he made his way to Pete's bark. He pushed them away or used his body to force them to break or loosen their grip. Finally as the barks sounded closer, the flash light picked up Pete's paws and then all of Pete.

Pete looked at Jon and started to moan as Jon approached. He looked back at something at front of him, looked back at Jon moaning, and then went back to staring at something in front of him. His head lay on his front paws.

Jon moved the light to see what had Pete's attention. Jon could see nothing but some scrub bushes, a lot of pines and a small holly bush nestled below one of the pines. Jon remembered what Lance had said something about a holly bush. Jon shined the light back to Pete and then back to the holly bush. Lance's words came back to him. "The bush Dad, the holly bush, it lit up."

Slowly, Jon got down on one knee. Again he played the light back and forth from Pete to the holly bush which seemed to have Pete's attention.

"I'm sorry Pete; I just don't get the connection. It's nothing but a holly bush and not a very healthy one at that."

Jon got up. He moved closer to the holly bush. Looking for snakes or something that might warrant Pete's attention, and seeing nothing, Jon kicked at the holly bush to show Pete there was nothing there.

In less time than it takes to blink, a wisp of light came out of the bush catching Jon's foot before he could strike the bush. Jon found himself being flipped through the air. With a thud he landed on some pine needles right beside Pete. His chest hurt where he had landed over a large surface root.

He quickly scrambled for the flash light and frantically looked around for the assailant. Pete hadn't budged. He just remained looking at the bush. Again Jon played the light back and forth from Pete to the holly bush.

"What the hell…," He picked up a small pine branch and tried to prod the bush. The branch exploded in flames as it touched the holly.

"*Please help me.*" The voice seemed to come from the holly and it lit up with a white and blue pulsing light.

"What the hell'"" Jon repeated to himself in a low tone not knowing what else to say.

"Who is out there?" The words sputtered out of Jon as if he was being made a fool of by someone playing a practical joke. Jon frantically shined the light again back from Pete to the bush and then around the area.

Pete was continuing his surveillance. Now he was groaning in what might be described as a low wail. He looked back and forth from his master to the bush.

"Please." the voice continued. *"I am a traveler from another world. I am marooned here and I need your help or I will die..."*

Jon said nothing quietly expecting any minute for someone to jump out of the bushes and tell him he is on candid camera.

The life form, or whatever it was, explained. It was a presence, a form of energy which had been shipwrecked on this planet. It went on to share its need. It could survive in its own form for decades, but every so often it needed a host. The holly bush was only a temporary resting spot. It needed a human organic host to act as a catalyst allowing the traveler to regenerate the energy it needed to survive.

"What the hell does this have to do with me," thought Jon whose mind was already racing back to his disbelief of Lance's story.

Jon could hardly detect the smallest of a wisp emanating from the bush and encircling him sensing his every thought.

In response to Jon's thoughts, the presence continued. It told Jon of how its presence within Jon was only a temporary thing. It told Jon it would leave Jon any time there were not great benefits for Jon to realize. It continued, telling Jon it could and would repair Jon's systems and upgrade them to their optimum performance. It would be a power source for Jon such that he could actually heal others. In addition there would be other powers Jon would possess so long as they were not used to attack others unless it was self-defense.

Finally Jon spoke out.

"Look, I guess I'm sorry for your situation… which I don't all together understand… but the answer is no… NO!" Then Jon looked down at Pete who was now looking at him.

"Now come on Pete, for the last time come on."

As if released from the trance he was in, the dog followed his master home.

Getting closer to the doublewide, Jon could hear the phone ringing off the hook. Jon looked down at his watch and shined the flashlight on it so he could see.

"Good God!" he exclaimed. It was 2:10 a.m. "If this is Judy, I'll…" He hurried into the kitchen and picked up his phone and roughly said, "WHAT!"

Dorothy was on the other end of the line. She was in hysterics.

"Dot… Is that you Dot?"

She kept on crying. Finally she said, "Jon where have you been? I have been trying to get you all night dammit!"

Jon held the phone away from him at arm's length and gave it a hateful look. "What am I still in the twilight zone?" he thought.

"IT'S LANCE…" she started to cry incoherently now.

Suddenly a new voice came on the line.

"Jon, this is Margie Templeton. I am one of Dorothy's neighbors. Lance was hit by a car earlier tonight… apparently a drunken driver. He is in critical condition and … and… they don't expect he will survive the week. There is extensive head trauma and massive internal damage. You need to come up as soon as you can." There was a pause

"Jon?"

Jon was stunned. He was trying to come to grips with everything and now this. He was close to losing control.

Finally, Jon came to grips with the situation. "Yes… uh, Margie is it?… uh… okay… uh… where is my son now?"

"He is in Massachusetts General Hospital in Boston."

"Uh… okay… ah… thanks for being a friend… uh tell Dot… uh I'll catch the first flight up."

"OK Jon. Let us know when you get in and we will meet you."

"Uh, thanks anyway, but you need to stay with Dot. I'll be okay. Uh… I'll get a cab and go straight to the hospital."

When Jon hung up he collapsed on the couch.

"Oh my god," he prayed out loud, "don't let Lance die. Please dear Lord don't let him die. Take me instead. I'll do anything, please don't take him."

After gathering his thoughts, Jon called the Greensboro airport. The earliest flight would not be until 10:00 a.m. tomorrow. "Wait a minute that was today," he thought. He looked at his watch it was 2:45 a.m. already. He booked the flight and collapsed on the couch.

"What am I going to do?" he thought.

Suddenly he remembered. The presence said, "*I would be a power source for you such that you could actually heal others.*"

"Man, I hope this wasn't a dream." With that Jon jumped up from the couch, grabbed his flashlight and headed out the door, with Pete right at his heels.

Finding the holy bush, Jon shined his light at it. "Are you still here?"

Jon prayed this was not all part of his imagination. "*Yes.*"

"Is the deal still open?"

"*Yes.*"

"Will the powers I receive allow me to help someone who has been hurt to recover?"

"*Yes.*"

"What do I have to do to do my part?"

"*Walk into the bush and open up your mind as if relaxing and about to take in information you wanted to have. It will be sometime before I will be re-oriented and then I can upgrade your systems.*"

"I don't care about my 'systems.' How soon will I be able to help someone who is critically hurt?"

"*I will be functional within four to five of your Earth hours.*"

Pushing the point, Jon continued. "Okay then within four to five hours. I will have the capability to help someone recover from being critically hurt."

"*Unless the person is in the last stages of irreversible damage you can.*"

Jon did not want to hear that. However, having no other choice, Jon did as he was instructed.

Pete watched his master walk into the bush and be encircled by a glowing white light flowing from the holy. The light turned light blue and created an aura around his master covering his entire body. Then as if pulled in by a vacuum, the light disappeared within Jon.

His master continued to stand there for a few minutes after the light disappeared.

Finally, after some moments, Jon turned to Pete.

"Come on Pete, we need to go home."

As Jon turned to leave, he furtively glanced at the holy bush. He tentatively kicked it. Nothing happened.

CHAPTER 3

FULFILLING THE AGREEMENT

It was pitch dark when Jon returned to his home. His mind was having difficulty comprehending what had just happened in the woods. He felt he was insane to have agreed to the strange bargain he had made.

"I have to do this, if there is any hope it might help Lance," he thought to himself.

At the same time he was trying to rationalize what he had just done, the first tremor struck. From the middle of his back up thru his neck into his head, the pain was so deep, so intense. Surely someone or something had just laid into him with a heavy axe. For a moment his mind took him back to the beating he had survived near the road house.

Yet there was no one there. At least there was no one there he could see. Now the pain began to come in waves. So excruciating were they, he began to spin around at the door way. He lurched forward. His subconscious led him to the bedroom wherein Lance had spent some precious time before he had to leave for home. The thought of his son brought a flicker of relief. It was much too brief. Then the relentless pain, now in his buttocks, grasped him as a dog might grab its favorite toy before shaking it in feverous motion.

A slight grasp at consciousness, the thought he was having a brutal heart attack. Before he could linger with rationale thought he lost consciousness and complete control as his body collapsed on the bed. Now he was no longer able to feel any pain. An observer would have thought otherwise. Surely he must be feeling pain as his face grimaced one minute and then relaxed the next only to go back to another strange distorted grimace. His eyes, wide opened, stared as his body pulsated with the tremors that would be expected of someone in the middle of seizures. Throughout the night his body would react this way.

Within him, Jon's organs, his pathology, the science of the mechanical, physical, and biochemical functions of his tissues and organs was in a state of change. The 1.3 gallons of blood flowing through almost 100,000 kilometers (62,000 miles) of blood vessels every single minute were in a raging storm. Every cell was undergoing examination and change as desired by some outside source that was now inside. Jon's molecular makeup was in the middle of a raging storm.

Likened to a race car being tuned up while in the middle of a Daytona 500 as it was flying down the track, Jon's body heaved up and down, back and forth as his internal and external mechanical, physical and biochemical make up was changed or adjusted. Every fiber and muscle was examined and reexamined until they were in perfect condition.

From the view point of a molecule within him it was like an explosion of the universe wherein a new planet is created. From the outside to a visitor looking in, it would look like a beautiful multicolor light show with glowing pastels and sharp colors intermingled over and under and through Jon's helpless body as he heaved up and down and back and forth on the bed.

As the night lingered on the intensity of the light storm lessened. Jon's body became more relaxed and soon he was lying quietly. His breathing was deep. A medical examination of him at this time would reveal a body of a much younger man. Imperfections were changed to perfections. The old was changed to new.

Now Jon lay peaceful engaged in a deep resting sleep.

At 6:30 a.m., the alarm clock announced the beginning of a new day.

Jon opened his eyes. As he laid there in the same clothes he had worn the day before, he had a sense there were some changes. He couldn't at first put his finger on what it was. Perhaps it was an after effect of the beers he had the night before. But as soon as he thought that he dismissed the thought. He began to stretch. As he shrugged his shoulders, he realized the pain he was always waking up to in his injured back was not there. As he sat up to turn and get out of bed, he saw the blood on the pillow.

"What the… ?"

Then he noticed the teeth rolling around in the bed.

Again, he exclaimed "What the… ? He began to feel freaked out. Immediately he jumped out of the bed and ran into the bathroom. As he hesitantly looked into the mirror, he stood there startled by what he saw.

He couldn't believe what he saw. The face looking back at him was not the one he went to bed with. The slight childhood scar he had under his right eye was gone. His skin was absent of the few freckles he had and was clear and vibrant. And his teeth… It was like someone had pulled all his teeth and replaced them with clean, new, white dentures. He reached into his mouth and pulled on his teeth. They were real.

"How can this be?" He said to himself.

Suddenly he was caught up with the thought he had to be on a plane at 10:00 a.m. Even so, Jon was mesmerized and dumbfounded by this new him.

Looking at his arm where the burn scars had been, they were no longer visible. Instead, his arm was clear. His back, despite being sore from a 4x4, which had fallen on it at work, felt strong and without pain.

Quickly pulling of his clothes and getting into the shower to get ready for work, Jon could not help but try to find reality, some explanation as to what was going on. As the water beat down, Jon began to remember the night before. He remembered the deal he had made with the energy source who claimed he could heal Lance who was in a hospital in Massachusetts after being hit by a hit and run driver. He remembered the strange source had asked to be allowed to reside within Jon.

He forced his thoughts to come back to reality. "It will take about an hour to drive. If I allow half an hour to park and get to the gate I will just have enough time. I better leave at 8:00 a.m. to allow for any problems. That should be enough."

He let out a deep yawn. He felt the need to stretch his arms and legs. Getting more of a bearing on things he saw it was a beautiful day. As he stood up, he felt a spring in his feet. "Gosh," he thought, as he looked at the bed. "It looks like somebody had a fight in it." He continued to observe. As he stretched like a cat to loosen up the joints and get the kinks out, he couldn't help but notice how good he was feeling. Despite have had hardly any shut eye, his back wasn't bothering him at all as it normally did during the early morning hours. In fact, Jon felt absolutely terrific physically. If it weren't for the terrible trip ahead and Lance's crisis, it would have been the start of a wonderful day.

Jon slipped into his slacks and wandered into the kitchen to start a cup of coffee. Last night's weirdness flashed ever so briefly in front of him. Suddenly Pete started to bark. Jon pushed the coffee maker button and looked out the front window to see what had Pete's attention. As he looked outside Betsy was walking down from the house.

"Oh good," he said to himself, "this will save me from having to write her a note."

Jon went back to the coffee and pulled out a second cup from the cabinet. While he waited for Betsy to arrive he took Pete's dog food and poured some into Pete's bowl. As he was getting Pete's meal ready, Betsy arrived at the back door.

She knocked.

"Hey, Betsy, come on in." Jon was smiling at her but Betsy looked serious and forlorn.

"Well, I see Pete's back," she said somberly. "He came up to the house and gently grabbed me by the hand and started to pull me down here."

Jon looked at Pete mischievously through the door. He laughed. "Well, Pete's no dummy. He always was a sucker for a pretty face."

He could see Betsy pull back a bit when he said that

Jon looked into Betsy's eyes. He put Pete's bowl down. He walked over to her and put both his hands on her shoulders. She didn't resist him.

"Look, I didn't mean to offend you by what I said. No more than I meant to when I kissed you yesterday. The remark I just made was meant to be cute, I guess cause I feel a little uneasy about having put you off so yesterday. I was just trying to put a little humor into the situation." He paused. "The kiss yesterday was real. It felt right and I would be lying if I told you I was sorry for doing it. There, I… I guess I am really being a jerk. I am sorry. I wouldn't hurt you for anything."

Jon turned away from Betsy. He reached for Pete's bowl and put it outside for Pete who devoured it all in three bites. When he came back inside, Betsy stood right in his way. This time she put her hands flat on his chest.

"Look, Jon, this is hard for me to get out, so be patient. It has been a long time since I have been stirred inside as you did with… with your kiss. It scared me. We have had such a great relationship. I was afraid it would go away I have spent a lot of time thinking about it. I even drove to the coast by myself just to be alone and think about who I was and what I wanted.

Jon opened up his mouth as if to say something. Betsy put her hand over his mouth. She continued. "Don't apologize for the kiss. It was beautiful. It felt good being in your arms. If things change, they change. If one can't smell the flowers when they have bloomed what good are they? You... You are a flower Jon. If I can be something for you, no matter how little, I am the lucky one."

Betsy took Jon's face in her hands and slowly, with her eyes caressing his face, brought her lips to his. Her mouth was open and willing. The softness, the tenderness of her embrace caused Jon to tremble. He felt ashamed as flash backs of the previous night came.

Betsy was breathing deeply. It was obvious she wanted more than an embrace.

Jon slowly and reluctantly pulled himself away and held Betsy at arm's length.

"Oh Betsy, you just can't believe how I need you and"—he paused—"want you... but..."

Betsy felt choked when she heard the "but."

"But there has been a terrible accident. Lance was hit by a drunk driver...," Jon's head fell down and he stared at the floor. "He is not expected to survive. I've got to catch the ten o'clock flight this morning to get up there as soon as possible."

"Oh Jon," she moved within his arms and held him close. "Here I am prattling on so... I am so sorry. I... I didn't know."

"Look Betsy," Jon said as he wrapped her in his arms. "You weren't prattling. You were making great sense. I want us to be close. But right now I have got to leave and be at Lance's side. The flight I need to catch takes off from Greensboro at ten this morning."

"What can I do to help?" Betsy said as she stepped away from Jon.

"Just be here. Wait for me to return. Take care of Pete... and... and... pray."

"Oh I will Jon. I will." With that Betsy threw herself into Jon's arms and nestled her head into his shoulder. She couldn't see the aura of light surrounding them both. She just felt warmer and more secure than she had ever felt in her life.

After talking things over, it had been agreed Betsy would drive Jon to the airport. It wasn't until he reached for the door on the passenger side of Betsy's car that he noticed.

The large black and blue bruise on his thumb had disappeared. The burn scars were no longer there. Betsy wanted to say something about it but respect for the crisis he was dealing with kept her from saying anything.

When they pulled into the airport, traffic was heavy. Jon told Betsy to pull over to a "no parking" area near the airline entrance. After she had done that, Jon reached over and put his arm around her neck. He looked longingly at her. "Where have you been all my life," he said. Betsy kissed him just as she saw an officer approaching the car through the rearview mirror.

"Uh-oh. Jon I don't think we can unload here."

"Excuse me, ma'am, but you can't..."

The officer stopped midstream as he looked past the driver at the passenger.

"Oh, uh, good morning, sir, uh, I didn't see it was you. Then looking back at Betsy he said, "Ma'am, you just park right here and take your time. Good day, ma'am," then looking across at Jon he nodded his head and said, "Sir," with a tone of respect.

Officer Scott moved hurriedly down to the next car illegally parked.

"Well, good morning to you also, Officer," Betsy said sarcastically with a smile in her voice and moving her head like a bobble head as Officer Scott moved along. Then she looked back at Jon with a smile that said, "What was that all about?"

Jon smiled sheepishly.

"Some people are just VIPs I guess," he replied giving her one of those crazy looks that drove Lance wild.

When she pulled her chin back and gave him one of those 'wait a minute' looks, they both laughed.

"I'll tell ya about it later, "he said. "I have a lot to tell you about. "He leaned over and gave her a kiss. He found it hard to pull away from her.

As he got out he told Betsy he would call her from the hospital. Betsy told Jon not to worry about work. She would call Mr. Trusky and explain the situation. He got his baggage out of the trunk, gave her a wave and hurried up the walk to the entrance.

He stood at the US Air counter waiting his turn. Suddenly he heard the ticket agent tell the person in front of him the airline flight to Boston was overbooked and she could only issue a standby ticket.

"Oh no!" thought Jon, "how am I going to make this flight?"

"Yes, sir, how may I help you?"

"Well," Jon began, "I have a family emergency and I called last night to reserve a seat on the flight to Boston this morning, and I…"

The tall attractive lissome brunette interrupted him.

"Well, sir, as I'm sure you heard me tell the last person, we are overbooked. I am sorry but standby is the…" This time Jon interrupted. He leaned over and smiled. "Can you please check for me? The name is Sullivan, Jon Sullivan."

Neither one of them were consciously aware of the aura of light flowing from Jon's fingertips to the computer console in front of the agent.

"Sir, you don't understand," the agent started to say, knowing this one was going to be a problem. She had an eye for problem people of the world. Meanwhile just going through the paces she punched up his name again, knowing it would show unconfirmed.

"Sir, I apologize I can't do anything for you but…" She stopped midsentence. Her eyes got as big as saucers. She looked up at Jon and then, double checking, punched up his name again. "Yes, ah… we can't…"

Suddenly she became quite flushed. "Please excuse me, sir, uh, Mr. Sullivan… hold on just a moment. Thank you so much." With that she backed away from the screen as if it had burned her fingers and hurried over to another individual behind the counter area. She talked rapidly to the individual. Then they both approached Jon.

Jon looked out at the terminal. "Oh please Lord let me catch this flight."

A man in his fifties, obviously a supervisor, came up to the ticket terminal where Jon stood along with the agent who had been waiting on Jon. She still looked flushed. Jon looked exasperated at the situation.

He punched in some information. Then he looked at Jon. "Yes, sir, Mr. Sullivan," he said as he verified the screen readings, "We have a first class ticket for you…"

The agent processed the ticket, and Jon pulled out his credit card to pay. The man smiling waved it off. Neither noticed the aura around the screen which was now becoming a wisp of light playing off the supervisor's hand.

"Oh no, Mr. Sullivan, this flight is on us. We are grateful you have chosen US Air and if there is anything we can do to make your trip more enjoyable, please let us know,"

The ticket agent looked dumbfounded, as she looked at the supervisor.

Jon looked totally puzzled, but he took the ticket, thanked the agents, and hurried down to gate.

As he passed through the metal detector, he wondered what had just transpired. Then he just shook his head to himself. "It's not worth thinking about," he thought. What was important was getting on the flight and locating his son.

As he walked away, he couldn't hear that ticket supervisor say to the lady agent, "that's ok; you had no way of knowing he is an FAA inspector." You see," he continued as he manipulated the terminal display, "the entry is made in the VIP section of the passenger record. That is what this flag is for just above his name. Next time just be more careful before you tell a VIP passenger they have to fly standby."

The lady agent looked down at the screen. "There is no such notation there," she thought to herself. The supervisor was moving away to another terminal. She looked back at him and started to call him back. "Uh… Mr…" Then after thinking about it she changed her mind "He has always been a Mr. Know-it-all," she thought. "When that ticket goes through audit, he can explain it to them. No sense in me getting my nose in it." As she turned to address the next customer, she couldn't help the slow smile that suddenly appeared.

Jon settled into the first class aisle seat at 2B. Just as he made himself comfortable, a lad in his twenties with long black greasy hair and a tee shirt that read "Purple Vengeance," brushed by him and plopped into the window seat.

"What's up old man?" the lad quipped sarcastically. "You one of those traveling sales men types or just a tired dude trying to get away from it all, eh what?"

Jon gave him a look that could kill. Then reminding himself of the purpose of the trip and they would be together for a little over an hour, he sighed deeply. "Boy," he thought, "first time in a long time, I get to fly never mind first class, and I've got to get seated next to some drug crazed punk."

The young man was staring at Jon waiting, no, expecting a reply. He bent his head down as he looked over his blue tinted shades at Jon.

"No," Jon softly replied trying to remain civil. "Just traveling to be with family during a medical crisis."

"Oh man, that's heavy, eh what?"

Having no reply, the lad settled down in his seat and looked out the window as the baggage handlers loaded the cargo bay with luggage.

From Jon's arm on the center rest, an aura of blue light appeared. It was hardly perceptible as it left Jon's arm and encircled the hairy arm of his companion in 2A.

Suddenly the stewardess slammed the plane door shut. She took her place at the front of the plane as a recording played out the instructions for the passengers with information they would need for a safe flight as well what steps should be taken in the advent of a problem.

The plane lurched forward and began its move toward the take off point as the stewardess walked the aisle to make sure all seat belts were fastened. The stewardess took her seat and the plane lurched forward with its turbines roaring as it fought to obtain lift. Soon the plane was rising upward away from the Greensboro airport on its flight to Boston.

The plane interior lights flashed that it was now safe for passengers to move about the cabin.

The young man no longer mesmerized by the rising aircraft and the disappearing landscape, turned toward Jon. Again he looked over his blue tinted glasses as he thought about the companion he had ended up with.

"Man," he thought to himself as he remembered telling his buddy K how he was going to sit next to some beauty who would crave his bod. "Man," he thought again, "where are the young chicks who usually make this flight. Man what goddamn bad luck. I've got to get a seat next to some asshole on a medical mission. Where are the fucking broads who usually make this flight?" He thought to himself as he looked back and forth at Jon and then out the window.

Jon could not believe the absolute insolent gall of this young punk. Who did he think he was talking to? Jon turned with a vengeance on his unsuspecting traveling companion.

"Look, you little piece of shit," Jon commanded in a low but deep and commanding tone. "Having you sit next to me is not my idea of a picnic either. If I hear another swear come out of your mouth or you make another reference to assholes or medical missions, I will rework your face for you, do you get it?"

The young man retreated so far into his seat all one could see passing by would have been a sea of black hair.

"Jesus, what in the hell is wrong with this dude?" he thought.

Jon began to get further upset, and then he realized the kid never opened his mouth. Yet Jon could distinctly hear what he was thinking.

Jon whipped off his seat belt and got up. He made a bee line to the men's room. He went in, closed and locked the door and looked into the mirror.

"What in the hell is going on?" Jon exclaimed out loud.

There was no sound except for the roar of the noise the turbines make as it echoes throughout the plane.

Jon repeated his inquiry.

"You, the thing that was in the holly bush… what in the hell is going on?

"*I don't understand the inquiry,*" came a voice which could only be heard in Jon's head.

Quite impatient, Jon turned away from the mirror. It was too weird getting upset at his mirror image. "We had a deal. You said if I wanted you out you would leave. Now what is going on? Talk to me." The absurdity of what Jon was doing made him extremely frustrated.

"It has taken me a while to put your systems in order, correct various deficiencies and begin the process of enhancing all capabilities."

"WHAT!" Jon shouted.

In order to minimize any physical reaction to my presence, I have had to carefully organize the necessary tasks for an optimal interface. You are 70.478 percent fluid. It is basically what you call water. Your system has been carrying a dangerously high level of toxic waste. I have been detoxifying your system. Now the cleansing process is complete. I am proceeding to enhancing your capabilities."

"Look, goddamn it!" If you think I have any idea what you are talking about… thinking… or whatever, you're crazy. I almost lit into some jerk because of what he said, or what I thought he had said. But his lips weren't moving and I know he is not a ventriloquist!"

"Jerk Slang. A contemptibly naive, fatuous, foolish, or inconsequential person. You were picking up his brain patterns as they were formed into communication elements… what you refer to as words."

Jon leaned against the small sink in the tight compartment. "You mean I was reading his mind?"

There was silence. The presence sought to communicate the essence of the answer without it being too difficult for Jon to understand it. Jon had no way of knowing he was specifically chosen for specific tasks ahead. Jon was not ready yet to understand all that would eventually be revealed to him. Yet little by little Jon would become a full partner in this union which was now just beginning. The words were chosen very carefully.

"You were not as you would say reading his mind. You were in his mind. His totality of thoughts, of experiences, belonged to you."

Outside the men's room where Jon was, a stewardess leaned toward the door thinking she was hearing a loud and contentious conversation.

"Sheila… Sheila." she called to another flight attendant.

When Sheila got closer, the stewardess motioned for her to listen at what was going on in the men's room. "Listen… there is a man in there carrying on a conversation, a loud conversation with himself. Do you think there is a problem?"

"Well, let's get one thing straight," Jon continued. "If I am in threat of bodily harm, or I think I might be in danger, your help is welcomed. If I want to read someone's mind, thoughts, whatever or jump into someone's mind or whatever the hell it is you call it, I'll tell you. Until then, don't do it. Do you understand me?"

"Yes."

Jon began to calm down. As he did he realized there might be some usefulness to these new talents. "If you sense information about someone that I might need to know to protect myself; or there is information it would be helpful to know in order to better communicate with someone; or I need to know something in order to avoid danger, then share it with me. Otherwise keep a lid on it. Do you know what that means?"

Jon thought about what he had just said. Before he could ask the presence whether or not the presence understood, his question was answered.

"Yes, I understand." There was no need at this point to tell Jon he was vital to the presence's mission and there was no way the presence would let any harm come to Jon.

"I wonder if you can understand me if I just think out my question," Jon thought to himself.

"Yes," came the reply.

"Oh my god," thought Jon.

Suddenly there was a knock on the door.

"I'll be right out," Jon replied, hastily slapping his face with cold water.

"Are you all right, sir?" came the voice on the other side of the door.

Jon opened up the door. "Excuse me?"

"Are you okay, sir? We heard some loud talking and were concerned you were okay."

"Yes… uh, yes… thanks… uh I have got to give a speech when we land and I was just going over some things," Jon laughingly explained, trying to look as much in control as he could.

"Oh," laughed one of the stewardesses, "Well, good, we hope you will do well."

Jon smiled. "Thanks," he said as he left the bathroom and headed back to his seat.

Each of the stewardesses looked at each other, exchanging weak smiles and exasperated looks that said… it takes all kinds of people to make up a passenger list.

"Now I won't have a thought to myself," thought Jon as he sat down next to his fellow seat companion. By now the lad had pulled himself as far away from Jon's seat as he could and was busy looking out the window just so he wouldn't get Jon's ire.

"I can at least be decent," thought Jon. "Presence," he commanded through his thoughts, in an effort to find out how this new power works, "give me enough information about this young man for me to be able to communicate to him effectively."

Almost instantly, as one might pull up a screen of information on the monitor at a computer terminal, Jon knew all about his flight companion.

Jon turned to engage the young man in conversation and reverse the situation he had created with his outbursts.

"Say... uh excuse me."

The lad turned his head slowly toward the voice. He had a dire look of apprehension on his face not knowing what to expect from this madman.

"Look. I know I acted like a... a..." *What's a word he would understand?* Jon thought to himself. Finding the word he continued, "A... a... squeeze, but I've got like a lot on my tubes, ya know where I'm coming from dude?"

"I can't believe this is coming from me!" Jon thought to himself.

Suddenly the lad stirred in his seat. He swung himself around and stared at Jon. He looked closely over his glasses like he hadn't seen him before. He turned his body around in his seat to make himself more comfortable.

"Ya, man, I can relate to the word," he said softly.

Jon stuck his thumb in the air. "The word," he said.

Now looking more comfortable than ever, the young man began to open up. "Ya know man, when you first started putting on, well man, I don't mind saying I thought you were a piece of upside down cake."

"I can relate to that," Jon replied with his face all squinted up and his head nodding as if he really did understand. Jon decided he would test his new found ability. "Give me more information about this kid," Jon requested of the presence, by merely thinking and not speaking out loud.

"Where are you flying out of originally, Raleigh?" asked Jon.

"No dude, I just got through working a jig in Memphis."

"You weren't by any chance hanging at Spartas?

The lad's eyes opened as wide as they had ever been.

"Dam doodle oodle, how do you know Spartas?"

Jon couldn't help but smile impishly while his insides were shaking with laughter.

"Uh... good friend of mine goes there all the time, works sometimes as a bartender when he isn't playing the fiddle."

"Yur putting it to me dude, what's the word?"

"Beebe... Beebe Walters."

"You know Beebe... Dam who would have guessed it?'

Now with a friendly connection established the lad opened up. "Listen dude, I'm DD Ransom, my friends call me shooter," and with that Shooter stuck out a dirty paw.

"Name's Jon." Jon shook the paw.

"Ya know, I'll bet you play in that quartet, uh, let's see, called uh... Moon Glow, dontcha?"

Shooter bolted up in his seat.

"Man, you're just one shocker after another, why I sure do. Have ya heard us?"

"Uh no, but Beebe speaks highly of the group."

"What? Beebe speaks highly of us? Oh my god wait till the troops hear this. Why that Kozinski puller is always givin' us a hard time, and here he is telling good things about us to strangers."

The conversation from this point on went on and on, until finally the Captain announced they were approaching the runway at Washington Dulles International Airport.

DD, shooter, got up to leave as the plane taxied along the runway up to the arrival gate.

"Listen, dude, it's been great rappen with you man. I hope I run into you at Spartas some time."

"Ya same here," returned Jon. When the airline came to a halt, shooter explained he was going to have to bolt to the door to get out and catch another flight. Shooter crossed over in front of Jon. As he was leaving he turned to Jon, with thumb up and said, "The word, man."

"Ya, all right, the word dude," Jon replied.

Amidst strange looks from fellow passengers, Jon sat uncomfortably while he awaited the plane's departure out of Washington and onto Boston's Logan airport.

As the plane readied itself in position for take-off, Jon, now alone in his aisle, found himself suddenly very tired. He was not aware of the takeoff. Nor was he aware of the forty five minute flight from Washington to Boston.

Jon's mind became not his own. His mind floated in space as he began to see and understand this presence and begin to sense the mission of which his acceptance of the presence had started him on.

Unbeknownst to Jon, the presence was beginning to give Jon the awareness of the presence's world, which Jon would need to know later. The presence began to weave a story for Jon of the world from which the presence came.

Jon saw a world of beings. He sensed a great warmth and love amongst the inhabitants of this world. They seemed similar to humans but not in the physical sense by which humans see and sense other humans. They had form and yet they didn't have form. They were like living energy. Yes, that was it. They were living beings consisting of pure energy.

Suddenly for the first time in his life, Jon saw the human creature, saw himself, differently than ever before. He saw man and woman as entities consisting of a physical shell operating on the principles of an electro-magnetic, chemical, and mechanical machine. This is a shell surrounded and immersed in an ether of energy; the fluid within which the machine worked. Bonding the two together was an aura of spirituality, the unknown mystery, the essence of it all.

As Jon was shown the relationships, it became clear there was more than mere existence claiming a bond between the presence and the human. But Jon couldn't grasp it yet. There was something about life and death and the interchangeability between the two, like one led to the other. It was there. The answer was there. Jon just couldn't seem to grasp it.

There was a relationship between the worlds also; the world of the presence and Jon's world. And there was a threat to both worlds caused by some occurrence in Jon's world. It was this threat which caused the presence to visit Jon's world. The presence needed Jon's help in a mission upon which could depend the very survival of Earth.

Each world existed in its own universe. Mankind was now beginning to harness the technology that would allow Earthlings to travel to other universes. They had been monitored for centuries by this alien planet inhabited by a race of aliens called mrows. Now fearful of Earth's terroristic society invading their peaceful existence, by solving the secrets of limitless space travel, the mrow race decided action had to be taken.

The presence was not the first of the energy beings to be cast through the universe onto Earth's surface. Many before had tried and failed. As the mrows, what the presence called his species, harnessed the technology necessary for the trip to be made to Jon's world successfully, some mrows made it through. Others did not. Some made it to Jon's world but expired. However, some had been able to transmit back much information which allowed other attempts.

Within the mrow community all options available to make the trip from their dimension to that of Jon's were fully explored. This became of greater urgency to the mrow species after they had abandoned the option of totally annihilating life on Earth. Long ago, the mrow had given up the pride and anger that rationalize destruction of life as an easy option. Such options could only be considered when all else failed and total destruction was imminent.

The presence within Jon was the greatest breakthrough of all for the mrow world. Other mrows were already on Earth. They occupied human hosts all of whom had been taken without human consent. However, without the human consent, the prior mrows had found limited abilities with the use of their human host. It was determined that only with a host who invited the mrow to coexist within it, was the potential for super-human mrow powers possible.

The creed of the mrow had been violated by the forced presence of the mrow into the human hosts initially made during the first years of their occupancy on Earth in the Earth years between 1945 and 1987. These forced habitations were felt to be necessary as they believed they were in a hostile world and their mission was paramount to saving the mrow world from destruction thought to be inevitable if humans succeeded in unlimited space travel.

Many mrows lives were lost, sacrificed in an effort to avoid the pending doom day scenario. With the new understanding that only with a willing human host could the mrow's powers be used to proceed in the ultimate mission, the attempts to find willing hosts were embarked upon and minor successes had been achieved.

It was after these early experiences the mrow council decided to launch the quest to make contacts with humans and seek their permission for this cohabitation. In return the humans would be rewarded with powers and gifts the humans considered of great value.

Only three other humans had been tested with a human host who had willingly invited the mrow to share its existence. The first, a simple but harmless man had died because it refused to let the mrow presence help unless he specifically asked. When a massive stroke occurred, the mrow was forced to wait for a request which never came. Both the man, name of Clyde, and the mrow expired.

Two others, street people, had been cultivated and were now positioned, one at a learning facility known as MIT, and the other in Washington, DC, one of the human's capital, as a special Senate representative to the Secret Service Agency. Each was awaiting the instructions to assist Jon's presence in the undertaking designed to either save both worlds, or destroy one so the other could survive.

In addition, the mrows already on Earth had found certain DNA characteristics yielded the most perfect bond between the mrow and the human. Jon had been specifically picked from a national DNA data base accessed by one of the two mrows already positioned. The challenge had been to make contact with Jon and obtain his willingness.

Jon's presence was the culmination of everything the mrow world had learned about the Earth humans. All the prior Earth mrow experiences were part of the data base made available to the mrow now residing within Jon. Now buried within Jon were capabilities he couldn't imagine; capabilities which would bring Earth to the brink of annihilation.

Suddenly Jon was startled out of his state, by the stewardess.

"Sir… Sir… Sir, can you hear me… ? Sir… Sir… ?"

"Yes… yes… yes… uh, what is it, uh, um, what's going on?"

Jon opened his eyes, no knowing at first where he was. The stewardess was leaning over him and the other stewardess was standing behind her to get a look. People from across the aisles were staring, as were the people in front of Jon. They had turned around to see what was going on.

"Sir… Mr., uh, Sullivan… are you all right?"

Jon sat up realizing sweat was rolling down his face and his hair was soaked. He squinted his eyes at the bright light illuminating the cabin.

"We have arrived at Logan Airport, Mr. Sullivan."

Seeing the passenger was now alert and probably had been awakened from a bad dream, the stewardesses moved on to alert any other passengers who might have fallen off to sleep and had not yet awakened.

As Jon left the plane and ambled toward the luggage terminal he felt overcome with a tiredness he hadn't felt in a long time. He tried to recall the essence of the dream he had but he could only connect with bits and pieces. He had no idea how close he was to the answers to many of life's mysteries. Nor could he image the programming now being set in place for the time when Jon would need to know it all.

After picking up his bags, Jon walked outside. He stood in line waiting for a cab. As he waited he thought about everything that had happened since the presence entered him.

"Boy, I hope I haven't made a colossal mistake," Jon thought to himself.

Instantly Jon realized the presence was probably monitoring his every thought.

"Can you hear every thought I have?" Jon thought.

"*Yes.*"

"Is there any way for me to keep my thoughts to myself, that is, from you?"

The presence did not respond. Instead, Jon could hear in his mind his own words previously spoken but now repeated by the presence. "*If you sense information about someone that I might need to know to protect myself; or there is information it would be helpful to know in order to better communicate with someone; or I need to know something in order to avoid danger, then share it with me. Otherwise keep a lid on it. Do you know what that means?"*

"Yes, okay, yes, I recall. Boy though it is weird hearing your thoughts played back in your own voice." Jon couldn't help but smile.

"Do I just think out any question and you answer or is there a better way to get your attention?"

"You may either think it out as an inquiry, or you may call me by my name David, or you may just think of the holly bush."

Suddenly Jon became alarmed. "Suppose I get hurt and can't control my thoughts to focus on the holly or call you by name?

"You must trust my judgment in such situations."

"Well, David, I guess I don't have much choice."

There was no response.

"You know it is rather weird having to have a conversation in my mind. If anyone would know this they would put me away as a paranoid schizophrenic. Isn't there some way I could see you so I didn't feel so weird talking to myself?"

"Yes. I can create an image for you. Yet wouldn't that create a problem if people say you talking as if to yourself?"

"I guess it could. But I would feel more comfortable."

"Very well. What image would you like me to have?"

"I don't know. Can't you just create something from my memory banks?"

"Very well."

Suddenly the image of Sylvester Stallone appeared standing beside Jon. "Oh my god!" exclaimed Jon. "I am not believing this."

"Does this not suit you?" The image said in the voice of Sylvester.

Jon started to laugh. "Ah, no, that's not what I had in mind." Jon was now speaking out loud. Several people standing waiting for a cab as Jon was were taking note of this man talking to himself. They looked at one another and shook their head sadly at this obviously deranged man. "How sad." Said one as they all moved away from where Jon was standing.

As Jon became aware of the attention he was causing, he quickly shut up. "Look maybe this is not a good idea," he thought to himself. "I am only looking for a relevant image of a guy who I can relate to as you. You know someone whose image especially in the face will reflect your feelings so we can better communicate. Someone who doesn't have to be a famous image, just someone I can relate to."

"How would you feel about the image of your brother?"

The idea took Jon aback. His brother David had died in Vietnam in 1969, two weeks before he was to come home. Ten years older than Jon, David was more than a big brother. Jon had cried and cried when at seventeen, David had joined the Marines right out of High School. Jon had been seven years old but he had loved his older brother and to this day could never understand why he felt the need to fight in that war.

Suddenly David's image appeared next to him. *"Will this be sufficient?"* The image of David said.

Jon was speechless. Beside him stood an exact image of his brother David as he remembered him at the age of seventeen. Suddenly the image began to age in front of Jon.

"Perhaps this is how your brother might have looked today at the age of forty-eight."

The image was that of a man about the same height as Jon. He had a distinctive skin, slightly freckled. His shoulders were broad, with a muscular frame. His eyes sparkled and his teeth were a beautiful shade of white. He had a broad German nose and although he was about the same height of Jon to Jon he appeared taller. He smiled at Jon who now had a tear slowly flowing across his cheek. Jon was so taken aback he couldn't speak.

"Sir... Sir... did you still want a cab."

Jon looked up. The cab driver was shouting at Jon.

Other cabs in the line waiting to pick up customers were beginning to beep impatiently.

A uniformed man rushed up to Jon's side. "Sir, if you want this cab, please take it. Otherwise other people are willing to take your place."

Jon looked at the sidewalk attendant who had rushed over when the other cabs started to beep their horns.

"Yes, ah yes. Thank you," Jon said. With that he opened up the cab rear passenger door, threw his bags in and climbed in. "Winchester Hospital in Winchester, please."

The cabbie put the cab in gear and spun away from the airport curb and headed toward Sumner tunnel. Beside Jon sat the image of his brother David. Dressed in a white pole shirt and khaki slacks, he looked like just another passenger traveling, although only Jon could see him.

As the driver turned down Sumner Tunnel, Jon caught the driver's glance in the rearview mirror. Jon sensed something was not right. Looking at David, Jon decided to test his newly acquired power. "What is the driver thinking?" Jon thought.

Suddenly, the driver's thoughts were Jon's.

"This fare is worth around eighty-five bucks. But by taking the long way through Sumner Tunnel and going the long way around Rt. 1A, rather than the Ted Nicholass Tunnel to Rt. 93, I should make an extra forty bucks or so. This will be beer money for the game later tonight and Margie shan't be the wiser." The cabbie thought to himself.

Suddenly Jon tapped the driver's Plexiglass shield separating the driver from the rear seated passengers. As the startled cabbie turned to see what the problem was, Jon said, "Driver take the next exit."

The driver looked confused. "What's say?"

"The next exit please," Jon repeated.

The cabbie took the exit and stopped at the bottom of the ramp, and looked back at Jon. "Hmmm," he thought, this guy don't look like no crook."

"Look driver, I am not "no" crook. I am also not going to be the victim of one. You are taking me way around the country and I am in a hurry. You figure you'll increase the normal fare by forty bucks or so. I'll have no part of it. You get back on Sumner and go back and take the Ted Nicholass Tunnel out to Rt. 93. If you keep your mouth shut, don't get in an accident, and get there in less than forty-five minutes, I'll give you an extra forty bucks. Otherwise, take me back to the airport *now*!"

Then, after a small pause, Jon said, "Do yourself a favor. Give the money to Margie and see how nice she'll treat you."

The cabbie didn't take much time to decide. He turned the taxi up the return exit and headed for Ted Nicholass Tunnel. As he drove, he kept looking back at Jon. In fifteen years as a cabbie, he had never run across something like this.

It was now 2:30 p.m. At the visitor's desk of Winchester hospital, Jon asked the attendant for the room where Lance Sullivan might be. Jon left his bag with the attendant and headed up to room 367.

Turning left off the elevator, Jon had to take a right which led to the nurse's station. Behind the station was a double door with a large sign saying:

No
Visitors Beyond
This Point

After introducing himself to the nurse at the station, he put on the visitor's pass and latex gloves and a mask to prevent infection. Lance was in isolation and Jon was informed Lance had contracted MSRA, methicillin-resistant Staphylococcus aureus. The nurse informed that Lance's condition was critical and he could only be allowed in with his son for no more than ten minutes.

A nurse escorted Jon to lance's room. She told him Lance was not conscious and he should prepare himself for what he would see. She also informed him there was an elderly gentleman sharing the room with a barrier between them.

"I don't understand. I was told Lance was in isolation."

"We are presently experiencing a shortage of rooms," the nurse curtly informed Jon. "The gentleman is not expected to make it through the evening, and at that point Lance will have the room to himself." Then after a small pause, she added "If he is still with us."

Jon was about to explode all over the nurse, when David appeared beside him.

"Patience... have patience."

Jon turned to David and said out loud "What the hell!"

The nurse, startled, said, "Excuse me sir. Were you talking to me?"

Jon just shook his head no and continued on to room 367 where the nurse waited for him to enter Lance's room alone. At the door, Jon paused.

As Jon entered he was staggered by the frail figure on the bed closest to the door. The name tag said LANCE SULLIVAN. Yet the figure did not in any way resemble the high energy, athletic fourteen-year-old Jon had put on a plane to go back to his mother. A sign as one enters requests all visitors and medical personnel to wash hands if gloves are not worn and to be careful not to bring any foreign objects in contact with the patient which may not be sanitized.

Slowly Jon made his way to Lance's bedside. Lance lay on his back. His head was slightly turned. An oxygen tent covered him. Tubes were coming out of his head, his nose, his arms, and his side. He was surrounded with numerous hi-tech equipment blinking, or with displays with moving graphs. The only sign of life was a cardiac machine reflecting in wave form Lance's heart beats.

"Remember Mr. Sullivan only ten minutes." With that said, the nurse turned and left.

The room did not smell good at all. The lighting in the room was dim and the life support equipment tied into Lance gurgled as tubes and hoses handled a plethora of fluids and gases which defined the decreasing life source within the small figure.

Except for the mechanical sounds and the electrical blips audible on the screens overhead, the room felt eerie. It was certainly no place for the living.

Looking down at Lance from the foot of his bed, everything within Jon's being began to ache. Tears of pain and sorrow forced themselves down Jon's cheek and fell to his cheek.

The torment of lost opportunities and the threat of the loss of his son flooded Jon's mind.

"O God," pleaded Jon audibly. "Dear Jesus, help me to help my son."

Overwhelmed by the trip and the circumstances exploding into his life, Jon suddenly just gave in to the emotion of it all. He cried continuously and sobbed uncontrollably.

Finally as he seemed to be overwhelmed with feelings of despair, he again cried for help.

"Dear Jesus, I know I do not deserve the grace only you can provide. But please, please give me the strength to do as you would have me do for my son.

David was shocked to suddenly sense a force within the human, other than himself. Such a force had never been previously detected. David sought without success to identify without success the location and function of the force.

Across the room lay a figure partially separated by a screen that ran half way down the length of the floor.

Jon threw his coat over a chair setting beside the wall. He moved another chair over to the side of Lance's bed. Slowly he sat down and bowed his head such that it lay on Lance's bed. His hand crept over to where Lance's pale hand was sticking out from under the covers.

"O dear God," he called out again. "I know I am not deserving of any favors, but I plead for my son's life." His mind turned to David's presence. David was there standing beside him although only Jon could see him. "Can you help me David? Can you heal my son?"

"*Yes,*" came the reply.

An aura of light passed from Jon's hand to and into Lance. It was 3:15 p.m.

The nurse came in every fifteen minutes or so as was the custom for such critically ill patients. At first she started to remind Jon his time was up. But as she put her hand on his shoulder to ask him to leave, her hand was immediately immersed in a white light she could not see. Soon she forgot Jon was even there. She went about her chores, and whenever she came back into the room, she just worked around Jon, almost as if she couldn't see him.

At 5:45 p.m. Dorothy entered the room.

"Oh Jon, oh Jon, I am so glad you are here."

Jon raised his head. He looked groggily at Dorothy.

"Hi Dot." For some reason he felt completely worn out. He shook his head as if to get rid of the cobwebs. "It must be the price I'm paying for the previous twenty-four hours," he thought.

"How long have you been here? How come you didn't call? Have you talked to the Doctor yet? What are we going to do?'

Jon smiled and shook his head slightly. "Good old Dorothy," he thought. "When she is under pressure she becomes crazy with impatience."

"Here, Dot." Jon got up and gave Dorothy his chair. Dorothy continued to throw out questions as she sat down and grabbed Lance's hand.

"Dot slow down. I am sure Lance will be okay."

"Okay, what do you mean okay? We are about to lose our son and you say you're sure he will be okay?" Dorothy looked at Jon with a bit of disgust as she shook her head negatively slightly at what Jon had said.

Jon moved over to the other side of the room. Jon couldn't understand why he felt so depleted.

"David?" Jon called the presence from his thoughts. David appeared with Jon on the side of Lance's bed next to the room separation curtain. As they exchanged thoughts, a wisp of color made its way to the bed on the other side of the curtain where the dying elderly man lay.

Jon looked at the image of David. Jon's mind spun the question, "Will my son make it?"

David spoke. "*Yes, it is certain.*"

Jon's heart filled with hope.

It was now 6:15 p.m. A man, looking like a doctor of some kind entered the room, stethoscope around his neck. He looked serious and glanced at Jon and Dot as he moved over to Lance's bed.

"Hello Mrs. Sullivan, is this Lance's dad?"

"Yes," replied Dot.

"Mr. Sullivan," the doctor acknowledged Jon. "I am Doctor Remfro," and then without looking at them further he moved over to Lance while taking off his stethoscope and putting it on his ears as he prepared to check Lance's pulse.

"Don't let him put that on Lance. It is full of bacteria. Make sure the doctor washes his hands," David cautioned Jon.

"Excuse me Doctor, you didn't wash your hands when you came in."

The doctor looked abruptly at Jon. He pursed his lips as if to hold back a comment. Then he smiled and turned back to the sink located near the entrance to the room.

"I washed my hands after leaving the last patient," he said in a slightly condescending manner. Then after reflection, as he proceeded to wash, he said, "But you are right to question anyone who does not do so."

Jon again addressed the doctor as he finished washing his hands and turned toward Lance. "Doctor, I apologize for being so nitpicky, but I would prefer you not use that stethoscope since it may be carrying bacteria or a virus since you see so many patients in the intensive care unit.

The doctor stopped. Slowly he turned around to face Jon. Then with a smile on his face, he took off the stethoscope and proceeded to take one out of a drawer near the bed which was in a sanitary package. Opening up the package, the doctor looked at Jon again, smiled, gave him a nod of approval and then proceeded to take Lance's pulse.

After checking the equipment, looking at Lance's chart hanging at the foot of his bed and adjusting several of the drip tubes going into Lance, the Doctor turned to face the Sullivans.

"Mr. and Mrs. Sullivan," he began.

"Oh we are divorced Doctor," Dorothy interrupted as though this fact had any significance on the matter being discussed.

Jon rolled his eyes upward and then smiled to himself. As he looked back at the doctor, the doctor continued.

"Lance's injuries are so severe, we are scheduling him for a liver transplant tomorrow and a proctoloectomy in 2 weeks.

"A what?" Dorothy lamented.

"A proctoloectomy involves the removal of the large intestine, rectum, and anus.

"Oh my god!" screamed Dorothy. "Isn't there another way?'

"No, Mrs. Sullivan, not if we are to save his life. Normally the liver transplant would not even be considered for a patient in Lance's condition. However, in Lance's case we do not feel there is any alternative."

Dorothy began to cry and weep to herself.

"Doctor what is your prognosis?', Jon inquired.

Mr. Sullivan, your son has such severe internal injuries, the fact he has lived this long is nothing short of a miracle.

"Do not allow any operations!" David spoke to Jon.

"WHAT?" Jon exclaimed so loudly both Dorothy and the doctor looked at him with surprise.

"Excuse me, Mr. Sullivan?" the doctor inquired.

"Ah… ah…" Jon tried to pull himself together. "Is there any reason why the operation has to be done tomorrow, Dr.?"

Jon smiled weakly at the doctor, not knowing where he was headed with this line of reasoning.

"Why would you have a concern about our doing it tomorrow, Mr. Sullivan?"

"Well, ah, well ah, maybe there are some more tests we can run on Lance. He may be responding better than you think to the treatment."

"Jon?" Dorothy exclaimed in disbelief at Jon's intrusion in the doctor's advice.

"Mr. Sullivan," the doctor spoke slowly and calmly realizing the father was not dealing with this rationally. He had seen this reaction before. "The tests indicate this is the only option left. Mr. Sullivan, this is not a decision that is made lightly. First any patient requiring a transplant is ranked according to need and urgency. Lance is ranked on a scale from 1 to 4 as a 1. Status 1, acute severe disease, is defined as a patient with only recent development of liver disease who is in the ICU unit of the hospital with a life expectancy without a liver transplant of fewer than 7 days. Based on this system, livers are first offered locally to status 1 patients. We have located a liver we feel will be compatible. Lance has been evaluated by a transplantation team. The transplantation team consists of a transplant coordinator, a hepatologist, a liver specialist, and a transplant surgeon. It also has on it a cardiologist and a pulmonologist. There is much expertise and experience from which this decision was made. And… if I may add, it takes difficult scheduling to get all the medical team required to one event."

"Jon?" Again Dorothy looked at Jon as though he had lost all his marbles.

"Well,… ah… ah… would it hurt to run the tests one more time Doctor? If there is still a need, I will volunteer my liver for use in Lance."

The doctor again pursed his lips. He wondered if he should give them the option of having another doctor. Then thinking better on it said, "All right Mr. Sullivan, if it will help you feel more reassured, we will run another series of tests this evening. If the tests do not show any substantial changes, we will proceed to qualify you as a donor for the transplant and we will proceed the day after tomorrow with the operation. Agreed?"

"Agreed," said Jon. They both looked at Dorothy who suddenly looked nervous as the two men stared at her, awaiting her agreement.

"Why yes… yes… of course," she said weakly and then looked at the doctor and then at Jon as if to see if that was the right answer.

The doctor shook both their hands and proceeded out the door. It was now 6:45 p.m.

Dorothy invited Jon to stay with her. She insisted he could use the guest room. Then in an attempt to lighten the conversation, she shared that since Margie, her divorced next door neighbor, was also staying to look after Dorothy, he would have two women to look after him.

Jon refused. He had a room already booked at a nearby Quality Inn. Since it was within walking distance to the hospital, he wanted to stay there.

Meekly Dorothy had asked if he would like her to stay with him through this ordeal. He smiled at her and said, "Thank you but no."

Dorothy gave Jon a brief hug and left.

David appeared and indicated they should stay longer. As Jon moved around the room so his back was to the room barrier, he leaned on the rail that was raised on Lance's bed. He found himself deep in thought as the aura from David permeated the entire room. It went in and out and around Lance. It also went into and around the old man on the other side of the barrier.

After some time, a team of nurses appeared at the doorway. They were there they said to conduct tests ordered by Dr. Remfro.

Jon walked out of the hospital and headed back to the hotel. The weather was pleasantly mild with the temperature at 63 degrees F and a slight breeze. On the way to his motel, he came across a bookmobile setup outside a senior citizen's rest home. Thinking he needed something to get the problems he was trying to deal with out of his mind for a bit, Jon stopped and entered.

It was now 7:05 p.m. "May I help you?" asked a kindly looking lady probably in her mid-seventies.

"Huh, well… I was visiting my son who is in the hospital here… and was on my way back to the motel where I am staying and I saw your mobile library," the lady looked on with an inviting smile. With a gentle tone she told Jon to feel free to make himself comfortable.

"We are really quite functional with the recently installed computer consoles. They tie in to all the computers accessible to the library including the Boston

Public Library as well as the Joseph P Healey library at the University of Massachusetts. Why not make yourself at home and see if you can't find some magazine articles or other area of interest to take your mind off your present situation. If you don't mind me asking, what is your son's name? I would like to pray for his recovery."

"His name is Lance Sullivan and thank you very much."

"Oh you are quite welcome. Winchester Hospital is a fine hospital." With that she moved back to her desk and the paperwork she was involved in before Jon had entered.

"It is really impressive," thought Jon as he looked at the computer console equipped with a modem to allow a tap-in to the various main library resources.

The moment was not lost on David who saw this favorable opportunity to acquire massive amounts of human knowledge to supplement the extensive training provided by the mrow council.

Jon felt himself drawn to the computer hook-up. Before he realized it the computer screen was asking for the level of inquiry. Suddenly Jon's countenance became still. He sat as if in a trance. In fact, he was in a trance. David had put Jon in a sleep mode while from all appearances he was actively using the computer. Using his mrow power David initiated control over the electrical flow of data as a massive exchange of information began. In the same way David's unique powers worked on Earth people, David began to inhale every bit of information offered by the system. This had been David's first opportunity to gather an abundance of information about this alien race and it would not be lost.

As she straightened out the books on the far side of the mobile library, Lizzy was beaming. She was happy to have a visitor. She couldn't understand why the library system would set the mobile unit up in such an obscure location where it was unlikely to draw many users. She had hardly any employees or visitors from the hospital. It had been a nice gesture for the folks in the senior citizens home. But the fact was, most of them had trouble reading and needed someone to read for them. What a strange location she thought.

Occasionally she would look up at Jon. She was so happy to have a visitor; especially one who was so willing to utilize all the resources the library had to offer. Jon's dropping in made her feel so useful. She looked caringly over at her visitor who had made himself at home at the computer.

Suddenly her smile turned to a look of dismay. The man was sitting stiffly looking at the monitor which was scrolling gibberish at high speed screen after screen.

Quickly she went over to Jon.

"Excuse me sir," she said excitedly. "The computer must be malfunctioning. If you will hang up and connect again, it may clear up the screen…"

Slowly Jon reached out and gently put his hand on her arm. A glow of energy flowed between the two.

The librarian turned and her smile returned. "Oh I see. Thank you very much," she said as if someone had communicated convincingly everything was all right, her presence was not needed and for her to continue with what she was doing and to pay no mind to what she saw.

She returned to what she was doing, humming a tune she thought she had forgotten long ago. Suddenly she shook her head as she realized she couldn't see well. She took off her glasses and looking at a row of books. She did a double take. Suddenly what she was looking at across the room was in as good of focus as when she wore her glasses. She put her glasses back on and everything looked fuzzy. Taking them off again she couldn't believe she could see without her glasses which she had worn since she was 7 years old.

"Oh my," she thought. "Wait till Dr. Sokolosky hears I don't need glasses anymore."

Little did she know the surprises which lay in store for her when she would suddenly discover her body free from ailment and returning with the youthfulness of many years ago.

For several more hours Jon sat at the computer terminal. The energy exchange continued as screen after screen of machine language scrolled across the monitor.

It was 8:30 p.m. Abruptly Jon became conscious of his surroundings. He looked down at his watch. He couldn't believe the time. He must have been so tired; he had fallen asleep in the chair.

Jon stood up to leave. "Thank you, ma'am."

"Oh you are so welcomed. I am supposed to close at 8 but you seemed so engrossed, I was hesitant to disturb you."

"I appreciate it. But I am through now. Thanks again."

"Oh by the way, the system tracks users. I should have told you but it probably doesn't matter. They like to see what interests' people. I hope that is okay."

"Goodnight."

"Good night, sir."

Shortly after checking in to his room, Jon took a hot shower and flopped down on the bed. It was 9:25 p.m.

At 9:45 p.m., there was a knock on the door. Jon got up, slipped on his robe and went to the door. It was Betsy!

Jon's look of surprise must have scared her.

"Jon, I know this is crazy. It is an impetuous thing to do…," she stammered, "but I wanted to be with you and Lance during this…"

Jon pulled her into the room and into his arms and married his lips to hers.

After a long embrace, Betsy explained how she had gone down to feed Pete and as she was getting his food, she noticed his trip itinerary on the counter. Her dad had agreed to take care of Pete and she took the first flight into Logan and then a taxi to the motel.

Jon Laughed. "I hope the cabbie didn't take you by way of Sumner Tunnel."

"Well, yes he did. Was that a problem?"

"No, sweetheart, it is not a problem. I am so glad you are here. I have much to tell you."

"Could I take a shower first?"

"Absolutely."

Betsy went in to take a hot shower all the time talking to Jon, explaining why she came and how she felt it was the right thing to do and so on and so on………

When she stepped out of the bathroom she stopped in mid-sentence. Jon was asleep.

She lay down beside him, having replaced her top and pants with a clean outfit. Almost instinctively, Jon draped his arm over her. "You smell so good," Betsy thought to herself.

Jon rolled to his side and began rubbing her back; as Betsy's smell awoke all his senses and a thirsting desire. "David," Jon thought, "do not be a part of this. Do nothing and say nothing. Do you understand?"

"Yes."

"Wait a minute, Jon," Betsy began to protest, but she was also already caught up in Jon's touch, his smell and her desires. Jon's stroking gently on the inside of her thigh had suddenly pulled up the kindling flame more than a notch or two.

Jon needed Betsy. He needed to escape the pain of the previous hours. More than that Betsy's presence, her smell, the feel of her seemed to complete Jon in a way he could not remember ever happening before. Betsy gave way to his touch. Her body arched itself closer. Her breathing became more rapid as she tried to resist him and at the same time pulled him closer.

His hands moved skillfully under her shirt and were already gently but firmly squeezing the already hard nipples. Betsy was arching her back and strange gurgling sounds were coming from her. Betsy was wriggling out of the pants she had just put on. As Jon kept one hand stroking her nipple, he caressed her with his tongue starting at her right breast and moving down to her navel. Slowly ever so slowly he kissed every part of her. His lips and hands, as if in concert, harmoniously played up and down her, taking their time, as if to feel and love every pore they found.

Betsy had her eyes closed as she kept undulating and writhing at his touch. She stroked his head and rubbed his neck and shoulders. Soon she was returning Jon's kisses and touch all over him. She parted her legs which were already moist. His hand found her and he stroked her in rhythm with her sighs. She was throbbing with pleasure she had not known in a long time, perhaps never like this. He drove her more than once into ecstasy with his hands. When his tongue came down on her, she tried to resist. Then giving way to his insistence to be a part of her, she grabbed at his back and held on for all she was worth.

The moist milk fluid glistened as it flowed across her soft skin. When he mounted her, she moaned with feelings she could not remember experiencing.

He plunged into her darkness and her mouth could not get enough of him. He was in her. She was in him. He plunged over and over, driving her from one climax to another. Finally as his thrust became more intense, she felt herself climbing a new mountain; a mountain higher than she had ever experienced. She was so close to the top, she wanted, needed to pass over its edge and fall into the sunny valley below.

Suddenly she could feel him let go inside her. Yet he continued to drive her upward. Finally she dared to fly over the edge. With her nails pressed into his back, her whole body released itself as it had never done before.

She screamed.

Jon held her tight. She held him tight. Jon lay beside her. She looked over at him.

"Oh Jon," she said softly and then lay her head on his chest. They both went fast to sleep. An aura of light wrapped them both as it swirled around and through them.

David for the second time since arriving in this world felt something within Jon he couldn't account for. He was not alone within the man known as Jon. For the second time he detected a spirit, another presence. It wasn't Jon. Yet it was Jon. There was a great strength to it. For the first time David sensed a power of equal or perhaps greater strength than his. He must try to understand this.

At 10:45 p.m. the phone rang, and rang. Jon sleepily rolled over to get to the phone.

"Yes?" he said into the phone.

"Jon," Dorothy said, "Doctor Remfro wants us to come to the hospital as soon as we can."

"Is it Lance?" Jon hesitated expecting the worst.

"He wouldn't say, but Jon… I think something is wrong… I am so afraid… I could just hear it in his voice."

"I'm on my way." Jon hung up the phone, jumped from the bed and started to get dressed.

"What is it Jon?" Betsy inquired in a worried voice.

"The doctor needs to see Dot and me right away."

"Anything I can do, Jon?"

Jon went over and put his hands on her shoulders. Her hands went immediately to his.

"Just stay the special person you are. This is a dark road for me right now. Be here for me when I return."

"I love you Jon."

"And, I love you Betsy."

As Jon withdrew his arms, Betsy suddenly reacted. "Jon, your arm?" She had seen that it was clear before but hadn't mentioned it because of Jon's worry over Lance. Suddenly it just popped out of her.

Jon looked down. Yes, his scarred arm was no longer scarred. His skin was smooth, tan and fit like the rest of him.

Jon sighed deeply. "Yes, uh, yes… when I get back we have a lot to talk about okay?"

"Yes," Betsy said in a low uneven voice.

"Do you trust me Betsy?"

Betsy reached out and took Jon's hand. "Yes," she said smiling and with confidence, "I do"

As fate would have it, a cab was just about to leave the motel, when Jon caught up to it. Even though he could have walked to the hospital in less than ten minutes, it was worth the six dollars to get there in three minutes.

CHAPTER 4

.........•••••••••••

THE DISCOVERY

Arriving at the hospital, Jon went immediately to Lance's floor. As he got off the elevator, he got a weird feeling. He could sense the nurses at the station look at him in an unusual way. When they would initially see him, they would do a double take. As he approached the nurse's station, the nurse who was manning the reception counter immediately got up and went over to another nurse in the corner. As he stood waiting, he observed them hurriedly talking back and forth while casting glances at Jon in between words.

Then one of the nurses came over to Jon, while the other one immediately got on a phone, turning her back to Jon as she talked quietly into the phone.

"Hello, Mr. Sullivan. I am sorry, Lance has been moved out of this unit, and um… we have put in a page to Dr. Remfro who is on the floor this evening. If you would like, you may wait here until he arrives.

Fearing the worse, Jon pleaded with the nurse to share with him what was going on and what condition his son was in.

"I am sorry Mr. Sullivan. I wish I could. We are not allowed to share that information." She smiled weakly. Jon could see fear and concern in her face. As he pleaded for information, an indiscernible white aura of light touched the nurse's arm.

Jon went over to a bench and sat down. "David what is going on?"

"The nurse is not really sure. There was a major incident earlier investigating why the tests on Lance all came back with solid indicators of recovery."

"Oh my god. Thank God. Thank God."

"Excuse me did I not come here with a purpose?"

"Well, yes, yes, of course you did. That was our agreement. I am just thanking my God for allowing all this to happen. The key is for us to get Lance out of here and returned to his normal life."

David was now sitting beside Jon on the bench.

"They have taken Lance off of life support and moved Lance to the second floor. He is in room 244."

Immediately Jon got up off the bench and proceeded back to the elevator.

"Mr. Sullivan, Mr. Sullivan please don't leave, the doctor will be here momentarily," the nurse called out as Jon and David stepped onto the elevator and pushed 2.

"Oh damn," the nurse called out. "Call security and tell them Mr. Sullivan just left the floor."

Getting off at the second floor, Jon looked at the signs. Finding the direction for room 244 he hurriedly proceeded down the hallway. As he got closer to room 244 he noticed two security personnel standing outside Lance's room.

Approaching the security guards, Jon smiled and introduced himself.

"Hi I am Mr. Sullivan. I understand my son may be here in room 244."

The room seemed full of people. One of the guards reached for the door and closed it. The other stood to face Jon.

"I am sorry, sir, your son is being attended to and no one can have access at the moment. Here let me get someone to assist you." With that the guard used his Nextel phone to call into it. "We have a code Gray second floor room 244. Code Gray room 244." The response was "detain and hold."

"David what are we getting into here?"

"Lance is recovering beyond their wildest imaginations and they don't know how to deal with it."

"Well, my god, that should be something to celebrate!"

Two additional security guards were now getting off the elevator. While the previous security personnel had no weapons, these men had Glock pistols strapped to their waist.

"Mr. Sullivan?" said the first guard to approach. "I apologize for this intrusion but I have been asked to escort you to a meeting being held to discuss your son's condition."

This whole situation was now beginning to get Jon's ire. "Look, since when is a hospital visitor coming to visit his son in ICU met with armed guards? I want to know what is happening. I want to know now."

The guard started to speak and Jon called out "David what the hell is going on?"

The guard suddenly became nervous and all four guards began to look around for who the "David" was. One put his hand on his weapon and began to turn around trying to locate the person called "David." David stood right beside them but they couldn't see him.

"These humans do not know what is going on. They only have instructions to take you to a meeting room. It would be best to go. Have no fear."

"OK," said Jon. Then sarcastically, "Take me to your leader."

The guards accompanied Jon to the elevators. When they got into the elevator, one of the guards took out a key, inserted it into the slot marked "E," and turned it. Immediately a flashing light beside the key slot started to blink. The elevator doors closed and the elevator moved its passengers upward to the executive offices of the hospital.

When the elevator stopped, the two guards, Jon and David stepped out. The surroundings could only be described as plush. Mahogany walls lined the open area and thick Constantine rugs covered the floor. The ivory design complemented the rich dark walls. Chandeliers made of Swarovski crystal dropped from above highlighting the white pressed metal ceilings. Nothing had been spared to keep the suite as elegant as possible.

Walking into the reception area, and off to the left was a large executive conference room. There were ten individuals standing around talking excitedly. As Jon and David approached, all eyes from the room turned toward them. They all sat down in their appointed seats and waited for Jon who was now at the sliding glass doorway. As the door slid open, Dr. Renfro came forward, his hand outstretched to greet Jon. Jon shook the doctor's hand and looked around at the room full of people.

"Good evening Mr. Sullivan. May I call you Jon?"

"Yes, sure," said Jon hesitantly as he proceeded into the room and stood at the head of the table with Dr. Remfro.

"Doctors, I am pleased to introduce you to Mr. Jon Sullivan, Lance's father," The room of people nodded or said softly a hello but there was no mistaken the serious faces which greeted Jon.

"Ah Jon we are waiting for," and then looking up he said, "Ahh she is here." Then leaving Jon, Dr. Remfro went to the doorway to greet Dorothy who was also being escorted by security personnel.

"Please come in Mrs. Sullivan."

Dorothy went in and stood by Jon. "Jon what is going on? Lance has been moved and no one will tell me anything." Dorothy looked scared and nervous.

"Dot I don't know. I have no clue as to what is going on."

"Would you both have a seat?" Dr. Remfro pulled a chair for Dorothy who sat down. Jon sat beside her. David stood at Jon's side.

Dr. Remfro went to the side of the room where he took a chair. As he sat, an older gentleman stood.

"Mr. and Mrs. Sullivan thank you for returning to the hospital so late at night. We know you have dire concerns about your child Lance Sullivan. To begin with and before I introduce myself and others let me tell you that Lance is doing beautifully and believe it or not should recover fully.

Dorothy grabbed Jon's arm and began to sob. "Oh thank you Jesus, thank you, thank you. Did you hear that Jon?"

"Yes," Jon responded softly while at the same time watching everyone at the table who seemed to be engrossed with his and Dorothy's reactions to this good news.

Suddenly a gentleman sitting at the other end of the conference room Table rose.

"Mr. and Mrs. Sullivan please allow me to introduce ourselves here tonight. I am Dr. Zachary Hereford, I am a paranormal psychiatrist. My expertise of study is of paranormal phenomena, that is, phenomena that cannot be explained by natural processes and are not the result of deception.

Jon and Dorothy sat confused but attentive as Dr. Hereford continued.

"You know of course, Lance's doctor, Dr. Remfro. Seated next to him is Dr. Clara Older, a psychiatrist, and proceeding around the table in the same direction Dr. Winfrey Slate the head of oncology, Dr. Bill Stewart, the head neurologist, Dr. Fred Steele, in charge of the gastrology dept., Dr. Freda Heinz a visiting psychiatrist from the University of Massachusetts, Dr. James Elliot specializing in paranormal activity and Dr. Jane Neely the president of the hospital.

As each was introduced, they briefly smiled and nodded in Jon and Dorothy's direction.

Dr. Hereford, a tall slender and very dignified looking man in his eighties remained standing.

Dr. Hereford continued "Mr. and Mrs. Sullivan, the reason we are here tonight… the reason you were called here tonight… and thank you again for being so gracious as to come… is because we need your help. Your son Lance was brought to Winchester Hospital after a brutal accident in which Lance suffered a ruptured spleen, a torn kidney, assorted broken bones and an abdomen that had been literally carved open with his guts torn and mutilated."

Dorothy gasped. She knew Lance had been hurt badly but this was the first detail as to the extent of his injuries. She began to sob again. Dr. Neely, who was sitting closest to her, offered a box of tissues which Dorothy took immediately and began to use.

"Please forgive me Mr. and Mrs. Sullivan for being so detailed in my description of Lance's injuries. But… It is important, however, for us to understand what has happened. Because what has happened is that within hours of the visit from you both, Lance's body has regenerated itself and may now be in better physical shape than before he was even in the accident."

Dr. Hereford sat down and stopped talking. All eyes were on Jon and Dorothy. Dorothy continued to sob. Jon sat stoically listening and watching the body language of the others in the room. They in turn watched Jon and Dorothy.

There was silence in the room. If anyone was expecting either Jon or Dorothy to speak, they were disappointed. Except for Dorothy occasionally sobbing, a pin could have been heard dropping on the long cherry wood conference room table.

Dr. Neely spoke next. "Mr. and Mrs. Sullivan, we are delighted in what must be an extraordinary joy on your part that Lance has so miraculously recovered." She paused.

"However, there is no medical justification for his recovery never mind the short amount of time in which it occurred."

"Perhaps," Jon finally spoke. "Perhaps Lance was not as critically hurt as was originally suspected."

"Bill Stewart here Mr. Sullivan. Yes, we thought of that and in that direction we have all been pouring over all the tests and their results. The explanation is not there. Something else had to have happened."

"Well, I don't understand why we are here," Jon spoke up. "Why are Lance's parents not allowed to see him? What does this all have to do with us?"

Dr. Heinz spoke. "Mr. Sullivan the reason you and your wife are here... were asked to join us is what has happened here has no explanation except for the supernatural. There is not a doctor here, and these doctors are renown in their field, who can come even close to coming up with any earthly reason to explain what has happened. Since you and your wife were the only two visitors we are hoping you can help us with an explanation."

Jon looked around the room. "I don't know what to say. We just want to be with our son. Please just take us to our son." Jon stood up to go. Dorothy looking up at Jon looked at the group then also began to slowly stand up.

Dr. Elliot also stood up. Dr. Elliot who had been quiet until now was a man who had retired from the intelligence branch of the secret service at sixty-two and for the last 6 years had given himself to paranormal activity with a specialty of UFO investigations. He was a stocky man about 5'8", in fit condition, who had found he had to use his deep voice along with an aggressive approach to intimidate those who would take him lightly. Dr. Elliot was the grandson of Gen. Roger Ramey, one of the principle Air Force investigators at the Roswell investigations in 1947. General Ramsey had left a profound impression on his grandson who to this day has dedicated much of his life to uncovering alien life on Earth.

"Look Sullivan, I am in no mood to play a game with you or indulge you in some fantasy. You are obviously delighted your son has recovered so miraculously. We are happy for you. With that said, we are of the opinion that either you or your wife has had some role in this phenomenal recovery. We want and we expect to get your compliance in cooperating with us in determining how this happened."

Again, the room was quiet.

"Jon," Dorothy said meekly grabbing Jon's arm, "what does he mean? Why can't we get to see Lance?"

The entire room was quiet as Dr. Elliot and Jon stood looking at each other as if waiting for the other to make a move.

"Gentleman," Jon said breaking the silence. "My ex-wife and I are overwhelmed at this proceeding. We are leaving now and going down to see our son." With that said, Jon turned and moved toward the door. Dorothy was holding Jon's arm and looking back with a frightened look at the table of doctors.

"Jon?" Dr. Heinz spoke up. "Jon, we have one more thing before you go."

Jon turned to look at the doctor.

"Do you know a Peter Slavak?"

"No, I do not," Jon replied curtly and with a tone that said he did not care to entertain whatever direction this would take.

.

"Well, Jon he was the gentleman in the same room as your son. He was suffering from lymphatic cancer. He was riddled with the disease and had less than forty-eight hours to live."

"Okay," said Jon. After pausing briefly Jon said, "So how does that have any effect on our son?"

"Jon it has no effect on your son. It does have an effect on you and your ex-wife. Since you both were in the room, Mr. Slavak has had a complete recovery. Jon he is cancer free."

Jon's face contorted into a confused look. "Well, we are happy for Mr. Slavak and his family. What does that have to do with us?"

"We don't know… yet. However Jon we feel there is a connection. We would like you and your wife to agree to a series of tests, at our expense of course."

Dorothy looked in shock.

"Hey," Jon brusquely said, "Right now our thoughts are on our son and our need to see him and take him home."

Dr. Neely spoke next. "Yes, Mr. and Mrs. Sullivan we can appreciate that. Lance needs some additional tests, nothing major, we just need to confirm everything is okay. He should be ready for discharge tomorrow. Please let me take you to him now." Dr. Neely looked around to see if there were any objections to her suggestion. There being none, Dr. Neely got up and escorted Jon and Dorothy out to the elevator and down to the second floor.

Once they were at Lance's room, Dr. Neely thanked them again and told them if there was anything they needed, to call her personally.

"Thank you Dr. Neely," Jon responded.

"Oh yes, we can't thank you enough," said Dorothy.

With that, Jon and Dorothy entered Lance's room. It was a private room. The walls were a pleasant teal in color and the TV was already on.

- - -

When Dr. Neely arrived back in the conference room, everyone was involved with discussions. What had happened? Was there paranormal activity? How could this have happened? Who actually is Jon Sullivan? How do we initiate an investigation?

Everyone stopped talking when Dr. Neely entered the room. "Well, the Sullivans are now with their son. How do we proceed from here?"

Dr. Slate spoke for the first time. "I couldn't be happier for either the Slavak family or the Sullivan family. But speaking from twenty years as a doctor of oncology, there is no, none, nada explanation for Mr. Slavak's recovery. Mr. Slavak came to us with advanced lymphoma. Only because he is one of the richest men in the state of Massachusetts, and who knows, maybe even the world did he have performed every test known to man to discover the extent of his cancer and find a viable prognosis. He had biopsies both incisional and excisional; endoscopy both upper and lower series, x-rays, CT scanning, MR scanning, and ultrasound. Every diagnostic method known to man was employed. We even used scintigraphy; single photon emission computed tomography. The family was paying a fortune to keep this patient alive and to find some way to get the cancer in remission. It was useless. Even though he is only fifty-eight, he had emaciated into an old man twenty years older. The last time we spoke to the family and advised them it would only be a short time before Mr. Slavak would expire, they had him given his last rights and were waiting to hear of his passing. He was on large doses of morphine which by itself should have killed the man.

Dr. Slate slowly looked around the room. "Now not only is Mr. Slavak in remission, he does not have a single cancerous cell in his entire body. Old scars have healed. New teeth have grown in forcing out his dentures. He looks like he is thirty years old. He has been taking off all medicine and is active and talking. He thinks the hospital has worked a miracle. He wants to build a new wing onto the hospital."

There was silence. "Mr. Slavak's younger son is a surgeon at Massachusetts General and he wants to know what the hell we did."

Dr. Remfro added his comments. "What mystifies me as well as what you all have covered is the lack of any scars. We opened the boy up, stuck needles and tubes in him galore and yet there is absolutely no indication of any intrusion whatsoever."

Dr. Elliot was the next to speak. "I am sure Dr. Heinz will agree. We have a full faced case of paranormal activity. It will be critical for us to study Mr. and Mrs. Sullivan. Don't you agree Dr. Heinz?"

"I fully concur, Doctor," Heinz responded. "But it seems as though Mr. Sullivan may not be receptive to this approach."

There was a hush of silence.

"He will have no choice. I will shortly be contacting the National Security Council, and if we have to quarantine the whole family it will be done." With that said, Dr. Elliot brought his fist down upon the tabletop with a thud. "Perhaps the cameras will help."

＊　＊　＊

As Jon and Dot turned the corner into Lance's room, there was Lance eating a bowl of ice cream and watching a basketball game on TV. His eyes lit up when he saw his Mom and Dad.

"Hey, Mom, hey, Dad," Lance exclaimed with excitement. "Wow is it good to see you guys."

Both Dorothy and Jon looked at Lance in amazement. Lance might as well be in bed at home none the worse for wear. He looked energetic, healthy and seemed full of energy.

"Why am I here? Dad? Mom? When can I go home?"

Jon and Dorothy were speechless.

"Son, "Jon finally responded, "You were in a terrible accident. The hospital has to run some tests and perhaps we can take you home tomorrow."

"An accident? I don't remember anything. I really want to go home."

Dorothy ran over and put her arms around Lance. "What's wrong Mom?"

"Nothing is wrong son," Jon spoke out as Dorothy broke into tears. "We have been very worried but now everything is going to be all right."

"Oh, okay, and I won't say any more about the bush that talks dad."

David stepped forward.

"Be careful I detect electrical emanations coming from a video device planted in Lance's bedside lamp and overhead in the light."

"Oh, Lance that was nothing but a bad dream. Don't think another thing of it," Jon replied.

Suddenly a nurse appeared. "Oh I am sorry, I need to take some blood and do an examination."

Dorothy let go of Lance and backed up.

"Son your mother and I will be back tomorrow. Sleep well. We love you."

"Me too Dad, Mom."

Dorothy and Jon left Lance's room. They couldn't help but notice two of the security personnel sitting down at the end of the corridor. When Jon looked at them, they turned away.

Dorothy dropped Jon off at his motel and they both agreed to meet at the hospital at 10:00 a.m. the next day.

Jon slid his room key through the door reader and entered the room. Betsy was sleeping in a chair by the window. She had fallen asleep while reading a local newspaper. The TV was on the local WHDH channel 7. The sound was low and the local news station was covering the views of the hurricane season. One of the country's top hurricane experts was predicting twelve named storms. Eight were forecast to develop into hurricanes with four of them being very intense.

As Jon moved around the room taking off the shirt he wore and slipping out of his slacks, Betsy stirred and opened one eye.

"Jon," she said pushing the paper onto the floor and jumping up to greet him. "How is Lance doing?"

Jon sat down on the bed and hung his head low not responding to Betsy's greeting. Betsy came over and sensing things had not gone well, got up from her side of the bed, came over and sat down beside him. She was still aglow from their love making earlier and she hated that things might not be going well for Lance and Jon now.

"Sweetheart," she said as she placed her head gently on the back of Jon's head. Jon looked up and turned his head to Betsy.

"Betsy," he said with a despondent tone that had Betsy afraid of what might follow. "We have to talk."

Betsy took her hand off Jon's neck and put both her hands in her lap not knowing what to expect.

"Betsy, I love you. I love you with a deep passion. You are the one I want to spend the rest of my life with." His words were so loving and caring and yet he seemed so down.

"Lance?" Betsy asked so very quietly.

"Lance is better than we could expect. Lance is better than he was. Lance is like a new Lance." Jon turned as he put his own hands in his lap and looked down at them.

"Honey, I don't understand."

"Betsy," Jon said while still looking down at his lap. "I need to apologize to you. I need for you to forgive me. I am afraid you won't."

Now Betsy looked alarmed. "Jon I love you also. I am ready to commit myself, everything I am, and everything I have, to you, to us. What could there be that would make you say that?"

Jon expelled a large volume of air out of his lungs. "We need to talk. I don't want to, I am afraid to, but I love you too much not to."

"Jon, you are making me afraid. There should be nothing we can't talk about. Whatever it is, we will deal with it together."

"Okay." Jon stood up and began to pace around the room. After another couple of sighs, Jon began.

"First of all, I am half negro. My Mother is German and my Father." Jon stopped there as if that might be enough.

"Yes," Betsy countered, and I am Irish and French and there is some German thrown in there somewhere." She laughed lightly hoping this was the worst of what was to be explained.

Jon sighed deeply and continued. "Now don't flip out on me, okay?"

"Okay," Betsy said quietly.

"I may also now be part alien." Jon paused and looked at Betsy as he paced the room, looking for her reaction.

"Part alien? What does that mean?"

Jon then proceeded to tell Betsy about Lance's visit to Carthage, he and Pete's involvement with the holly, his being told about Lance being on the edge of death and the agreement he made with a force to allow it to reside inside of him and how it has regenerated new skin tissue on his arm, old sores having cleared up and now not only Lance's miracle but that of a man called Slavak who was Lance's roommate.

When Jon finished he sat down beside Betsy. Again his head drooped low as he looked into his hands which lay in his lap.

Betsy turned to Jon, took his hands in her and put her head on his shoulder. "Wow," she said.

"Jon you are the most wonderful, caring man I have ever known. You touch me and I feel like I am on fire. You give me pleasure beyond what I ever believed I would have. I will go anywhere with you. Alien or no alien, German, French, Negro, Russian, or whatever, you have my undying, unrequited love from now until forever. I want Lance to be well; I want you to be my soul mate. Other than that I could not care less."

Jon felt a burden of overwhelming weight lifted from his shoulders. With this commitment from Betsy, this pledge of love, Jon went on to explain what he knew of the presence. He told her everything, but he didn't tell Betsy about his ability to read thoughts. He had told David not to ever share Betsy's inner thoughts with him.

"So Lance is recovered. That is wonderful news. Does that mean we can go home and start our life together?'

"Jon?" Betsy asked in a pleading manner assuming the answer was yes.

"No, I am afraid things have become a bit sticky."

"What does that mean Jon?"

"It means there are individuals who now have an interest as to how Lance recovered. In addition, I didn't know David was going to regenerate the Slavak man. In addition David has not revealed to me his entire purpose and what role I am to be."

Betsy's shoulders dropped. "What should we do now? I will do whatever you need me to do."

Jon took Betsy gently by the shoulders. "My love, I need for you to go home. I need for you to prepare our life together. I want you to tell your Dad everything I have shared with you and listen to his advice. I sense he is a good man. I also need for you to research this man Slavak. I don't know why but I feel he may have a role to play in whatever is to happen. In addition you need to think seriously about whether or not you should hang with me because I am not sure where all this is headed."

Betsy sat quietly staring at the floor. Several minutes passed. Jon wondered if the last thing he said was what she was thinking about.

"Well, David," Jon thought to himself, "you have not had much to say."

"*I am observing.*" With that David appeared to Jon wearing a smirk on his face.

"Okay," Betsy said finally. I will do all that you requested. That is all but the last suggestion. Jon you have my heart. We are in whatever we are in together." She turned and looked in directly in his eyes. "But… only if you will do just one thing for me."

"Honey, I will do whatever you need. What is it?"

And with that, Betsy pushed Jon back down on the bed. She climbed on top of him. She put her face within inches of his. "I want you to make love to me as if this were the last thing you had to do on this Earth."

Jon slowly smiled and pulled her body down to his.

"David this is to be just me, please don't be involved."

"*As you wish.*"

Then they each melted into each other's arms and did everything people do behind closed doors and don't confess.

David became part of Jon and observed the raw emotions. Needless to say he couldn't resist flowing through both of them and providing energy when and where they needed it.

Anyone entering the room that evening would have been able to see the fireworks, the sparks and the explosions that took place that night. The room was full of flashing pulsating colors.

⚓ ⚓ ⚓

"Standing near the desk in Dr. Heinz's office, Dr. Elliot barked into the phone. "I don't give a good god damn what time it is you get him to the phone immediately; this is a matter of national security!"

After some time, a voice barked into the phone, "Scruggs here, what's the friggen problem?"

In a calm but aggressive tone, Elliot got Scruggs' attention. "Scruggs, you know who this is?"

"Yes," came the response.

"Scruggs, we have an AI red alert."

Immediately Scruggs' attention was focused on Elliot's call. This is the first time this code had ever been used with regards to "Alien Intrusion."

"Location?" Scruggs asked.

"Winchester Hospital, Winchester, Massachusetts. One subject in the hospital, major concern's location is not known but within ten-mile perimeter and should be within hospital perimeter between 6:00 a.m. and 12:00 p.m. tomorrow."

Peter Scruggs was a senior secret service agent who, five years ago, had been assigned to head up the NSA, National

Security Agency. The NSA had, as a result of the terrorist attack on the United States September 11, 2001, taken on terrorism investigation in conflict with the FBI. At that time focus was also being brought on the potential of alien presence on Earth. The scientific community was supporting the probability of life on other planets. This support combined with UFO (unidentified Flying Objects) incidents not available to the public, was the genesis of a new department within the NSA called the Alien Task Force. The similarity of the two acronyms ATF for the bureau of alcohol, tobacco, firearms and explosives, and the Alien Task Force was thought to create some confusion. However, to play down the fact the group was concentrating on alien life as a separate entity within the NSA, it was decided to incorporate it into the same three letters used by the Bureau of Alcohol, Tobacco and Firearms and Explosives. However the badges of those within the Alien Task Force were identified with a small skull and cross bones, wherein the skull was replaced with the stereotype image of a Martian with an oblong face, two large black eyes and two small slits representing a nose. In written and conversational reference to this special unit of the NSA, the initials ATFa were used.

However, lately there had been and continued much conflict between the NSA and the Federal Bureau of Investigation (FBI) as to who had the prime role over terrorism in the United States. A Justice Department inspector general's report had found that the FBI and the NSA were not coordinating their efforts. Much rancor existed between the two departments, and as a result, Scruggs found himself under intense pressure to get results from the ATFa that dealt with Alien Life Forms.

To head up the ATFa group he had put Lizzy Richmond in charge. Richmond was an MIT graduate, who had been selected to join the NSA at about the same time Scruggs took it over. Richmond was at the top of the NSA graduating class out of all those who must complete a twenty-seven week training program at the Federal Law Enforcement Training Center in Glynco, Georgia. As the top agent in the special ATFa group, Richmond was eager to get her hands on a specific case. She was a tough, no nonsense agent who secured the trust and allegiance of her staff by being willing to do anything she asked of others and proving her abilities in the field. Nevertheless, she never allowed any social time between herself and her staff. So while the staff respected her ability and willingness to do what was necessary, they sensed something stand offish about her.

The majority of her unit's time had been spent on backing up other NSA activities in the normal assignments that typically come to the NSA. The rest of the ATFa work had been tracking down and investigating UFO claims. Although there had been some substantiated UFO claims no details had ever emerged of substance. When Scruggs called her and told her about the possible existence of an alien presence in Winchester, Mass., she was chewing at the bit to get her ATFa unit there and attempt to substantiate the claim. "Now finally," Lizzy thought, "This may be the break to launch my career."

— — —

The light from the window woke Betsy. She slowly turned and looked at Jon. The clock said it was 7:00 a.m. Now carefully, so as not to wake Jon, Betsy slid out of the bed. She went to the window and looked out at a beautiful morning.

As she stood there thinking about how lucky she was to have found Jon, she thought and worried over how the events and what Jon revealed to her might impact their relationship.

Jon stirred. On his side he opened his eyes to see his Naked Betsy silhouetted by the sun's rays. His eyes swallowed her up. "What a woman," he thought to himself. Then as if to check he thought "Good morning David, are you here?"

David's image appeared before him. *"Good morning Jon. I hope you rested well."*

"Humph, you should know." Jon silently chuckled to himself. "Good Morning sweetheart," he called out to Betsy.

Betsy turned around. She smiled. Unabashed at her nakedness, she strolled over to Jon. She sat down on the bed beside him and took his hand. "I don't want to leave you today," she said.

Jon rolled closer and placed his head on her arm. "I know. I feel the same way. My love for you is busting out all over. I just hate that I have to stay. But I have to make sure Lance is okay and gets home safely. Then we will be able to return home."

Betsy bowed her head. She knew he was right. She picked up the phone and rang the front desk. "Would you please call a cab for me? Yes, that's right, room 101. I will need the cab to be here in an hour and one half. What? It will be taking me to Logan Airport. Yes. Thank you."

Jon laid his head back down into the pillow. He smiled up at Betsy. "Last night was absolutely unbelievable."

Betsy leaned down and put her mouth next to his ear. "You haven't seen anything yet." She chuckled an impish little sound.

Jon grabbed her and pulled her into him. Betsy pushed her nakedness into his. Neither one could keep their hands off the other. Jon enveloped her, made love to her and each brought the other up to and through an orgasmic explosion.

Finally, Betsy pushed away, jumped out of the bed and sashayed over to the bathroom door. "I believe I will take a shower. It would be lovely to have someone special rub my back." She looked back with a coy little smile, went into the bathroom and closed the door such that it was opened just a crack.

Jon could hear her singing. He smiled, swung his feet out of the bed and proceeded into the bathroom. There they played, rubbed each other, made love once again and caressed each other as they enjoyed the shower. This would be the last time they would spend in this way for some time.

* * *

Jon opened the cab door for Betsy, put her suitcase in and embraced her. "As soon as I can I will come to you."

"I know, sweetheart. Make sure Lance is well and safe. Do what you have to do. I will be waiting"

As the cab pulled off a black escalade SUV pulled up. Four men and a woman got out. The four men stood in front of the SUV. A tall statuesque brunette, her hair worn short with bangs and dressed in a svelte black suit that enhanced her finely shaped legs, disembarked from the escalade.

Jon walked back to his room. He began to pack his bags, when there was a knock at the door. Jumping up in anticipation it might be Betsy and she decided to stay a bit longer, Jon rushed to the door and opened it up in anticipation. He was taken aback by a lady surrounded by four rough looking characters.

"Mr. Sullivan, Mr. Jon Sullivan," the woman asked sweetly.

"Yes," said Jon confused by this group entering his room without invitation. Jon was forced to back up.

"Mr. Sullivan, may I call you Jon?" she inquired.

David appeared before Jon. *"Be careful, these people do mean you harm."*

"Hey," Jon said aggressively walking forward toward the group. "I need to go somewhere and don't…"

Jon was cut short by a blow to his chin that sent him over the corner of the bed. As he felt his jaw, two of the men picked him up and roughly threw him into the chair in the corner.

The woman walked over to the bed and sat down. Dusting her lap as she looked down at it she said, "Jon we need to have a heart to heart talk."

Jon began to interrupt and one of the thugs slapped him hard across the mouth causing a trickle of blood from his nose. "Shut the frig up and listen to the lady or you will see the worse of it."

David leaned down looking into Jon's face. *"Hmm I would bet that stung."*

Jon thought, "Are you going to just enjoy this or are we going to do something about this?"

"Let's see what they are about first."

"My name is Lizzy Richmond, ATFa special agent Lizzy Richmond Jon. You may call me Lizzy."

She paused to let that sink in.

"Jon we are in the pursuit of an alien force here on Earth. We need your help? Will you help us Jon?"

"Listen," Jon said as he felt his jaw and his nose, "I am here for my son and nothing…" The thug who had first hit him delivered another damaging blow to Jon's jaw.

"You fracken jerk, I am going to mess you up if you don't answer agent Richmond's question without a lot of fracken crap." The man stood poised to deliver another blow.

"Geese David," thought Jon, "feel free to join in anytime."

"Look, mister," Jon said looking directly at the man who had delivered the blows, "one more shot like that and I am going to put you on your ass."

The man snarled and launched another punch aimed at Jon's eye. As his fist came within 6 inches from Jon's face, Jon's hand clamped on to it. Each man was looking at each other eye to eye. Suddenly Jon with a rapid twist of his wrist flipped the man head over heels onto the floor. The man sat dazed and surprised as the other three rapidly approached Jon.

Liz called out "stop."

The men backed off. "Do we really have to do this the hard way?" She said to Jon. Silently she was quite impressed with how Jon had flipped the 200 lb. agent with such little effort.

"Look I don't want to do anything except see that my son gets safely home with his mother."

"Fine," she said sternly. "You go with us to the hospital, take the tests they have set up for you and your wife. If they turn out to be nothing, you all are free to go. Agreed?"

"Okay," quipped Jon. "Let me continue to get dressed and I will meet you in the lobby in five minutes."

With that Lizzy stood up. She smiled at Jon and turned for the door. "We are out of here."

"In the 5 minutes Jon had, he cleaned up his face, put on another shirt and sat down to talk to David.

"What are we going to do?" Jon asked.

Jon I am going to have to put you back in the shape I found you in terms of outside appearances and the appendix you had taken out as a child. I will make it so that bone fractures you have had earlier in your life which were healed but evident, still show on the x-rays. In addition, your arm scars and any black and blue marks you had originally will have to come back."

"That makes sense. I hope I don't get back that awful back pain I suffered with at night," Jon said sarcastically.

"You won't."

"I was being sarcastic," Jon said wondering, if David understood what that meant.

"I understand."

"Do you understand sense of humor?" Jon said rhetorically.

David tilted his head as if to say give me a break, but he said nothing.

As Jon came into the lobby area, Lizzy and her four thugs got up and accompanied Jon out to the escalade. Jon sat in back with an agent on either side. Lizzy sat up front with the driver.

Jon would have to admit the situation and environment he was being put in was very intimidating.

When they got to the hospital, Dorothy was already in the Hospital lobby. She had already been examined, x-rayed and gone through an MRI scan. As soon as she saw him she hurriedly went up to Jon.

"Jon they have run me through all these examinations. It has been very embarrassing."

"Well, as long as Lance is okay, whatever it takes to get us out of here!" Jon turned to see Lizzy at his side but the other four agents fell back to positions around the lobby.

"Who is this, Jon?"

"Uh… this is Lizzy Richmond, an ATFa agent who has an interest she says in seeing whether or not we are aliens."

Lizzy looked at Dorothy and smiled. Dorothy gave her a weak smile in return.

"Oh my god, Jon, where did they come up with that idea?"

Jon just shrugged and gave Lizzy one of those locks like "what am I supposed to say."

An agent came forward and whispered something in Lizzy's ear. Lizzy said to Jon, "They are ready. We have to go up to the eighth floor, and Dr. Elliot shall meet us there." Then she turned to Dorothy. "Mrs. Sullivan you may go to be with your son he is still in room 244."

Dorothy immediately turned to go to the elevators and then upon reflection she turned to Jon, "I assume we will see you later." Then without waiting for an answer she proceeded around the corner to the elevators. Lizzy smiled. Jon said, "She is an ex."

"Oh," Lizzy replied as if she was surprised to get that bit of clarification.

Lizzy stopped at the door of Rm. 812 and motioned for Jon to go in. Dr. Elliot was approaching from the opposite direction. They greeted, said a few words, She then walked down the hall a short distance talking into her Nextel phone to the other agents.

Inside Rm. 812, Jon was asked to disrobe and put on a hospital gown. He was then put through an extensive exam and subjected to X-ray and MRI scans. When he was released after three hours, he was told he could see his son in Rm. 244. There would be an agent accompanying him and he would not be able to leave the hospital until they cleared him to leave.

Jon went down to see his son. Lance was doing well and was delighted to see him. They talked about Pete, Betsy and about the next time Lance might get to be able to come down to North Carolina.

Upstairs in the executive conference room, Dr. Elliot was surrounded by Lizzy and the agents not currently monitoring Jon or Dorothy,

Dr. Smith, an ATFa medical doctor who had been brought in to oversee the testing, came in with the test results for both Dorothy and Jon. "Gentlemen and Miss Richmond, I have the test results for both subjects." Dr. Elliot and the rest of the group scanned the results.

"What is your opinion Dr. Smith?"

"Well," Dr. Smith began; "we know that the son has gone through a complete and unexplained regeneration of organs. However, both the mother and father show the same scars and body defects noted from their prior medical history. Personally, we have no indication that either the mother or the father possesses any supernatural abilities reflected by their own physical make-up."

"Damn," responded Dr. Elliot.

"So, this trip was wasted time?" quipped Lizzy.

"Release them all for the time being but I want a periodic surveillance set up on the father." Dr. Elliot commanded.

"Okay, boys," Lizzy barked into her Nextel, "Stand down and lets go get something to eat."

It wasn't long before Dr. Remfro entered Lance's room to let Jon and Dorothy know they could take their son home.

They thanked the doctor and proceeded to pack up Lance's things. An orderly came by to take Lance out to his mother's car as was the practice for patients released from ICU.

Jon gave his son a hug good-bye and told him he would call from Carthage.

"What was all that about anyway, Jon," Dorothy asked as she was getting ready to drive away.

"Don't really know, Dorothy. But we have been blessed big time by Lance's miraculous recovery. You all have a safe trip home and we will talk later."

"You know you could come back to the house and visit for a while."

"Thanks Dorothy but I really have to book a flight and get back. But thanks." He waved as they drove out of the hospital parking lot and headed back to Boston.

Dr. Remfro ran into Lizzy and her band of thugs as they were preparing to leave the hospital. "Dr. Remfro." Lizzy acknowledged the doctor.

"Miss Lizzy.", the doctor acknowledged back. "It seems like we all got caught up on a wild goose chase," Lizzy commented.

"Yes, yes, it does," Dr. Remfro replied.

"It is hard to understand why Dr. Elliot thought we were in the middle of an alien episode when both the mother had validated histories of scarring and physical injuries.

"Yes," Dr. Remfro agreed than on second thought said, "scarring? What scarring are we talking about?"

"Not sure exactly, Dr. Smith gave the exams and compared them to their histories." Lizzy replied. He said Jon had some massive scarring that would have been regenerated if in fact he had that ability to regenerate."

"Oh my god," said Dr. Remfro as he seemed startled by what he remembered. "How could I have missed that?" Dr. Remfro sat on a lobby bench as he tried to mentally recapture his conflicting thoughts.

"What is it?" Lizzy pursued, as she felt some undetected secret was about to be revealed.

"Jon Sullivan's arm!" the doctor exclaimed. Then he said it over and over. "How did I miss that?"

"What about his arm?" asked Lizzy now impatient with the doctor's lack of explanation.

The doctor began to slowly explain. When Jon Sullivan first came to the hospital he had no scarring visible on his arm. They were smooth as silk. Yet this morning when I saw him in Lance's room, his right arm was massively scarred as if it at some time had suffered severe burns."

The impact of this revelation hit Lizzy hard. "What the frig?" she exclaimed. Immediately she announced to her team. "We have a red alert, again!"

She left the team in the lobby and had Dr. Elliot paged to meet her in the executive conference room again.

Dr. Elliot and Dr. Heinz were there when Lizzy charged in. Lizzy hurriedly told them about her conversation with Dr. Remfro. Elliot and Heinz looked at each other in a panic.

"What condition did Sullivan have on his arms, when you picked him up?" Dr. Elliot inquired of Lizzy.

"There was no scarring. I am sure of that!"

"He must have regenerated his previous physical defects to escape any detection," offered Dr. Heinz.

"That god damn alien," Lizzy cursed.

"Go get him, now." Dr. Elliot barked.

CHAPTER 5

UNRAVELING THE PURPOSE

After checking out of the motel, Jon, at David's suggestion, told the desk clerk, he was on his way to the airport and thanked him for his hospitality.

"Thank you for treating us cordially," Jon said to the desk clerk as he signed out and paid his room bill."

"Oh that is our pleasure, sir," The desk clerk responded. Knowing Jon had come from the airport in a cab, he asked "Will you be needing a cab to get to the airport?"

"Yes, kind of you to ask."

"There will be one in front within five minutes," the desk clerk reported after making a call to the cab dispatch.

As they left the motel, David announced they would need to go to Washington where they would meet with the other two presences who have been successful in finding a host. They would need to purchase a car in which to take the trip but that going to the airport would throw anyone off their trail who might be following them.

"Do you really feel we will be followed?" asked Jon.

"*Most definitely*," responded David.

Jon informed David they needed money in order to pay cash and not leave a trail anyone could follow.

David said he had made arrangements for that through the presence who was in Boston and who would meet them at Logan Airport and then take them to the Crossroads, an Irish Pub and restaurant on Beacon Street in Boston's Back Bay area.

The cab arrived and to prevent any misunderstandings, Jon instructed the driver to take them to the airport, the United Airlines entrance and to go via the Ted Nicholass Tunnel.

On the way, David explained their immediate course of action.

"We will rendezvous with the others in Washington. While we are on our way Jon, I will reveal the true extent of my mission here."

"Am I going to regret my role in this?" asked Jon.

"Do you regret saving your son?" answered David.

Jon gave a deep sigh. "Of course not," he thought.

Neither spoke or shared thoughts for the rest of the trip to the airport.

— — —

Lizzy and her team arrived at Jon's motel ten minutes after Jon had left. She went to the front desk and showed her badge. "Jon Sullivan, is he still here?"

"No ma'am, he left by cab I believe to the airport."

Without so much as a thank you, Lizzie turned and headed out the door. She was busily given directions into her phone.

It wasn't long before the cabbie taking Jon and David to the airport was given an alert over the intercom. The alert was for the cabbie to press his trouble light button. This light is just what it is called, a trouble light. It is located on the back of the Taxi, inside and just to the left of the trunk lock. It is used to send out a silent distress call in the event of a crime. A driver who is being robbed can press a button in the cab, which causes the light to flash and alerts passing police cars. It is also used by a cabbie for whatever reason to alert a passing police car of other kinds of trouble. It was to be used now as a result of instructions coming ultimately through Lizzy Richmond through local law enforcement and then through the cabby's dispatcher.

Jon's cabbie pressed the trouble light button. David quickly picked up the electrical signal and an aura of light passed between Jon and the cab driver. The cab driver was instructed to turn off the trouble light. However, once turned on it can only be turned off from within the cab's trunk. This is to eliminate the possibility of a passenger, being aware of the trouble light, trying to get it turned off.

David's aura passed into the car's circuits and the trouble light was extinguished just as they passed two state patrol cars sitting by the side of the highway on alert to a cab with its trouble light blinking. Fortunately they were close to the airport and the road was filled with too many cabs for the state patrol to stop every one of them.

Twenty minutes after Lizzy had given her instruction to get the cab with Jon Sullivan in it stopped, there was still no feedback he had been found. She cussed and slammed her fist against the door of the car she was riding in.

Meanwhile…

After turning into the airport entrance, the cabbie was given instruction to pull over at the United Airlines entrance. A black Mercedes pulled up behind them. Jon got out of the cab. He paid the driver and stood at the curb waiting for the driver to leave. After the cab driver left and was out of sight, Jon took his bag and at David's direction got into the Mercedes.

Navigating the back streets of Boston, the trio arrived at the Crossroads. After they pulled up to a parking spot and parked, the driver leaned over the seat and introduced himself. "Hi Jon. I am Nicholas. I, like you, have a presence. It has been a wonderful experience for me. I hope it is for you also." They exchanged pleasantries and walked into the restaurant. It had a pleasant and comfortable ambiance. As they slid into a booth, two others appeared beside them. One was David.

"Jon this is the visual of Mikka. Mikka has been with Nicholas for years preparing a way for us."

Jon nodded and looked at Nicholas. "Can you see them?" Jon asked. Nicholas laughed. "Yes, I can see them."

The waitress appeared and asked what they would like to drink. Nicholas said he would like a coffee and a Reuben sandwich. Jon hesitated.

"We have a long way to go Jon; it would be good for you to eat something." Nicholas followed up his suggestion with an encouraging smile.

"Ah, right… ah give me an ice tea and a club sandwich."

The waitress took their order and left.

"Did David give you a lecture of all the toxic wastes you ingest and urge you to have a better life style?" Nicholas asked with a chuckle.

"Um no, not really. Well, I guess he did say something about cleaning out some toxicity. But he helped save my son who was fatally injured in a hit and run."

"Oh, sorry to hear that. Is your son okay?"

"Yes, thanks to David."

Mikka looked at David and they shared a look.

"Well," Nicholas said as he began his further introduction, "I was a homeless tramp, wandering the streets of Boston when Mikka found me. He cleaned me up and mentored me to where I am today."

"Where is that Nicholas?"

"Jon, I am a research scientist in the CUA."

"The what… ?"

"The Center for Ultra cold Atoms. It is a MIT project, government funded, which brings together a community of scientists from the Massachusetts Institute of Technology (MIT) and Harvard University to pursue research in the new fields that have been opened by the creation of ultra-cold atoms and quantum gases. The research is currently organized around the themes of strongly correlated states of ultra-cold atoms and quantum state control of atoms and photons. The research is carried out in dedicated facilities at MIT and Harvard University by a community of approximately one hundred graduate students, postdoctoral researchers, undergraduate students and visitors who work under the supervision of the Center's senior investigators in collaborative projects."

"Okay," laughed Jon. "I am just a dumb engineering graduate from Boston University. I don't have the foggiest what you are talking about."

"Ya, sorry," laughed Nicholas in return. "I am not even a GED graduate but here I am on the front line of quantum physics. I know how you feel. But with Mikka's help I stand tall with the smartest of my colleagues."

"Wow, I should be so smart," Jon replied.

"Oh, be patient Jon. You will be."

With Jon looking at Nicholas with a stunned "huh" look, the waitress came with the drinks and sandwiches.

As they chowed down, Nicholas continued to fill Jon in on the MIT work. "This is all very hush, hush, in fact I have a top secret clearance and what I am about to tell you could put me behind bars for a long time." As he said that, Nicholas looked around to see if there was any chance he might be overheard.

Nicholas took a deep breath and then began, only stopping periodically to enjoy his meal before the long trip.

"We at the CUA are on the verge of discovering how to leap across galaxies in a fraction of a second. Light travels at the rate of 670, 616, 629 miles per hour. We are into the final stages of being able to travel trillions of miles through the galaxies within a human's lifetime."

"What a minute," responded Jon, taking a break from his meal. "Einstein's quantum mechanics revolves around E=MC squared. To move at such speeds means a mass would get so large as to explode on itself, wouldn't it?"

Nicholas laughed. "Yes, Jon, you are absolutely correct. That is why our discovery of negative energy is so fantastic."

"Negative energy?"

"Yes, Jon. We have developed a breakthrough to time/ space travel without violating Einstein's Law. We have actually created the "warp drive" idea of Captain Kirk and the Starship Enterprise." Nicholas stopped to gage Jon's reaction.

Nicholas continued. "Isn't it amazing Jon, how our world has been able to replicate the fantasy of the original "Buck Roger's" movies when even primitive space travel was only the figment of someone's imagination? Who would have even imagined back in 1939 and a cartoon strip by Dick Calkins and Phil Nolan you would today be living in a world that is more like the Buck Rogers imaginary adventures than it is different?"

"A warp drive, Nicholas, I can't even imagine how that could be."

Nicholas laughed. It was that kind of laugh that precedes telling someone how to do what they think is impossible.

"The scary part," Nicholas continued, "is that what we are doing is analogous to giving a monkey a gun and expecting he will be able to shoot it without killing or maiming the rest of the animals."

"I am not sure I understand, Nicholas."

"Jon, the point is that as humans our technology far exceeds our maturity to handle it."

Jon thought "Oh my god, what have I gotten myself into." The table was quiet for a bit except for Nicholas and Jon finishing their meal.

Finally, his engineering background itching to understand, Jon couldn't resist asking a question. "Nicholas, if the theory of relativity is not the basis for long distance through space, how do you propose it would be done?"

"Ahh Jon didn't think you would ask. The key is the relationship between space and time. An energy bubble is created to bend the relationship between space and time. Through a combination of positive and negative energy, we can produce an expansion and shrinking of space. Negative energy is the key to this and, if you will, the fuel for this phenomena. By expanding space in back of the object while compressing it in front, the ship can move at speeds far exceeding the speed of light."

"Negative energy?"

"Yes, negative energy. In our associate lab at Harvard, our team has been able to produce negative energy by shooting sub atomic particles with microwaves and measuring them with atomic microscopes."

"Wow. This is hard to comprehend."

"Don't worry, your presence, ah David, is already as we talk working on increasing your brain's ability to take this all in and understand it. You probably, as with most of us, use about 5 percent of your brain's capacity. I now use about 35 percent. You will feel your increase over time. It is just one of the many gifts the presence shares with you. In fact, given David's increased functions over the previous visitors, I wouldn't be surprised if you didn't find your mental ability "off the chart" as we say."

"I am not sure I want to be that smart."

"Ahh, feel cozy where you are, huh?"

"Well, not that, I don't think. But I remember a psychology professor who said to me, "When you are in a room full of crazy people, they are not the ones who are crazy."

"Oh, I like that," Nicholas said with a chuckle. With that, he put down his utensils and pushed his plate away. Both had finished. They both got up and Nicholas paid the bill as all four walked out of the restaurant.

Once they were all back in the Mercedes, Nicholas at the wheel, it pulled away from the curb and proceeded to the I90 turnpike headed toward Washington, DC. The trip would take approximately 8.5 hrs. and they would travel approximately 450 miles.

In the meantime Lizzy had initiated a check with each airlines but no Jon Sullivan was shown ticketed. In anticipation, she also authorized road blocks on the main highways out of Boston going in any and all directions. Each road block had been supplied with a picture of Jon and he had been labeled as armed and dangerous even though Lizzy knew that not to be the case.

As the Mercedes approached the last toll booth on the Mass turnpike, the traffic became unusually heavy and within a mile of the booths proceeded at a crawl.

"There may be a road block ahead," Nicholas said to Jon who was in the back seat.

"Oh great, Jon exclaimed in a nervous tone, "If it is, they probably have a picture of me."

"Everything will be fine Jon. Sit back and look at ease."

Sure enough, as the Mercedes got close enough to the toll booths, they could see each vehicle being stopped to collect the toll by hand rather than let the cars deposit the toll amount into the collection bin. Alongside each booth was a State Highway Patrol person holding a picture and looking at all the occupants of vehicles coming through.

As the Mercedes inched closer, Jon exclaimed "Oh my god, they have a picture they are looking at."

"Jon be calm everything is fine. Trust me."

"OK, OK… I trust you… I think."

They were now the next vehicle to get inspected. When the vehicle in front moved off, the Mercedes moved up to where the patrolman was standing.

"How are you today, sir?" the Highway Patrol person asked Nicholas.

"Fine Officer, is there a problem?"

"No, not at all," he said as he looked at Jon and then back at the picture he had. Then he said, "Okay, you may proceed. Thank you."

"You're welcome, Officer."

With that, the Mercedes moved on down the high-way, merging with the other vehicles coming out of the toll booths.

"Man, I don't believe that," Jon said out loud. The driver looked at Jon in the rearview mirror and smiled.

"Look in the mirror Jon."

Jon looked in the mirror and jumped. The man looking back at him had black hair, a scar on one side of his face, black eyes, and facial features not at all like Jon's.

David smiled. "Wow," said Jon. "Is this my new look? I hate it." Then Jon began to laugh. They all laughed.

As the Mercedes continued on its way, David began to explain more of his purpose on Earth. As he did, Jon was put into a semi coma so that David could bring Jon back to his original condition wherein he had no scars or defects.

"My home", David reveals, *is a planet just under 31 trillion kilometers away from Earth. This is the equivalent of*

3.26 light years. It is called by your world an exoplanet because it revolves around a sun different then Earth's sun. Your people have sent exploratory vessels called "Voyager," one of which we deciphered in your year 1977. This began our awareness of an inhabited planet close enough to be called neighbor, your Earth. We began to study Earth just as Earth astronomers and scientists were attempting to better understand the solar system. We were, at first, delighted to find another planet with a race of inhabitants we hoped would be compatible with us. Unfortunately as our studies intensified, we came to view this planet you call Earth as potentially a threat to our way of living. Increasingly we studied the wars, the killing, the ravaging of one another and we began to develop a strategy to first explore, validate our fears and then to deal with the threat. We are now in the stage of validating whether or not our fears are justified. As a result of our highly technological development we managed to design a way to visit Earth and determine what this neighbor was like. As we visited we lost some travelers along the way. Yet we acquired much information on the Earth people species. What we found was a planet of an increasingly innovative almost intelligent species whose technical achievement, just as Nicholas had said earlier, far outweighed their maturity to handle them. As soon as Earth people develop a better way to kill, they deploy it on their own species. My assignment is to determine if we need to take action to terminate this threat."

David could sense Jon's increasing blood pressure and mental panic set in as Jon realized some of David's real reasons for visiting Earth.

"Then you lied to me," Jon thought.

"Lie? No. What lie did you hear me say that was a lie?'

"Did you not say you could be a source of healing power?"

"Have I not proven I am?"

"You told me you needed a human organic host to act as a catalyst allowing you to regenerate the energy it needs to survive."

"Yes, and has that not been so."

"You… you told me how your presence within me was only a temporary thing and that you would leave anytime I requested it."

Then David played back for Jon exactly what he had said. *"I shall leave you any time there are not great benefits for you to realize."*

"Well, what the hell are these benefits you offer if you are here to annihilate the human race?"

"All life is temporary, even ours although ours is considerably longer than Earth lives."

"Temporary my ass, David. You are mincing words with me."

"Mincing, used with an object as:

1. *To cut or chop into very small pieces;*
2. *To soften, moderate, or weaken (one's words), esp. for the sake of decorum or courtesy;*
3. *To perform or utter with affected elegance;*
4. *To subdivide minutely, as land or a topic for study."*

Jon was angry. "I feel betrayed. You sucked me in because my son was near death. You are considering annihilating the human race which means me, my son, my loved ones, good people everywhere."

"Good people everywhere? Where are these good people Jon? Your people get all upset over a war where 3000–5000 deaths occur. Yet in your country alone over 65 people a day are murdered; not killed in defense but outright murdered. That is 23, 725 people murdered, each year! Where are Earth's priorities?

In this region, you call America, the land of the free and home of the brave, you all live sequestered lives without care for those who are less fortunate, especially if it means you have to give up something to help others.

You place your children in front of televisions and expose them to what you call entertainment; drama and music, and replay over and over violence and hatred not only in words but also in deeds. You compensate actors and actresses with excessively exaggerated incomes who play out such anger and hatred and murder on your various media while you pay little to teachers and those who care for others. Adults are mesmerized with these soap operas and talk shows that delight in the basest actions of your race. They function with a mentality that can't focus more than one half an hour and expect all problems to be solved within the same amount of time as their TV shows. They have many opinions, mostly negative about others, can't even get off their couches to vote and then wonder why their government works the way it does.

You spawn groups who use religious beliefs as the basis for hatred and attack on others. You remain oblivious to the torture, rape and killing of your young, your women and your weak.

It is the same in all other regions and in some much worse. You allow yourselves to be governed by those who are self-centered, greedy, and power hungry. You complain about the laws

*they make for you to follow but all you do is talk while enter-
taining yourselves with perversion. You allow laws and actions
that rape your planet of its ability to flourish and support life
yet you let the powerful reign so that they may continue their
pillaging and destruction of the planet."*

*Finally David looked directly at Jon. "Jon. Where are
these good people?"*

Jon was taken aback by this diatribe against the values of the human race. There was anger in David's tone.
Jon had not ever perceived any emotion from David except
calm rationale. Perhaps his anger might not be perceptible to others, but after hearing David handle matters, Jon
could sense the definite angry emotion in David's words.
Silently Jon gave way to a prayer to have the ability to convince David the human race was salvageable.

Once again, David could feel within Jon a force he had
no control over and of which he had no understanding.

Jon, in turn, was now angry. "You deceived me David.
I don't care how you put it. You arranged your words and
veiled your intent so as to get what you wanted."

David was now concerned. Not only did he have no
idea as to what the unknown force was inside of Jon, but
now Jon was building up a wall of defiance which could dis-
rupt David's immediate purpose to determine if there was
any reason the mrow planet should not annihilate Earth.
Should Jon make a decision to destroy himself, David
would not, even with all his powers be able to reverse that
course of action. In turn, defiance from Jon would handicap David's efforts to determine whether or not the planet
was worth saving. A new tact must be employed.

"Jon, do you disagree with what I shared with you?"

Jon thought deeply. "No, in all honesty, many of your observations are correct about the baser aspect of mankind. But you do not have a complete picture."

"Jon, tell me how so."

"Humans were created by a God. This God, whom I refer to as the creator of heaven and Earth, asked his creations to trust him, and to love him with their heart, their mind, and their soul."

"Excuse me," David interrupted. *"What is this soul?"*

Jon fought in his mind to make this clear to David. He said a prayer asking for divine intervention.

"I do not hold myself as one who can articulate such things. But I will try. A soul is an internal spirit within men and women who accept God through the sacrifice of God's son Jesus Christ. The body which is created from the crass material aspects of this world is subject to decay and demise but the soul which is a pure extension of God transcends our physical limitations of creation. When created, mankind was given what we refer to as free will. It is the ability to decide what we will believe or not believe. Only this way does God want to receive the love he asks of us. From this free will, many have taken different paths in their beliefs. From this have come many different belief systems. Most, if not all, have an ultimate belief in a creator. However, there are some whose believers or disbelievers, if you will, choose not to believe except in their own ways. This "soul" which some refer to as our conscience, gives us, those who are Christians, our innate knowledge of what is right and what is wrong. Some, like atheists do not believe in a creator but still hold to a knowledge of what is right and what is wrong. We don't have any proof of what we believe except for our faith which God tells us will lead us to eternal happiness."

After a brief pause, Jon continued. "I look around and see many with hearts heavy with grief. I see many impoverished and unable to afford the basics of life. There is a great deal I cannot do. But I can make it my mission to do more acts of kindness. I would be the first to tell you I have let my life's disappointments create a distance from myself and God. As well there are many who claim to believe in a God and many who like me believe in God through his only son Jesus Christ who gave his earthly life to save us from punishment for our sins and yet who don't follow what we know to be the teachings of God. We call this: talking the talk and not walking the walk"

"So do you just talk the talk and not walk the walk?"

After some pause, Jon said, "Yes, I am guilty of just talking the talk. But there are many who do walk the walk, who love and care in the way God would have us do."

"How would I find such people?"

"Well, they are everywhere. History documents very good and very bad people. In addition there are many people who do evil things because of mental problems, defects in their make-up."

"Yes, from your libraries I have compiled much information about those who are what you would label, evil. The issue we have is that your world seems set on spreading its evil into the solar systems and eventually to where we exist. We cannot have that."

"Well, let's talk about your civilization for a moment. Have you or your people never known what you would agree are evil beings?"

"We learned that the ultimate of joy and happiness comes from working together on common goals."

"Yes, but you didn't answer my question. Before you got to that point, what was your world like?"

"Our planet's civilization is over 20,000 of your Earth years old. Our history shares there were many clashes before we learned to share common values and destiny."

"Wow, 20,000 years? Well, can't you see, from the time God's Son came our planet is much younger? We are like babies just learning how to crawl. We are still learning what it took your people thousands and thousands of years to learn."

"Yes, that is true. But we were never a threat to other civilizations."

"Well, okay. Why can't your people help ours develop and learn the secrets of your many centuries?"

"Would such an effort be worthwhile? Will your planet just continue to explore and eventually find success in polluting the universe with its technological achievements guided by ill tempered, power hungry, destructive people? That is what I have to decide."

"Well, what if I can show you we can learn and follow a better path?"

"Do you think you can?"

"I can try. Let me guide you to what is the potential of this planet."

"I would be willing to do that but what if I can't be convinced?"

"Then it will be as it will be. I have faith that God through Christ Jesus will guide me."

Again, David felt the force yet to be identified move within Jon.

"*I do not detect, Jon, your mental awareness of a predicted end to your world.*"

"A predicted end? Jon laughed. "No, I am not aware of such."

"A *sacred Aztec calendar properly called the Eagle Bowl forecast such. It represents the solar deity Tonatiuh, alleged to be the foreseer of such. The amazingly accurate calendar has been in use in various forms for more than 2,000 years. A Zapotec prophecy, based on the Eagle Bowl, states:*

"*After Thirteen Heavens of Decreasing Choice, and Nine Hells of Increasing Doom, the Tree of Life shall blossom with a fruit never before known in the creation, and that fruit shall be the New Spirit of Men.*"

The 13 Heavens and 9 Hells were each 52 years long (1,144 years total). Each of the 9 Hells were to be worse than the last. On the final day of the last Hell (August 17, 1987), Tezcatlipoca, god of death, would remove his mask of jade to reveal himself as Quetzelcoatl, god of peace.

In the mythology of the Aztecs, the first age of mankind ended with the animals devouring humans. The second age was finished by wind, the third by fire, and the fourth by water. The present fifth epoch is called Nahui-Olin (Sun of Earthquake), which began in 3113 BC and will end on December 24, 2011. It will be the last destruction of human existence on Earth. The date coincides closely with that determined by the brothers McKenna in The Invisible Landscape as "the end of history" indicated by their computer analysis of the ancient Chinese oracle-calendar, the I Ching.

The Mayan calendar is divided into Seven Ages of Man. The fourth epoch ended in August 1987. The Mayan calendar comes to an end on Sunday, December 23, 2012. Only a few people will survive the catastrophe that ensues. In the fifth age, humanity will realize its spiritual destiny. In the sixth age, people who survive will realize God within themselves, and in the seventh age they will become so spiritual that they will be telepathic."

"I don't know what to tell you. You are right. I have no knowledge of such a prophecy."

"Perhaps it is this "God within ourselves," which I feel within you."

"What are you talking about David?"

"You have a strange force within you that moves about, especially when you are doing or thinking beneficial thoughts."

"Beneficial to whom?"

"Others. It occurs most notably when you think of your faith, or you do this thing you call prayer."

"Hmmm. I don't know about that. I can only tell you how I think and feel."

"Well, perhaps if all thought and felt as you do, there would be no need for an end."

"Oh, there will be an end. And I am not so perfect. I sin every day. Every day I sin against my God. I betray him through my tongue, my mind, my heart. It is just that… I… that we… those of us you have faith in God through Christ just try to pick ourselves back up and keep trying."

"Do you think others who do not have your faith, or have no faith at all don't keep trying to be what you call good?"

"David, I am not smart enough to question anyone else's faith. Certainly we are influenced by the environment we grow up in. When I turned over my life to Christ, accepted him as I was guided to through God's word, the Bible, I felt a new me. Even though I stumbled in my life, and still do, I have felt I am a better person."

"Do these people of faith gather some place, a place where I could find them?"

"Well, many Christians go to churches; others of different faiths go to such gathering places called Temples or Mosques or other names."

"Do you go to this place called church?"

"No. I don't go to Church because I feel many Priests, Pastors, Bishops, many of these people who are supposed to help guide us in our walk with Christ are themselves polluted with blinders made of personal interest, power and prestige. That does not mean there are not good leaders of some Churches. It just means I have not found those "good" leaders."

"Well, Jon doesn't that help make the argument there is no hope?"

"No it doesn't. Life is a struggle of good and bad. It plagues all of us. But good, will eventually reign. I believe in that."

"So, how do you propose convincing me of the justification to save life on this planet?"

Jon thought to himself for quite some time. "I want you to let me take you to neighborhoods within the United States. I will determine where and how we go. You will have the ability to decide whether the people you meet are worth saving."

"Why just in the United States? What about the rest of the world?"

"Well, this can be a start. If you are not satisfied by what you find here, then you may go elsewhere. Deal?"

"All right as you say, a deal."

- - -

Sitting behind a large office table, Lizzy called her staff together at the NSA Charlotte, North Carolina office. Once everyone had assembled, she announced they would be stationed temporarily out of this branch location of the NSA. Everyone was told that no one in that branch was to know anything about the ATFa or their mission.

"Effectively immediately, we will dispatch ourselves to the area of North Carolina last lived in by Jon Sullivan. We will leave this evening. We will be in four black GMC sports utility vehicles. We will rendezvous in Carthage at the White Horse Motel at 136 Union Church Road. At 6 a.m., we will dispatch two vehicles to the employer of Sullivan and two to his home. You have maps and directions. I want every bit of information about anyone and everything having to do with Jon Sullivan. Those of you being dispatched to Sullivan's home will have warrants to allow you to turn his place upside down. We will meet at 7 p.m. back at the hotel. Does anyone have any questions?"

There being no questions, everyone got up and proceeded to gather what they would need prior to leaving Charlotte for Carthage.

- - -

"You said you wanted to meet someone in Washington, DC. Would it be acceptable to start there?"

"*That would certainly be acceptable Jon.*"

Nicholas continued into Baltimore and across the Patapsco River.

"Mikka, we will need to stop for fuel."

Mikka acknowledged for Nicholas to stop as he thought best. Nicholas brought the shiny new Mercedes off the exit in Baltimore onto the bypass 695. At exit 34, the Mercedes turned onto Philadelphia Rd. Nicholas pulled into a convenience store and up to the gas pumps that provided diesel gas. Both Nicholas and Jon left the car with the diesel fuel on automatic fill and entered the store. Nicholas went to the soda machine and got himself a cold drink. Jon went in and used the rest room. Jon came out and wandered over to the front of the store. Nicholas was paying for the drink and the fuel, when Jon was approached by a man. The man had ripped jeans, and an old air force jacket, torn at the collar. "Could you help me out?" said the man to Jon.

"What do you need?" Jon said to the man with a smile.

"I need some money for some fuel," the man replied. "My car is broke down about a mile from here. I had to leave my wife and kid and try to find help. Can you lend me some money?"

"I can do better than that," said Jon. "I can take you and some fuel to your car. How would that be?"

"You would do that? I mean, let me ride in that new car and bring me and some fuel to help us?"

"Sure we can," said Jon.

The black face bent down and the man shifted so Jon might not see his eyes water and him holding back his emotions. Jon noticed the man's face and he could see his eyes water. The man started to sniffle to hold back the fluid in his nose.

"Excuse me," the man said, "I'm tired. I had given up on anyone helping. I really didn't know what I was going to do."

Nicholas watched as did Mikka and David as Jon put his hand on the man's shoulder. "Well, what we are going to do is to get you and this gas to your family."

"Thank you, sir," the man said. He was obviously tired and worn out. Jon introduced himself and Nicholas. The black man introduced himself as Tyrone Whitaker, an unemployed textile worker. He explained he had family in Washington who might be able to find him work and he was trying to get his family there.

"Ahh, he finally found a sucker, huh?" A loud voice came from over the beer cooler. "He has been hitting up on everyone. I am betting he doesn't even have a car." With that the man reached down for his beer and started to laugh sarcastically at the black man and the stooges he had gotten to give him money.

Jon slowly picked up a gas container, and ignoring the man's sneers, slowly walked over to the counter. He paid for the container and 5 gallons of gas. Then he, Nicholas, and the black man walked out to the Mercedes. As they were filling up the gas can, the loud patron came out and went over to his work truck with a twelve pack of beer. He said some things to the other three guys in the truck. Then the guy turned and he and his three buddies walked over to Jon who was filling the gas can.

"A couple of rich whitey liberals. You guys make me sick. A hard working person has no chance once you fracken liberals hold up the slugs of society. You think you are better than guys who work hard like us and that trash like this free loader should get your lousy handout."

The men encircled Jon as he continued to fill up the gas can. Suddenly the loud guy in the group kicked the can out of Jon's hands.

"Someone needs to teach you a lesson," he said.

Jon slowly stood and turned to face the loud leader of the group. Slowly Jon asked, "And exactly what lesson might that be?"

With that, the leader shot out a fist at Jon's face. Jon's arm came up and his hand opened and caught the man's fist square in the palm of his hand. It was so quick. The man had hoped to sucker punch Jon. Jon reacted quicker than the human eye could see what happened. The thud was similar to the sound the man would have caused if he had struck a piece of steel. Jon's hand never moved as the man's hand slammed into it as it was on its way to Jon's face. Jon's hand held the man's hand in his grip as the man went to his knees writhing in agony. The man's three companions backed away, their eyes as big as large marbles, not believing what they had seen. Jon slowly turned his head to one side and then slowly to the other watching the man's friends as the man on his knees pleaded for Jon to let him go.

"David," Jon thought, "Please restore this man's hand to its normal condition."

Jon released the man's hand. The man suddenly realizing he was free from Jon's grip and that his hand wasn't broken, got up from his knees.

"Now, what were you saying?" Jon asked.

The man didn't reply. He and his companions hurried back to their truck, looking around at Jon who had gone over to pick up the gas can and had resumed filling it with gas.

Tyrone was now afraid and unsure if he should go with these men. Even though Jon was fairly reacting to the anger of the man and his companions, Tyrone was concerned his family might be in danger. He stepped back from Jon and Nicholas and his face showed his fear. Jon instructed David to let Tyrone know he was in safe company. As David's presence was felt by Tyrone, he became calm. When Jon opened the passenger door on the driver's side, Tyrone got in. After all were in the car, they drove to where Tyrone had left his family.

In the 1995 white Aerostar Ford van parked where Tyrone had brought them were his wife and twelve-year-old son. Tyrone introduced his wife and son Anthony to Jon and Nicholas. "Hello, Mrs. Whitaker," Jon said with a smile.

"Oh thank you for helping us. I prayed the Lord would send someone to help Tyrone."

"You are very welcome," Nicholas responded.

They emptied the gas into the car and turned the ignition. The engine would not fire. Jon put the hood up and began to check out the engine. It was obvious the engine had not received any care in quite some time. Tyrone and his family huddled in the car hoping it would start. Tyrone's son got out of the car and looked on at what Jon was doing. Jon glanced sideways and noticed the young man had a pronounced limp.

"What happened to your leg Anthony?" As Jon waited for an answer Tyrone came up behind his son and put his arm over his shoulders.

"I don't know," the young man replied. "It has always been like this."

Jon looked at Tyrone for an answer. "Ah, Anthony was born with it. We think there was an interruption in his blood flow when he was born. His umbilical cord got twisted around his neck and there was a delay in untangling it. He suffered some mental impairments but he has not been as disabled as some. We have been lucky. Haven't we Anthony?"

Anthony's dad put his arm around him. "He just misses being able to run and play like the rest of the kids. There is some amount of teasing but we have learned to deal with that haven't we son?"

"Yes, Dad," Anthony replied looking sad. Anthony turned and went back to sit with his Mom. "He is a great kid. We are blessed," said Tyrone.

Jon turned his attention to the engine. Nicholas came over and looked also.

"Watcha think Nicholas?" Jon asked.

"Time for a new engine," Nicholas replied wincing his eyes at an engine which had obviously reached its last moments among the world of operable engines.

"Anything we can do David?" thought Jon.

"I think we might be able to handle this. Have Nicholas take the family back to that diner we passed and lets you and I see what we can do."

Nicholas huddled Tyrone, his wife and son into the Mercedes and they left Jon standing there looking at the engine.

"It looks like the head gasket is gone, the ignition wires aren't connecting as they are supposed to and God knows what else is wrong with this."

David's aura filled the old van with what looked like a wisp of smoke. The wisp of smoke covered the engine, the van, and all its insides. The smoke became visible just as a police cruiser happened to come by. The officer stopped and rolled down his window.

"Sir, sir," he inquired of Jon who was hovering over the smoking engine. Jon looked up and turned toward the officer. "Yes, Officer?" Jon replied.

"Are you okay? Do you need some help?"

"Oh no," Jon replied, thinking quickly. "I shorted out an ignition wire and it caused all this smoke." The officer looked puzzled. "Do you need any help? I can call you a tow truck."

"Oh no, thanks but it will clear in a moment and I have friends on the way."

"Well, okay. I will be back this way in about an hour. I will check on you and make sure everything is okay."

"Thanks. Hopefully we will be back on the road by then." The officer moved away. As the smoke was clearing from around the van, the officer couldn't help but notice what wonderful shape the van was in. "Boy," he thought to himself, "that van looks like it was brand new. It's an older model for sure but it looks like brand new." Shaking his head at what a good looking old van it was, the officer got a dispatcher call, turned on his lights and headed toward what was being reported as an accident.

Shortly Nicholas and his passengers showed back up. As Tyrone's family got out of the Mercedes, their eyes were big as saucers. Their old van looked like new. The upholstery was repaired, it glistened and the engine looked clean and spanking new.

"What happened?" Tyrone could hardly get the words out of his mouth."

"Oh nothing, really," Jon replied nonchalantly. "I got the engine fixed and took it to get it washed. Hope you don't mind?"

Tyrone looked at the engine, he looked inside the van and he walked around it several times. All of a sudden he started to cry. He had tried to hold it back but it was all too much for him. His wife came running over to him and put her arms around him. "Who are you people?" she demanded in a scared tone.

"What do you mean," Jon replied. "We are just folks trying to help."

"No, something else is going on. Are you angels for certainly you aren't of Satan."

"Just regular folks," Jon replied.

"No, you can't be." She continued. "While we were eating, Anthony discovered his legs were no longer hurting him. He can walk without a limp. I don't feel any back pain. Now this. Please we are scared."

"Blessings are not to be something one should feel afraid of," Jon replied.

"Oh my god, you are angels!"

"Well, we have been called worse. Please don't despair. We hope we have helped and that you find what you are looking for in Washington." With that Jon turned toward Nicholas and motioned to him to get in their vehicle. With a window turned down, Jon looked at the family as he also got in. "Glad we could help and…" Suddenly Tyrone ran over to Jon's side of the car. He grasped Jon's arm. "We can never thank you all enough," he said as tears rolled down his face.

"Oh you can," Jon replied. "Be good to each other and others you meet. And be patient with those who are not good. Blessings on you all."

With that said Nicholas pulled the Mercedes out onto the road and they were back on their way. Anthony and his family waved good-bye as the Mercedes pulled away and proceeded on its way. As they got back in their new van, they were like children at Christmas after receiving what they had always wanted. Anthony's mother opened the glove compartment and found $5,000 in $100 bills. "Oh, Tyrone," she said as she pulled out the bills and a note that said, "spend it wisely and continue to have and live your faith."

- - -

Two black SUVs sped down 2427 on route to Jon's home. As they turned down McCrary Rd., they unstrapped their weapons, and the vehicles slowed down. As they reached the end of the cul-de-sac, they turned into Betsy's driveway. There were no vehicles there. They stopped and surveyed the area. Checking the mail box for the correct address, they proceeded down to the doublewide. Slowly they got out of their vehicles.

There were three agents in each vehicle. Lizzy was the lead agent who went around to the back while three approached the seldom used front door. As Lizzy turned the corner, Pete who had been sleeping came up off the deck. Growling at the intruders, Pete kept his ground. Lizzy aimed her weapon at the dog and fired.

Betsy sat in her Dad's kitchen still going over the events she and Jon had experienced in Boston.

"Dad it was incredible." Max Sumler listened to his daughter recount her relationship with Jon and what had happened to them in Boston. He got up with his cup of coffee and stood over by the kitchen sink overlooking the pond where he would go sometimes to enjoy the solitude and think.

"Betsy, my sweetheart, Ever since your Mom passed away, I have thought about my own deep secrets and sharing them with you as you have just shared some of yours.'

Betsy looked surprised. She had been wondering whether or not her dad could swallow the whole alien thing and everything she and Jon had encountered in Boston. She didn't tell her dad about her intimacy with Jon but she had shared her growing love for him. Now without comment or question, he has something to share with her? She felt like she was in the twilight zone.

"Betsy when I was a young man, my dad had died. He had treated me pretty rough. I got beat almost every day. I became pretty rebellious. I had a gang then and we did some awful things. I stole things. I beat people up." He turned to look at his daughter. She looked stunned like she couldn't believe what she was hearing.

He continued. "Your Mom knew. We never kept any secrets between us. I just never thought I would be sharing this with you."

"Well, Dad," Betsy gained control over her composure. "Everyone does stupid things when they are young." She paused.

"It was more than just stupid things. They were cruel, evil things. Then one day three of us encountered this old man on the railroad tracks. It was an old abandoned spur. We knew he came that way after he had collected what little wages he was paid for cleaning up and such. We were going to rob him. We were prepared to do worse."

Betsy gasped, afraid of what was going to come next. "What do you mean Dad?"

"When I was a young man I was more like a young thug. A group of us were like the bullies you read about accosting people on the street. We just seemed to be driven by the devil. We did bad things. Once we even tried to mug the old man. We encountered him and were prepared to rob him." Max paused and took a deep breath. "God forgive us we were prepared to do much worse. Then something happened to us. This old man had the strength of ten men. We felt ah this ah this presence coming from the old man. It actually filled us full of awareness of what we might be and a life of helping rather than destroying. I… I… It could have been alien. I have tried not to think about it before. It was almost more than I could comprehend. Yet after that time, I began to learn things… things I had

had difficulty understanding before like math and abstract thinking. I became a new person. I became socially and politically active. It was the greatest thing to ever happen to me. I guess what I am trying to say is, I understand somewhat what Jon experienced. But his experience must have empowered him with awesome powers if he is able to heal."

Betsy and Dad talked for some time. Then Betsy bid her Dad good-bye and headed back to her home.

Pulling into her driveway, she could see strange tire tracks leading down to Jon's home. Betsy parked and walked down to the doublewide. "Is it possible Jon came home?" she wondered. As she turned the corner to the back entrance, she could see the door was opened. When she walked in, she was shocked. The place had been torn up. Things were scattered. Drawers had been yanked out and thrown about the place. Glasses, plates broken and strewn all over the place. Betsy was staggered. She made her way out the door. "Pete? Pete?" She called. As she walked along the path she looked down and gasped. "Oh my god!" she exclaimed. There along the path into the bushes lay Pete.

— — —

Nicholas and Jon continued their travel into Washington, DC.

"David?" Jon broke the silence as the powerful machine chewed up the miles.

"Yes."

"That was an awesome thing you did for those people." There was silence and Jon continued. "You present yourself as a potential executioner and yet you save my son, you heal the man in Lance's room, and now you do such a wonderful thing for Anthony and his family. I am having difficulty understanding your role as this potential executioner of the human race. In addition to that I am overburdened with questions and don't know how to begin."

Nicholas cast a glance in the rearview mirror as he sat in anticipation of David's response.

"Jon, what do you think your people did when they invaded this land you call America?"

Jon looked at David thoughtfully before speaking. "Well, we were a people looking to escape tyrannies. People settled here looking to start new, fresh lives for their families."

"What about the people who already resided here?" Jon asked.

"Well, I am not exactly a student of US history, but surely there was some attempt to establish civilized relations with the Indians and whoever people ran into."

"Ran into? Is that a quaint euphemism for ran over?

Jon was silent as David allowed a flurry of images and information to flood his consciousness about the story of American colonization as a territorial invasion. David allowed Jon to see the invasion of America shorn of old mythology and rationalizations, Jon watched in his mind the raw invasion of the "Puritan" whose actions could only be seen in all due honesty in the cold light of material interest and naked expansion.

Jon hung his head. He felt ashamed in the revelation of the baser instincts of mankind. "Do we have no redeeming features?" he quietly asked.

"If there were none, do you think we would be having this exchange? By the way and as we have noted you and Nicholas handled yourselves well today."

Jon sighed deeply. "No, I guess we wouldn't be having this exchange. But then if we have some redeeming qualities why is destruction of my race even contemplated?"

"Jon, what will the posture of nations be against countries labeled as terrorists who come into possession of massively destructive weapons, weapons referred to as "WMDs?"

Jon rhetorically said, "They would have to be willing to cease such efforts, give up such capability to destroy others or be destroyed themselves."

Jon sighed deeply again. He now better understood David's mission.

Jon's mind began to fill with question after question. "There is so much I want, need to ask you. Why have you chosen me? Why have you chosen the US to begin this query? Why did you not only save my son but also the old man next to Lance? We, that is Christians, believe in a creator and a savior called Christ. We follow God's word from what we call a Bible. When our Christ was sacrificed and left to return to God, we were left with the Holy Spirit. That is hopefully the force you sense within me. What beliefs does your species have? Isn't there a better reason to help us as people rather than destroy us with the same evil mentality that has lead our nation as well as others to do to one another? What am I supposed to do now that I have found my love in Betsy?"

"Hmmm Jon. That is a wide assortment of questions. However you deserve an answer to all you ask. First, the US as a country was chosen because of its wealth, stature in this

world and it represents the highest level of civilization in the world. One would expect to find the qualities here over any place else which would warrant a redemption of the fate otherwise planned. You were chosen because Nicholas, and Orson, the secret service agent you have yet to meet, reviewed all the DNAs on file in the US data bases to come up with the optimum fit for my mission. Saving your son was important to securing your willingness to let me be within you. The old man who was next to Lance is a Peter Slavak. He is a multi-millionaire founder of Estron Electronics. He was riddled with cancer. His son had dumped him in the hospital understanding he had essentially expired and they needed to get a death certificate to continue with the business. He was moments away from death and it was so not necessary. It is another example of how your race has exceeded its pursuits of so many technologies yet when it comes to those dealing with increasing the quality of life you move at a snail's pace. It was easy to pin point the cancer stem cells at the heart of Slavak's illness, turn them off and allow his body to begin its repair efforts along with some help. So I decided to do it. Your medical scientists are occupied with bombarding all of cancer cells with toxic radioactive rays and in doing so miss the critical stem cells. As a result they miss what causes destructive cancer to grow and propagate even after massive and sometimes destructive radiation and chemotherapy. It was child's play to save Slavak. The irony Jon is that your planet's inhuman ways has led to the very cancer most fear."

"What do you mean by that?"

"Jon, the majorities of cancer suffered by your race are caused by the way meat is processed. Rather than quickly killing animals intended for food such as beef or chicken, your

needs for mass production include barbaric ways of death for these creatures. These methods are so traumatic they cause great fear and pain in the animals prior to their actual death. The chemical changes in these animals that are so processed become cancer causing agents when ingested by humans."

"I thought animals are killed quickly in slaughter houses prior to being made into food parts."

"Yes, Jon your race eats their burgers, chicken fillets, fish and are oblivious to the fact that how these animals are killed for processing as food affects their own chemical make-up when ingested. The consumers, the slaughterers, the farmers and the butchers, have not understood the division of the nervous system into sensory and motor systems. Your medical professionals and scientists ignore this reality and are content to just deal with the outcome: Cancer. No one wants to know that animals might have suffered severe pain every time they eat a ham sandwich, hold a barbecue, eat fish, have a "Happy Meal" or consumed turkey, or chicken. And it is just not only meat products. You spray highly toxic chemicals on your fruits and vegetables and are oblivious to the effect on consumption."

"Well, most wash them off before eating."

"Jon, take apples as an example. Before packing they are sprayed with high pressure washers. Why do you think washing them under a faucet will get the residue, the cancer causing toxins, off? In addition, your FDA, food and drug administration, accepts putting extreme poisons, like roundup, within seeds for such vegetables as corn, soy bean and others. They do it because it keeps the crop weed free. Then people wonder where autism, cancer, and a multiple of other diseases come from."

Jon, your race is led by money and power. Regardless of the outcome or method used, the end result for your people seems to be all about that. If we had the time we could wait till you all destroyed yourselves.

"Help us. Educate us. "If you are so enlightened, work with us rather than playing the role of barbarians who are intent on annihilating us."

We are not barbarians Jon. We have a high consciousness of existence and caring for one another. Our only resort to destroy your species became an option when our own existence is in peril such as it is now with the combination of your species technology in the area of space travel and your immaturity in the areas of power and material gain."

In a moment of silence Jon said, "Wow. There is so much involved. It is almost mind boggling to take it all in.

"Yes, it is Jon. However I have been working on that. Human minds only function at 5 percent of their capacity. You will soon be at 50 percent; a level far higher than your smartest at least in the area of IQ. For some that would or could be turned into ruthless control and a destructive evil. You have been determined to be not such a threat and someone who will use your newly acquired capabilities in positive ways. Combined with attributes I will leave you with Jon you may very well be in the category of what your comic books call a super hero."

"Well, I don't understand that."

"You will. Now, continuing with your other questions brings us to an interesting point. Your own scientists have already discovered the Christian Holy Grail of your branch of philosophy dealing with the origin and general structure of the universe, with its parts, elements, and laws, and esp. with

much of its characteristics as space, time, causality, and free-dom. How your world keeps such information from being uni-versally known must have to do with its need to hide anything that threatens man's wealth and power. Your Christians did this in the early centuries of mankind. Fearful people would not understand, the so called churches translated your God's word into an esoteric language called Latin. This is the part of mankind we fear. It is the extent of this which I am here to measure."

"What? Are you saying science already has the proof of God's existence?"

"Yes! The "Big Bang Theory" of the creation of your uni-verse appears to be generally known. What is not generally known except for those scientists who seem to agree is that contrary to the thought the universe is either expanding or is static, it is actually decelerating. Your Albert Einstein's general theory of relativity proves that. Einstein became convinced of the existence of a creator through his studies. Unfortunately he died before he could realize the scientific proof. This proof of difficult nonlinear equations gave testament that your creator, or as you call it, God, exists. He is intelligent. He is creative. He is responsible for the universe. Even the renowned phys-icist Stephen Hawken pointed out, if you prove time has no beginning; all possibilities are eliminated except your Christ. Among the wide variety and numbers of faiths on your planet, only one describes the creator independent of time, space mat-ter and energy. That is the Christian Bible although there are some ambiguities in its translation which veil actual meanings of scripture."

"Yes," exclaimed Jon with the excitement of one making an awesome discovery. "I see it. Wow it is so clear now. What about your beliefs?"

We have always believed in a creator. We were also once of material form. We were able to surpass the need to outdo each other and were able to develop a society which focuses on the common good. It has brought us great achievements and pleasure beyond description. We did have from our early years, information about the creator left by visitors who came to our planet just as they came to yours. We developed to where we are today. But unlike your race we never saw the need to fight over material things. We learned to enjoy the pleasures we had. It allowed us to grow spiritually and achieve much.

"I am staggered by the flow of information and enlightenment I feel. Visitors from another planet led to our creation? I thought the creator, God, created us."

Jon, when your species clones a living organism, animal or human, do you not think God empowered you with the ability to do so? And as I can see you do, is it the person who cultivates the test tube or the creator who allowed the life to begin?"

"Okay, I see your point. Then with your beliefs how can you process taking our lives? Our Bible says not to kill as it is a sin."

Jon the Hebrew translation is not to murder. There is a difference. Your race employs that difference whenever it feels it has justification to attack others in an effort to prevent murder or mayhem or a loss of power or oil. Your world fights terrorism, and with that justification invades other countries."

"I feel overwhelmed. Why doesn't your world then focus on teaching us and, as the first visitors knowingly walking among us, lead us to the kind of existence where we are no longer a threat?"

"Jon, the latter part of your question we will address another time. However, as to the first part, you will be the one to lead the way to convincing us such a relationship is worthwhile."

"Whoa. How am I supposed to do that?"

"You made the point many of your people are good people. I decided to give you the opportunity to test that. When we meet the man we have in Washington, Orson Willoby, whose icon is Nicholas, I will be leaving you for a time as the three of us need to deliberate on what we have found. You will proceed on your own, with the powers I grant you to explore your thesis that there are many more people with good generous hearts than there are of those who seek only their personal gain at the expense of others."

"Wait. I don't want to go on some kind of crusade. I need to get back to my home; my family, my life. I don't have any powers. I have come to enjoy your companionship. Besides how would you know what I have found?"

"You might say a part of me will be with you. It will function as you need. You can dispense a variety of powers. Only your imagination will be your limiting force. What you imagine you will be able to do. The part of me with you will record all I need to know to make a decision when we meet."

"When will that be?"

"Jon it will be when I am ready. I will tell you when. Trust me you will have great emotional challenges. I wish your increased IQ coupled with your powers good luck. You will need it"

"Well, first I need to see Betsy. She has become my soul mate and I need to return home."

"Fine, Jon. I put no requirements on you. You will do as you decide. I am only interested in your proof of the "good" people you say there are which fact would negate our destruction of your species."

"How much time do I have?"

"In two months, sixty of your days, you will come to L Street NW and Ninth Street NW, Washington, DC. We will await your arrival. We will evaluate your progress then."

"What if something happens to me in the mean time?"

"Jon remember. You are a super power now. Nothing will happen. Just choose your powers wisely."

"What powers? I don't know what you are talking about. Can't you be a little more specific?"

"The knowledge is within you. Just use it. But to ease your mind, take this knife."

A knife suddenly appeared in David's hand. Jon took the knife handed to him. *"Now thrust it into your right thigh."*

"What?" Why would you want me to do that? *"Jon, this is an issue of trust. It is also a sample of the powers within you."*

Jon took the knife. He caught Nicholas's eye looking at him in the rearview mirror. "Oh my god what am I thinking of." Then he closed his eyes and plunged the knife into his thigh. Jon pulled the knife up. Blood was on the knife edge. "Oh my god, oh my god, what have I done?" Jon frantically unbuckled his pants and slipped them off. There was a hole in the pants where the knife had gone through. There were traces of blood on the knife blade. However, there no signs of the knife penetrating his leg. Jon was breathing heavily not understanding what he had just done and what he had just witnessed. The Mercedes pulled up alongside a coupe in which two men were talking furiously at each other. As they got along side, Nicholas rolled down Jon's window on the side closest to the car. *"Jon, use your hearing. You need to want to hear what they are saying. Use your ears and concentrate."*

In a second the conversation of the two occupants in the car traveling next to theirs was as clear as if they were in the car with them. "Wow," Jon said. "But they are speaking a foreign language." *Listen to them very carefully Jon and decide you want their conversation translated into your language. Your mind can do that."*

Again, Jon focused his mind on doing as Jon directed. Now the conversation of the two men in the car riding next to him, Jon could hear in English.

"Remember Jon, not only do you have the invincibility against harm, but you have a super mind with an IQ of 300 and it's growing. There is little you can't figure out.

"Okay, Okay," said Jon finally convinced of powers in his possession he would not in his wildest imagination dreamed he would ever have.

"Now rest Jon. You have a great adventure ahead of you.

Jon laid his head back. Exhausted mentally, he fell into a deep slumber. Little did he know David had brought this about in preparation for Jon's quest.

The Mercedes pulled up at the corner of L Street and Ninth Street, Washington, DC, and parked.

Jon woke to a uniformed patrolman knocking on the backseat car window with a night stick. Jon looked at his watch. It was 6:00 p.m.

THE QUEST

"Hey, buddy, you can't park here. What are you doing? You can't park in front of the convention center." Jon looked at the officer. His face had the look of someone disheveled and groggy. "Get out of the car Sir."

Jon slowly got out of the backseat of the Mercedes. He found himself stumbling forward as he tried to come back to consciousness. The officer stared at Jon closely, moving closer to detect any give away smell. "Is this your car sir?"

"Uh, no, uh actually it belongs to a friend; uh they must have left me for a moment."

"Do you have any ID, Sir?"

"Well, uh yes, of course I do." Jon reached into his back pocket and suddenly realized the officer was going to run the information on his ID to see if there were any wants or warrants. As Jon handed the officer his billfold, he touched the officer's hand. As he did, Jon looked into the officer's face and subconsciously told him "everything checks out and I need to be on my way."

The officer looked at Jon. Then after briefly turning to go back to his vehicle and run Jon's information, stopped.

He turned back around to Jon. "Sir, everything checks out okay. You need to be on your way now."

"Yes, thank you officer," and with that Jon jumped into the driver's seat to get on his way. He was startled to see there was no ignition key. "Oh no, what next?" Jon put his hand over the ignition and told the car to start. The Mercedes engine roared. Jon put it into gear and sped away. Using the GPS, Jon moved out of the city and proceeded back to North Carolina. "Hmmm," Jon thought to himself, "I am beginning to like this." Then, thinking about David, Jon called out. "David? David, are you there? Are you here?" Having no sense of David, Jon tried to get his wits about him. He had sixty days. Sixty days to do what, find enough good people to justify David from annihilating the planet?"

Crossing the Potomac River, Jon noticed the mobile phone. Picking it up, he called Betsy's home.

"Hello," she answered.

"Betsy, it's Jon."

Betsy broke into tears. "Oh my god, Jon, where are you? They have been here." She was crying uncontrollably.

"Betsy, I am on my way. Who has been there?"

"Jon I don't exactly know. But they have ransacked your place… and Pete… and Pete…"

"What about Pete?" Jon asked frantically. Betsy couldn't seem to stop crying.

"Jon… Pete is dead."

Jon felt like something had punched him in the stomach. Suddenly a rush of anger swelled up inside him unlike anything he had felt in a long time. He found it hard to speak. Then in a calm voice he said, "Betsy are you okay?"

"Yes," she whimpered.

"Okay," Jon replied. "That's what is important." Jon thought for a moment. Suddenly he realized their conversation was being overheard. "Betsy?"

"Yes, Jon, tell me what to do. I am afraid."

"Okay. Sweetheart. I am on my way back to Boston. I am going to track down the agent who was responsible for this. I know it is unfair to ask you to wait further because I don't know how long it will take me. Listen I am about to board a flight. You won't hear from me for a while. Please be patient. OK?"

"Jon, I love you. I don't understand any of this but I will be here waiting."

With that the phone went dead.

Lizzy's phone rang. "Richmond," she answered.

"Chief, Jon Sullivan did make contact with the Collingswood woman. He told her he was boarding a flight to Boston to track us down and that he won't be seeing her anytime soon."

Liz barked her orders into the phone. "Pull out of there and get back here as soon as you can but maintain minimum surveillance. We have preparations to make."

The drive to Carthage was posted by MapQuest at 5 ½ hours. Jon made it in just fewer than 4. Pulling up onto Gilbert Trusky's street. Jon pulled over and parked the Mercedes several houses away from the Trusky house. Slowly Jon got out of the Mercedes and quietly scoped out the neighborhood. As he approached Gilbert's house he stopped at a stone wall from behind which he could see the entrance and front. As he looked at the house he concentrated on whether or not he could see anyone inside or outside the house. Suddenly flashes of orange appeared inside the home. Jon blinked his eyes. He looked again. They were gone. Again he concentrated and the orange glows appeared again. Jon realized he was actually able to pick up heat signatures off bodies inside the home. He looked around at the adjoining homes and realized, if he concentrated, he could also see them there. It was now 10:30 p.m. One of the glows was that of someone taking a shower; probably Judy. Another was one which appeared to be lying down; probably Gilbert. But wait a third glow came from the same area of the shower. Jon continued to give the area surveillance. Seeing nothing to make him concerned except for the third glow, Jon decided to risk his entry. As Jon reached the side entrance closest to Gilbert's bedroom, he thought about how he would make entry.

Standing at the door, Jon wondered if he could just float through the door. David had told him that reality is merely an illusion, albeit a very persistent one. He had gone on to explain the molecules making up matter are spaced very far apart such that we can actually pass through objects if we view things in a different reality. David had demonstrated that by having Jon rethink his thoughts about material things and with David's presence within him, Jon actually passed an arm through a tabletop and back again. Thinking on that Jon wondered if he could do the same to this door. Concentrating, Jon just walked through the door. The results were exhilarating. It made goose bumps appear on Jon's arm. As he stood inside Gilbert's house he looked around. "Awesome," he said to himself as the extent of these new powers were becoming a reality.

Getting his bearings, Jon slowly walked through the living room to the small narrow hall leading to Gilbert's room. The door was closed. Jon smiled as he briefly thought about walking through that one also. "Hmm, why not," he thought. With that Jon passed through Gilbert's bedroom door only to face a snarling Doberman.

Panic briefly rushed through Jon before he quickly used his thoughts to calm the Doberman. As he had done with the policeman, Jon focused on the dog who now lay silently with his eyes peeled on Jon.

Gilbert's eyes opened. "What the hell?" Gilbert yelped as he saw Jon standing there.

"Shhh Gilbert it's me Jon Sullivan."

"I know who the hell you are, Jon." Gilbert said groggily as he sat up in his bed now looking over at his Doberman Dennis with a "what good are you" look. "What in the hell are you doing in my bedroom, Jon?" Then after a brief pause, "Where the hell have you been?" Gilbert turned on the light at his bedside table, flipped off the bed covers and swung his long legs over the side of the bed and sat up.

"Gilbert," Jon said in a very quiet tone. "I know this looks crazy but I need your help and this is the only way I could come to you."

"Jesus, Jon," Gilbert moaned as he turned on his bedside light and looked at his clock. It read 11:30 p.m. He ran his large hand through his hair. "I had just fallen asleep. What is going on?" Then after a moment of reflection, he asked "How is Lance?"

"Lance is fine, Gilbert but I am in a messy situation." Gilbert reached out his hand and Jon helped Gilbert to his feet and over to the oversized recliner Gilbert kept in his large bedroom.

Grabbing a partially full but old cup of coffee from the small table beside the recliner, Gilbert took a sip. Leaning back into the recliner, Gilbert said, "Tell me what is going on that would make you break into an old man's house at almost midnight."

Jon sat on the side of the bed and told Gilbert the entire story about the Holly Bush, the presence, his trip to Boston, the healing of Lance, the cure for an old man with cancer and now the pursuit of him by the government agents and his requirement to find enough "good" people to keep their world from being destroyed.

Gilbert sat there, sipping on his cup, watching his dog Dennis who was laying there with his head on his front paws watching them, and occasionally sighing and shaking as if he was getting the chills. Finally when Jon stopped, Gilbert coughed. He looked up at Jon, and after a brief stare said, "Am I in a fracking nightmare or what?"

Suddenly there was a knock on Gilbert's bedroom door, it opened and Judy stuck her head in. She saw her Dad, the dog, but never saw Jon. "Dad are you okay? Can't you sleep?"

"I am fine Judy. There is too much damn noise in this house tonight and it's hard to sleep. What's going on? Is someone here?"

"Oh yes Dad, uh, I was taking a shower. Sorry, I'll try to be more quiet."

"Fine do that. Now close the door. I am going to listen to some news and try to sleep, okay?"

"Uh, okay, Dad. Goodnight." With that said Judy closed the door and went back to her room.

Gilbert scratched his head. "How did she not see you?" Gilbert looked at Jon bewildered.

"Well, I saw her coming and uh I disappeared."

"Someone please pinch me," Gilbert said as a smirk crossed his face. "Jon let me see your arms." Jon rolled up his sleeves and Gilbert examined both his arms. "Jesus," Gilbert exclaimed, "all the burn scars have left. Your arms look like you never had them." Gilbert looked up at Jon with an astonished look on his face.

Anticipating Gilbert's thoughts, Jon replied, "Yes, I know Gilbert. It is amazing."

"Jesus, Jon," what else can you do other than remove scars and control Dobermans?"

Jon laughed; well believe it or not, just about anything I put my mind to. Gilbert looked at Jon still having a hard time taking it all in. Jon picked up a 6 inch hunting knife off of Gilbert's dresser. He pulled it out of its sheath and handed it handle first to Gilbert.

"Gilbert," Jon said as he put his hand on the table beside Gilbert. "Stab me with this knife."

"Are you stone cold crazy Jon?

Jon smiled understanding Gilbert's reluctance and took the knife from Gilbert. Jon then plunged it through his hand resting on the table. The knife went through Jon's hand pinning it to the table. Gilbert jumped. "My god, Jon, why in the hell would you do that?"

Jon pulled the knife up leaving his hand on the table. Gilbert watched as the knife wound in Jon's hand healed itself before his eyes.

"God Almighty, God Almighty, "Gilbert mumbled as he rose from his chair and pulled out a small bottle of "Wild Turkey" bourbon from a dresser drawer and took a long swig. He put the bottle back in its place and closed the drawer. He let out a long breath of air. He went back and sat in the recliner. After a few moments when the conversation and demonstration was over, he looked at Jon.

"Jon, I have always felt about you as a son I never had. I have heard your story. I have seen what you can do. I don't understand any of it but I trust you. What do you need for me to do?"

Jon continued to tell Gilbert about the danger Betsy was in, and Pete's death. "Gilbert I need to get Betsy away. I want you to drive a Trusky truck over to Betsy's in the morning. I will be wearing a Trusky uniform. You will go to the door and give Betsy a clipboard with a paper on it which shall explain I am there. She will be instructed to act like it is a maintenance call. Once she indicates she understands, you will signal me by waving at me to come. I will be wearing a wig and I will carry a ladder to shield most of me. When we are inside we will wait for about ½ hour. Betsy will get dressed in the Trusky uniform and you and she will leave. Don't worry about me. I will be okay. You will take her to her Dad's."

"Just where do you think you will find a wig between now and tomorrow morning?"

"I don't know, but I will figure it out."

"Take a seat. I will be right back." Gilbert got up and left the room. Within minutes he returned with a woman's wig and a Trusky uniform. "Here, try this wig on for size."

Jon started to laugh. "Shhh" Gilbert cautioned, "Do you want Judy here?"

"Right," Jon acknowledged. Jon tried on the wig and now it was Gilbert who had to hold his mouth to keep from laughing. "You would make a great broad," he managed to get out between smirks and stifled laughs.

"Thanks a lot," Jon replied as he gave Gilbert a cutie wink. "You can pick me up at the Shell Station down the road at 9 a.m." With that Jon left.

9:00 a.m.

The Trusky truck pulled into the Shell station. Gilbert could see the Mercedes parked over by the side. Jon came out of the station wearing the Trusky uniform including an oversized ball cap to cover the brunette wig he was wearing. He was carrying two cups of coffee and a bag of doughnuts. As Jon got in the truck Gilbert looked at Jon, gave him a smile and a wink and said, "I hope this doesn't get around town."

"Ha, Ha," said Jon facetiously as he handed Gilbert the coffee and put the bag down between them in the middle seat. They rode in quiet, sipping coffee and eating a doughnut as they proceeded to McCrory road. "Do you think they will be watching?" Gilbert inquired.

"I think we can count on it," replied Jon.

As they pulled off of 24-27 onto McCrory Rd. Jon pointed to a big blue van parked on the shoulder. Looking intently at the van, Jon said, "They have tapped the phones and have a visual on the house."

Pulling into the driveway, Jon noticed the curtains part as someone peered outside as the Trusky truck pulled in. Gilbert shut the truck off, looked at Jon, grabbed the clipboard and headed for the front door. He rang the bell several times before Betsy answered.

As she opened the door, Jon got a big lump in his throat. He could feel his insides wanting to jump out of the truck and run into her arms. Gilbert showed her the clip board. She said something and looked out at the truck. "Be brave sweetheart," Jon said to himself as he could image the fear in Betsy's heart.

Gilbert waved at the" man" in the truck. Jon got out and shouldered a small, light aluminum ladder but moved slowly as if the ladder was very heavy. He moved to the door. Betsy's eyes got as big as saucers. Jon went in with the ladder. He put it down. Then he turned to make sure the curtains were closed. He turned back toward Betsy who took a flying leap into his arms. They embraced and kissed until Gilbert was getting embarrassed. "Gees Jon, you didn't tell me the kiss was what would be half hour long."

Betsy pulled away. "Oh, I am sorry Gilbert." Then she laughed and jumped back in Jon's arms. "Well, what an adventure we have started on."

"Ya, babe, I am so sorry I have pulled you into this." Jon said sorrowfully.

Betsy took his face in her hands, looked him square in the eyes. "You have nothing to be sorry about. If I had to do this all over again as opposed to being my miserable self, I would do it in a heartbeat. Is David with you she asked?"

"No I am all on my own but I will explain after we get you over to your Dad's" Gilbert looked puzzled but said nothing.

Jon stood there with Betsy's arm around his waist. "Boys, Have you all eaten this morning?"

"Uh"—Jon looked at Gilbert—"nothing except a doughnut."

"Nothing here," Gilbert replied.

"Okay, breakfast it is. You two just relax or fix whatever you are supposed to fix," she said as she laughed and went into the kitchen.

After a fine breakfast of eggs, grits, bacon and muffins, Betsy cleaned up and went into the bedroom with her wig and Trusky uniform. When she came out she caringly asked Jon if he was going to be all right.

Jon put his arm around her and said. "I will be fine. Just carry the ladder out like you are a worker. Throw the ladder into the back of the truck. Keep your head down and get into the truck. Shield your face with your hat as there is a van at the top of the road with a man who is looking this way."

Betsy took the ladder and headed out the door. Gilbert went out after her and turned as if to thank the lady of the house for the "work" they had just done.

The agent saw the two workers come out of the house at what he noted was forty-eight minutes after they went in. As the truck came up McCrory Rd, the agent inside the van gave them a brief look and then turned his attention back to the house.

Inside the house, Jon was leaving out the back door. He furtively made his way down to the double wide without detection. As soon as he came close, he could see where Betsy had buried Pete. He lingered there for a moment. Tears swelled up in his eyes. They became replaced with anger as he thought about this needless death of his dear friend. Inside it was obvious Betsy had picked things up and neatened the place up the best she could. Jon smiled at Betsy's forethought, as he looked at the Polaroid's she had taken of the place after the agents got through ransack-ing the place. He went out to the back deck and thought about the times he and Pete had shared. Then the thought came to him. Pete had sired some pups for a friend. Jon wondered if there might be any available. "After this ordeal is over"—he paused—"maybe Betsy and I can check that out."

Jon spent the day at the doublewide. He felt depressed. Opening up the refrigerator he found a six pack of beer still there. Even though he knew better, he sat on the back porch near where Betsy had buried Pete and started drinking. "How did he ever get involved with all this?" he thought. "Why did Lance have to get hit requiring him to make this pact with an alien force?"

Jon slipped into a deep sleep. It was nearly 10:00 p.m. when he awoke. Hungry he could not find anything of substance to eat.

Jon went down into the woods and then began to work his way up to the agents van. He could see the agent's infra-red image. Anger surged within Jon after thinking about seeing Pete's burial plot. Jon opened the passenger door of the van. "Let's see how good I am," Jon thought. The agent, who was already nodding off, looked up in surprise as Jon told him not to worry and to focus on what he was doing.

The agent turned back to monitor Betsy's house. Jon used his mind to explore what the agent knew about those who had pillaged his home and killed Pete. The agent in the van wasn't part of that crew but was stationed here days ago to keep surveillance and to report back to Boston, if any developments occurred. The agent had heard it was Liz Richmond who killed the dog and enjoyed doing it. Jon instructed the agent he needed to get something to eat and to drive. Rather than risk the chance of having the driver take him near Max's house, Jon directed the agent to drive to a café just alongside Route 24-27 just outside the Carthage city limits.

It was now dark. Rather than go back to Betsy's Dad's house, Jon sought out someplace to eat. As Jon directed the agent to drive up Rt. 24-27, toward the community of Robbins, Jon directed the agent to stop at a small dimly lit café called Rusty's. Jon touched the GPS and made it inoperative so that there would be no trail to where the driver had driven. Then Jon instructed the driver to go back to where he was set up and resume his surveillance.

As the agent turned the vehicle around and headed back, Jon watched him. Then Jon looked at the café where there were over a dozen motorcycles parked. Suddenly David appeared beside him.

"Hello Jon, I thought I would drop in and see how you were doing."

Jon looked at David with a surprised look. Then he grinned. "Good to see you again my friend."

"Did you stop here because you were hungry?"

Jon looked at David and gave him a look that said, "Perhaps this is not a good choice."

David smiled. *"Nothing ventured, nothing gained, isn't that a well-known Earth saying."*

"Hmpf," Jon responded, casting a glance a furtive glance at David.

The lights in the café were dim and the noise was loud. When Jon entered, silence prevailed as the café's customers stopped their chatter and looked over at the new customer. Jon stopped and looked around. These were big ugly men hugging their beer bottles and giving Jon a look that was not inviting.

Jon approached the café counter at the back part of the café in front of a kitchen. A surly looking gal who would be a contender in a contest for the most body piercings, stared at this man who approached her.

"This guy must not have any idea what he has walked into," she thought.

"Any chance I can get something to eat?" Jon said as he stood before her. From his left Jon could see a tall man approaching him and turned to see a man about 6'7" walking up to the counter. He stood beside Jon. Before the gal could respond to Jon's question, the man spoke.

"Hey, stranger," He said and smiled to show a mouth full of many missing teeth. "Can I get you something?"

"Well, I was hoping to get something to eat."

"You a citizen?"

"A citizen?" Jon asked.

"Jon a citizen, to these folks, is anyone who is not a member of a Biker Organization."

"Ahh, yes, sir. Just walked in hoping to get a bite to eat."

"Name is Too Tall," the stranger offered and stuck out a large dirty paw. Jon shook it and then turned to the gal. "Any specialties?"

"Specialties?" the young gal repeated looking at Too Tall.

Too Tall laughed. Then in a voice loud enough for all to hear, "Yes, sir we do have specialties. Tonight specialty is beans and franks." The bikers laughed.

"Here young man, there is a table over in the side here. Let's get you seated and Ms. Sandy will bring you your specialty." Again the whole place filled with laughter.

Jon moved to a table beside a door that led to a back room. The room was still laughing and looking at Jon as they drank their beers and ate.

"Well, Jon a whole room full of 'good people' just waiting to give you a good time."

Jon gave a big sigh. The gal brought over a bottle of beer, some napkins and utensils. "Too Tall sent this beer over to you on his tab."

Jon looked over at Too Tall and nodded his appreciation.

Shortly the gal returned with Jon's meal and put it on the table along with a ticket showing twenty dollars owed."

Jon shook his head. He knew they were trying to soak him with a ridiculous bill. "Don't forget you also owe me a five-dollar tip," the gal said as she laughed and turned back to the counter.

The bikers were all laughing among themselves as word spread about how much Ms. Sandy was charging the citizen.

Suddenly the front door opened and in came this young gal pushed behind by another biker. As soon as she spotted the bikers in the room she tried to turn and make her way back out. Her smile turned to a frightened look as the biker forced her into the café and blocked the door.

"I have got you a 'hard belly' fellas," the biker at the door yelled.

David clarified for Jon what he meant by that term. *"That's a young gal with a tight belly."*

"Get her over here Pan Handle," someone yelled to the biker who had brought her in.

"Ya," said another. "We'll make her into a Mama." The room laughed and the young girl looked terrified.

"A Mama is a woman who makes herself available to service any biker. They are going to take her into the back and gang rape her.

"How we gonna decide who gets firsts?" One of the bikers yelled.

Suddenly Jon stood up. "I am the guest here, I should get firsts."

The room suddenly got very quiet. Too Tall stood up. "Well, now citizen, the only way you can get firsts is to defeat a biker of our choosing. That is the way we settle that." Too Tall was laughing and smiling at the bikers. The bikers cheered and yelled their approval.

"Bam Bam, can you handle this citizen?" Too Tall asked.

From the back of the room, a bear size of a man with arms of steel stood up. He wiped the froth from the beer he had been drinking off his lips and smiled. There was not a tooth in his mouth.

The bikers moved the tables back off the floor to give the fighters a chance. "Okay citizen," Too Tall whined in a girly voice. "Come out here and earn your reward."

The bikers roared, yelled profanity at Jon as Bam Bam made his way to the floor space that had been vacated. As Bam Bam stood in front of Jon, Too Tall said he would share the rules of the match. "The rules are, there are no rules." Before Too Tall finished, Bam Bam struck Jon in the face with a sucker punch with such force it knocked Jon back against the wall. The bikers hooted and hollered. Normally most men would not have survived such a blow from the sledge hammer like fists of Bam Bam. Jon looked at Bam Bam and just smiled. Bam Bam came rushing forward to pin his quarry against the wall and continue to pound him into the floor. Bam Bam rushed forward with great force, but at the last second before he hit Jon, Jon moved so fast later the bikers would argue it seemed one second he was standing in front of Bam Bam and the next he wasn't as if they had blinked and missed the move.

As Bam Bam passed beside Jon, Jon put his hand on his back which added to Bam Bam's momentum such that Bam Bam couldn't stop and slammed into the wall so hard the café shook and Bam Bam fell to the floor like a wash rag.

The room became very quiet. Then the bikers began to protest and cuss Jon out. They appeared to becoming aggressive. "Quiet… quiet," Too Tall commanded. "They fought fair and square. We don't like the outcome but the rules are the rules. The citizen gets first with our soon to be Mama."

Despite the protests, Too Tall ordered Jon to take the gal into the back room. "You have fifteen minutes with her and then you come out and the next person goes in."

Jon took the scared young woman into the back room and closed the door. Looking around there was a dirty bed and one window covered with bars as a security measure.

"Please I want to leave," the young girl pleaded.

"Look," Jon commanded. "If you want to leave here unhurt, listen to me and do as I say."

David had located phone wires on the wall hanging loose. Using his powers he held the wires and called 911.

"911," the police dispatcher answered. "What is your emergency?" Repeatedly she asked. Hearing no response but seeing the line remained opened, the dispatcher determined where the call had originated from and dispatched officers to Rusty's Café.

The café room was full of wild bikers waiting for the back room to become available so their fun could start. "Hey, it's been more than fifteen minutes. Why ain't he out yet?"

Too Tall went and tried to get the door opened but it wouldn't budge. Several bikers joined him. Just as they broke in, sirens could be heard and red lights seen outside as several police cruisers pulled up to the café. Just as he got the door opened, Too Tall looked in briefly to see that the window was wide open and no one was in the room.

Up the road, Jon rode on the motorcycle he had taken belonging to Pan Handle, the biker who had brought the girl in on the pretense there was a great party going on. The young homeless girl, Amy, rode on the back. Jon took her to a rooming house where she said she had a room and where Jon could spend the night on a couch.

The next morning Jon rode his newly acquired motorcycle to the street where Betsy's Dad lived and slid it under the bushes a few houses away from Max Sumler's house. Carefully walking down the street, Jon came to Max Sumler's home. He slid around back to the patio entrance. He looked through the French doors and say Max and Betsy sitting at the kitchen table engrossed in conversation.

Jon looked around slowly. Seeing no one was aware of his presence, he tapped lightly on the window on the French door.

Max stood up as he heard the tapping. Looking, he saw it was Jon. Betsy had already seen who it was and rushed to the door. She opened up, pulled Jon in and wrapped her arms around him, placing her head on his shoulders.

"Jon are you okay?" Betsy asked, pulling her head off his shoulder and looking up at him.

Jon put his hands on Betsy's arms in a loving way. As Betsy moved slightly away from Jon, he said, "Yes, thank God. I am okay." Then as an afterthought, he added. "In fact, I am probably better than I have ever been in many ways."

Both Max and his daughter looked quizzically at Jon as he moved to the table and sat down beside Max.

"Max, before we begin, I want you to know I love your daughter and want to marry her."

Betsy put her hand up to her mouth. Her eyes were wide and full of a look of surprise.

"Well, uh Jon, uh I appreciate you sharing that with me but don't you think you should share that with Betsy."

"Yes, Max. Betsy knows. But I am asking your permission. And before you give it to me; I need to share with you what has happened in my life."

Max nodded as if to say, "OK."

Jon began by telling Max the entire story about himself, Lance's accident, David and the quest he was now on to try and convince David's race not to annihilate Earth.

Max listened intently and Betsy pulled up another chair slightly behind Jon and glowed with love as Jon explained all he had experienced.

Jon stopped talking. Then he resumed. "Max now you can see that my love for and relationship with Betsy could expose her, and you for that matter, to some danger."

"Well, Jon first allow me to share an experience I had." Then Max told Jon about his experience with a presence just as he had shared with Betsy. Finishing his story, Max went on to say, "As far as I am concerned, you and Betsy have my blessing. I am not afraid of any danger and Betsy will speak for herself."

Betsy put her arm around Jon's neck and looking at her Dad and then at Jon said, "Dad I have already made that decision. Jon is where I want to be regardless of the potential outcomes."

Jon put his arm around Betsy's waist as she stood beside him. He looked up at her. "Sweetheart, this mission I am to go on has its danger. I am sure the AFTa will be pursuing me."

"Hey, I will be with a super hero," Betsy said flippantly with a smile that showed she was ready.

Suddenly, Max spoke up. "Jon this all seems so surreal. It is hard to imagine someone being a superhero and then all that stuff about proof there is a creator. I love it. But is that all real?"

Jon got up and went over to the sink. He picked up two sharp steak knives. He came back to the table and sat down again. Looking at Max, Jon put both of the knives through his hand just as he had done with one for Gilbert. Max jumped out of his seat and backed up to the kitchen wall. Betsy squealed quietly. "I will never get use to that."

Jon pulled the knives out of his hand, one by one. Then with Max watching, he kept his hand laid on the table as the puncture wounds healed before his eyes.

"Wow," Max exclaimed. He was at a loss for words. Finally Max spoke. "Okay, I am stunned but you have made a believer out of me." Then upon reflection Max asked, "But what about that "Big Bang" stuff. Do you really think that gives evidence for a creator? Saying the "Big Bang" equals Christ is a pretty big leap. Don'tcha think? You know I am part Jewish."

Both Max and Betsy looked at Jon waiting for a response. Jon stood up and took the knives back to the kitchen sink. He dropped them in the sink. Then he turned and leaning against the sink he spoke. "Max, the Old Testament deals with the origin and general structure of the universe, with its parts, elements, and laws. It also details the characteristics of time which matches modern scientific discoveries. Therefore Judaism at a minimum is validated by modern science. How does that bring me to say the "Big Bang equals Jesus Christ?"

Hebrews 11:3 notes that the universe we know was made from that which we cannot detect. We can detect matter, energy, length, width, height and time, but not beyond.

Eight places in the Bible tell us that God created time. Two examples: 2 Timothy 1:9 which states, "The Grace of God that we now experience was put into effect before the beginning of time," and Titus 1:2, which states, "The hope that we have in Jesus Christ was given to us before the beginning of time." Jon paused to see if he still had Max and Betsy's attention. They were attentive and waiting for more so Jon continued.

"Max we can find in the Bible, specifically John 1:1 where it tells us in the beginning was the Word, and the Word was with God, and the Word was God. Later we learn that the Word became flesh in the form of Jesus. He was with God in the beginning. Through him all things are made. Without him nothing was made. Only through our discoveries of this century and DNA do we know that words and language are the basis of all creative acts. DNA is a code just as music is a code. Without this genetic code replication of cells any kind of evolution would be impossible. John 1:1 is a theological statement. This statement extends to science and philosophy. This statement is that conception always precedes embodiment. It is the basic fact that an idea must come before implementation: mind over matter. Only Judeo-Christian theology describes our world, describes our universe in that fashion. In the Christian New Testament, both John chapter 1 and Colossians chapter 1 follow this claim by God. God has no beginning. God has no end. God is not created. Among the world's religions, only the Christian Bible says this about God.

"In Titus 1:2 Paul recounts that eternal life was promised by God before the beginning of time. This apostle Paul was saying that God created the time dimension and of importance only God has the capacity to operate through cause and effect before the time dimension of our universe ever existed. Time is that dimension, that place in which causes and effects take place. What we are told here through Paul's inspired account is that we humans are confined to a single line of time. That line of time cannot be stopped or reversed. No matter what we do, it just keeps on going forward in one direction. I can walk home tonight. That's it. It is a simple but rigorous proof of the existence of God. We are confined and the entire universe is confined to a single line of time. Therefore the universe must be created. We must be created. However, God is not so confined. What I have just shared with you is the doctrine of the independence transcendence of the Creator. We can now go beyond this proof of the existence of God of the Bible. We can thus prove the existence of Jesus Christ because we can prove that God, our creator, is an independent, transcendent being."

Both Max and Betsy stared in amazement.

"May I pour myself some water?"

"Of course Jon," Betsy quickly replied. "I have some ice tea if you would like that."

"No thanks, the water will suffice." As Max and Betsy still mesmerized watched Jon, he slowly went over to the cupboards, got a glass and poured himself some water. He watched Betsy and Max intently as he drank the glass.

Max was the first to speak again. "Jon may I see your arm where the burn scars were? Jon walked over after placing the glass in the sink and showed Max his arm. Max rubbed his hands on Jon's arms where the burn scars were.

Suddenly Betsy turned her eyes. "Jon with all that you are now, I can hardly see why you would want, would need me." A tear began to roll down her cheek.

Jon quickly put his arms around her. "Betsy you are part of my soul. Without you, I would be like a horn without noise, a plant without blossoms. Forgive me if I have made you feel that way."

Encouraged Betsy put her arms around Jon as he held her and nestled her head on his shoulders.

Max spoke up. "Jon we would both be lying if we didn't say what you shared, what you can do, is more than overwhelming. However, your clarity makes so much sense it's scary. It's hard to see how others would not get what you have shared. You truly are a blessing. Now, how can we help you on your quest?"

"Well, that's it. I don't know. I mean I could just travel around, go to churches, or visit organizations where people are truly helping other people. I just don't know. One would think with this increased mental power I have I could figure this out." Jon sat down and looked a bit forlorn thinking about his quest and how to go about it.

Betsy put her hand on Jon's shoulder. "Jon why not do as you suggest. Go to people who serve other people. Certainly it shows how we have that capability within us."

"Yes, Betsy, that makes sense. But it seems to me we should be able to find good people throughout our communities, from the top down and from the bottom up."

Max started to talk, and then stopped. Jon caught Max's hesitation. "What is it Max, what were you going to say?"

"Well, I know this sounds silly. I was just thinking most of us were pretty good as children. Then because of material wants, and competitive urges we seem to learn how to fight for what we want. Then as we get older we rationalize getting things, power, etc., at the expense of others. Not everyone does but many do."

"Yes?" said Jon in an encouraging tone hoping Max would continue with his train of thought.

Max continued. "Well, I mean, why not stay on the path you were thinking except concentrate on children. Wouldn't that show what we are truly capable of being?"

Betsy looked at Jon. Jon looked at Betsy. Then looking back at Max, Jon smiled. "Max I think you are the one with the highest IQ. I think you are right. Then as frosting on the cake we, er, I mean I will go right to the top."

Betsy's head went back as if pulled from behind. "What do you mean the top Jon?"

"I mean the president of the United States. Who better to show the caliber of leaders we have—"

Max interrupted as he hung his head. "Or don't have."

"Cheer up Max. You have got us on the right path I think."

"Huh, Mr. Sullivan, what was that "we, er, I mean I stuff a second ago?"

Jon put an arm around Betsy who playfully pushed it off waiting for an answer. "Well, to be honest sweetheart it would probably be safer for you to stay here with your Dad. That way I could contact you all if I needed any help."

Betsy pulled away from Jon. "No Jon," she began to whine, "Now that I have found you, I don't want to lose you."

Max interrupted. "Betsy, Jon makes a great point. With the ATFa or whoever breathing down his back, it would be safer for you to hang here."

Now Betsy was facing down both men. "Now look here you two. I am not going to have a difficult time with both of you am I?"

Max and Jon looked at each other and shrugged their shoulders. They laughed. "Okay, okay," Jon conceded, "we will do it your way."

"Well, that's better," Betsy said proudly as she walked over to Jon and again put her arm around his waist. "Who would be better than I at warming up to children and getting them to share their beautiful inner selves?"

"Well, good. Now that that is settled, I am ready for something to eat. How about you Jon?"

"Sounds good to me," said Jon in answer to Max.

"Okay, you guys settle back and I will get us a biscuit and some hot coffee for brunch." With that Betsy smacked Jon on the butt and both men moved from the kitchen into the den.

As both men moved into the den, Jon commented on the task. "There will come a time when repulsive, evil and barbaric behavior will become extremely rare and even cease to be. Yet we as a people are not there yet. I pray David will see we have the potential to move away from such behavior.

⟶ ⟶ ⟶

At the command quarters Lizzy had made for herself and her men at the hospital where the results of Mr. Slavak and Lance's discovery were being studied, she called Otto into her office. Otto was a Russian Special Forces operative who had been drafted by the US Secret Service during a joint Russian US mission to investigate and validate the complaints of the Bosnia Muslim government who sought UN help from Bosnia Serb forces. The atrocities reported were large in number. It was shortly after the Russian US team of which Otto was the leader of the Russian contingent, at which time it became evident how brutal the man Otto was. His US counterparts complained about the terrorist tendencies of the man. He was known for being very intolerant of any view different than his own. He beat prisoners, tearing the thumbs off one. For another prisoner he raped the man's wife in front of him. He then threatened to rape his daughter. The prisoner confessed and gave the unit the information they wanted. Otto went ahead, brutally raped the man's daughter and then shot the man. Despite Otto's psychotic behavior, a member of the US forces, a man by the name of Scruggs, who was now the head of the NSA, recommended him to Lizzy.

It was rumored Lizzy established a weird relationship with Otto some of which was sexual and some sadistic. The rumor was Lizzy enjoyed Otto's physical aggression in private. Whatever the connection, Otto soon became the one Lizzy would call on when she had difficult assignments.

Otto closed the door behind him. He threw the dead bolt lock on the door and turned to face Lizzy. She got up from her desk.

"Look Otto," she said in her serious tone, "this is not the time for horseplay."

"We have a problem Otto. We have lost track of a man we are sure may be affiliated with an alien group.

"Oh so you want horse play Lizzy." Otto smiled a cruel smile and moved toward Lizzy in a menacing manner. Lizzy stood her ground in front of the large desk.

"Damn you Otto. This is not the time to frack around. We have a serious issue here."

Otto was now standing directly in front of Lizzy. "You don't worry about serious. Otto takes care of serious. Right now Otto is hungry and Lizzy wants to be fracked by horseplay."

Lizzy started to interrupt Otto, "Look, I tol…" Otto grabbed Lizzy by the shoulders and twirled her around to face her desk. Lizzy would not have taken this from any other man but Otto had always been able to manipulate her. She hated it but she loved it at the same time. Lizzy grunted as Otto slammed her over her desk and pulled up her skirt to reveal her tight pink buttock which she hardly ever wore pants to cover.

"Damn you, Otto, I…"

"Shh," Otto whispered with a deep guttural growl, "Lizzy wants to play horsey."

Outside the office door, Lizzy's seductive whine and gasps could be heard by those passing close enough to the door. Fellow agents looked at each other but no one said a word. To be accused of witnessing this relationship would mean a painful disappearance.

After eating the meal Betsy had prepared, all three shared the kitchen table peering over maps to decide how and when to travel such a way to maximize their coverage of children's schools, homeless shelters, churches, non-profit organizations, health care organizations right into Washington and eventually a meeting with the president of the United States.

"I don't know, Jon. Do you think you and Betsy can cover all this ground?"

Jon looked over at Betsy. "Betsy has done an awesome job mapping out a strategy." Betsy put her arm around Jon's neck.

"Dad, I think we can do it. We will certainly do our best."

"What about the government agents after you Jon?"

"Well, we won't be using credit cards nor doing anything which might facilitate anyone tracking us. You will be our prime contact. I would like you to do something though."

"What is that Jon?"

The guy in Lance's room at the hospital was a Peter Slavak. Can you see if you can contact him and get a contact number for us? He could be of tremendous help when it comes to contacting the president. Slavak was the head of Estron Electronics. His family may be heading it up now. However, now that Peter is back to health, he may have retaken his role."

"Will he remember you?"

"I am sure he will. After the long and intensive investigation they did on him, I am sure he knows my name."

"Okay. I will work on that and send a message on Betsy's mobile."

"Uh Max, we are going to use a number of mobile phones. After we call or have conversation we will be throwing that phone away. You will know the new number from text messages you will receive with three asterisks after the number."

"Okay, sounds like a plan. When will you start out?"

"I need you to take me back to where I left the Mercedes. We will fill it up and be out of here at the crack of dawn."

＊ ＊ ＊

After her session with Otto, Lizzy pulled together the team leaders under her control for a meeting to discuss strategy.

As they all sat around the conference room table, they began to discuss how to track Jon down. All of Jon's personal information and that of anyone who knows him was compiled and circulated.

"He is probably too smart to use a credit card or get in the public view but we need to monitor all those avenues anyway."

"What about the gal in Carthage where he lives, the one he may have a relationship with?" One of the agents asked.

"That's a good point," responded Lizzy. "We haven't got anything back from the agent down there monitoring. Fred," Lizzy asked one of the agents, "do we have anything on this broad's family?"

Fred rifled through some papers. He scanned a document and then offered, "The gal Betsy Collingswood, a thirty-two-year-old widow has a father a Max Sumler who lives in the town where she lives."

"Well, what do we have on him? "Demanded Lizzy.

There was silence at the table. "Damn it. We better get this information pretty damn quick or someone's ass is going to be hanging high."

Fred got up quickly and left the room. The discussion of logistics and strategy as to finding Jon continued until Fred came back into the room.

Fred waited till Lizzy addressed him. "Well, don't sit there like a stone. What the hell do we have on the father?"

"This Max Sumler is a former bigwig on the town council. He lives by himself. There are no negative aspects to his record. He is a widower and his only relative is the daughter Betsy and his granddaughter who is away at college." Fred shrunk in his chair as Lizzy bored a hole through him with her eyes.

"Okay, get a tap on his phones and I want another agent down there to keep him under surveillance. Also, under some ruse, I want confirmation that this broad is still at her house and we have tight surveillance on her."

"Under what basis do we get the court order for a wire-tap signed?"

Lizzy turned and stared at the agent who asked that question. "Sonny are you new with us?

Lizzy looked over at one of the senior agents and gave him a flick of her head toward the agent who had asked about the wiretap order. The senior agent got up and with a nod of his head motioned for the agent to get up and follow him.

When they left, Lizzy looked carefully around the table. "I don't know how that piece of work got into this meeting but it better not happen again. There was a pregnant pause. "If there is anyone here who does not understand the importance of our mission and may let some law, policy or whatever get in the way of finding this alien speak up now."

Again there was a long pause. No one spoke. "Now let's get to work. You each have an assignment. With that Lizzy got up and went back to her office followed by the senior agent who had taken the fairly new agent out of the meeting.

"Jesus, Jimmy," Lizzy spoke sharply to him. "If we can't get better hold on our own mission and who is on the team, we will be in deep shit. Do I make myself clear?"

"Yes, Lizzy," Jimmy responded. "That guy will be shipping out tomorrow to a NSA location in North Dakota. It won't happen again."

"It better not Jimmy or he will have company. Do I make myself clear?"

"Yes, ma'am."

"I want anyone associated with this alien covered like a blanket. I want to know the flavor of gum they are chewing. Got it?"

"Yes, ma'am."

After a full lunch, Betsy and Jon said their good-byes to Max, They re-confirmed their phone signals. Leaving the driveway, they went to the end of the street and turned right. Coming the other way was a black SUV which turned left onto Max Sumler's street and parked just past Max's house. The agent inside the SUV contacted the ATFa headquarters to let them know he was on location set up to do surveillance.

— — —

"Well, Jon, our first stop will be a childcare and the churches in Sanford."

"Yes. How should we approach the childcare or schools we visit?"

"I don't know. What are you concerned about?"

"Well, these days, people are on the alert for stalkers, pedophiles, you know, people who just don't seem to be appropriate for what is going on."

"Well, why don't we represent ourselves as a couple checking the area for a place for our children?" Betsy squeezed Jon's arm as she said that.

Jon gave Betsy a loving look and a warm chuckle. "Someday." Then after a pause Jon said, "that is a great idea. We can use the same approach for the churches."

"Yes, Jon. Oh I love this. Maybe someday we can just ramble through the country on our own; visiting little communities and seeing the sites."

Again Jon chuckled. "Well, sweetheart that's what we are doing now."

"Well, yes, but we have an agenda. I am talking about when we can spend 2 days, a week or whatever without have to worry about some mission."

"Yes, that would be nice."

Betsy turned on the radio and picked up a station they both enjoyed listening to.

As they pulled into Sanford, they came across the First Baptist Church. Betsy was the first to point it out. "How about this for our first stop? It isn't Sunday but they have a day school and there seem to be a lot of cars in the parking lot."

Jon pulled the Mercedes in and parked.

As they got out of the car, a mother with two children pulled up next to them. They exchanged pleasantries and followed the mother as she shepherded her children into the section of the church where day care was held.

Seeing two faces she did not recognize, one of the teachers walked over to Jon and Betsy. "Hi," she said. "I am Ruth one of the teachers here. I didn't recognize you and thought I could be of assistance."

"Well, thank you," Betsy responded excitedly. "Jon and I are considering moving into the area and we wanted to come by and look at the day care facilities here."

"Well, great," said Ruth. "Please allow me to give you the guided tour. How many children and what ages do you have?"

"We have a three-year-old son." Said Betsy. "Oh wonderful, well that is the youngest we handle here. There is an infant to two-year-old class on the other side, but here we work with the three- to six-year-olds."

Ruth took Jon and Betsy on a tour pointing out the facilities, schedule of activities and hours of child care. More interested in the children Jon asked if they might say hello to them. "Well, Mr. Sullivan, the children are about to start their show and tell. This is a time when we allow them to get up and tell whatever they would like to about events and experiences they have had.

"Well, great. I have a show and tell. I am a bit of a magician. Do you think I might share that with the children?"

Ruth thought for a moment and then asked to be excused. While Jon and Betsy waited, Ruth went over and spoke to several of the other teachers. They would all cast looks in the direction of Jon and Betsy. Finally Ruth returned. "Let me introduce you to the children. I am sure they would love to see some magic."

After introducing Jon to the children, Jon pulled out a teacher's chair and began to talk to the children. He pointed out he was traveling today looking for good people. He asked if the children knew any good people. They all said they did and one little boy said that was something his parents wanted him to be. Everyone laughed.

"Well, said Jon, I have the ability to identify good people. I just shake their hand. And it seems that every time I shake their hand, I can tell whether or not they are good. If they are good, I usually find a quarter hidden somewhere on their body where they didn't know it was." Immediately the little boy who had spoken up reached up behind his ears. He was looking to check and see if anything was there because his uncle Bobby would occasionally find a dime there. But he never found any quarters and Bobby wanted to make sure there was nothing there.

One by one the children came up to Jon. One by one he took their hand. He would smile at each one and ask them if they had been good. When each one would shake their head yes, Jon would first take a piece of paper from a small pad of post-it notes he picked up from the teacher's desk. He would crumple the paper up in a small ball. Then he would reach behind their ears and pull out a quarter. The teacher's eyes got big as saucers as they wondered where all those quarters came from. They looked hard to find out Jon's secret but never did.

When Jon got through he and Betsy thanked the teachers and excused themselves. As they were leaving, the church minister ran into them in the hallway. Ruth was walking behind them and she introduced them to Pastor Wolfe.

"What line of work are you in Mr. Sullivan," asked Pastor Wolfe.

"I am in the construction business Pastor."

"Oh that's wonderful," the Pastor replied. "Might I ask you a professional question?"

"Of course Pastor."

"I mean it may not be in your line of expertise but if you will allow me I will ask anyway."

"We are not a wealthy church. Years ago the church spent quite a bit of money on church bells that would play a variety of melodies. The bells are in our steeple. When they work the sounds are wonderful and very enjoyable to most. However, something has happened and we don't seem to be able to make them ring anymore. We don't know if the bells are the problem, the amplifier or what. We have received several bids to resolve the problem. However the least amount bid is several thousands of dollars, an amount beyond our budget. Would you have any suggestions?"

"Where is the amplifier located?" asked Jon.

"Why it is up in the balcony. May I show you?"

Betsy looked a bit startled by this sudden wayward direction in their schedule. But Jon just winked and smiled at her.

The pastor took Jon up to the balcony where he showed Jon the amplifier. Jon put his hands on the amplifier. He picked it up and checked each of the connections. The pastor who stood there watched Jon yet he could not see the flow of energy moving from Jon to the electrical apparatus and back to Jon.

"There," said Jon. I believe it should operate as it is supposed to."

"Oh my word. Thank God. Can I try it?"

"Of course."

The Pastor flipped the amplifier and waited. Suddenly the melodious sounds from bells could be heard filling the air waves.

When Jon returned down stairs with the pastor, Betsy was there with Ruth. "Oh Mr. Sullivan you fixed the bells. Thank you, thank you."

"I was glad I could help. It was only a communication problem between the amplifier and the bell transformer."

"Now may I ask you a professional question Pastor?"

"Well, of course, Mr. Sullivan."

"Please call me Jon."

"Yes, of course, Jon. Thank you. How can I help?

"This is going to sound strange but how do you go about finding "good" people?"

The Pastor laughed. "Please excuse my laughing. I would never have expected that to be your request." He paused. "Jon, 'good' is an abstract term. Like most abstract words, they take on the meaning of the listener. What is good to one person may not be good to another. In the church, we define *good* as people caring for one another and loving God which we believe creates that desire to care.

But like the old saying goes there are many who talk the talk but have difficulty walking the walk."

"Yes," agreed Jon.

"Jon, why this pursuit of good people?"

Betsy watched Jon wondering how he would explain this. "Well, I have a friend who feels that God would have a hard time finding enough good people to justify continuing." "Huh?" "Like when he left Noah and his family alive and destroyed everyone else."

Betsy had this look about her with her lips pursed in a "well that's okay" look.

"God has much patience with us Jon. He has watched his children certainly improve over the centuries. And he promised never again to do as he did when he destroyed all people except Noah and his family."

"Ah yes. Well, thank you Pastor."

"No, thank you Jon."

Jon and Betsy bid good-bye and headed out to the Mercedes. Suddenly he heard someone behind him. "Jon, "the pastor was calling. Huffing he came up to Jon and Betsy and gave each one of his business cards. "Please call if I can help in any way."

Both Jon and Betsy agreed they would and then they left with the music from the church steeple behind them.

"That was a wonderful thing you did back there Jon."

"You mean giving each child a quarter?" Jon said kiddingly.

Betsy punched Jon playfully, "No you big hunk. I meant fixing the church steeple."

"Well, the connections were all corroded. All I did was clean them off so they could communicate better."

"Well, it was beautiful. Oh and how did you do that quarter trick?"

"Why? Do you need a quarter?" Jon said kidding again.

"Well, not exactly, but you would be nice to have around if a gal wanted to do some shopping." They both laughed.

Throughout the next 6 weeks Jon and Betsy proceeded up the East Coast toward DC. They stopped at day care centers, churches, nonprofit organizations any place they felt they could collect experiences of young and old alike who would give David evidence of the potential of the human race.

"Okay," Betsy said. "Next stop is to get some lunch.

Just off Burbank Lane, Dale Virginia, just off Route 95, Jon and Betsy found a little café called "Patsy's."

"I have to admit," said Jon, "I am more than a tight bit hungry." Betsy smiled. She said, "Tight bit hungry? That's a good one hadn't heard that one before." She giggled. Jon held the door of the café open as two gentleman came out and gave Betsy a loving pat on her behind as she slipped past him to enter first.

"Let's go over there", she said pointing to a table against the side wall. The place was about half full. The smells were enticing and even Betsy was now feeling a bit hungry. They sat down and a young waitress approached the table. She welcomed them, introduced herself and shared with them the special which was a Salisbury steak with gravy, mashed potatoes and choice of salad or side vegetable. She took their drink order and left to get them and to give Jon and Betsy time to think. As she headed behind the counter, Betsy noticed her getting into a quiet but agitated discussion with what seemed to be a kitchen helper. As she and Jon talked about what they wanted to eat, Betsy kept looking up at the waitress and the man involved in a disagreeable discussion based upon the looks each was giving the other.

The waitress returned to the table with the drink order. "Sweet tea for you ma'am, and water for you sir. Betsy couldn't help but ask if everything was okay. Her question took the waitress back a little. Then realizing Betsy had seen her in an agitated discussion, she responded with resignation. "Oh, I have told the owner several times about the frayed wires behind the counter and the hazard they present. I mentioned it again and he told me to pay attention to my job and let him worry about such things."

"Sorry," Betsy said consolingly. Jon and Betsy gave the waitress their food order and began to discuss their visit to the church. "Well," Jon offered, "I think it went well." Betsy agreed. Soon their food was there. They said grace and began to eat.

In the middle of their meal, everyone's attention was turned to the counter area. Jon and Betsy's waitress was screaming as if she had just seen a dead body. The owner came racing out of the back and yelled for someone to call 911.

Everyone was standing. Some were leaving the café in a hurry. Some were crowding the counter looking over it to see what was causing the commotion.

Jon and Betsy got up and moved to one end of the counter. Peering around the corner, they could see an older waitress lying on the floor. She was in a puddle created by some drinks she was attempting to take to a table. Sparks were flying everywhere. The woman who lay unconscious was flopping slightly as electricity jumped around her body, into the puddle and back and forth. There was a hissing sound.

"Get back, get back," the owner was screaming trying to keep anyone from getting close to the prone figure.

"Help her someone, help her please," the young waitress pleaded." She is my momma please don't let her die."

Then the waitress turned on the owner. "Call 911 you pig. This is your fault," she screamed. More people were leaving the café. Jon could hear some calling 911. Quickly he went around the counter to where the woman lay. "Stop," said the owner, "my son has gone to shut the power off."

Ignoring the owner's commands, Jon walked into the puddle and electricity flowed through him. He reached down and threw the live 220 watt electrical wire which had come loose to the other end of the counter. He touched the woman, realizing quickly her heart had stopped. Without a hesitation he picked her up in his arms and brought her out to the front of the counter. He cleared a table with his left hand and as dishes bounced off the floor he laid her limp body on the table. Quickly Betsy was at her side.

"Do CPR," he whispered to Betsy. Betsy began compressions, remembering the beat to the Bee Gees song "Staying Alive," to coordinate her beat as she was taught in the Carthage YMCA class for CPR. She had yearly taken a refresher course because her Dad was getting older and she was afraid if anything happened she wouldn't know what to do.

The woman's daughter was screaming and crying at the same time. People crowded around the table to see what was happening. Jon took the woman's hand and closed his eyes. "Look," a small boy said," There's electricity flowing from the man's hand!"

Incredibly the small boy had detected a wisp of aura flowing from Jon into the woman. The crowd pushed forward. However, before they could understand what the young man was getting to, the EMS truck and fire truck, with sirens and lights flashing had pulled up to the café. Bill Dobey, however, had heard the young man. He had witnessed Jon walk into the electrified pool, cast the live wire aside and pick the woman up with no fear for his own safety.

Bill Dobey was a recent graduate who had just started as a cub reporter for the Sanford Herald. He was young and wet behind the ears but he knew a story when he saw it or heard it and there was no doubt about this. He could see the headlines now. "Man walks into electrified pool at the Sanford Café and saves a woman whose heart has stopped by flowing electricity from him into the woman's otherwise dead heart."

He began to drool over the prospects of such an award winning story.

The EMS personnel rushed into the café along with bystanders who were now hearing how some guy walked through electricity to save an electrified woman. Rumors ran rampant through the crowd. The EMS workers pushed Betsy and Jon aside and began to evaluate the woman's condition. Quickly Jon and Betsy worked their way through the crowd just as the woman began to cough and breathe on her own.

The woman's daughter rushed to her mother, who was now just gaining consciousness. Seeing her mother was going to be okay, she looked around to find the man who had risked his life to save her mom. Not seeing him but catching sight of the owner, the daughter began to scream at him again about how he knew the wiring was bad and he should be arrested.

Jon and Betsy had just gotten out onto the side walk when they realized their car was among all the emergency vehicles and they wouldn't be able to get out until those vehicles left. Jon tugged at Betsy's hand and they began to stroll down the street to window shop and use time until they would be able to have access to their car.

Bill Dobey had tried to make his way out of the now crowded café to catch up with the man who had risked his life to save the waitress. As he stood outside he had trouble seeing through the crowd. He jumped up and down to get a better view. He would have seen them except Jon and Betsy had just moved down a side street and away from the view of the restaurant.

Finally the EMS was gone. The fire engine was gone. The police had left. The café was closed. Jon and Betsy returned to their car. They were not aware that Bill Dobey had hung around. Later he would tell the news media it was based on a hunch.

It was midafternoon. They decided to drive to the town of Lorton, VA. It was right off 95 in the direction they were going and they would stop, get a bite to eat and find a place to stay for the night. In the morning they would plan the next day.

However, not being able to find a place to stay in Lorton, Jon and Betsy agreed to go closer to Alexandria. They stopped at a Comfort Inn in a quiet community called Huntington, just off 95. After a brief run to a supermarket, they took their provisions back to the Inn.

Betsy decided to run a shower while Jon laid out their food. It was about time for the six o'clock news and Jon turned on the TV to catch the news highlights. As Betsy came out for her shower, Jon was staring at the TV news coverage of an event in the town of Dale, Virginia.

There on CNN was an interview with a Bill Dobey talking about the couple who saved a woman from being electrocuted. "They disappeared from the café," Dobey reported. Then as he was asked questions, he offered to show a video he had made. There on Dobey's video were Jon and Betsy getting into their Mercedes and driving off. "On a hunch," Dobey recounted, "I hung around hoping they would appear again. It was a miracle," pronounced Dobey. "They were like two angels who put their life in danger and saved this woman…" Jon turned the TV off.

"Oh Jon? What should we do? "Betsy asked with a tone of utter desperation.

Jon sat on the edge of the bed. His head was in his hands and he was in deep thought.

"Betsy"—he paused—"there is much I have not shared with you about David and the powers he has provided me." He looked up at Betsy who was standing at the window looking out. She turned around and put her hand over her mouth as if to hold back the thoughts swirling around in her head which were trying to get organized into words and fly out.

"Jon," she said calmly. "There is nothing we can't face together. I don't understand all this, but I have faith we can deal with it together." Now, for some reason, as she watched Jon again cover his face with his hands, she began to feel fearful. It was the first time. She didn't know why and she desperately needed Jon's confidence that all would be well.

Jon looked up and stared at Betsy in a way that scared her. "Betsy, I have put you and your Dad in danger. I have put everyone I know and love in danger."

Trying to hold back a sudden trembling, Betsy sat down beside Jon and took his hand in her lap. "Jon, it will be okay," she tried to be reassuring, while needing reassurance herself.

Jon's gaze softened and he looked down at her hand. "Betsy look at the hand you are holding." Betsy looked as Jon had requested. Suddenly her body stiffened as her eyes could not believe what she was seeing. Jon's hand literally came up through Betsy's hand without her hand moving. His hand actually moved through her hand. While she sat there staring at her now empty hand, she glanced up to see Jon's other hand touch the side of the bedside table. She watched in awe as the wood around his hand began to swirl and shimmer as water might do as you put your fingers into it. Then he drew out the Gideon Bible that had been in the bedside table drawer. His hand and the Bible passed through the wood and he slowly put it down on the bed. The wood stopped swirling where his hand had entered and it now looked solid as before. Betsy jumped off the bed and slowly walked over to it. With hesitation she touched the place where Jon's hand had entered as if to confirm to her it was solid,

"Oh my god, Jon how did you do that?" she exclaimed as she backed herself into the wall. "First the knife through the hand and now the hand through solid wood, Jon what is the explanation for all of this."

"Betsy, there is no limit to what I can do," he said dejectedly. Without looking up he continued. "Now that we have agents of the Federal government after us, I just don't know what will happen. I know that I am not to do harm with what I can do, but I also can defend those who need to be defended. Yet my mind is spinning as to how I am to handle all the power David has given me. He said one major problem of Earth is that its people have developed tremendous technical knowledge yet they have not kept pace with their maturity to handle such knowledge. I am beginning to feel that way now. I am not sure I can handle the growing sets of powers I seem to be developing.

Betsy, now sensing Jon's pain in his voice, moved back to the bed and put her arms around him. Suddenly the pressure welling up within him caused him to put his head on her shoulder and he began to cry.

For some time, Betsy held Jon as he wore himself out crying into her shoulder. Like someone who has taken on more than they can handle, Jon seemed consumed by the thoughts of loved ones being the target by those seeking David.

Slowly, Betsy laid Jon down on the bed. She lay beside him. He put his arm around her. They both fell into a deep sleep.

Betsy opened her eyes and looked over at Jon. Then looking over at the clock on the radio on the bedside table on her side, she could see it was now 9:45 p.m. Slowly she swung her legs over the side of the bed. Then ever so quietly, she stood up. Feeling that Jon might like something cold to drink when he got up, Betsy decided to go out to the front office where the ice machine was. After checking herself in the mirror to make sure she looked decent, she picked up the empty ice bucket from the desk and left the room.

Turning the corner to where the motel front desk was located, she realized she had not taken any money. Approaching the front desk, she stood waiting for the motel's clerk's attention. His eyes glued to the TV, it was a few moments before the attendant realized someone was standing there. Turning, he saw Betsy. "Oh, excuse me. It has been a quiet night and I didn't realize you were standing there."

"Oh that's okay," Betsy replied. I am in room 124, and I came down to get some ice. However, I forgot to bring some money. May I charge my room for the ice?"

"Oh, uh, you don't need money for that but the ice machine is broken. I am sorry. But we have a lounge and you can probably get some ice there. Just use your room key to charge it to your room, if they charge you anything I will remove it from your bill when you check out."

"Thanks," replied Betsy. She swung around and headed down the hall in the direction the attendant was pointing.

The attendant turned back to the TV. The station's news was coming on, preceded by a banner on the bottom of the screen. The banner read "Virginia law enforcement presently looking for couple involved in electrocution of woman in Dale City restaurant." Suddenly the face of Betsy and Jon appeared on the TV screen as a reporter talked about how the couple, a Betsy Collingwood and Jon Sullivan, was being looked for and wanted for questioning regarding an attempted electrocution of a waitress. The attendant did a double take as he recognized the woman who had just asked for ice as the same one on the TV screen. Immediately, the attendant picked up the phone and dialed 911.

As Betsy entered the lounge, she could see it was sparsely populated with few people. She went up to the bar. The bar tender came over and she asked for some ice and if she could charge it to her room. "I can give you the ice dear, but if you need any soft drinks, except for what we use for mixers, you have to get the drinks out of the drink machine over against the wall." "Oh," laughed Betsy. "All I need is the ice but thanks for that information. The bar tender filled her bucket with ice and Betsy thanked him and turned around to leave. She had almost gotten to the lounge exit when a large burly man stepped in her way.

"Hey, sweetie, where ya going so fast?" Betsy stopped short. "Please excuse me," she replied and attempted to get around the man. The man laughed and moved sideways to prevent her from going around him. "Sir, please allow me to pass," Betsy said in a determined voice not understanding why this man kept blocking her.

"Look sweetie, my friend and I are looking for some company tonight. The pickins are slim but you just fill the bill. So why don't you just bring your pretty self over to the corner with me and ole Mike and we can all have a good ole time." With that the man grabbed Betsy's ice bucket with one hand and using his other and his body pushed Betsy over to a corner booth forcing her to sit down. Another man sitting at the booth grabbed at Betsy and pulled her into the booth. It was dark. The music was fairly loud and Betsy's attempt at getting the bar tender's attention were of no avail. What she didn't know was that the bar tender was trying not to notice. These two would come in the lounge once a month or so on their way to NY. They were rough truck drivers who after a few drinks were loud and obnoxious. More than once they had caused fights and once threatened the bar tender if he should interfere.

As they pulled Betsy further into the booth, Betsy could smell the alcohol and a pungent smell that came from being around diesel oil and few baths. The men were in their forties. They were unshaven, hair dirty and crude. The one who was already in the booth when Betsy was first forced in grabbed at her breasts. He just laughed when Betsy swung at him. He caught her arm and attempted to plant a kiss on her lips. As Betsy turned her face, the man who had brought Betsy over to the booth said, "Hey, Mike wait for me. There is enough of this pretty thing for both of us." Both men laughed and they took another drink as they conjured up how they would take her to their truck. Trying to keep her wits about her, Betsy came up with a plan. In the sweetest tone she could muster, she said, "Look boys why don't we go back to my room. That way we can have a comfortable time rather than being jammed up in a truck. Wouldn't that be better?"

"Damn Robert if the broad ain't got a grand idea." Robert reached over and planted one hand on Betsy's thigh.

Then he planted a big juicy kiss on her neck. "Sounds good to me Mike. Where is your room sweetie?"

Betsy handed Robert the key. "Oops" Robert laughed. "It looks like I get firsts." Laughing in return, Mike quipped, "Just as long as you save enough for me Robert." Both men laughed as they, with Betsy between them, walked out of the lounge. As they walked in front of the office attendant, Mike had his face in Betsy's neck and Robert looked at the attendant and laughed as they turned the corner and headed down to room 124.

⚓ ⚓ ⚓

At the Alexandria State Trooper headquarters, the dispatcher took a call from the police station at Huntington who had just taken a call from the attendant at a local motel that the woman being sought for questioning in the attempted electrocution of a Dale City woman had checked in at the motel. Police were advised and were already on their way to the local Comfort Inn where she was supposed to be staying along with a male who had registered as a Jon Sullivan. Police were asking for back up since the all state bulletin had come in from the ATFa with a "not to be made public" notice that their apprehension was a national security matter.

Within minutes five state trooper vehicles were on their way to Huntington. However Police were now at the Comfort Inn and were awaiting the trooper back up before making entrance.

⚓ ⚓ ⚓

"Lizzy, Lizzy… wake up." Lizzy turned over in the cot she was napping in at the hospital. She opened one eye to see Fred leaning over her. "Lizzy?"

"What is it?" Lizzy coldly asked. "They have located Jon Sullivan in a Comfort Inn in Huntington, NC." It took a few seconds for it to register. She jumped up and began to shout orders at Fred to organize and go after him. "Lizzy, I have already sent a squad out and we are in contact with the police who at this moment are about to make an arrest." After letting that sink in, Lizzy ran a hand through her hair. "Good, good. Get Otto and let's be on our way."

"Lizzy," Fred replied.

"No. Otto is in the other location with the woman's father and her daughter, remember?"

"Oh yes," she said, "yes. I am still half asleep. Let's put another crew together and get to Huntington."

"Right Lizzy, I am on it. We will be ready in five." With that Fred left and Lizzy put on her shoulder holster. Looking in a mirror, she smiled at herself. Then she headed through the door.

＊ ＊ ＊

Jon had opened his eyes shortly after Betsy had left their room. At first he was concerned. Then he noticed the ice bucket was gone. That was over five minutes ago. She should have been back by now. Jon got up and was prepared to leave the room, when he heard loud talking and laughing. Suddenly a key was in the door. As the door swung open, Robert pushed Betsy through. He and Mike followed and Mike closed the door. Betsy looked around frightened when she could not see Jon. "Hey, baby, look at that nice bed. That's where we are going to play rodeo." Robert and Mike laughed and Mike grabbed Betsy and threw her on the bed. "Hey, wait a minute Mike," Robert yelped, "You get seconds buddy." Again both men laughed.

Suddenly Robert who was still behind Mike was grabbed by something and his 255 pound body was thrown against the wall like a wet dish rag. Mike turned around, and seeing a man for the first time and Robert lay up against the wall, charged at Jon. Jon moved like a matador, stepping aside at the last second and assisting Mike's momentum to crash just like Robert up against the other wall where he landed with a thud and stayed motionless.

"Oh my god," Betsy uttered as she flew into Jon's arms where she started to whimper. "It's okay sweetheart." Betsy looked up at him and sobbed out how she had been accosted by the two men and after they threatened to take her out to their truck, she proposed they come back here where she would find Jon.

"That was good, quick thinking Betsy. Now we need to get out of here and on our way."

"I couldn't see you when I came in the room. I was so scared."

"Sorry, honey, I had made myself difficult to see. I didn't know who was coming in."

"I understand darling. How did you do that?"

"I made my outer layer reflective so that if you looked right at me, I was blended into the image of the room."

"Wow, is there no end to your new abilities."

"I told you. You are part of a strange new world."

"Well, as long as I am with you, I am okay with whatever."

"Thank you, sweetheart. Now, if you will, go down and check us out. I will make sure these two thugs are not going to wake up for a while. I will meet you out at the car."

Betsy smiled. "Good, let's get out of here." Betsy left the room and headed down to the front desk to check out.

The State Troopers had arrived and with the Huntington Police, they entered the Comfort Inn. As Betsy was checking out, an officer came up behind her. "This is one of them, Officer," the attendant said. Quickly the officer grabbed Betsy, introduced himself, and pulled Betsy's arms behind her and slapped cuffs on her. Two other officers took Betsy out the front door while the attendant pointed out where their room was.

⁕ ⁕ ⁕

After putting both men into a deep sleep, Jon felt something was not right. He left the room and went out the back entrance just as the officers turned the corner to the hallway where his room was located.

Now outside, Jon saw the police cars. He quickly moved to a dumpster and jumped inside as several officers came by and entered the back entrance.

Inside the officers found no trace of Jon. Instead they found the two thugs who they revived. Robert was the first to awake. As he saw the officers around him, he uttered, "Hey, we meant no harm. The girl invited us to her room."

After talking to the attendant and later the lounge bar tender, it became obvious the two men had accosted Betsy and forced her to her room. However, having no evidence, the officers let the two men go with a stern warning not to visit the Comfort Inn again.

Searching around the motel, an officer jumped up on the edge of the dumpster and peered in. "Nothing here but trash," he exclaimed. "Okay, said the officer in charge, we have the girl. Let's put out an APB and find this guy. He must be awful important if the ATFa needs to locate him "

Hearing that, Jon knew Betsy had been detained by the police and that ATFa agents would be close behind. Jon struggled trying to decide what course of action was best. He had limited time to answer. They only had less than two weeks to get back to David. Should Jon fail, there was no doubt it could affect the planet. Even if they did get back, Jon had no idea whether or not his and Betsy's efforts would be enough to placate David. Trying to decide what to do prevented Jon from noticing the two figures approaching him from the back of the motel.

"Mr. Sullivan?"

Jon swung around not knowing what to expect. Every sense he had went on alert.

CHAPTER 7

A FRIEND

"Mr. Sullivan?" Again the first man asked. The two men were dressed like twin mannequins. Each wore a fine black suit with burgundy ties. They looked fit and not at all like the police. Perhaps they were with the NSA Jon thought.

At a loss as to how to react but seeing the men knew who he was, Jon, although surprised, decided to deal with the two straight on.

"Yes?" Jon replied.

"Mr. Sullivan, we have come to ask you to come with us for a meeting with Mr. Peter Slavak."

"Peter Slavak?" thought Jon. "That was the man who was in the hospital room with Lance." Jon's mind was racing. "Yes, Max must have contacted him and elicited his help. But how could they have known where he was. I hadn't spoken to Max in a while."

Suddenly, as the two men stood there for a while, Jon decided to ask a few questions. "How do you know Mr. Slavak? More importantly how do I know you represent Mr. Slavak.?"

The two men looked at each other and then the one who hadn't spoken said, "We are Peter Slavak's sons. I am Robert and he is Arthur." Each of the men slowly pulled out some identification and handed it to Jon. The driver's licenses they offered identified each as Robert had indicated.

"Wow, how did you ever find me here?"

"We can discuss that later," Arthur spoke. "We are in danger of being discovered and I would suggest we leave this area immediately."

Nodding agreement, Jon followed as the two men turned and went back around the motel to a black Escalade parked at the rear of the motel. Robert suggested Jon get in the rear as it would be more difficult for him to be seen. As Jon settled into his seat and buckled up, Arthur in the front passenger seat was on the telephone. "Positive contact, we are moving."

As Jon got settled into the back seat, Arthur turned back to Jon. "Thank you for saving our Dad."

Jon nodded with a smile and caught a responding look from Arthur in the rearview mirror. The Escalade pulled out onto the main road and after turning onto 95 headed into Washington, DC. Jon looked around the Escalade. It was outfitted with a number of pieces of electronic equipment. There was what looked like a police scanner roaming through the frequencies used as well as sophisticated radar equipment. The windows had the emblem "Kevlar," indicating they were probably bullet proof. A sophisticated mapping system tied into a GPS highlighted with blinking dots, the locations of any police transmissions, Jon assumed. So long as the police were communicating with each other or the dispatcher, blips appeared on the screen showing the location of the unit when transmitting. However, noticing red, blue and purple blips, Jon asked why the different colors.

Looking in the mirror, Arthur said. "The blue blips are police. The red are fire related and the purple are Federal Government cars."

"Like the NSA," asked Jon.

"Yes," Robert replied, and then he added "like the ATFa."

"What is the ATFa?"

"Jon," Arthur replied. "Those are the special NSA alien task force hunting you."

With a large sigh, Jon sank into his seat. "Wow, what have I gotten Betsy and me into?" He thought to himself.

It was only about 28 miles from Huntington to Washington, DC. The ride would be about thirty-seven minutes. However, at the rate of speed of the escalade, they would make Washington in less than thirty minutes. As they passed the exit to Alexandria, Jon couldn't help but think about Betsy. He was tormented by the desire to leave the car and pursue the authorities who would have her. He rationalized she would be in some kind of protective custody by now and there would be time for him to get her. Besides she was not involved in any way with any crime.

As route 95 turned into 395, they soon crossed over into the District of Columbia, Jon's thoughts turned to David. "He should be ready to receive us, um I mean me by now," he thought. "It doesn't seem like we have done enough to convince David to save the Earth." Jon fell into despair over the thought of having failed with his assignment.

Soon the car was speeding down US1 via exit one toward the National Mall. Down Constitution Avenue they rode. Soon they pulled up at the infamous Watergate Hotel. The escalade pulled around the hotel to a private back entrance. Robert and Arthur got out of the car and Arthur opened Jon's door. As Jon stepped out, he could not help but remember The *Watergate* scandal; a 1970s United States political scandal resulting from the break-in to the Democratic National Committee headquarters resulting ultimately in President Richard Nixon's resignation to avoid impeachment.

Jon followed the brothers into a private entrance leading to some elevators. The building was originally slated to be luxury apartments. Later, however, it became a hotel with luxury business offices. Arthur inserted a key into the elevator and the elevator quickly moved up to the fourteenth floor. The elevator doors opened onto a lustrous marble with light streaming in from large windows overlooking the Potomac River. A security guard armed with a Glock met them as they left the elevator. He stood back at ease when he recognized the Slavak sons. There seemed to be only a one room entrance on this level. They moved to the door and Robert punched in a combination on a combination lock and he opened the door and ushered Jon in with Arthur and Robert following. The door opened to a short corridor against the right wall of which was a mahogany secretary with a small but elaborate gold lamp under a large gold framed mirror. To the left was a beautiful cherry wood chest of drawers. A man stood up from the secretary and turned to greet the visitors. As they approached him an electronic sensor buzzed as they detected weapons Robert and Arthur were carrying. The man who stood up was also armed with a Glock. With a nod exchanged between the man and the brothers, the man reached under the secretary and pushed a button which opened the panel doors at the end of the corridor.

As Jon entered, he was greeted by a young lady who asked if she could get him some refreshments or anything. "No, but thank you," was Jon's brief reply. The woman bowed in respect and backed off into what seemed to be a side kitchen area. Continuing to enter what was an enormous room; Jon's breath was taken away. He stopped to survey the room he had entered. There were fresh gorgeous arrays of flowers everywhere in the room which was the size of most people's houses. Large TVs were mounted on the walls, at least eight in number. Some flashing information from computer terminals, one with the stock exchange and the rest showing without sound at the moment what was going on in selected board rooms and manufacturing sites of interest to Mr. Slavak.

On a table off to the far side of the room were an array of security cameras with flashing views of various points around the hotel including where they had parked and the elevator they had entered. A gentleman sat by the security cameras. He was writing on a log and had an array of electronic equipment around him to monitor what was going on. He wore headphones as he monitored the sounds from the different views and never looked up as the three entered the room.

On the far end of the room past a number of sitting areas made up by elaborate couches and chairs was a fireplace. There was a large mahogany desk on the top of which, shielding the view of the person sitting there, another computer screen. As they proceeded further into the room, the person stood up and proceeded out to greet them. Jon did not recognize the man who was approaching with his hand outstretched. As the man came closer, Jon reached out and shook the extended hand.

"Please Jon, won't you sit here with me?" the man moved to a couch area where he pointed a place for Jon to sit. As Jon sat down, the man pulled a chair up close to Jon. The brothers looked at each other as they stood apart from the two. Never had they seen this no nonsense man who dealt with facts, only facts, take such a personal interest in another. But then this was just not any other person. And their father had changed a lot in his dealings with people since returning from the hospital.

Jon sat and waited for the man to speak. The man reached over and took Jon's hands in his, making Jon feel uneasy. "Jon. I am Peter Slavak."

Although Jon thought the man might be related to Peter Slavak, there was no way he would ever have recognized who he was. The man looked like he was in his late thirties. His hair was black and full. He had a robust tan, a firm grip and was obviously very fit. He was not at all like the old withered up man he had seen in Lance's room at the hospital.

"Yes, Mr. Slavak. I didn't recognize you," Jon softly said.

"Ha," Slavak replied as he laughed. "How could you. When you saw me I was an emaciated old man, hours away from death." Then he stopped. He looked at Jon intently. Slowly and with great feeling he said, "Jon you took me from the grip of death and brought me back for another time. Not only that, as you can see I am in essence a new man. Not only physically but spiritually you have allowed me to have a better life, be a better person than I have ever been."

Tears began to flow from this man who was once a cold hearted capitalist who only lived for the dollar he could make from the electronic genius he was. He bowed his head as the tears flowed. He kept holding Jon's hand. "You have allowed me to see the essence of life; the beauty of creating caring relationships, the benefit my riches can mean to others less fortunate, the gift of life."

The brothers fidgeted nervously. Arthur, who had given up his post at Massachusetts General Hospital where he was an impressive surgeon to be with his Dad, knew he was in the presence of someone with incredible power. As a Doctor, he knew full well his Dad could not survive long at Winchester. His Dad's recovery also took on a miraculous tone in terms of his new persona. Their Dad had become a new person, a more giving person than they had ever known. However, they had never seen their Dad so emotional and drawn to tears by anyone outside the family. They looked back and forth at each other.

Jon wasn't sure what to say. Slavak could see that Jon felt embarrassed and released his hands. He started to speak but Slavak stopped him. "Jon I apologize. I don't mean to get so emotional. What you have given me is beyond words. I now have a faith in God Almighty through Christ Jesus. Beyond my physical self which by itself is a great gift, you have given me an understanding of how helping others really is the essence of life on this Earth."

There was a great pause between the two. Now Slavak, taking Jon's hands again into his own said, "Jon everything I have is at your disposal to defeat these evil people who are intent on hunting you down and destroying you and the ones you love."

Jon, not sure how to respond to this just said, "Thank you."

Now Peter sat back. He looked at Jon more seriously. "Have you thought about how you might get Betsy back?" This reality check of Betsy's situation caused Jon to feel insecure. "I... I am trying to decide how I should proceed. I have to go to the state trooper quarters in Alexandria and get her out."

Peter stood up. "Jon, Betsy is not with any police. The ATFa have her."

Jon stood up. "I am sorry. It was great seeing you. I am happy for you. But I must leave and figure out what to do."

"Jon, we know exactly where they have taken her!"

Jon stood silent. He waited for Peter to continue.

"Betsy has been taken to a building located in North Carolina. We have been tracking them for some time since I left the hospital and got back on my feet so to speak."

"Is she all right?"

"Yes, for the moment." Peter paused and then added, "For the moment."

The ominous sound of that implication made Jon cringe. He felt surges of anger and the anxiety of wanting to flee away from here and to where his love was.

Jon sat down as if a huge weight had landed on his shoulders. He forced his mind to engage a plan.

"Peter," Jon said sternly. "I need to go to the corner of L Street and Ninth Street here in Washington."

Peter thought for a moment. "Hmm, okay, that's the Washington Convention Center." Slavak's face looked puzzled.

"I know it sounds bizarre. I have to"—Jon paused—"meet an associate, someone who is crucial for what I need to do now."

"Okay, well, we can get you there." Peter studied Jon as if to find an understanding as to this strange request.

"And," Jon added. "I need to have a meeting with the president of the United States."

Now Peter sat down. "Wow, you take my breath away. What about Betsy?"

Jon looked down at his lap. "I have to pray I will have enough time to do what I have to do, what Betsy would insist I do, before I can go after her."

Jon looked up and stared intently at Peter who was now looking around the room and who was in obvious deep thought as he tried to figure out a way for him to help this man who gave him life.

"Okay, okay," Peter finally said as if he had resolved what to do. He looked back at his sons. "I put this man in your protective custody. Take him to the location he needs to go to. I will make calls and try to use my influence to set something up at the Whitehouse. I believe the president is meeting today with the Premier of China. I will let you know what can be done."

He turned to Jon who was now standing beside him. "My brother, I hope I can help. My sons will make sure you have whatever you require and I wish you well in your pursuit."

Both men stood up.

Jon reached out his hand to shake Peter's. Peter avoided Jon's outstretched hand but rather took Jon and wrapped his arms around him and planted a kiss on his cheek. "May our Lord guide you my brother, "he whispered.

As the escalade sped to L and Ninth, Jon couldn't help but wonder if he would be able to contact David and complete his journey. Never could he imagine how his journey was far from over.

As They left the hotel, a large SUV, black and with government plates pulled out of a side area and followed them.

"Arthur?" "I know Robert I see them." A red blip appeared on the special GPS grid. Immediately Arthur turned on the rear cameras and activated a homing device which brought a satellite picture of themselves and the traffic behind them onto the screens in the Slavak offices.

"Mr. Slavak?" Peter looked up from his desk. "Please look at screen 5." Immediately the satellite image of his son's vehicle and the car behind them came into view. "Deploy immediate rescue," Peter Slavak barked at the man and into the transmitter on his desk.

Arthur increased speed as the Escalade moved down Virginia Ave. NW toward the Potomac River Circle. The black SUV following them kept up. "Look," Jon said, "I don't want to get anyone hurt. If you will find a place to let me out, I will get away and you both will be safe."

Robert and Arthur looked at each other and started to laugh. "What's so funny?" Jon asked. Robert turned and looked at Jon. "If you think we would be safe by going back and telling Dad we just dropped you off as the ATFa was following us, you really don't know Dad." With that Robert turned back to look at Arthur who was looking at him again. They both started to laugh again.

As the Escalade headed into the circle, blips were still on the screen. The red blip was gaining. Robert called Arthur's attention to a flashing green light on what appeared to be a transmitter device. Robert pressed a button. A voice could be heard. "Twenty-Fifth Street NW and First NW, right hand side contact," the voice said. Arthur steered the Escalade skillfully around the circle. Suddenly Arthur turned against traffic and up H St NW against oncoming traffic. Fortunately the traffic was light. The black SUV followed. After briefly going a short distance, Arthur turned up Twenty-Fifth Street NW. The black SUV was right on their heels. Flashing blue lights appeared on the dash of the SUV in an attempt to get Arthur to pull over. "Oops" Arthur chuckled, "am I going to get a ticket?" Jon sat quietly waiting for something to happen. Then it did.

The Escalade slid past First Street NW. Then as the black SUV began to cross the intersection of Twenty-Fifth St NW and First Street NW, a large dump truck pulled out of First Street in front of the black SUV. The SUV was going so fast, the driver could only jam on the brakes and veer sharply off to the left. Through several ornamental bushes and into the corner of a building went the SUV. The crash disabled the SUV, as the trucker continued on its way down First and Jon's vehicle headed down Twenty-Fifth and turned onto L Street NW. Blue blips showed up on the screen headed toward the red blip. Arthur was laughing so hard, he could hardly contain himself. "I just love it when a plan comes together." With that comment both brothers laughed. Even Jon had a smirk on his face.

It wasn't long before they were at the corner of L and Ninth. Arthur pulled over. "Shall we wait?"

"Yes, please," came the reply. Slowly getting out of the vehicle, Jon surveyed the large convention center. "Hmm." he uttered solemnly. "How am I going to locate you David?"

Jon entered the convention center from the L Street entrance. A guard at the entrance inquired as to whether or not Jon needed help. "No, thank you," Jon replied. "I am just browsing today."

"Yes, sir," the guard replied. "Have you ever been here before?"

"No, sir," Jon politely again replied as he looked around to get his bearings and perhaps get a hint as to how he was going to find David. The walls were glass and the deep golden tones of Macore wood. "Ah, mister, you look like a golfing friend I once knew. Any chance you ever play around Pinehurst, North Carolina?"

With that comment, Jon turned and looked at the guard more closely. He was a tall lightly skinned black man, probably older than Jon, or at least Jon thought so from his frosted gray hair which could be seen under his guard's cap. He was at least as tall as Jon and he looked fit in his uniform. He had a friendly air about him and it was obvious he was a good choice to greet people. The guard smiled and there was a twinkle in his eye. Jon felt compelled to ask; "What was your friend's name?" "Why it was David," the guard replied with his smile even larger now. "Oh, I would love to meet him sometime." Jon continued the chit chat not knowing where it would lead but amused at the irony of the conversation. "Yes, sir, he is a fine fellow. When he visits here, he enjoys going to the third level to the L Street level and watching people travel below. "Thank you, I will check that out." With that Jon returned the man's smile and proceeded to the elevators.

Getting out on Level 3, Jon slowly walked out to the L Street Bridge which crossed over to convention center ballrooms. As he entered the glass enclosed structure, he sat on a bench and looked down at the traffic below.

Suddenly a voice from behind him spoke. *"Hello Jon. Is your mission complete?"*

Jon swung around to see David, who sat down beside him. "Well, no, it is not. And I am afraid I may have failed. I am afraid I have failed you, failed Betsy." Jon's voice dropped off. "I am afraid I may have failed the world I live in." Jon's was now not looking at David but rather had turned and was now staring at the traffic below. There was silence.

"Would you like to share it with me Jon?"

Jon was feeling despondent but turned to face David. Slowly Jon shared with David all the events since they had last met. David listened intently even though Jon felt David already knew what had happened.

"Yes, Jon," David suddenly interrupted. *"Perhaps I am aware of everything. However it is important I hear them from you and more importantly understand how you feel."*

Jon stopped, looked down at the floor and then back to David. He proceeded to continue and talked about everything right up to where the Slavak brothers dropped him off outside the convention center.

"*Well, Jon. What do you think we need to do now?*"

Jon thought for a second. "I need to find Betsy. However, it was our plan when we got to Washington to see the president."

"*The president of the United States?*" David looked at Jon with raised eyebrows.

"Yes," Jon replied looking down at the floor. "Once we had had a chance to mingle among people, we had planned to visit the president."

"*Okay. So which direction should we proceed?*"

"What do you mean 'we'?"

David tilted his head as if to get a better look at Jon's eyes. "*Jon. Your quest is not complete. You have a decision to make. How should we proceed? Now that we have rejoined with each other, let's go in the direction you decide upon.*"

Jon was silent. He worried about Betsy's safety. Yet he knew if she were here she would be upset if he didn't complete their mission in light of the number of lives it could affect. With a sigh, Jon looked at David. He was experiencing a weird feeling. He at this moment for some reason felt closer to David than he had since he agreed to let David be a part of him. David was still tilting his head back and forth looking at Jon intently.

"We need to see the president, and then we need to pursue Betsy's captors."

David smiled. "*Yes. The sacrifice of one for the safety of the many. That, my Dear Jon is what visitors from my planet to yours have been doing. That is what your "freedom fighters" do for their country.*" And how do we proceed now Jon?"

"There are two young men waiting outside. They are the sons of the Peter Slavak you cured, ah repaired, when we visited Lance. I… ah we, need to get back and proceed with our plan to meet with the president assuming Peter has been able to set something up."

Jon stood up and went back to the Seventh Street Lobby entrance. As they approached the door to exit, the guard looked up. "Good Luck, Jon." Jon did a double take. The guard smiled and looked down as he was greeting other visitors. "Do I know that man?" Jon asked. *"No, you don't," David replied, "but I do."*

As they approached the Escalade, Robert jumped out and opened the back door for Jon. Jon and David slid in the back seat. "The White House please," Jon commanded of Arthur. "Yes, sir," was the reply and the Escalade moved into traffic.

By the time the Escalade reached the South face of the residence portion of the White House, evening was falling. The lights on the White House lawn were on and the fountains were now being shut down. Over the car radio came the message that Peter had contacted the president. He was willing as a favor to Peter meet with Jon but he wasn't sure when he could schedule such a meeting and would have to get back on that. The president did have a window of available time but it would have to be within the next couple of hours and he understood that such a quick meeting was probably not possible."

"Arthur let us," and then he corrected himself, "let me off here. Come back in 3 hours with the information we need to pursue those who took Betsy and we will go after her."

Not understanding this revised strategy, since his Dad had, through his contacts, made an alternative arrangement for a visit to be made to one of the president's aides, Robert looked back at Jon. "Well, Dad had told us…" Jon interrupted. "Yes, I understand. "This will be sufficient. Thank you. Can I assume you will be here in three hours?" Robert turned back and looked at his brother. "Yes, Jon we will be here with the information you need in 3 hours," Arthur spoke as he looked at Jon in the rearview mirror.

Jon and David left the vehicle and stood there as it sped away. Looking around and seeing no one watching them, Jon and David walked through the wrought iron fence and the numerous infrared detectors in their path to the back of the White House Residence. Jon was still in awe of what he seemed to be able to do. "Are we doing this together David?" "*Yes, Jon we are.*"

As they reached the South entrance there were two Marines stationed outside. Standing behind a tree just outside of their view, David directed Jon's attention to the third floor. David spoke. "*That is where we are supposed to meet with the president who has agreed as a favor to meet with an influential friend of Peter Slavak, but only if it can happen within the next couple of hours.*"

Jon turned and looked surprised at David. "How would you know that?"

"*Arthur and Robert shared that information with me.*"

"Hmm" thought Jon. "Yes," he thought to himself, "like shared their thoughts while we were driving here?"

"*Yes, Jon of course.*" David directed Jon's attention to the top balcony. "*That is what they call a round portico or balcony. It leads into the "Yellow Room" where we are scheduled to meet with the president. In fact, I believe he is already there enjoying some reading by the fireplace at the back of the room. Look Jon."*

Jon stared at the window on the portico. As he stared, he could see red/orange images like had happened to him when visiting Trusky. Several people were coming and going but one remained stationary over by what appeared to be a fireplace. As Jon stared intently he began to see the room and the president sitting there as David had indicated, with a book in his hand.

"Now, Jon, we need to make our entrance but before we do we need to change our appearance somewhat. If you were a Marine Jon what rank would you like to hold?"

"What?" Jon asked incredulously. "What kind of quest…"

David interrupted. *"I think a five-star general might be appropriate."* Suddenly as if transformed, Jon found himself in the uniform of a five-star general. David continued. *"Now Jon let's expand your knowledge of what you can do if you put your mind to it. Look at that portico and visualize yourself standing there."* Jon did. Suddenly he was standing on the third floor portico looking in at the president.

Suddenly someone entered the room and set a cup of tea down beside the president. "Will there be anything else Mr. President," the person asked. "No John, I will ring if I need anything else."

"Thank you, Mr. President." With that, the person left. David's energy swept into the room, around the room, touching all the doors and other items. The president paused in his reading as if he sensed something, looked up and after a few seconds resumed reading his book.

"Are you ready Jon?" David asked. Taking a deep breath, Jon said, "I guess so." Then with an afterthought, Jon added; "nothing ventured, nothing gained." David gave Jon a quizzical look. With that Jon found himself suddenly inside what was commonly referred to as the "Yellow Oval Room," at the White House. The Yellow Oval Room is a room often used for formal private receptions for important guests. The president's wife uses it often to entertain female dignitaries. The room has three doors. They lead to the Central Hall, the Truman Library, and the Living Room. The room is traditionally decorated with yellow. The furnishings are in the Louis XVI style, assembled during the Jacqueline Kennedy renovation. Like the Blue Room below it, this room is not quite 40 feet by 30 feet. Across from the portico doors through which Jon passed is a fireplace. Above the fireplace hangs a large gold framed mirror. Jon notices he can see his own reflection in it but not David's. He looks to his side and although David's reflection cannot be seen, David stands beside him.

The president is immersed in a book "Waiting For Superman." The book essentially convicts the AFT and NEA teacher unions for causing the failure of the American education system. Normally he would be reading something much lighter but his wife had talked about the dilemma of the US education system and had referenced this book often. Wanting to gain an understanding of where his wife's view point was coming from, President Foster decided to gain some knowledge of the subject. His critics who often accused the president of having little intellectual curiosity would have been surprised at this side of the man.

Sensing movement to his left, President Foster cast a glance toward the portico doors where Jon stood in the splendor of his Marine general's uniform. Startled initially, Foster's mind tried to wrestle with the dichotomy of a Marine and his presence inside the Yellow Room without permission. "Mr. President, sir, may I speak with you?" Jon stood still as Foster's book fell from his lap and he reached for the panic button, one of several placed strategically around the room. Feeling security personnel would come into the room within seconds; Foster pushed himself back into the yellow plush couch and waited. With what he thought was the knowledge protection was moments away, Foster took the time to more closely scrutinize the interloper. There was no recognition of this Marine Officer. Yet he didn't appear to be threatening. Was this a coup of some sort? All this and more streamed through Foster's mind. Irritated no one had come to rescue him, Foster beat on the panic button several times. Now he called out. Yet as he opened his mouth no sound came out. The room was silent. The only movement was Foster struggling to make a sound, his face constricted at the sense he could not.

Now Jon moved forward. Slowly he sat down on the far end of the couch where Foster sat. Foster felt unable to move and his panic escalated as his only ability to move seemed to be to push himself as deep into the couch as possible. Jon slowly extended his hand, his palms turned upward in a sign of peace. Jon smiled gently. "Mr. President, I know my presence is shocking but I present no danger to you." Jon paused. Foster slowly relaxed from his attempted immersion into the couch. Realizing the "panic" button was not working and his ability to call for help was not possible, Foster began to accept the presence of a superior force that seemed to offer no danger, at least for the moment.

"Mr. President I represent no harm to you. Please forgive my intrusion and my need to insure no intrusion on our meeting. What I have to share with you represents an imminent threat to our world. Foster took note of the fact the intruder said, "A threat to our world," not to the United States. He relaxed a bit more and sat more upright giving a more dignified look than his previous posture. "I don't understand." Foster said, surprised that his voice now made sound. Thinking briefly of making an attempt to call for help, Foster's thoughts were interrupted with a caution from Jon. "Please don't think about calling for help," Jon pleaded. "There is much we need to share with you." In a renewed panic, Foster latched onto the word "we" and looked about the small room frantically to see if there were others here that he had not seen. "There is no one else here other than what you see Mr. President." The president turned sharply at Jon as the president thought.

"What? Can you read my thoughts now?"

"Yes, Mr. President we can read your thoughts. Now please allow us to communicate our concern to you and we will leave."

With the thought of being free from this intrusion just by listening, the president thought "Okay, I am willing to listen." An aura slowly entwined around the president of the United States. During what seemed like one hour but in fact was two and one half, George Foster was allowed to see in his mind everything Jon had seen and learned about David and his world.

President Foster sat in utter amazement as Jon permeated his mind with the actual technical achievements of which he, even as the leader of the United States had little or no knowledge. "On the verge of space travel?" Foster knew about or thought he knew all there was to know about NASA, the National Aeronautical Space Association. As well, he was slightly aware of the funding granted to the prestigious schools seeking innovative scientific breakthrough in the areas of weaponry and space travel. However, he was not aware of the depths of achievements. That is not until now. In addition, although he was aware of and approved research and funding devoted to penetrating the universe with electromagnetic pulses, he had never been advised there had been any results.

"Be careful of what you seek," the president heard, "lest you find it."

"What do you mean?" the president said. "Is it so wrong to want to explore the universe to find others like us?"

"It could be," came the reply. When you attract others who would view you as food, or a commodity not to be friendly with but to control and enslave you, do you invite such?"

The president sat immobile as he became more and more aware of the predicament his world could be facing.

Foster's face turned to shock as he took in David's threat of annihilation of the human race; if David could not leave the planet able to give assurances to his world that Earth did not represent a threat to the mrows existence. "Surely, you cannot do that," Foster briefly thought smugly.

Suddenly the room turned dark. Foster found himself on a road leading from Washington. Lines of people struggled past the burned out buildings. Overhead streams of fire rained from the sky. Cries of screaming and the sound of fire and explosions filled the air. Foster looked around. He was alone. In the background he could see the shattered edges of what was left of the White House of the United States of America. He sat on the ground and cried.

As quick as he had left the White House in the vision, Foster found himself back on the couch in the Yellow Room. His pants were soaked as he had had an accident. The sweat was pouring from him and his clothes were wet. "Oh my god, what happened?"

"What happened was an insight as to what will be, if the people on Earth continue to develop technically but without the maturity to handle their innovations; representing a threat to other worlds."

"Why have you come here to us, to me, when the whole world has much at stake?"

"The United States is at the pinnacle of what you call civilization. If The United States cannot change its direction, the world will not."

"Do you have any idea what it is like trying to deal with US politicians never mind world leaders? There is no one who will believe what I have experienced here tonight. World leaders need to be aware of what future awaits us. If they can be convinced, certainly they will comply." Then as an afterthought, he said softly to himself, "They must."

Jon sat back on the couch. Thank you. We hoped you would be convinced."

"But how will you convince such a diverse group all with their own individual agendas?"

Jon rose from the couch. He walked over to the center of the room. David spoke. *"Hold on Jon. This will be a new experience for you. Have no fear."*

"David I trust you."

Slowly the Marine general, standing in the middle of the room, began to vibrate. The vibration turned to a shine with a subdued flickering light. Suddenly Jon's body became stripped to just muscle like one would see in an anatomical book about the human body. Then the sinew glowed within the increasing flickering of light. As it the muscle and sinew disappeared, there was nothing but bones; a human skeleton stood in the middle of the Yellow Room. In a poof Jon was no longer there replaced by different waves of light. The multicolored bright lights moved around in rapid fashion encircling Foster and the contents of the room. For Foster it was like being inside a sparkler on the fourth of July. As quickly as it happened, the process reversed itself. Jon now appeared in front of Foster, no longer as a Marine general but as he was before the transition.

The president smiled. No longer in fear but in awe he said, "Wow. Yes, I think that should do the trick."

"Good," Jon replied through David. "If we can reach an understanding, we may be willing to help you find peaceful solutions for many of your civilization's problems not yet solved in the areas of medicine and cures for various inflictions. But…" Jon's voice turned to a serious tone… "There needs to be a lessening on technical achievement and more emphasis on interpersonal harmony."

"I will do everything I can to make this happen."

"Thank you Mr. President." Jon slowly walked around the room and approached the president. "In the interim you have a group, an offshoot of the NSA, which you need to harness. It has been seeking me because of healing I have performed of a paranormal nature, on my son and then on a Mr. Slavak."

"Oh my god," reeled Foster. "That is why Peter, my friend, made such a miraculous recovery."

"Yes, Mr. President."

After sharing the details of the National Security Agencies renegade group dealing with alien searches, Jon got president's assurance it would be disbanded.

"Thank you, Mr. President. You might also want to stop inviting invaders from outer space to visit you just now." Again the president nodded in agreement. "But I don't know what influence I can have on that since it is the scientific community which wants to continue sending pulses into space."

"Yes," said Jon now smiling, "we can help be convincing in that area also. Now it is probably time for us to leave." The president agreed to set up a meeting with the National Security Council and invite Jon as a guest. He would let Peter know the details.

After a brief pause, the president got control over himself. "May I suggest you leave by the front door this time?" Foster and Jon laughed. "Yes," Jon replied. "We would be happy to."

With that Foster got up and escorted Jon to the door. As he opened it, the butler looked up in surprise as did the Marine standing at attention. The butler looked at the Marine who returned the look. They both wondered how this man got passed them. The president was engrossed in conversation with the man and neither was about to interrupt. However, they could not help but notice the president looked worn out. Perspiration still filled his face and his clothes looked as if he had spilled something on them.

After hearing the two Slavak boys would be waiting in a car parked outside the South side, Foster sent personnel out to find them and escort them into the White House grounds. As Jon left, he shook hands with President Foster. The Slavak car was waiting.

As the Slavak car pulled away from the White House, no one said a thing for a minute or two. Arthur was the first to say anything. "I hope, I assume, everything went all right?" Again there was silence. "Yes," Jon replied. "Everything went well, everything went very well."

"Didn't everything go well David? Jon thought. "*We will see*," came the reply. David's lack of optimism concerned Jon. However, David made no comments to Jon's thoughts concerning that. They weren't a minute into the drive back to the Slavak location when a burst of noise came over the car speakers. "Under attack," was the only thing that could be heard over the garbled transmission. Suddenly all communication ceased. Robert kept trying to initiate a response but it was all to no avail. Traffic for the time of night seemed heavy. Robert took out a blue light from a container under the dash board and placed it on the roof of the car. Arthur accelerated the car and a siren was activated to try and clear away any slow moving vehicles. Suddenly on the uniquely designed scanner/GPS blue blips appeared. They were all converging on the area to which they were headed. Then as they got closer still, red blips could be seen, four of them, headed out of the area to which they were headed. Robert looked at Arthur who returned the look and accelerated even more.

As they came into sight of the Watergate Hotel, numerous blue lights could be seen flashing. Rounding the Hotel, flames could be seen coming out of the Slavak floor. Arthur found a place to park just as a third fire engine on the scene almost hit them as it inched closer to support the fire engine teams already trying to quench the fires.

Arthur and Robert couldn't get out of the car fast enough. They ran up to the entrance they usually used but the entrance was barricaded and two police officers were preventing anyone from getting any closer. Despite their identification as to whom they were and that their Dad was probably inside, the officers would not give way. Through all the shouting and arguing anyone looking at Jon would see him one moment and the next he would be gone.

CHAPTER 8

AN ATTACK

Jon suddenly found himself on the fourteenth floor of the Watergate hotel, where David had put them. Jon had a look of despair. "David can we help anyone here?" "*I don't know,*" came the response. "*We need to find out what happened and whether or not Slavak survived this attack.*"

An explosion had ripped through the main entrance door and destroyed the elevator lift. David surveyed the scene as a forensic scientist might do, looking for the smallest of clues as to what had happened and in what order. "*The elevator was bombed last as they left,*" David said as if talking to himself. Large junks of flooring were no longer in place and there were dark holes where if one were to try and walk, they would fall through to floors below, some of which had already been heavily damaged. Jon was nervous and his face showed the fear now running through him. He was concerned about the stability of the place and concerned about the floors. However, he felt himself guided by another force, the power of which allowed him to glide right over holes which would have swallowed any other human. Jon could have been on a trapeze as a performer of Cirque de Sol. With ease and yet without a conscious effort he floated across the open areas. Now entering the main room, there was much destruction and much signs of gunfire. Even though beams were charcoal encrusted, bullet holes from a high powered machine gun could be seen splattered around the premises. Several bodies lay on the floor. One was in parts where one of the explosions had destroyed his limbs. Another lay slumped over one of the smoking TV screens and what was left of electronic equipment. The explosion had not burned away the large pool of blood still being fed by the drips coming from the body.

As they entered the area where Slavak's desk was, there were no bodies. As Jon turned he found a figure lying near one of the couches that although burned was still intact. Water was gushing through the walls as the fire fighters below were trying to extinguish all flames and burning coals. Jon rushed over to the body. It was still faintly alive. *"This is one of the attackers."* David said to Jon.

Jon stayed near the body while his hands in David's control delicately held the man's head. Jon could see the man's chest moving ever so slightly as the man hung on to life. Just as suddenly Jon could feel that the man had now stopped breathing. Yet he couldn't release his hands as David continued to hold his head.

Suddenly David stopped. He released the man's head and stood up. *"This was a covert action intended to extract Slavak to find out where we were. In addition it was a plan to terminate any operations out of this location. There was a fierce fire fight. They also wanted to terminate or secure the sons but of course they were with us."*

"Why," Jon asked. "Why did they want Slavak?" David looked at Jon trying to appraise how he would take the additional information. "*Max and his granddaughter are now in their hands. So far they have not had any luck getting substantive information from them. They have turned Max and the granddaughter over to a brute named "Otto" and his henchmen and decided to come after Slavak. They figured Slavak was either an alien, had ties to aliens, or had information that would be useful to them. He has been taken to this Otto.*"

"My god no!" Jon felt anger surge within him. David stood beside him. His head slowly turned toward Jon. Slowly David spoke. "*Jon you also need to know Betsy is presently being held at the ATFa headquarters in a community called Charlotte.*" David looked at Jon introspectively. Jon was tense. Anger flew through him and his adrenalin was pulsing through every muscle. His jaw was tight and his breathing was measured. Then with carefully considered tone David spoke again. "*This is the time to be measured and deliberate in our thinking. We need to work together if we are to get this successfully resolved. Anger will just get in our way, as it always does.*"

There was a pause as Jon considered the logic of David's comment. "Yes. I know," Said Jon, with much humility in his voice and a demure manner. Then with determined and deliberate speech, he added "You mentioned the "world," David. Well, Betsy is my world."

"*And Lance?*" David shot back.

"Yes, Lance is also my world!"

"*Your emotions are of high interest to me. They have their benefits. They also have their failings. You believe when you die, you go to heaven, correct?*"

"Well, yes, but—"

"*There is no but,*" David interrupted. "*Until your world is able to reach the level of existence we have reached, your life time is relatively short. It is this emotional overreaction that pervades your species when it comes to possession, and power, which gets you unable to maturely handle the technical innovations you create. It is like giving a three-year-old a grenade to play with and just hoping the child doesn't pull the pin.*"

"*We need to find Slavak.*"

"Wait," appealed Jon. With the pained look of a child just told by his parents to go to his room, Jon whined "What about Betsy?"

"*Jon, Betsy is with the ATFa agent called Lizzy who heads up the ATFa team. Presumably Betsy is safe. Slavak, however, is with a sociopath as is Betsy's father and his granddaughter. Slavak will be instrumental in assisting the president in convincing world leaders to reevaluate their methods. There are three people in danger with this Otto. Betsy is only one. Is there a better approach?*"

Jon, resigned to David's continued logic; his shoulders slumped said, "No." Sadly, Jon had to admit David was right. He ached over the logical choice of abandoning his Betsy for the moment. His inside ached over the decision.

At the entrance to the building the Slavak brothers were still arguing with the fire marshal and local authorities about gaining entrance to the building when Jon appeared behind them and called them away.

"Your father is not in the building. A covert operation team has kidnapped him. For the moment I am sure he is alive. However we need to pursue the kidnappers if we are to have a chance to save him." The brothers looked at each other in shock and amazement at this information. Then they looked at Jon. "You know... Dad is alive?"

"Yes," Jon replied. "Now it is imperative we locate him and secure his release. We know where he is located?" "We?" repeated the brothers almost in unison. "This is not the time to explain such things. You are going to have to trust me without question, if we are to get your father back safely."

Nodding in agreement, and abandoning any further questions, the two brothers followed Jon back to the car. This time Jon got into the driver's seat. He sped out of the parking lot deftly making his way around the enforcement vehicles parked or moving into the area. The special GPS system in the car began to sputter directions. Jon without even looking reached down with one hand as his other one controlled the car and shut all the systems down. The brothers again looked at each other as if to question how he could find the airport without navigational assistance or asking them for help. However, Jon was now relying on David's directions from his vast knowledge bank of the area absorbed from his visit to the library in Winchester. Jon drove directly to Washington International airport using some alleys, and roads unbeknownst to the brothers. Using David's abilities, Jon was able to drive past security points onto the airfield over to a remote area where a National Guard helicopter sat. The brothers sat in shock. Surely, they thought, this man is far more empowered then we initially gave him credit for being. As they closed in on the helicopter, a vehicle came speeding over to their location to determine who they were. Men carrying weapons in their hands got out and approached their car. Jon instructed the brothers to get into the helicopter as he strode over to meet the advancing men. The brothers started to hesitate and then went immediately to the helicopter. Jon approached the advancing armed men. Jon held out his hand and smiled at the lead officer. The officer shook Jon's hand as the others trained their weapons on him. Touching the man's hand, suddenly Jon knew everything about the man including his background, who they were and more importantly what needed to be said to the officer to defuse the situation and allow Jon and the Brothers to be on their way. "Officer Conway?" The officer appeared stunned. He looked closely at Jon to recognize who this man was who recognized him. "We are on a critical alert sequence Alpha Omega 44." Stunned again the officer recognized the code words for any covert action authorized at the highest level. The head of the security team who advanced on them as they approached the helicopter, radioed in his approval for the flight of the helicopter. Jon joined the brothers and took control over the helicopter. Robert noted they had managed to get several weapons on board. "Hopefully." Jon spoke, "we will not need those." Then with David's guidance and instruction, the copter took off. It would be approximately one hour and forty-five minutes before they would be in the area of the secret ATFa location David had learned about from the now dead ATFa man in the Slavak office.

As the helicopter headed for the location; a warehouse located in an obscure North Carolina town called Mocksville, David briefed Jon as to what they might expect to find. *"Since you and Betsy became the main targets of the ATFa, the ATFa has set up temporary headquarters in North Carolina. We are headed to an abandoned manufacturing plant in a town known as Mocksville. They have used this location before and it is set up to do the kind of interrogation this man Otto specializes in."*

Jon passed on the essentials of the conversation to the brothers.

"What do you mean by "kind of interrogation?" Robert Slavak asked.

Jon felt the words flow through him even though they came from David. "This man is what your psychologists would label a sociopath."

"You mean a psychopath?"

Jon turned to Arthur. He smiled. "Yes, that is an acceptable label also. He is a man with an antisocial personality disorder. He defines the words brutality and cruelty."

Robert and Arthur looked at each other. For the next hour and one half there was silence. David's aura swept the cabin of the helicopter and noticed and measured with interest the spirit of each as they became engaged in prayer. Soon the helicopter, already flying low to remain under any radar, began to land in an open parking lot on Bethel Church Road, Mocksville North Carolina at a factory approximately one hundred yards from where the ATFa crew had gathered with their prisoners.

Inside the abandoned manufacturing plant, behind the weeds that shielded any looks from the road, Max and his granddaughter sat as prisoners. Max had been worked over pretty good. He had several broken bones, a smashed eye and blood trickled from his mouth where most of his teeth were broken. Even through the pain, Max could not help but think of all the movies he had seen where the bad guys worked over someone's face yet their teeth always remained pretty. Max was in a great deal of pain but he had shed little light on the alien his captors were seeking. Even with the threat of the rape and torture of his granddaughter who sat handcuffed to a bed in shock in a corner of the room, Max's attempts to placate his captives were to no avail.

Otto and his team were now ready to interview Slavak. All the windows of the plant were barricaded with special fabric preventing any light or sound from escaping. Slavak had been taken into an office entered from the back where no outsider could catch sight of anyone. He was weak from the explosions at the hotel and had to be dragged into the office and strapped into a chair. Otto had been out on what was once the main production floor, sizing up the granddaughter and playing his planned rape scene over in his mind, when he was told Slavak had arrived.

Otto had come into the office where Slavak was slumped in the chair to which he had been secured. The chair was similar to those used in schools which had a flat wooden arm where one would put their book or paper to be used for the daily lesson. One of Slavak's hands was tied to the side of the chair. The other was tied such that his hand lay flat, palm down, on top of the wooden arm. Otto had slowly entered and sat down in front of Slavak. He had walked in slowly with the air of someone who had casually come in to interview a potential job applicant. As he pulled up a chair to sit in front of Slavak, he had quietly and surprisingly to his companions politely called out his name. "Mr. Slavak?" He spoke in the most gentleness of manner. Slavak looked up at this man calling his name. The man was huge. He had a round gruff looking face and nostrils that resembled those of a pig. "Mr. Slavak." Again Otto addressed Slavak. Again his tone was quiet and gentlemanly. Otto was not looking at Slavak as he took off the black leather gloves he was wearing. The gloves dripped with a red liquid which Slavak, even in his weakened state recognized as blood. Without looking at anyone in particular, Otto said in a louder but still not very loud tone, "has anyone asked Mr. Slavak if he would like something to drink?" No one said a word. Otto again turned to Slavak. "Mr. Petro Medved Slavak." Again Otto repeated his name. "Mr. Petro Medved Slavak, my fine Slovenian friend, it is not polite not to greet your conquerors."

Slowly Slavak turned his head to study this man who knew his family name. Slavak looked doped as the explosions at his place had taken their toll. He slowly lifted his eyelids until he was looking into Otto's black eyes which were now staring at him in a way that was neither friendly nor polite. Slavak had seen that looked before in his native Carinthia, on the other side of the Karavanken Mountains. The cradle of Slovenian nationhood is Carinthia. It was in Carinthia that Petro Medved Slavak had stood with his fellow Slovenians and declared their independence from Yugoslavia. Yugoslavia was a multi-ethnic state in which the component peoples have a history of hating each other. The proclaimed secession of Slovenia and Croatia at the end of June 1991 led to an attack by the Serb controlled

Yugoslav Federal Army and Air Force on targets in Slovenia and later in Croatia. It was there Peter was captured by the Serbs and a group of mercenaries hired to strike terror into the hearts of the Slovenian freedom fighters. Before Peter escaped he witnessed such brutality few could imagine. Slavak recognized the evil who sat in front of him.

As Slavak's eyes told Otto, he was now aware of who his captor was, Otto smiled. He stood over Slavak. "Well, Peter. What are we to do? Are you an alien? Or are you an innocent bystander?" He paused. There was complete silence except for muffled noises coming from the main plant area. "Peter we need for you to tell us." Again there was silence. Otto turned his back on Slavak. "How about a form of torture Peter? As a Slovenian you undoubtedly have seen the worst." Then turning to face Slavak, Otto continued. "Let's see, there is keelhauling. Hmm well we are not at sea, that won't work. Oh but then there is water boarding, a favorite of the CIA." Then, and as Otto talked, he turned back to a shelf on which there was an assortment of tools, "there is always the removal of fingernails." Slavak seemed to shudder as Otto approached him with a tool much like pliers but with ends that curved inward. "Tell me Slavak," Otto now growled as he leaned over and took one of Slavak's fingers as Slavak struggled to pull it away. Otto watched with delight as Slavak's eyes exploded with pain as the special pliers pulled at the nail of his fore finger. Slavak convulsed in the chair, flailing his legs and pulling at his arms in a futile attempt to escape this brutality. Otto sat down to give himself more leverage. Otto pulled with a grunt until it was ripped away. Slavak reacted with a writhing scream, which told of the excruciating pain. The others in the room turned away. At the end of the scream, Slavak lost consciousness. Otto laughed uncontrollably. "Well, we certainly don't have an alien here do we?" The other men in the room tried to snicker or laugh even though their insides were turning inside out at what they had witnessed. No one wanted Otto to see them as weak.

"Get his hand wrapped up. Give him about 15 minutes. Then douse him with a bucket of cold water," Otto screamed. "We have more to talk about." With that, Otto got up, turning over his chair as he rose, and sauntered out of the room.

＋　＋　＋

At the landing zone in a field adjacent to the vacant plant where they believed Slavak was being held, Jon gathered Arthur and Robert around him. "Listen to me. I must do this alone." Despite the brother's protests, Jon continued. "I need you to call 911 and get the police and EMS over to this location. Give me fifteen minutes before you make the call."

Under protest, the brothers let Jon leave and walk through the field toward the plant where they believed their father had been taken. At about ten minutes, Arthur took a call on his cell. The call was coming in from Slavak's special Ops group who had been tracking the brothers and at the same time researching the location of the plant in Mocksville where they were now.

Cliff, the head of Slavak's Op team was on the phone. After Arthur said hello and identified himself, Cliff shared the information they had come up with. "That plant has been abandoned for a number of years, more than five. It was purchased by a black ops group part of the NSA. It is used as a location to question subversives who are caught around the world and brought there for interrogation."

"OK responded," Arthur. "That means we are probably at the right place."

"There is more," Cliff continued. "Over the last two weeks there has been a delivery of highly reactive material, a powerful resonance machine, and an unusual plastic coating impregnated with iron crystals."

"What could all that be used for?" asked Arthur.

"In experimental labs," Cliff continued, "doing testing on the creation of antimatter, it is used as a protective screen to prevent antimatter particles from hitting human operators. They use it to cloak the walls surrounding the antimatter device. It not only protects those outside the cloak but intensifies the effects of the antimatter within the room in which it operates. We are not sure what the end purpose is but the scientists tell us it could be used as some type of weapon. One thing is for sure. You don't want to be inside the cloak when the antimatter is discharged."

"Jesus," shouted Arthur. After hanging up, Arthur turned to his brother. "Robert make the 911 call and then grab a weapon, I think Jon may be running into a trap."

- - -

Lizzy came back into the room where Betsy had been sitting for hours. "Betsy?" Lizzy asked in a warm friendly fashion expecting she would get more by being sweet than by alternative means. There would always be time for other means.

Please may I have some water?" Betsy asked.

As Jon approached the abandoned factory he could see heat images coming from inside. There were several at the front entrance and a cluster of heat images toward the back middle of the building. Slowly moving around to the back, Jon detected one heat image coming from a rear entry door. It was not moving and Jon anticipated the person was perhaps sitting. As Jon approached the rear fence, he could see it was a chain link fence six feet high with coils of barbed wire attached to the top of the fence.

"*Jon,*" David spoke. "*Look carefully at the fence we are approaching and utilize your visual senses to their fullest.*" Jon complied and as he did, he could see vibrating crisp sparks of electricity pulsing through the fence fabric. "The fence is electrified." Jon said to himself. "*Yes,*" replied David. He looked at Jon with his lips pursed and a humorous smile on his lips. "*Shall we walk through it?*"

"Can we?" asked Jon. David's smile become broader, he tilted his head toward Jon and looked at him with a mischievous look. "*Let's give it a try, you think?*" Jon briefly glanced at David and continued to walk at the fence and then through it. "*Well, how was that?*" David asked almost rhetorically as he along with Jon surveyed the back entrance of the building. "Wow," exclaimed Jon in a whisper. "I got goose bumps from the electricity." A slight smile crept across Jon's face as they approached the loading dock.

"Is there anything that can stop us?" "*Let's hope not,*" replied David.

Once they were on top of the loading dock. Jon stopped. He looked at the heat image which they had previously seen. Now he could see it in much more detail. It was of a person who was sitting with his back against the wall. Suddenly he detected an instrument on his head and he could hear some communication coming across to the person.

Inside the man was sitting in an old chair with his back to the wall but watching the rear entrance. He could hear the chatter coming from the main part of the building where communications equipment was set up. In between electronic crackles, the message was sent. "Have received an electronic pulse coming from the fence but it has subsided and no intrusion is detected." The person monitoring the chain link fence electronic set up began to check on each of the team members stationed around the building. When he asked for number 12, the man on the other side of the back wall spoke into his head set "All clear."

Moving down along the side of the outside wall, Jon and David positioned themselves to come into the room behind that person. Jon moved against the wall and silently slid through. The man was still sitting facing the rear entrance. Suddenly as if from a sixth sense, the man slowly turned to look behind him. As Jon reached out and instantly touched the man, he fell to the floor unconscious. "Okay," Jon said as if to himself. "Now what's the next move?"

Jon walked to where the wall ended into a corridor which led to the main part of the building. Again with his power of vision, Jon peered across the plant, through its walls. The heat signatures remained essentially the same except for a strange phenomenon. There was what appeared to be a signature of sorts but it didn't show as a person's heat signature does.

"What is that all about?" asked Jon. There was a pause and Jon turned to David. "Did you hear me?"

"*Yes, Jon I did.*" David looked especially concerned. "*Jon,*" David said as he came close. "*Do you trust me?*"

Jon looked into David's eyes and his body language especially with his head as he pulled it back and looked surprised at David's comment, said he could hardly believe what he was hearing. "Do I trust you? We have come this far and you should ask that?"

David did not flinch but looked at Jon expectantly waiting for an answer.

Finally Jon replied. "Well, of course. You should know I do."

"*Jon you must trust me such that you give yourself to me wholly and willingly. You must give yourself over to me such that you will only be a spectator to the events that will unfold. You will not be able to speak. You will not be able to communicate with or to me. If in fact I am correct in what I think is happening, you will, you may even feel some pain. But to survive, I will need all of my powers concentrated through you.*"

Jon looked stunned. He shook his head nodding affirmatively but for the very first time Jon felt afraid. "*Jon,*" David spoke. "*Do not be afraid. You have my powers through me and you have a power source within you, one I have not been able to understand. Yet it is a powerful force through which you can and I urge you to pray and commit all of your own energy to the task.*"

"Yes, of course," Jon stumbled in his speech not knowing what to think of this strange conversation with David.

"All right then Jon. We will initiate my total control now." With that David moved into Jon and they became one. Jon didn't feel any different except he felt like someone who was just looking in from the outside.

Jon felt himself moving toward an opening where the corridor wall ended into the main plant area. Peering around the wall, Jon could see a large warehouse like area. In the middle was what looked like a huge revival tent. But it was not white like the traditional tents Jon had seen put up alongside the road for a religious revival. It was dark gray in texture with what looked like German helmets with a short stub like antenna coming out of the middle scattered across the surface of the tent. The tent like structure had solid metal doors. Inside there were three individuals. Above the tent and going down through the middle of it was a strange looking probe. It seemed to be turned on as sparks were emanating from the inside of the tent. It seemed to be turned on and waiting for something to happen.

Suddenly a siren sounded. Someone yelled "the fence has been breached." Within seconds there was an explosion coming from the front part of the building. Jon could see many armed men running toward the front of the building. Everyone was running except for one person who was running toward the wall where Jon stood. He was shouting "Otto pull the switch, the alien must be here. Then from the source of the strange heat scan which David had observed earlier came a deep voice. "Lure the alien into enclosure. Create enough action to keep him distracted.

He will see the people he came to save are inside and he will enter."

"*A trap,*" David thought. Sensing there was little time to spare; David looked up at the electrical wiring and followed it to a large transformer on a back wall. With focused thought, David drew Jon's arm back. A spur of lightening appeared in Jon's hand almost in the shape of a javelin. The silver streak of energy snapped and popped. The man who had been running toward Otto looked in amazement at the figure which came from behind the corridor with a bolt of lightning in his hand held over his head. Before he had even a chance to yell, David used Jon's strength magnified many times to fling the spear of lightening into the transformer. Sparks flew everywhere. Even as all electrical power ceased, sparks of gold flew around the plant. A fire was started in a back corner where sparks hit a container of oil.

Just as the Slavak brothers broke through the front entrance scattering any opposition, Jon called out to them to save those in the enclosure which was now on fire. The firefight between the brothers and the few still standing who decided to fight it out continued.

Quickly Jon went around the wall that separated him from the man they called Otto. Rounding the wall, Jon was hit with a round of gunfire which backed him up. As Jon put up a shield through the use of his energy, the Otto character was turning and running toward the back of the plant. As he ran he seemed to shed his clothes. But wait he was also shedding his human skin. "I should have known," thought Jon. A figure emerged. The figure was totally greenish gray in color with smooth feet without toes. His arms were thin and his head was sort of triangular in shape coming to a wedge shape at the top. He seemed to have no nostrils and he had sharp coal black eyes. Where one would expect ears to be there were slight indentations looking almost like slits.

Jon started to proceed after him, when he heard Robert call out for help. He turned to see the tent was ablaze. The brothers were with the hostages inside. Surrounded by flames, it looked as if there was no safe exit to remove the hostages who were hurt and unable to move quickly. Immediately Jon focused on the fire. Jon found himself picked up in the air and carried by David who grabbed onto the tent fabric and ripped it along with the flames back over the hostages so that the brothers who had by now subdued all the resistors could free everyone caught inside.

Once David saw the brothers had everything under control in rescuing the hostages, he immediately turned his attention to the Otto figure. Otto was dashing out the back, with strides so long he covered 10 yards each step. Reaching the outside, David could see the brake lights of a vehicle turning onto Bethel Church Road and heading for Rt. 64. David jumped on a motorcycle parked nearby and began his pursuit, using his senses to recognize the patterns on the road left by the vehicle Otto was driving.

— — —

As he came to the intersection of Bethel Church Road and Rt. 64, David like a blood hound, used his eyes to see the tire track impressions just left and turned right at high speed into the down town area of Mocksville, NC. Ahead of them, Otto, or the creature known as Otto, sped under the underpass which led suddenly around the curve to the intersection of Rt. 601 and Rt. 64. Traveling at a high speed, his vehicle could not stop at the red light. An oil truck proceeding through what was for it a green light entered the intersection just as Otto came through at a high rate of speed. The oil truck driver never saw the car coming. Otto's car made impact at the back end of the oil tanker. Otto's car broke into the oil tank causing an enormous and loud explosion to add to the metal to metal crash. The large truck bent like a twig in a hot fire. Fortunately for the oil truck driver the explosion broke the tank part of the truck free from the cab which was unceremoniously tossed across the intersection into a parking lot and subsequently come to rest against a vacant building. Otto's car was caught in the hull of the flaming tanker as it rushed forward now free of its cab into the cars waiting on 601 to take a left onto 64. Even as the car was dragged along with the tanker as if in the clutch of some formidable beast, Otto's new shape emerged from the car and hurtled over the truck. At the sight of this strange figure, people screamed as if the roaring inferno and crushed cars were not enough to make them yell. Otto ran into the Horn's gas station at the next corner and pulled a screaming older lady out of her pride and joy, a 1989 grand touring sport coupe from BMW's high-end luxury line. Equipped with a V-10 507 horse power engine which can get to 155 mph this BMW can hit 62 mph from a standstill in 5.1 seconds.

Jon came into the intersection just seconds after Otto had jumped out. He came to a screeching stop just avoiding the burning inferno by inches. He jumped off of the motorcycle. Then from the reaction of people who were staring up the street after Otto, Jon hurtled over the cars in front of him and took off up the street just as a BMW with the greenish gray figure in the driver's seat came roaring out of Horn's and racing down Rt. 64. People were left behind in shock and rubbing their eyes which must certainly be betraying them by seeing things not possible. Jon watched as the BMW roared away. Just as quickly a NC Highway patrolman ran from the gas station convenience store over to his vehicle which he had earlier pulled into the gas station and filled. As the patrolman Sgt. AJ Farmer jumped behind the driver's seat, Jon jumped into the passenger seat. "Hey, sir…" Farmer did not get but two words out before Jon reached over and grabbed his shoulder with his left hand. Suddenly the patrolman put his Dodge Challenger into gear and sped after the BMW. With lights blazing the patrol vehicle pulled up to the left turn on Rt. 64 at the next intersection taking it to NC Highway 40. There was no BMW insight. However, again using his eyes to pick up the distinctive tire markings the same as were left at the gas station as Otto sped away, Jon using his telepathic and mind control abilities directed Farmer to turn left which he did. Of course it was David doing all this but Jon was observing and as the observer it felt like watching a video game. As the Challenger stepped into high gear, Jon felt David's powers working on making changes to the car's engine capabilities even as it thundered down the road siren and lights blazing. Jon marveled at how David quickly custom-tuned the V-8 engine to make it capable of more than 400 horsepower and able to reach speeds of up to 165 mph.

Just as they completed the rise up Rt. 64, they could see the entrance ramps to I-40. There turning onto the west bound side of I-40 was the tail end of the BMW. Farmer accelerated and at the same time issued an all-points bulletin for the west bound BMW. Then after they were on pursuit on I-40, traffic began to get heavier. The BMW was now about a quarter of a mile ahead. Swerving in and out of traffic in a way Farmer never would have done on his own, the Dodge Challenger began to close the distance on Otto.

Otto now looked down at his gas gauge and realized the owner of the car had not begun to fill the tank before he hijacked it. Looking at less than a quarter of a tank of gas, Otto began to develop an alternate plan of escape. Traffic was now getting thicker. Otto had to use the breakdown lane for much of his travel.

Up ahead a young couple had just pulled over into the breakdown lane. "Oh Frank, we are not going to get to mothers on time and she is going to be so upset."

"Baby, I know it but I didn't plan for us to get a flat tire now did I?"

"Well, Frank I am not one to tell you so," she said with that I told you so look, "but you did say before we packed yesterday we should get some new tires." Exasperated, Frank reeled around. "Dammed Jesse, this is not the time to worry about who hit Annie in the fanny with a flounder. We will put on the spare and get the tires checked out at the next exit."

"Okay, I'm sorry," replied Jesse in that soft forgive me tone which always worked when she decided to end what could have been a knocked down dragged out argument. "Here let me help. What can I do?"

"Thanks sweetie. I tell you what, traffic is very heavy, it's dark and there are a lot of nuts out there, get junior. You and he sit up on that banking while I change this tire."

"Okay," Jesse replied as she began to pull junior out of his car seat. "Come on darling, let's sit up on the hill and watch the traffic while Daddy changes a tire." The air was cool and it was dark except for the light shed by passing traffic.

Frank and Jesse had no way of knowing what lay in store for them within minutes. As Otto flew down the breakdown lane he looked in the rearview mirror at the blue lights which were gaining ground. Then he looked at the fuel gauge and then frantically back at the blue lights on the state patrol car gaining ground. As Otto looked in front of him, a dark spot of something seemed to be emerging from the breakdown lane. Suddenly a car with no lights came into view. Now panic set in as there was no room to edge back into traffic which was now impossible anyway since every lane was backing up and there was no room. When he hit the car, it was with such force that the fuel tank of Frank's car exploded. The BMW shot straight up in the air as it used the car it just hit as a ramp. The BMW flew over Jesse and junior. Jesse was screaming as she looked down at the massive flames billowing from their only vehicle and no signs of her husband.

The BMW flew into the trees lining the edge of the top of the small incline where Jesse and junior had gone to be safe. The BMW hit a pine tree and came to a sudden stop. Flames began to creep out of the BMW's undercarriage. Grass was now on fire. Otto had been ejected through the front window as the air bags intended to prevent such an occurrence failed. Although Otto suffered a major gash to his head and a black liquid, his bodily fluid, poured from the opening, he came to his feet and began to run, stumble, fall, pick himself up and limp through the underbrush that covered the land he found himself in.

The State Patrol car pulled up in back of the car on fire. Jon instructed Farmer to call in for help. As the Trooper made the calls, Jon sprang from the car and started after the BMW and its driver. As Jesse screamed, Jon looked back at the car to see a man half out of the car which was now on top of him. Without hesitation, Jon turned his attention to the man. Jon picked up the rear end of the car which was trapping the man. The fire and heat were intense. So hot was the chassis of the car, the hot metal burned Jon's hand before his restorative powers came into play. Jon was still an observer to David's control and he felt a surge of gratification that David would stop what he knew was the primary mission to help this man who was most likely dead anyway.

Holding the car up with one hand and pulling Frank free with the other, Jon could see massive burns all over Frank's body. The flames from the explosion had burned away most of his clothing. As well, his left leg was gushing blood and was almost severed completely off.

Jesse screamed continuously as she could see the devastating injury to her husband. She held the baby close to her bosom and suddenly her screaming turned to prayers said over and over. As she prayed Jon felt David turn and look briefly at Jesse. Pulling the unconscious and presumable dead man into the grass away from the flames, Jon observed himself touch this man's body in such a gentle manner. A blue glow overwhelmed the man. Jon straddled

Frank's torso and held his leg together with his hands. The bleeding stopped and as Jon looked closer he could see the gash that threatened to separate the man from his leg pulsating from a golden glow that was so bright it was impossible to actually see the gash even as close as Jon was. Finally David made Jon roll away. Jon lay on the ground stunned. Was David exhausted, he wondered? Then as quickly Jon got back on his feet again under David's control and proceeded to climb the rise in pursuit of Otto. Jon wanted to ask David some questions but he realized the only way he could do that was when David allowed it. At the moment Jon's senses of which he had control over were limited to his eyesight and his mind. All else belonged to David.

Otto continued to run although somewhat hampered by his injuries but knowing he had a dangerous pursuer and there was no alternative, Otto knew he was running from one who might be able to turn off his life force. Off in the distance Otto could see lights from a development. If only he could reach there, he thought, he could find refuge and perhaps a way to contact Lizzy.

As Jon climbed over the earthen rise and headed through the woods after Otto, he finally heard David speak. "*Jon?*"

"Yes." Jon answered. David continued. "*Now you are going to meet an ultraterrestrial.*"

"What is that?"

"*Well, Earthlings would consider Angels and Demons as ultra-terrestrials, as they would consider any strange and mystical beings that supposedly originate in a reality slightly removed from our own. These are visitors from another dimen-*"

sion. The one we are following is certainly not an Angel by any definition you have Jon."

"How do you know that?"

"Because, actions speak louder than words. Now Jon you are going to see the power of sight you now possess when you ask for it."

With that said, all of a sudden Jon could see rays of light streaming upward from the Earth. Around them were streams of light in multi colors. Some came from the heavens. Some just seem to be moving all around them. "Wow. Where did these come from?"

"Electromagnetic radiation that has a wavelength in the range from about 4,000 (violet) to about 7,700 (red) angstroms may be perceived by the normal unaided human eye. Jon, you can and are now seeing wavelengths of all angstroms. You are looking at cell phone calls, TV cable transmissions, Earth radiation, satellite signals; you name it and it is in your vision capability."

"Wow," replied Jon. Then rhetorically he added "just what am I supposed to do with that capability."

"You will see Jon. You will see." Then after a pause David continued as they moved along the ground. *"Here is the scan you will use to detect the heat signature from living things. You have used this before."*

Jon scanned his range of vision. "Look I can see some images, rather weak though, coming from the development off in the distance."

"What about closer Jon?"

Jon looked intently. Suddenly he picked up a different type of heat signature. It was a weird one, grayish not orange. "Well, I can see a gray illumination moving across the field in front of us."

"*Yes, Jon. That is the creature we seek.*"

"Creature?"

"*Oh most definitely a creature; what your science refers to as an ultra-terrestrial. This is one bad guy. He seeks those such as me to destroy.*"

"Why?"

"*Because we are a threat to his kind's attempt to manipulate humans to be destructive. By so doing they seek to gain control over this dimension. Hold on Jon lets catch up with the figure called Otto.*" With that, Jon under David's control suddenly appeared in front of Otto. They had jumped through space just as they had done on the president's balcony.

The creature was demonic looking. His skin was solid greenish gray. His head was shaped like an axe. He seemed to have human like appendages. "*What happened to the real Otto?*" Jon asked.

Suddenly Jon felt David moving him back several paces away from the creature. "*Jon,*" David said in an alarmed tone unlike any Jon had heard from David. "*I can't explain this but you are going to have to fight this creature, I cannot.*"

"What?" said Jon incredulously? "Wha… wha… what do you mean I have to fight. Where the hell are you going?"

"*Jon. I am sorry. I can't explain this right now. Be assured you have all of the necessary skills. Your imagination is your only constraint. Think carefully and remember you can jump, you can change material things and you have electrical energy at your disposal. I am sorry. This is unfair to you but I have no other viable option available.*"

All of a sudden the look of the creature began to change. As if it weren't horrid enough, it was turning into a strange and ugly animal looking creature with large, long appendages, more like tentacles than arms. It sensed there was some hesitation on the human alien in front of him and so it began to advance on Jon.

"Jesus, David. What the hell is this? Help!" There was no reply. One of the creature's appendages hit Jon around the ankles. It yanked Jon off his feet and threw him with great force into a large tree. "Thud." Jon hit the tree back first. Slowly he slid down to the base of the tree with the creature now running at him. "Ouch," Jon said as he felt pain running through his back. The creature had a large mouth full of ugly looking but obviously very sharp teeth. They looked more like spikes than teeth. Its mouth was open and a large snarling noise came out of it as the creature approached. It began to run at increasing speed at Jon with its mouth wide open, appendages flailing. Just as the creature was about to physically attack Jon, Jon visualized himself flying up the tree away from his attacker. The creature was moving so fast he couldn't stop as Jon seemed to fly straight up the tree. The creature's teeth sank into the tree with such power combined with the force of his momentum, the tree began to crack. As Jon held onto a large branch, he could feel the tree begin to fall over. The creature pulled away from the tree and was positioning itself to attack Jon as he fell. Jon thought about being back where they had encountered the creature. The tree fell with a loud crash to the ground. Jon was not in it. The creature snorted and gave a god awful scream as it could not find its adversary. It swung around to see where Jon was standing.

"What the hell is wrong with me?" Jon thought to himself. "I have any power I want and yet I seem to be hesitant. Well, here goes nothing."

The creature rushed toward Jon. As it approached Jon's eyes met it with a laser like ray that stopped it in its track. Jon shot the creature another laser beam. The creature ducked this time and the laser beam hit what remained of the tree that had fallen. The beam cut right through the tree. It was not lost on Jon the fact the beam had severed the tree trunk but had only stopped the creature briefly. The creature began to encircle Jon looking for an advantage. Jon turned with the creature so as not to expose his back.

The creature suddenly lurched forward as if to attack but pulled back just as Jon shot another laser beam at it. The creature ducked and before Jon could do anything else shot a mouthful of what can only be described as goo out of its mouth at Jon. The goo landed on Jon's chest. It burned. Jon breathed heavily and was stunned his new alien like body could be so penetrated. The goo sizzled on Jon's chest and was burning a hole into Jon's abdomen. Jon reeled back and turned in pain exposing his back to the creature. The creature took advantage of Jon's dilemma and immediately jumped on Jon's back. It sank its teeth into Jon's shoulder penetrating his flesh and causing great pain. Jon mustered all his strength to create a tremendous release of electricity throughout his body. The shock had its effect on the creature that howled and released its grip on Jon. As it moved away, Jon realized he must neutralize the goo that was like an acid eating its way through Jon's flesh. The creature seeing the effect the goo was having, prepared to spit more on Jon. Suddenly Jon created a large pool of water from the ground that both he and the creature stood upon. Thinking the water might at the very least give him some relief from the goo, there was no way he could realize the effect it would have on the creature. As both Jon and the creature were surrounded by this pool of water covering the size of a large YMCA swimming pool, the creature began to scream and thrash around. As it did, steam appeared all around the creature. He kept thrashing until he disappeared. It was almost like dropping dry ice into a glass of water, or alka seltzer even.

The goo itself dissolved into the water. Jon pulled himself out of the pool he had created and fell to the side exhausted by what he had experienced.

Suddenly David appeared. He beamed down at Jon with an admiring look. Jon looked up at him. "Where in the hell have you been?" Jon exclaimed.

"*I have been here with you Jon but I could not interfere.*"

"You couldn't interfere? Why the hell not?"

"*You forget. My prime directive forbids me to directly cause the death of any living thing while on this mission. This confrontation was not anticipated. The only choice I had was to retreat if there was to be a violent confrontation. My only other choice was to let you deal with it using the powers I had given you.*" He paused. "*You did well.*" Then after a brief hesitation David asked, "*How did you come to create the pool of water. That was quite ingenious. I would have had no idea of the creature's insensitivity to water especially such that water would be the weapon it could not overcome.*"

"I had no idea either," Jon responded as he sat on the ground looking up at David. Jon shook his head like a dog shaking its body to get rid of water after a bath. Then Jon lay over on the ground.

Suddenly David realized Jon's life force was ebbing low to the point David might not be able to retrieve him. Regardless of how he tried, the effect of the acid goo had penetrated Jon's chest and he was failing. David tried but he was unable to reverse the damage that had been done.

CHAPTER 9

REFUGE IN ANOTHER WORLD

Jon's eyes began to flutter. He could hear noises. As he gained his senses, he tried to understand. It sounded like chatter. His eyelids flickered. Then one by one he opened his eyes. The light was bright. It was a bright blue light. Slowly as his eyes focused he could vaguely see what he assumed must be a white ceiling. He must be either in heaven or a hospital room he thought briefly. The thought gave rise to a slight chuckle. Feeling down where the bed should be in which he lay, he could feel no substance. He was laid out as if in a bed. It felt like he was laying on something. Yet there seemed to be nothing there. His senses tried to make reason out of the realization. Suddenly he realized he was actually suspended. He tried but he could not move. As he began to gain focus on his surroundings he could vaguely make out there were many instruments around where he lay. Nevertheless there were no tubes sticking out of him as one might expect lying up in a hospital bed. If he were in a hospital there should be instruments. "Why can't I move?" He wondered. He could still hear the chatter. He tried but he couldn't make out any details. There were figures or maybe it was one person moving around. He couldn't tell. He just couldn't make any sense out of any of it.

Suddenly he heard a female voice. "Jon." She paused. "Jon. If you can hear me Jon, blink your eyes." Jon did as he was told. He still couldn't see anything clearly. Suddenly he felt as if his arm had been released from something that had been holding it. With effort he reached out. Slowly with his right arm he reached out. It hit something. It was curved and it seemed to go completely around him.

"Jon," the voice commanded. Please put your arms down by your side. You are okay. We have placed you in a surgical cylinder to evaluate and fix your injuries."

Yes. Now Jon vaguely remembered. He had fought with that thing… that, what did David call it; an ultra-terrestrial thing. He had conquered it. Didn't he? He must be in a hospital. David must have gotten them to a hospital.

"David," Jon called out. "David… David," he called out repeatedly. Suddenly he heard a strange whooshing sound. Something was penetrating the cylinder and was coming down toward him. He could see a long needle coming out of a tube and coming down straight down into his chest. Again he felt something hold him. He couldn't reach out any more. Again he called out for David. Then there was blackness.

⸙ ⸙ ⸙

Lizzy entered the interrogation room where Betsy had been placed. Betsy was tired. She wanted to go home. Her head lay on the table as if to try and get some shut eye. However, each time she tried to raise her right arm and put it under her head, the cuffs she was in restrained her. She had told them she didn't know where Jon was. She had told them over and over that neither she nor her family were aliens. Nothing seemed to please her interrogators.

"Well, kiddo," Lizzy began with a sarcastic tone, "your alien lover has been terminated."

Betsy heard her but didn't move. Slowly tears swelled up in her eyes. Irritated at Betsy's response, Lizzy threw the cup of water she had carried into the room with her onto Betsy.

Betsy raised her head. Tears were flowing down her face as she looked angrily at Lizzy. "Why do you have to be so selfishly cruel? Are you so inhuman you have lost any sense of decency?" With that, Lizzy rushed around the table, took off Betsy's cuffs and slammed her up against the wall so hard it cracked Betsy's skull. As Betsy fell in a limp pile on the floor, Lizzy turned and walked calmly out of the room. "Jack," she commanded the officer standing near the door, "get that mass of human waste out of my interrogation room."

"Yes, ma'am," He looked as if he didn't know what to do. "What should I do with her?"

"I couldn't care less," Lizzy spit out in a disagreeable way as she walked away.

The officer went in the room. He walked around the table and found Betsy crumbled to the floor. Blood was forming a puddle under her head. Quickly he spoke into his collar microphone. "Call EMS, we have a situation in interrogation room 4."

Again Jon gained consciousness. This time it was easier to focus on the room. Once more he reached out with his hand to feel the cylinder which had surrounded him previously. It was gone.

Jon shook his head. He seemed to be conscious. He seemed to be alive. Yet here he was seemingly floating in space and around him were these circles. They were floating through the air almost without purpose. Wait, they weren't circles, they were spheres. Suddenly, they moved away as a person came to his bedside.

Jon looked at her. He had seen her somewhere but he couldn't place where he had seen her. All of a sudden he realized she looked just like the mother of his boyhood friend Paul Young. Jon and Paul had played together as childhood friends. They always ended up at Paul's house where his mother was always baking something. Oh how Jon loved the smell of homemade bread. Mrs. Young was always so happy to see Jon. She treated Jon as if he was another of her sons. He always felt at home and loved in Paul's house.

"Jon." The woman spoke. "Please don't be alarmed." She reached over and touched Jon's arm. Suddenly Jon could smell that same smell of his childhood years which brought back such good memories. It was the smell of homemade bread baking.

"Jon, I am an icon of a pleasant memory of someone in your past. You are here at David's home."

"David's home?" thought Jon. All of a sudden a panicked feeling rushed over him. "How could that be?" Jon mumbled.

Suddenly the vision of his fight with that ultra-terrestrial thing or whatever it was came back. He had defeated the alien thing. But he had been fatally wounded. He had been in the process of dying. The last thing he remembered was David saying "Hold on Jon we are going home."

Jon sat up. The spheres moved away from him. The woman put her arm around Jon's back as if to support him as he sat up. "What you see in me Jon is a familiar image we took from your mind. I am an icon which we hope is familiar and welcomed."

Jon looked at the image of what he remembered Mrs. Young as looking like. "Wow," he uttered. He paused and looked around him as the spheres moved closer to him again. "Am I alive or what? Where is David?"

The icon sighed. "Yes, you are what you call alive."

"And David, where is David?"

The spheres were now all around him. They pushed forward. "And, what are all these things, these, these spheres?"

The spheres moved back. "Jon these are David's brothers and sisters. What you are referring to as spheres is what we look like in our natural form."

Jon gazed in amazement at the spheres. They looked two dimensional but they were actually three dimensional. They were so perfectly formed. Their outer circumference was a band of color. Each one had a white dot on one side. It was about 6 inches in an oblong shape on the three to four foot diameter spheres which hovered around the room.

"Awesome," responded Jon. He watched them as they hovered around and over him. Then turning his attention back to the icon of Mrs. Young, he said, "Where is David?" Jon again asked only this time in a more insistent manner.

"David is still within you."

"Why can't I see him? I want to see him."

The icon looked at Jon in a sympathetic manner. "We will talk more about David in a moment. First we need to share with you our excitement that you made it here still functioning. This is a first ever endeavor on our part. We have only recently developed the technique to extract from your planet. Before we could only send visitors. Initially some made it but others did not. When you were fatally wounded, David initiated a new system we employed if we had to do an emergency extraction. However"—the icon paused—"we were only supposed to extract one of our own who was without a host."

"Okay," I appreciate that but where is David?" Jon asked again in a tone that insisted on an answer.

"David did not make it back in the form in which he was intended." Again the icon paused. "David is still within you."

"What do you mean?"

"Our tests show that David is, as a life form like he was originally, still alive within you. But it seems he has become so integrated with your life form, he cannot be extracted. Our senses show us he is functioning at some level within you but he seems to be in…" The icon paused for a way to explain. "He seems to be in what you might call a coma.

"I don't understand."

"Unfortunately, Jon, neither do we, at the moment but we are working on it. The fact you have made it to here in one piece is what you would call a miracle. It saved your life as we were able to neutralize and repair the fatal damage the ultra-terrestrial caused. We are ecstatic you have survived and we are in deep sorrow David has not in a form you, and we, are accustomed. This has been enough for you right now. You need to rest and we will discuss more later." With that the icon put her hands over Jon's eyes and he entered a deep sleep.

However long it was, Jon's eyes began to open again from the deep rest he had been put in. Mrs. Young was no longer there, nor were the numbers of spheres that had encircled him last time he was conscious. There were no longer any instruments in the room. Suddenly several spheres came into Jon's view.

"Hello Jon." Jon looked around to find Mrs. Young from whom he knew the voice came. Instead there was no one except the two spheres in front of him. One of the two spheres seemed to slightly glow when the voice came. Jon looked directly at the sphere.

"Yes, Jon I am the one speaking to you. If it would make you more comfortable I can resume my icon form of Mrs. Young or I can stay in my natural form. Which would please you?"

"Ah… you're fine as you are. I appreciate your efforts to make me comfortable. While I was in the deep sleep, I had a conversation with David."

The two spheres become illuminated and pulsed as if in response to one another. "Yes. David said I am his prodo."

"With that the two spheres began to pulse almost excitedly."

"Oh Jon. This is such good news. We are so over-whelmed with Joy. This means that for whatever reason although the energy form you know as David can't re-emerge, he is still alive within you."

"What is a prodo?"

"Jon, a prodo means you are David's brother."

The two spheres began to indicate they were messaging between themselves by the pulsing of the lighted band that encircled their circumference. For some time this went on.

Finally Jon spoke up. "Is something wrong?"

The pulsing stopped. "Well, Jon I am being reminded of David's mission. He was to bring back the results of his determination as to whether or not your peoples should be allowed to survive."

"Yes," David responded as he hung his head. "I was on a mission to determine whether or not there were enough good people to justify our being allowed to continue as a race of people."

"What was the result of that mission Jon?"

"I don't honestly know. My…" Jon struggled to describe what Betsy was to him. "My love and I were trying to mingle among people enough so David could feel whether or not we were worthy."

Jon looked at the spheres as they talked amongst themselves as indicated by their pulsing color. He now wondered as to whether or not this miraculous trip to a far end of the universe would end here.

"Jon you should know we were able to download much of David's mission."

"Yes?" Jon replied questioning.

"We also downloaded your brain history and all that has transpired in the time David joined with you."

Jon pursed his lips, and his body language did not show pleasure over this knowledge. Jon looked out the large opening to his left which revealed a beautiful landscape of green foliage and large looming brown cliffs in the background. For the first time he realized he was breathing air on the planet. Out in the distance were what seemed like different colored balls. They flew about it seemed. Some moved with great speed. Some moved slowly. Some began to get closer to where Jon was. As they got closer they became larger until they had the size of the spheres hovering close to him.

His attention was brought back to the spheres in front of him as they spoke. "We were pleased with what we found in David's download. He speaks admiringly of you. From that and using you as a representative of your planet, we are pleased."

Jon began to relax and a slight smile flickered on his face.

"However, we still have a deep concern over the violence and greed which permeates the people of your planet. From the information David has brought us we have an even deeper concern over the ultra-terrestrials that have already become involved in driving the human race to even more violence."

Jon sat there wondering if he would ever get to see Betsy again or his son.

As if sensing Jon's thoughts, the spheres spoke again. "We feel we can get you back to Earth… in one piece. Our ability to get you here has answered many technical questions which previously remained unanswered."

"Awesome," spoke Jon enthusiastically.

"Ah… when do you think I can leave?"

The spheres pulsed. "Is this what you are discussing now?" Jon asked.

"Yes, Jon."

"You communicate by those pulses I see."

"Yes, Jon. We communicate through the process you would identify as harmonics. Our pulses are varying frequencies. The different frequencies we pulse produce communication in our world. In your science of physics you define harmonics as a wave whose frequency is a whole number multiple of that of another."

Jon's face reflected the look of "Hmm okay, I guess I can sort of understand that."

"Now getting back to the question of when you might leave. I think a week in our time which will equal about a day in Earth time. Would that be satisfactory?"

Jon could hardly speak. "You mean I will be here a week and yet when I return it will only be a day later than when I left Earth?"

"Yes, plus or minus some minutes. But that is close enough for round figures."

"Ok!" Jon said enthusiastically, what shall we do during the week?"

"Well, of course we will have to verify various parameters to properly define the electrical pulse to carry you back. We do want to run some more tests to see if we can contact David before you leave. Other than that you are welcome to enjoy our world."

"Well, I am ready to start."

Then as if talking to himself, Jon blurted out "no one at home is going to believe this."

"Jon few will believe the talents and attributes you will have either."

"What do you mean by that?"

"Well, the main reason you were able to make the trip here successfully and will be able to return is that David rewired you so to speak in a way that kept you in sync with the transmission wave we use. This re-wiring is what has given your native intelligence and your physical and mental prowess an increase beyond human years."

Suddenly a sphere appeared and rapid pulsations occurred between the three spheres. "Jon we are going to place you back into a deep sleep while we meet with our senior council. We shall return."

"But I…" Jon was immediately put back into a deep sleep.

Upon awakening, Jon was introduced to several of the spheres who enlightened Jon about the various aspects of their world. Jon learned that the color rings designated rank which would change over the years based upon age and accomplishments. The small white dot on one side of the sphere was used to propagate through a process of energy sharing which produced a smaller sphere. The smaller sphere had no colored outer ring but as soon as it was created became very busy communicating with other spheres gathering information.

Jon walked among the spheres. Although there was no solid ground on this mostly gaseous planet, the spheres had given Jon the perception of solid walk ways and an environment closer to Jon's familiarity.

Finally the day of departure came.

Jon was taken back to the room, or what he envisioned as a room, where he first regained consciousness. The icon of Mrs. Young was there to greet him.

"Jon. Are you ready to return to your home?"

"Oh yes I am," Jon replied excitedly. "What about David and where will I arrive at on Earth?"

"Unfortunately, there has been no change in David's status. We do not know what effect the travel back will have on his relationship with you. You should be aware of the fact your powers may be diminished for a while, perhaps a day or even a week of your Earth days but they should return. We have installed a guard against the weapon the ultra-terrestrial used against you but we have no way of knowing at this time, if they have other weapons or techniques which could prove detrimental to your shell. You should be aware you have a great healing power. However, should that be depleted due to a great exertion of this power it may become significantly diminished. You would know this is happening when the white and blue glow produced during the healing power turns to red. If it does, you must disengage your healing power before the glow goes to black or suffer a significant decrease in future applications. As to where you will arrive, we have notified our fellow spheres presently on Earth to be prepared to greet you. Where would you like to arrive?

After thinking for a moment, Jon replied, "Carthage, North Carolina at the home of Betsy's dad."

"That will be possible. Are you ready?"

"Yes." Jon looked at the icon and extended his hand. The icon took Jon's hand and smiled.

"Jon?"

"Yes."

"One more thing; David was under command not to do harm to any living being on Earth. For this reason David could not terminate the life of the ultra-terrestrial. This command almost took your life. We have made the decision you personally represent the kind of race we could work with and the kind of race who does not present the kind of threat we initially were concerned about. However, there are others on your planet; many others perhaps, who do represent a threat. It is our hope you can influence your planet's inhabitants to turn away from their quest for greed and power at the expense of others."

"Thank you," replied Jon.

"The powers you have are unrestricted except as I have shared with you. That is you are free to use your best judgment as to how to use them without the restrictions we placed upon David and the other spheres on your planet." Jon shook his head affirmatively acknowledging what was being said.

"We will be monitoring your planet's activities. If you are unsuccessful or we feel there is a potential threat created by others of your race, we reserve the right to take whatever action we deem necessary."

Jon quietly nodded that he understood.

"Now, Jon please lay down."

Although Jon could see nothing, this time he could feel a solid table like structure behind him. He lay down on the table he could not see. The icon leaned over. "Jon?"

He looked up at the icon who was smiling over him. "Yes?" Jon replied.

"Jon on your planet years before your time, there was a phrase good friends left one another with as they departed." Jon listened eagerly. "The phrase was the words 'God be with you.' Over time that phrase became shortened to the word Good-bye... Jon, Good-bye."

CHAPTER 10

THE STING OF DEATH

The next voice Jon heard was that of Nicholas. "Jon... Jon, it is Nicholas and Mikka." As Jon opened his eyes he found himself in a back yard close to Max's house. He was naked. Despite the temperatures of late July, Jon felt a coldness as shivers ran through his limbs.

"Here Jon, we have clothes for you." Jon looked up to see Nicholas who was carrying a bag of clothes. As he dressed himself he tried to get his bearings. Sensing Jon might be a bit disoriented, Mikka told Jon where they were in respect to Max's house.

"Yes, thank you," Jon said in a whisper to Nicholas and Mikka as he got himself up and looking around.

"Jon," Nicholas began, "Max is in a bad way. He was injured severely. He was brought back to the hospital and is using a wheel chair to get around."

Upon hearing that Jon started for Max's house. "I must see him. I must help him and then go to get Betsy."

As Jon approached Max's house his scan told him there was only one individual in the house. The person was moving slowly toward the kitchen and seemed to be in a sitting position as he moved.

Going around to the sliding door entrance to the kitchen area, Jon tapped gently on the glass. A bruised and battered old man came to the door in a wheel chair. As he opened the door, his sad face turned to a happy one as he saw Jon.

"Jon… oh Jon. I am so glad to see you my son. Please come in."

Jon quickly entered with Nicholas and Mikka following right behind him.

Max shared with Jon, Nicholas and Mikka the details as he could remember of what Otto and his men did to him. Fortunately they had not gotten to Julie before Jon showed up.

Jon and Mikka and Nicholas all encircled Max and began the healing process. Within minutes under the combined powers of the three men, Max began to look like his old self. "Look guys," Max jokingly pleaded, "Don't make me look much younger. They won't let me in the Senior Citizen's Center if you do." They all laughed.

Then Max lowered his head and said, "But my baby is dead." The tears flowed and Max had a hard time controlling them.

When Max said Betsy was dead, Jon's body trembled with sadness and extreme despair. Mikki reached over and put his hand on Jon's shoulder. Suddenly Jon shook as if someone had just walked over his grave. He looked at Max sternly.

"Max how do you know this?"

With slow deliberation Max explained one of the AFTa men while they were torturing him laughed in his face as he told of how Betsy had been taken off to the AFTa office in Charlotte. He was told that after they worked her over she had been slapped up against a wall so hard it cracked her skull and she died. It had seemed to delight the AFTa men. Hearing that Max had gotten so angry he strained to get out of the chair he was strapped in. He yelled, screamed and cried until he had neither voice nor energy to resist anymore. But he still resisted telling anything about Jon and they pounded him and cut him incessantly.

"Finally, when you came Jon, there was the sense we might be rescued. Then there were explosions and gunfire. Two young men put down most of those who stayed and resisted. Many fled. Then EMS showed up along with a variety of other law enforcement officers. That's when they took me to Davie County Hospital where they did what they could and sent me home to recover. I was supposed to schedule a visit to Baptist Memorial Hospital in Winston Salem. I guess I won't have to do that now. If I did, it would start this "alien" thing all over again." Max almost began to laugh.

"No, Max. You will be fine now." Jon paused. "But you really don't have any proof Betsy is not alive do you?"

"No Jon, but I made some calls and that is what I am being told."

"Max, do you know what the story is with Slavak?"

"I know that creep Otto had hurt him; not as bad as me. Then he was thrown in with my granddaughter and me. It was shortly after that when you showed up. Then everything erupted and we were separated. I assumed he went back to wherever he came from."

"How hurt was Slavak?"

"Well, he looked pretty weak when he came in. I think they had just started to work him over. His hand was wrapped up like they had done something to it just before he was thrown in with us. We didn't talk, just exchanged looks. Several times he cringed and tried to put his hands to his chest. I was worried he was having a heart attack. I called out for help but I was just laughed at. When everything went down he was whisked away and I was sent to the hospital."

"Well, my dear friend," Jon replied, "it looks like you took the worst of it."

"No Jon." Max looked down. "I am afraid Betsy took the worst of it." He paused and looked at the floor. "Perhaps Slavak did also. He might have had a heart attack and died. I never knew."

Jon hung his head for a while as they all watched in silence. Then Jon spoke. "Mikki you and Nicholas see if you can track Slavak down. Hopefully he is still alive. Let him know what has happened; that I am still alive and that as soon as I find Betsy, I will search him out."

Both Nicholas and Mikki nodded in agreement.

Max wished them all good luck and watched them leave. Jon waited till Mikki and Nicholas were out of sight. Then he got on the Harley he had commandeered from Pan Handle which Max had allowed him to bring to his house and store there in the garage. Jon took off toward Charlotte. Before they had left, Nicholas had made some calls and found out where the ATFa location in Charlotte was.

As Jon started out going north on Court House Square toward Dowd Street, who should he run into coming the opposite way but Too Tall and about 6 of the outlaw bikers. Too Tall and the others did a double take when Jon flew by them. They started screaming and tires started to screech as their bikes turned around and they headed after Jon. As Jon turned right onto McReynolds Street onto what was now 24-27, the bikers were in high gear about a half a mile behind. Jon smiled to himself as he slowed down to let them catch up.

"We have that bastard now," thought Too Tall to himself knowing the bike Jon was riding was not as fast as theirs. He knew the bike Jon was on belonged to PanHandle and that bike severely needed a tune up.

Seeing themselves catching up, the bikers were relishing what they were going to do to Jon when they caught him. They hit the gas and roared after their soon to be victim.

When they were only 1/8th of a mile behind him, Jon reached down and put his hand on the cycle's engine. Suddenly it came alive with power.

Too Tall couldn't understand it. They were catching up. Yet now they couldn't seem to get any closer than where they were.

The bikers were now going 80 mph down 24-27 where the maximum allowable speed was 55 mph. Up ahead Jon could sense radar rays. He could sense the intermittent light waves emanating from a lidar gun. Concentrated light is the basic element in what is generally known as a light detection and ranging gun or lidar. "Hmm" thought Jon, "light is what I am all about these days. As Jon's bike bore down on the lidar with Too Tall and his hooligans in pursuit, Jon began to sense the emitted light and he absorbed it as it struck him. The bikers behind were not so lucky. The light bounced off them and returned to the awaiting officer's gun.

As Jon's bike went by the state patrol car, the officer couldn't understand why he wasn't getting readings on that bike indicating that it was speeding. However, when Too Tall and the other bikers immediately came into range, the radar gun continued to pop with feedback showing they were definitely speeding.

Too Tall saw the Highway patrol car and attempted to back off on the throttle. It was too late. As they passed the patrolman, they knew he would be pulling out after them. He looked straight at the officer at the same time the officer was eye balling him. "Well," Too Tall thought "If they get us they will get that prick in front also." Using that as his rationale, Too Tall ratcheted up his cycle. The others followed. Soon they were streaming after Jon at 85–90 mph with the State Highway Patrol in fast pursuit.

Jon increased his speed accordingly. Then Jon used his powers to slowly veil himself and the bike in an electromagnetic covering that, except for dirt flying up under the wheels, made Jon and the bike invisible to the human eye. Jon pulled off the highway and slowed the bike down.

Too Tall and his group suddenly lost sight of Jon's bike. As they flew along at outrageous speeds, Too Tall couldn't help but notice a patch of dirt flying up along the side of the road as if something was kicking the dirt up. It seemed to be going in their direction yet at a much slower speed. Soon Too Tall and his bikers were well beyond the strange sight and the Highway Patrol was in pursuit. Unbeknownst to Too Tall, there would be several Highway Patrol cars further up on 24-27 waiting to escort him and his crew to jail.

As Jon watched the speeding bikes go by, he couldn't help but smile. "Couldn't happen to a nicer group," he thought to himself. Moving back onto the highway, Jon resumed his trip now focusing again at getting to Charlotte as soon as he could. Maintaining a speed of 55 mph, Jon eventually passed by Too Tall in handcuffs and three highway patrol cars with officers putting the bikers inside their vehicles.

As Jon passed by, the first Highway Patrol man who had first spotted the speeding bikes looked up. He shook his head. He couldn't figure out how that motorcyclist had gotten behind him. He stood there in amazement watching Jon head down the road toward Charlotte, as did Too Tall.

Once Jon came into Charlotte, he picked up the 277 loop and headed for South Caldwell St. Once there, he turned down East Stonewall and stopped at what appeared to be an abandoned building. Jon found a parking spot and proceeded to the front entrance.

As he approached the entrance, Jon noticed people going in and out. Each person going in or out of the building had to flash a badge to the security people at the front of the building. Looking around, he spotted a pizza delivery guy parking his vehicle and going into his back seat for a stack of pizzas. Hurrying over, Jon put his hand on the man's back causing him to immediately pass out. After helping the man into his car, Jon placed his hand gently on the man's head. After reading the man's brainwaves, Jon knew the man's name. It was Juan and he was on his way to this address to deliver pizzas. Jon took the man's hat and the stack of pizzas and headed up to the front door. Wearing the hat so as to shield some of his face and causing a slight distortion to his facial features so as not to be recognized, Jon encountered one of the security personnel. "Hey, Mac," the security agent said to his fellow security guard, "The pizzas are finally here." Then looking at Jon, the agent lifted Jon's hat and said, "Hey, you aren't the regular guy."

"No," Jon replied hoarsely, "Juan had some problems and couldn't come."

"Well," the second agent said, "If you know Juan, it must be okay."

"Wait, Jim, you know the procedure, no one gets to come in who hasn't been cleared. Juan was cleared. This dude hasn't been." "It's okay," Jon replied. "I understand I will take the pizzas back and tell them." "Whoa," said Jim. He looked at the first security agent, Mike, who was holding Jon back from entering the building. "Are you going to go up there and tell them they won't be getting their pizzas?"

After thinking about it briefly, Mike asked Jon what Juan's wife's name was. "Margarita," Jon replied.

"See Mike, geese."

"Okay, okay," Mike said then he asked "you know how to get to where they go?"

"Yes, sir," Jon said.

With that said the security officers took one of the pizzas and sent Jon into the building. As soon as he got out of their sight, Jon entered a men's room and put the pizzas down. As he did, a young man came into the men's room and stood at a urinal. Jon went up behind him, quickly put him to sleep and then put him into one of the stalls with the pizzas on his lap.

As Jon left he swiped the man's badge and clipped it to his shirt.

Jon came to the elevators but not wanting to encounter anyone until he was ready, Jon took the stairs to the third floor where the ATFa administrative offices were located. As he passed his badge under the entry device, the door clicked open. As he entered the main door, which was a steel security door, Jon fused the lock behind him with his hand so that no one could enter or leave.

A young lady at the front said hello, then she looked disconcerted at loud noises coming from the back of the office area. She appeared apologetic as they could hear yelling and screaming. The voices could be heard all the way to the front of the office.

"This was a major frack up of immense proportions. Someone's head is going to roll and it won't be mine." The young lady saw that Jon had the right kind of badge but didn't bother to check his badge photo. Instead she gave him a grimaced look as the shouting continued. Jon walked straight back past numerous cubicles where people were working but obviously aware of the commotion. Jon opened the door to where the yelling was coming from.

As the door opened Liz spun around. Suddenly terminating her discussion with the two agents who were giving her the latest lowdown on the aftermath of the mess that went down in Mocksville, she focused on the impertinence of someone entering her office without knocking.

"Who the hell do you think you are?"

"I am the one you have been looking for."

The look of shock and dismay on the face of Liz and the two agents was too great for words. "Ah no, you aren't," Liz replied. She continued with increased furor and tone in her voice, "you are not..." Jon's face was returning to his normal countenance and Liz could see this was the man who not so long ago she pushed around in a motel room at the Winchester Mass. Hospital. This was in fact the same man she had been seeking all this time. The two agents backed up to the wall and removed hand guns from their holsters. Jon looked right at them.

"Shoot you fools shoot." She said. One of the agents did shoot and the handgun exploded in his hand causing him to fall to the floor writhing in pain. Looking square at the other agent, Jon said in a calm voice. "You need to get your friend out of here. Do it now." The agent could not get himself and his wounded friend out of the room fast enough.

Now Liz was backing up to the back wall; the same wall she had slammed Betsy against. As the two agents left, Jon closed and locked the door without taking his eyes of the woman.

"Do you think this is going to get you anywhere?" she snarled.

"We shall see won't we?" Jon replied. Already Jon's scan of her returned the same weird scan image the ultra-terrestrial known as Otto had returned.

"I have little time or desire for discussion with you. I want to know where Betsy is. What have you done with her?"

"Done with her? Done with her?" Liz repeated. "Why we killed the bitch. That's what we 'done' with her." Jon sensed she was about to go to her alien form. Sure enough as she stood there in front of Jon she came out of her human suit and stepped toward Jon with the same snarl Otto had used. Then Jon heard the same guttural noise that preceded Otto's spit of that awful burning green stuff that almost did Jon and David in. As her mouth opened and the green stuff came out of her, Jon was ready. He slapped an electromagnetic shield in front of her that caught the glob. It dropped to the floor where it was beginning to burn through the carpet and then the concrete floor below. Suddenly Jon put his right hand out and a white substance came out of his hand coating it completely. Jon then reached down and collected the glob which he then held in his protected hand as he approached Liz. "One more time where is Betsy?"

"I tell you nothing." The ultra-terrestrial spit out at Jon. With that Jon grabbed the beast's throat and forced its mouth open. He pushed the glob down inside of her. The glob had come out of her mouth but after hitting the air it had transformed into a substance not intended to be consumed again. She screamed and shook as the glob began to eat through her skin. Finally she sank to the floor, dead.

Jon grabbed the alien and dragged it to the door. He opened it. Some were trying to open the main front door he had fused shut. Some were trying to break the bars on the windows in an effort to escape. Jon dragged the beast into the room outside the office and let it drop down to the floor. As agents looked aghast at what they were seeing, Jon spoke. "This is what you have been following, an alien trying to get you to find an alien."

Jon gave it a few minutes for it all to sink in.

The people in the room stopped their furtive efforts to get out. They all just stood around and stared, stunned at what they were seeing. They could hear security people outside the steel entrance door trying to gain entrance and shouting for people to respond. No one in the room spoke.

"I want to know what happened to Betsy Collingwood."

No one moved. No one spoke. With deliberate intention, Jon released lightening like waves of electricity. They came out of his mouth; out of the ends of his hands. For an outside spectator, it would have been a light show extravaganza. There were waves of blues from light to dark. They were combined with and mixed with waves of white light. Truly it appeared as if a lightning storm was happening within their office area. This office of agents stood or sat in fear. They could feel the electricity running through them. They didn't know it was all for show and actually harmless. "If you want to survive this," said Jon, "If you want to see your families again, you will tell me. What happened to Betsy Collingwood?"

Suddenly an agent stepped forward. "I knew there was something wrong with that agent, that Liz. She ran this entire department. When the woman you are looking for came in, it was she who took her into the office you just came out of to interrogate her. None of us really know what happened except Jack Cresto. We had the awareness she had been hurt badly and most of us thought she had died. Only Jack knew for sure because he took care of it."

Pulling the electrical pulses back into him, Jon approached the agent who had stepped forward. In a calm voice, Jon asked "Where is this Jack Cresto?"

The young lady at the front who Jon had encountered when he first came in spoke up next. "Mr. Cresto, uh he is"… then she looked around at the agents for fear she would be getting into trouble by telling. The first agent who spoke up told her it was okay. "Well," she continued, "Mr. Cresto is on leave. Ah I have his address."

Jon slowly walked back to the front where the girl sat. She gave him a cardex address card from her rolodex. Jon turned. He faced the agents. "Feel free to say whatever you want. However, I warn you not to contact this Mr. Cresto and forewarn him of my coming. If you do you will put yourselves and your families in jeopardy."

With that said, Jon distorted his face again back to what he looked like as Juan. He reached down and removed the weld he had put on the door. The security agents rushed in.

Mike was the first one in. "Please"; Jon said as Mike rushed by him There is a monster on the floor. "What the…" Mike exclaimed as he spotted the ultra-terrestrial, "what the hell is that?" The second security guard Mac rushed in looking over Mike's shoulder at the unbelievable sight of this green monster looking thing lying on the floor at the other end of the offices.

Jon rushed by them and was quickly out the door and off to find Jack Cresto.

Jack Cresto was a fairly big man. Trained in all the martial arts and a weapons expert, he had joined the NSA group feeling confident he could contribute to the protection of his country. The pay and the retirement weren't anything to sneeze at either. He had made a nice home for his family and children in one of the nicer suburbs of Charlotte. It was after his assignment to the ATFa he began to wonder if he had made the right choice. He was second in command but his superior Liz was demanding and often rude, crude and disrespectful to him and the other agents. He really didn't believe in the "alien" thing but he went along with it. Then the "Otto" character came into the picture. He was thinking about getting a transfer when this "alien" rumor started.

After Liz had manhandled the girl Betsy Collingwood, he became sick to his stomach. It was unspeakable what he did to her. She had taken her life and for what? He intended to use a few days off to make some contacts and actively seek another position even if he had to lose his present grade.

When Jon knocked on the Cresto front door, Jack's wife Mary answered it. "Yes, she said may I help you?" Jon had changed his features again and introduced himself as Roy Cochran.

"My wife and I have been looking at one of the houses for sale in the neighborhood and I hope you will excuse this presumption but I wanted to meet some of the neighbors." "Oh," Mary replied, "Why, certainly. I am Mary Cresto and my husband Jack and I and our three children live here. We love the neighborhood. It is very friendly and the school system here is great. Do you and your wife have any children?"

"No not yet. But we have plans. Would your husband be in by any chance?"

"Yes. Please come in. He is down in his work shop. Feel free to sit here in the den and I will fetch him."

As Jon sat and took in the décor, he noticed the pictures of Cresto in his Marine uniform dressed out as a Major. Along the fireplace mantle were pictures of the family at various outings as well as the children in sporting and craft events. It was a warm comfortable home not at all as Jon would have envisioned a home for the kind of animals that were ATFa agents.

Jack Cresto came into the room. He was a big man. Dressed in khakis and a plaid shirt, he looked like the picture of the all American guy.

"Mr. Cochran? Hi I am Jack Cresto." He smiled and reached to shake Jon's hand. Jon stood up and took the man's hand. Neither Jack nor his wife noticed a faint blue light exchanged between the two men.

Mary noticed they seemed to be shaking hands longer than one might expect. "Ah, could I get you some coffee Mr. Cochran?" She looked at her husband as they kept shaking hands. "Yes," Jon replied. "That would be delightful." Mary looked at her husband. "Jack you look like you are in a trance or something." She laughed hoping it would snap Jack out of his strange appearance. "No," Jack responded with a flat voice. "Everything is fine, please just get us some coffee." She gave her husband a strange look and left the room.

Now somewhat under Jon's control, he directed Jack to sit on the couch. Jack did so. Jon sat in a recliner. "Jack as you are now becoming aware, I am the individual you and the ATFa group have been pursuing. When I leave, you will call your office and they will tell you I was there.

They will also tell you I had an encounter with Liz who, as it turns out, is an ultra-terrestrial. She is dead."

Jack sat quietly and listened intently to Jon. He felt a panic but somehow was immobilized and unable to respond and fight or flee the usual alternatives to great fear. "Jack the reason I am here is to find out what happened to Betsy Collingwood. Please tell me what I want to know. It is not my intent to hurt you or your family... unless I am forced to."

Mary came in with the coffee and put a tray with cream, sugar and some cookies down on the coffee table in front of the couch. As she put the tray down she turned sideways so Jon couldn't see her and gave her husband a look like "what is going on?"

She stood up getting no response from her husband. "Jack are you okay?"

Jack looked up at her with a blank look. "Honey I am fine. Mr. Cochran and I are going to chat for a while." Still looking confused, Mary left the two men alone, although before she left, she gave her husband another of those "what is going on" looks.

Jack proceeded to share with Jon how Betsy came into the ATFa offices, how she was treated by Liz and how he was instructed to get rid of her, after Liz had apparently fatally wounded her. Jon winced with pain and anger as he heard what Betsy had been subjected to.

"Jon, I called EMS and they came and I believe took her to Carolinas Specialty Hospital. It is located on Vail Ave. here in Charlotte. I didn't think there was much if any hope for her. I am sorry. After that I am not aware of what happened. I assumed she passed"

Without commenting, Jon got up and left the home.

As Jon drove into the hospital parking area on 2001 Vail Avenue, he felt despondent. "At least I can let Max and Betsy's daughter know where she is buried," he thought.

Once inside, he found it difficult to get any information because of the HIPPA confidentiality laws. As he leaned over to talk to one of the receptionists, Jon was able to touch one of the computers on which she was entering data. He maintained a warm conversation with her as his powers searched the data base for a Betsy Collingwood. There was no data relating to Betsy. "How do you catalog people when they come in?" Jon asked casually. "Well," she said enjoying this encounter with such a handsome fellow. "By birth date and name of course." "Yes, of course," Jon said with a look of dejection. As he turned the receptionist who was taking a liking to Jon and looking for an excuse to keep him talking to her commented, "Of course if they come in without a name they would be entered in as a John Doe or a Jane Doe as the case may be."

Suddenly Jon's interest was piqued. He turned back toward her and smiled. "Yes, of course. Do you have many that come in like that?"

Well, not so many anymore. Let's see over the last month we actually only got two John Does' and uh one Jane Doe."

"Wow, you are good," Jon said giving the girl a warm encouraging smile. Again he found himself draped over her counter and touching her computer. "Honey," she gave Jon her best smile "I am good. You just ought to let me show you."

Now having some additional follow up information, Jon said he would certainly do that, took her number and said good-bye.

The hospital data base had showed an incoming Jane Doe within the right period who was treated and then sent to a nursing home in Advance, North Carolina. Jon got the address of the nursing home. As Jon left the hospital, he noticed a police cruiser parked behind the motorcycle. The officer had a pad he was writing something down on and was on the radio.

Jon walked by the cruiser and he could hear the officer say he had located the motorcycle reported as stolen.

Jon walked down the street and into a used car lot. Once he had the salesman in front of him Jon used his powers to get himself the use of a car to try it out. It was an older car but it would do.

Now Jon proceeded up I-77 toward Winston Salem. Soon he was on I-40 and headed toward Advance. At the Advance turn off onto 801, Jon proceeded straight until he got to the Bermuda Run Nursing Home and Rehabilitation Center.

Jon had not said many prayers since he returned. Now as he parked, he turned off the ignition, bowed his head and prayed. It was a warm pleasant day. It was a day for good things to happen. Jon was prepared for the worst.

He left the car and entered the facility. The entrance was a long corridor that led to a set of doors. Behind the doors was a nursing station. "May I help you?" a lady from behind the station asked.

"Yes, within the last week or so there was a Jane Doe brought here from Carolinas Specialty Hospital, I am thinking she may be a relative. Can you help me?"

"No I am sorry, I would but I am not authorized to give out that information because of confidentiality laws. However, the DON, uh excuse me the Director of Nursing might be able to help. If you will keep walking down to the next nurses' station, I believe she is there today."

"Thanks," Jon replied and proceeded down the hall as he was instructed.

After talking to the DON, Jon was told that there was a Jane Doe who arrived and subsequently passed away but that without more specific information she could not help him. Before Jon could reach out and shake her hand to transfer information he might be able to use, a woman to his left started to scream. "Oh Carol," stop that," the DON said sharply and then she quickly turned away to give her attention to another of the residents who was making a disturbance.

As Jon walked back down the hall toward the entrance trying to decide upon his next move, he couldn't help but wonder how he would break such news of Betsy's demise to Max. Even though Max had a pretty good idea he had lost Betsy, this news would remove any hope.

A young girl hurried up next to him. Just as she was passing, she said, "I am going out for a break. I will be right out front. See me." With that she hurriedly walked on in front of Jon.

As he went out the door, he could see the young girl sitting on the side on a bench about to light up a cigarette. He walked up to her. She sat there nervously looking to the right, then to the left. "I am only a CNA and I could get fired for what I am about to say." She paused briefly. "We still have a Jane Doe who came in last week. I doubt she will last too long." She paused. "At least that's what the Doc said. Anyway, she is such a pitiful soul, no visitors and young too." She looked up at Jon, "probably about your age. In any case, if there is any chance you might know her she could sure use the company. She can't talk. She just lies there staring without seeing it seems. My heart just broke when I saw her." Repeating herself, she said, "She could sure use some company, although maybe she wouldn't know." Again she glanced over at the front door as if she was afraid someone might see her. Suddenly she said, "Oh shit."

Jon looked back to see another nurse or CNA, he wasn't sure, approaching them "Hey, Clara," the approaching girl called out. "Trying to take a break without me?" She laughed

"Room 102 on the hall you were on" Clara quietly said to Jon as she stood up quickly and moved over to her friend.

Jon walked back to the car. After waiting a few minutes so that he couldn't be connected with the helpful CNA, Jon proceeded to re-enter the nursing home. He nodded to the lady at the first nursing station and proceeded down the hall to find room 102. Suddenly he saw it. His heart was pounding. Hoping beyond hope, Jon swung the door open. The room was dark. There were two beds. The first one closest to the door had an older lady who smiled at Jon when he came in. "Hello," she said. "Did you come in to see me? Are you the doctor? Can you please have my brother call me?"

Jon smiled at her and put his finger to his lips asking her to be quiet. There was a drape, a curtain between the two beds in the room. Moving the curtain aside, Jon leaped with joy.

There lay Betsy.

"Oh, Betsy, my dearest Betsy, what pray have I let happen to you?" Betsy lay still. Tubes came out of her arms. Her eyes were wide open. She was sickly pale looking. Her hair was matted and her bed was wet. Jon turned and made sure the door was closed. He fused the lock. As he turned back to Betsy, the first lady smiled "Are we going to do something secret?" Jon smiled back again raising his finger to his lips indicating we need to be quiet. "Oh good," the old lady said, "we are going to have a secret."

Jon came to Betsy's bed. Slowly he lay down beside her. He put his arms around her, his legs over hers, and nestled his head into her neck. Slowly at first waves of blue and white poured out from Jon and into and around Betsy.

Jon breathed himself into Betsy. He cried over her, begging her to come back to him. He asked for her forgiveness for what he had put her through. The colors were vivid now. The room was dancing in a beautiful array of electrical pulses in a variety of colors.

Outside the room, someone was trying to gain entrance. "Would someone call maintenance, this door is stuck again."

The old lady in the room with Betsy but on the other side of the curtain was delighted. She reached for the waves of color and they came to her. "Oh you are so beautiful," she said. "Oh you feel so good. Victor if only you could be here." This dehabilitative old woman was squirming around like a youngster.

Suddenly Betsy's color started to return. Jon kept talking to her and the streams of color energy waves streamed around the whole room. Her eyes began to flutter. They become clear. Suddenly she said, "Oh, Jon, where have you been. I have been waiting for you."

Her arms went around Jon and her lips went to his.

The little old lady was singing "Happy days are here again, the skies above are clear again. So let's sing a song of cheer again, happy times happy nights, happy days are here again."

Outside the room someone said, "Hey, Lucy is in here and she is singing Happy Days." The DON showed up and asked the maintenance worker what was going on. "Ma'am, I don't know. The door is stuck or something." The DON pushed the maintenance worker away and put all her weight behind the door. "What the...," she uttered. Suddenly she could her Lucy singing. "My god, this old woman is singing to beat all." All the CNAs' and nurses were gathered around the door.

"George," she shouted at the maintenance worker, you have to get this damn door open. I don't care how you do it, take it off at the hinges, break it down but I want access to the people in there."

George took out a hammer and a chisel. He began to take the door down, when someone opened the door from the other side.

Out came Lucy bright eyed and Bushy tail full of vim and vigor. "Whatcha doin boy?" She said to the maintenance man in her sweetest Southern drawl. Now looking stern she said to the crowd who had gathered at her door "Get outa my way people. I'm hungry and I'm gonna to get something to eat." With that she plowed her way through the absolutely astounded crowd of nursing home staff. Everyone was speech less.

"My god, Lucy can't walk," came an astounded voice from the group. "Lord Jesus it's a miracle," said another. "Look at her go."

Then Lucy stopped. She turned around. She looked at the group standing there with their mouths all open. Lucy shouted at the DON, "Hey, you!" The DON meekly pointed at herself as if to say you mean me. "Ya, you missy, think you're so special you treat everyone like a piece of shit. Call my brother. Tell him to get himself over here. I am headed home, after I get something to eat."

After getting over seeing Lucy, the old lady who was suffering from dementia and was bed ridden, unable to walk hopping down the hallway like a teenager, the DON quickly went into the room. She pushed the curtain aside to see an empty bed where Jane Doe ought to be. Then looking around the room she noticed the window was open. "Oh my god, oh my god" she went screaming down the hallway.

As Jon pulled out of the nursing home with Betsy in her night gown, nestled over next to him, he put his arm around her. All the way up Rt. 801 toward 158 they basked in each other's glow. As they came to the intersection of 801 and 158, Jon looked over at her. "Are you hungry?" "Famished" was her reply.

Back at the nursing home, the DON was in a panic making telephone calls. Clara was walking up the hall just a smiling and singing. "Don'tcha just love a miracle?"

Jon pulled into the drive thru of the McDonalds on the corner of I-158 and 801. "What would you like?"

"Everything," she said with a giggle and that smile Jon loved so much.

After gathering their food, Jon took them to the nearest motel. After getting a room, Jon parked opposite their door. He carried Betsy into the room. Then he went and got the food. Betsy had laid out a towel for their feast. As soon as Jon put it down, Betsy spread it all out. She reached out for Jon's hand and asked him to say a prayer.

For the next 4 hours well into the night Jon shared with Betsy all that had happened. Betsy couldn't remember anything after the last night they had spent together at the motel when a government agent had insisted she go with him. She listened with rapt attention as Jon shared with her all that had happened.

The next morning Betsy spent hours on the phone talking with her Dad and her daughter. While she was making contacts with family, Jon had gone to the nearest K Mart and had gotten Betsy some basic things she needed and a change of clothes. After coming back to the motel, Jon and Betsy made love; they checked out and then found a restaurant to get some breakfast. Betsy delighted in sharing with Jon how excited her Dad was. He had started a garden and hadn't felt that good since he was a young man.

"Well, Jon," Betsy said looking up from a bite of eggs and toast," I feel we are still on our trip out in the world looking for the "Good People."

Jon sat back and looked at this beautiful woman who had become his life. "Yes, sweetheart," and I am looking at one of the best right now."

Betsy took Jon's hand and smiled warmly. "Back atcha," she purred. Then after a minute or so, Betsy put down her coffee and looked seriously at Jon. "Jon do you think there is any chance you will get to see David again?" Then she added, "Or for that matter, go back to his world?"

Jon looked down at his coffee. "Sweetheart, the only thing I am sure of is how blessed I am to have you back in my arms and that I want to get married as soon as we can arrange it with Max."

Betsy reached over and grabbed Jon's hand. "We are both blessed to have each other Jon." Her smile was radiant. The waitress was suddenly there filling up their coffee. "Did ya'all just get married? I don't mean to be personal but you all look so sweet and into each other like newly married folks?"

Betsy looked up at the waitress. With a smile she said, "We are not married yet, just engaged."

"Oh well you all ought to be, you look perfect together."

"Thank you" replied Betsy and then she looked at Jon lovingly as the waitress moved to another table. "I guess we should leave a big tip huh?" Jon said. They both laughed.

Suddenly Betsy turned serious. "Jon, what must we do before we can go back home and resume our life together?"

Finally after a few minutes Jon spoke. "Well, we need to go up and see Slavak and make sure he is okay. Then we need to make another visit with the president."

"The president?" Betsy asked.

"Yes. I am afraid he has forgotten the meeting we had. It is important to our world we do everything we can to tone down the obsessive greed and power that permeates the world before it is too late."

"What about Mikki and Nicholas?"

"They are both back to their respective jobs. But we are able to maintain contact. They have a role to play. It is just a matter of timing."

"But the world is more than the U.S. Jon, how can you affect it all?"

"I am not sure. But the U.S. is a start. We will just have to wait until we know what to do next."

"Sweetheart, how will you know that?"

"It is strange Betsy. I am not sure how it works. But I can actually communicate with Mikki and Nicholas when I need to as well as receive and transmit messages to David's world. I know that sounds weird."

"I don't care how strange it is or how weird it gets, so long as we are together." Betsy reached across and again held Jon's hand.

After leaving the restaurant, Jon called the used auto place where he had gotten the car. He told them he was going to buy it and gave them the credit card information they needed to get the car paid for.

Then they went shopping for clothes, bought a mobile phone and Betsy called her Dad to let him know how to contact them. When she got off the phone, she turned to Jon.

"Jon," Dad says he was contacted by the Slavak sons. Their Dad has had a heart attack and is presently in intensive care. They did a bypass but the Doctor's feel he has little time left maybe weeks. In addition, the Whitehouse has refused to take their calls so they don't know what is going on there.

After talking it over Jon and Betsy agree to drive to Washington about 6 hours away.

CHAPTER 11

SNATCHED FROM THE GRAVE

Coming through Arlington Virginia, Jon took I-66. Crossing over the Roosevelt Bridge, the road became Constitution Avenue. Betsy turned from looking at the sights as they rode along. She looked straight ahead as she asked Jon, "What can you do for Mr. Slavak?" Jon looked briefly at Betsy. Thinking back on his first encounter with David's healing powers when they were used to save Lance, to repairing Peter and then his dramatic healing of Betsy, Jon smiled. Jon had shared with Betsy the details of his trip to David's world. He also shared how he had been told David is still within him but is in what they described as a comatose condition.

Suddenly, Betsy, realizing how ridiculous her question sounded, looked at Jon and blushed. "I mean... that is"— she paused—"I don't mean can you heal him. Of course you can. But beyond that is there a way Mr. Slavak can assist us in doing what has been asked to justify leaving Earth spared from some outside cataclysmic event?"

Passing the Washington Monument and the Whitehouse, Jon turned and looked at the president's house. "Slavak is a way to get into and maintain contact with the president." He paused. "Assuming that his son's comment about not being able to reach the Whitehouse does not mean Slavak has lost his influence in that area, Slavak is our way into this influential area."

"What will we do, if the Whitehouse distances itself from Slavak?"

Turning left onto Seventh Street, Jon continued down passing over Massachusetts, New Your, Rhode Island and Florida avenues. "Well, then," responded Jon, "we will have to make an impression they cannot deny."

Looking up at a passing street sign, Betsy could see the road changed its name to Georgia Avenue. Jon looked over at Betsy to see if he could read her body language.

Betsy turned to look at Jon as she felt him looking at her. Jon returned to paying attention to the road ahead.

Betsy bowed her head. "I know this sounds selfish." She paused as Jon looked again at her briefly and then turned back to the road. "But Jon, will there ever get to be a time for us. I mean… and I feel selfish for asking this… but will we ever be able to just get away… just the two of us… and not have to worry about… saving the world?"

Betsy could see the signs leading to the hospital. Jon turned right onto Irving Street and reached for Betsy's hand. He squeezed it lovingly and said, "Yes, sweetheart, there will be." It was a promise Jon did not know if he could keep. But it was a promise he knew Betsy needed to hear. Betsy squeezed his hand in return and they looked at each other lovingly.

Bearing to the left on Irving Street, the National Rehabilitation Hospital was on their right. They turned right at the entrance to the Washington Hospital Center Campus. Then they followed the signs to the Washington Hospital Center Parking Pavilion. It was Friday just past 4:15 p.m.

As they entered the hospital waiting area, Robert Slavak was there to greet them. Jon made the introductions between him and Betsy. Then Robert turned to Jon. "Thank you so much for coming. You have no idea how much it means to the family. Unfortunately Dad has not made it through surgery as well as they hoped and he is in an intensive care unit. I am going to pass you off as his brother so we can get you in to see him." Robert looked awkwardly at Betsy.

"Jon I am going to be right over there," Betsy said pointing at a corner of the waiting room, "okay?" With that she smiled at Robert and grabbed his hand. "Your Dad is going to be fine." Robert smiled weakly and said, "Thank you." Betsy smiled at Jon and then turned and went to find a seat.

"She is a gem, Jon." They watched Betsy as she walked away. "Yup she's a keeper," Jon said softly. Then he looked at Robert and said, "Let's go."

Getting off the elevator at the ICU, Robert rushed ahead to alert the head nurse, that his Dad's brother was here to see his Dad. The nurse nodded okay and looking up and seeing Jon looked at him in a puzzling manner as he walked by. "Hmm" she thought to herself as she looked back down at the paperwork she was dealing with, "there is no family resemblance at all."

As Jon walked into the hospital room, he was greeted by Arthur. In a soft voice Arthur thanked Jon for coming.

"Of course," Jon said as he moved over to the side of the bed where his friend lay. Sitting down by him, Jon looked over at his friend. "Well, brother, it seems we have been here before." The Slavak brothers looked at each other with a puzzled look. Jon could see Slavak had bandages around his right hand. He was on monitoring equipment. His eyes were closed and he was as pale as a ghost.

Arthur stepped closer to the bed, looking at his father he spoke to Jon. "The doctors said they fixed his valve which is the main problem but that the tissue is very weak as a result of trauma he has faced in his past. The thugs that took Dad and pulled nails out of his fingers acerbated his heart condition and the doctors consider it a miracle he is still alive because of the condition of his heart valve and arteries. Their prognosis is that he has maybe a week to a month to survive." Arthur put his hand on his Dad's chest lightly and with a tear rolling down his cheek said softly, "or less."

"Hmm" responded Jon as he began to unravel the bandages around Slavak's damaged hand. Once he had the bandages off, he grasped Slavak's hand with his left hand and put his right hand on Slavak's chest just over his heart.

As he bowed his head, he said, "A miracle he is still alive? Let's show them a real miracle."

Suddenly a nurse walked in. "Oh my god, what have you boys done," she muttered as she picked up the bandages Jon had taken off. "What are you doing?" She now yelled at Jon seeing him with his hands on the unconscious patient.

"Arthur," Jon spoke sharply, "Escort the nurse out please."

With that and under a loud protest by the nurse, Arthur and Robert forced the nurse to leave the room. Then they stood at the door to prevent anyone else from coming in.

Jon's hands began to pulse. The room was filled with energy waves of blue and white. They surged in and out and around Slavak.

Within minutes the area was filled with several doctors along with hospital security personnel who forced the door open.

"Excuse me," said the older of the two doctors entering the room. "We must ask everyone to leave. And someone shut off these lights. What the hell do you people think you are doing?" With that the two security personnel stood beside the door waiting to exit people out. The other doctor rushed over to Slavak's side. Noticing the medicine drip no longer connected to Slavak the doctor barked orders at one of the two nurses who had accompanied the doctors to get Mr. Slavak hooked back up immediately. One of the two nurses was looking for a light switch to turn of the waves of lights flowing through the room. The lights ceased and Jon stood up.

"Doctor," Jon said addressing the older doctor. "I must insist you leave the room immediately."

"Look here," the doctor began to protest angrily, until he noticed a weapon in Jon's hand.

"Okay… okay… everyone out." The doctor yelled out as he backed out of the room. The security personnel and the nurses looked confused. "Dammit," the older doctor again spoke, "everyone out of the room now."

They all left except for the Slavak brothers and Jon. Jon fused the door just as he had done at the nursing home. Jon went back to the position he was in with Slavak and the pulsating lights began again.

In the meantime, the doctor had called for police help and they were on the way.

In the meantime, Arthur softly asked Jon, "Is Dad going to be okay?" "Yes" came Jon's terse reply.

Within fifteen minutes, Jon stood up. He walked over to the back wall and sat down. The brothers looked at each other as if it was all over and their dad could not be helped. Suddenly, Slavak sat up. "Would one of you boys get me some water?"

There was a pounding on the door. Someone announced they were the police and to open the door immediately. Robert looked at Jon. Jon caused a beam to leave his hand and unfuse the door. Jon then nodded his head at Robert indicating it was okay for him to open it. Robert stepped to the door, opened it and found himself facing 4 uniformed Washington's finest. A doctor in the back pointed to Jon as the one who had the weapon.

"Stand up, sir," said the highest-ranking officer to Jon. "Turn and face the wall and don't make any sudden moves." Jon did as he was directed. Jon was searched thoroughly but no weapon was found. "Who are you?" The officer directed the question at the Slavak brothers. Each one gave their name and pointed out they were the patient's sons.

"Please tell me what the hell is going on. I wake up and ask for a glass of water and I have to put up with this? Why have you busted in here? I am a sick man on his death bed. Boys," he said now directing his words to his sons, "If I die because of complications due to the trauma created here, I want you to sue the Washington Police and this hospital," and then raising his voice and turning toward the doctors at the doorway, "and these damn doctors personally."

The senior ranking police officer looked at the doctor in a menacing fashion. Then he turned to the patient and said, "Please forgive us, sir, we were led to believe there was a problem and obviously there isn't."

The senior police officer looked over at the one who had patted Jon down and who was waiting for Jon to show some identification. "Come on Philipps."

"Ah Lt. I was just going to check this man's ID." Sternly the Lt. said, "Forget it. Let's get out of here."

With that said everyone left. Arthur went over and closed the door. Outside they could hear quite a commotion as the Lt. was laying in to the doctor's about the penalties for false arrest. Finally it was quiet. Robert had brought some water to his dad who was sipping it and looking at Jon. Slavak looked down at his hand which looked as good as new. He smiled, put the water over on the table and folded his hands over the sheet covering his stomach.

"It's good to see you Jon… again. We need to stop meeting like this? How many times do you have to save a guy's life?"

Slavak and Jon smiled and the brothers started to laugh. "As many as it takes," Jon said as he moved over to the bed and clasped Slavak's hand.

Peter Slavak told the attending physician he was ready to check out. Despite the physician demanding Slavak stay for some tests to confirm his condition, Slavak remained determined. "Look, if I am going to die, I want to die in a familiar surrounding with my family around me. Does that sound so illogical?"

Finally, seeing how determined Mr. Slavak was, the doctor had no choice but to sign him out.

As Slavak was accompanied by a nurse pushing his wheel chair, he made his way to his son's car. It was agreed Jon and Betsy would follow and they would all go to Slavak's place in Spring Valley, Washington, DC.

As Jon and Betsy followed the Slavak's Limousine down Massachusetts Ave NW, Betsy couldn't help but comment on the changing scenery as they drove into one of Washington's most elegant districts. "Wow, Jon. Just look at the size of these houses. It sure is a stark contrast to Appalachia."

"Yes, sweetheart it is. There is a growing disparity in this country between the haves and the haves not. The middle class is getting smaller and the rich are getting richer. It all just gives witness that we have lost sight of the most important priorities of life."

"Amid this entire quest for fame and fortune by the few at the expense of the many do you really think we have much hope in making the kind of change which will satisfy David's world?"

Jon was pondering the question as they followed the limousine into the property at 5122 Twenty-Second St.

Betsy couldn't believe the opulence. "Wow," she uttered as the cars rounded the circular paved drive around the large fountain and flowers everywhere. The guards and the weapons they carried at the front entrance also did not go unnoticed.

As they parked in front of the detached three story brick veneer home, Betsy could not help but be awed by the style and the elegance. It seemed they must be hundreds of miles away from the bustle of Washington, DC, instead of just minutes away in a cozy suburb.

A maid and a butler emerged from the front entrance and began taking bags into the home. Peter walked up to Jon and Betsy as Robert and Arthur followed the maid into the house. "Well, my friends, I hope you will be comfortable here during your stay. We have five bedrooms and five baths not including the servant's quarters. We enjoy a pool and hot tub by the patio. While you are here this is your home. The length of time you stay is up to you. When you leave, you may return whenever you wish. This is your home in Washington, DC."

"You are too gracious Peter. I doubt we will be here very long. We do need to have a discussion of how we should proceed with the president but we have much to do."

"Oh yes, oh yes, lots to do." Peter looked around the driveway and then back at Jon and Betsy. "Betsy," Peter said and then he looked sternly at Jon and then back at Betsy, "Has this great wonderful guy proposed to you yet?" He paused as Betsy blushed and Jon started to interrupt.

"Hey, Peter that isn't…" Peter interrupted. "Isn't what? Any of my business? You are wrong. You are family Jon. Family looks out for each other. You have looked out for me. Now I know you two are in love. I just want to know if you intend to make an honest woman out of this beautiful woman."

Jon swung his head back and forth nervously, as Betsy laughed and Peter stood there waiting for an answer. "Well, of course… ah we… Yes, we plan to be married." Now Jon was blushing and Betsy grabbed his arm and smiled at Peter.

"Good, then you won't mind if we have the ceremony here in one week. Next Friday is a splendid day one week from now. Don't you agree?"

Jon looked like he had been run over by a truck and Betsy also looked quite surprised. Then she looked up at Jon as he looked down at her. They certainly had planned to get married. They just hadn't put it into many words… until now.

"Jon?" Betsy inquired. Suddenly Jon broke into a wide smile. He put his arms around Betsy. "Wow Peter. Yes, we will be honored for you to do that for us." Betsy jumped up into Jon's arms planting a deep kiss.

"Well," Peter returned, "The honor is all mine. What is family for anyway?" he said as he turned and left Jon and Betsy embraced. Then as Peter walked away talking to himself. "What is family all about if they can't do for each other?"

Suddenly Betsy pulled away from Jon. "Darling we have to get Max and Julie here. How can we do that?"

"Sweetheart," Jon replied with a big smile on his face, "I don't know. But knowing Peter I am sure…"

Suddenly Peter stuck his head out from the door. "Oh, I forgot to tell you Betsy. Max and Julie are planning to be here at the end of the week for the ceremony." Then he disappeared into the house.

"What," Betsy exclaimed. With a gigantic smile on her face, she hung onto Jon's arm as they both entered the 5, 429 sq. ft. home.

At the door they were met by the butler. He introduced himself as Alfonso. "I and Marie the maid are at your service. Mr. Slavak has asked me to give you a tour of the home prior to taking you to your room if that would be satisfactory?"

Betsy was still holding onto Jon's arm like she might wake up if she let go. She looked up at Jon and then said. "Thank you Alfonso that would be wonderful."

Alfonso then turned and began to point out points of interest in the home. "This is of course the foyer with a classic chandelier and the stairs done in a modern style." Betsy looked at the beautiful white walls and polished hardwood flooring which gave balance to the mahogany staircase with white ballasts. The home was nicely appointed. A settee in the foyer added a nice touch. Then as Alfonso led them they turned into a huge sitting room with light blue and beige furniture giving accent to the light peach colored walls and the beautiful pink and gray carpet providing partial covering for the hard wood floor. A fire place gave warmth to the room.

Then they went back through the foyer into a small hallway leading to a well out fitted open spaced kitchen with gray marbled counters accenting the creamy white walls and ceiling. Just off the kitchen on one side was a spacious Victorian styled dining room done in a lavish pastel blue in the middle of which was a mahogany dining table that must have been at least twenty feet long. From there they were taken on a tour of the family room, the recreation room, the den, the library and the study. Last but not least was a beautiful triple deck back patio with gazebos, a hot tub, an Olympic sized pool, a sports court and anchoring one side of the back yard a four car garage.

Alfonso left them in the bedroom they were to occupy, but not until he informed them that Mr. Slavak was having their walk-in closet filled with the clothes they might need during their stay.

Betsy sat down on the oversized king bed. "My god, Jon, I am simply overwhelmed."

"Yes, I agree. There is, however, one thing that puzzles me greatly."

"What is that sweetheart?"

"How am I going to find you at night in this universe of a bed?"

Betsy started to laugh as Jon pulled her over and nuzzled her neck. Suddenly she pulled away. "Excuse me sir," she said dramatically, looking at him with a cute but demure grin. "If we are going to anoint our new quarters let's do it privately." With that she jumped from the bed, closed and locked the door and turned and jumped into Jon's waiting arms.

- - -

It was 9:00 a.m. Saturday, when someone knocked on their bedroom door. Jon turned over and looked at Betsy. Her head seemed to be a part of the satin pillow. He couldn't help but wonder as he looked at her, how he could ever be so blessed. "Thank you God thru Christ Jesus," he muttered. Then as an afterthought, he said, "Thank you also David."

Jumping up off the bed, Jon quickly slid into a pair of slacks he had put at the foot of the bed. Suddenly there was a knock.

Opening the door, Jon faced Alfonso who was standing by a small table on rollers. On the table on top of the white table cloth were two plates with eggs, bacon, and sausage, homemade hash browns, sliced tomatoes. A plate with buttered whole grain toast and accompanied by three different jams occupied a third plate. Then there were two cups of coffee, two glasses of juice, the local Washington paper and a note from Peter. The note read: "No hurry. Enjoy. See you down stairs when you are ready —Peter." Topping it off were two beautiful multi colored carnations, Betsy's favorite flower.

Jon thanked Alfonso and wheeled the table into the bedroom. Picking up the coffee and flavoring it with the cream and artificial sweetener provided, Jon sat down on Betsy's side and held the coffee such that the aromas wafted over her pillow. She turned with a sound almost like a kitten just awakened. As her eyes opened, she glanced at Jon and then the coffee. "Oh Jon, how thoughtful."

Jon smiled at her. "Not I this morning sweetheart. Alfonso has delivered a treat."

Hoisting herself up on one elbow, she looked over at the table. "Oh my word. Doesn't that look beautiful?"

Jon handed her the note. She read it and giggled as she slid out from between the sheets. Her slim beautiful legs took Jon's breath away. She laughed and slapped Jon playfully on the arm. "I am famished. This looks wonderful."

After they had both finished eating, Jon flopped back down on the bed. "That was wonderful."

"Yes, my darling it was. And I believe last night was even more wonderful," Betsy replied as she pushed the table away and curled up next to Jon. He held her in his arms, and they both melted into each other.

＊ ＊ ＊

It was 11:00 a.m. when Jon finally came down stairs. Alfonso came to greet him. "I hope you rested well, sir," Alfonso said. Jon unconsciously used his senses to determine Alfonso's state of mind which was only on the business of making sure Peter's guests were properly treated. "Thank you Alfonso, we did. It was a lovely room and we so enjoyed the breakfast. It has been some time since we have been able to rest like this. Please extend our thanks also to Marie."

"Excellent, sir. Mr. Slavak is out on the back lawn, if you would care to join him." "Yes. Thank you Alfonso." Jon watched as Alfonso turned and walked away. The sixty-two-year-old man was certainly of German heritage thought Jon. "He seems like a man with an interesting past; someone I would like to know more about," Jon watched as Alfonso turned the corner and disappeared. Jon turned and made his way out onto the back lawn where he found Peter sitting at a lawn table alone, reading a book and enjoying a drink of orange juice and cranberry juice.

As Jon walked up behind him, Peter greeted him. Without turning his head in Jon's direction, he looked up from his book, looked straight ahead and said, "Good morning my friend."

"Good morning Peter. May I join you?"

"Of course you can. Please sit down."

Jon and Peter discussed how good it was to be back in a somewhat normalcy compared to the way things were. Suddenly they were joined by Betsy.

After being greeted by Peter, Betsy shared how lovely the house was and how much they were enjoying their stay. "Oh good, I hope so," replied Peter to which Betsy and Jon looked at each other as if to say "what did that mean?"

Suddenly after a bit of chit chat, Peter turned to Betsy. "My dear friend Betsy, the soon to be bride of my brother Jon, I must apologize."

"For what?" Betsy responded with laughter in her voice unable to think of anything for which Peter should apologize.

"You have been gracious enough to allow me to prepare the wedding for you and Jon." He paused looking at both of them trying to gage their reaction. "I hope I have not stepped beyond what is proper in this regard." Again he paused. Jon and Betsy looked at each other with their eyes wide open and a slight shaking of their heads as if to say, "Tell us already."

"Your daughter Julie and Max flew in last night after you had retired. I felt you all needed to discuss wedding things and go shopping and all that great stuff." Betsy's eyes and mouth showed the great surprise on her face. "What...?" Betsy stammered as she looked around frantically to see her loved ones. "Betsy," Peter said in a way to get her attention. "They are in the family room now talking with Lydia a special friend of mine who is a wedding consultant. They are waiting for you to start the discussions, the arranging and the shopping that needs to take place."

Suddenly Alfonso appeared on the back deck, waiting to escort Betsy.

Betsy swung both her arms around Peter's neck and planted a big kiss on his cheek. "Now, now," Peter sputtered, "it's just a little thing I am doing for my dear friends."

Betsy looked at Jon who was grinning from ear to ear. "Sorry dear, I didn't know anything about this."

Peter interrupted before she could say any more. "Jon and I have some matters to discuss, so if you will excuse us, we will stay here while you all prepare for the wedding." Then looking up behind Betsy, he said, "I think Alfonso is waiting for you." With that Betsy took off running up the lawn to the deck and then to follow Alfonso to meet with her Dad and Daughter. Just as she got to the deck she turned and stopped. She looked back and then ran back to Jon. She put her arms around him, gave him a loving kiss and then turned back to follow Alfonso.

Peter laughed. Then after some small chit chat about the wedding, Peter turned to a more serious subject.

"Jon, we have a serious meeting with the president's National Security Council next week. I am sorry it may interfere with an immediate honeymoon but I was sure you would agree this is of the utmost importance." Peter paused, waiting to hear Jon's comments but hearing none and not getting any reading from Jon's body language he continued. "The president was, needless to say, overly impressed with you and the message you brought to him. However, he feels he cannot implement your suggestions without the unanimous consent of the NSC. Paving the way to such a meeting, I have invited several of the members of the NSC as well as leading members of Congress to the party I have prepared to have this Wednesday. At this meeting you will be able to meet and perhaps better measure the kind of people we have to persuade." Peter stopped talking. He began to light the pipe that had been sitting on the table, looking intently at Jon while he lit it.

Finally, after a long sigh, Jon began to speak. "I am sure Betsy and I will enjoy whatever you have planned Peter. You have proven to be the most magnificent host." With that said Peter smiled in appreciation as he shook the match he had used to light his pipe, put it in an ashtray and silently nodded for Jon to continue.

"I do understand the president's dilemma. I will be pleased to meet with the council and will hopefully impress them with the need for changes. Can you share with me who of influence shall be at the party?"

"Better than that Jon, Alfonso has put a brief on each of the party visitors who you will want to pay special attention to on your bed. Read that and if you have any questions I am at your disposal."

"Peter, Thank you." With that said Jon stood up. "If you will excuse me, I will seek out the briefs and do my homework so to speak."

Before Jon turned to leave, Peter removed the pipe from his mouth and placed it in the ashtray. Slowly he stood up. "You know Jon," Peter said quietly with a smile, I never know exactly whom I am addressing you or your alien friend. I hope you don't take offense with that comment "

Now it was Jon's turn to smile and then with a twinkle in his eye, "Well, Peter as it turns out we have become inseparable brothers. But have no fear; I have only the best interests of the human race at heart."

Peter nodded his understanding. "Well, I hope you consider 'us' brothers Jon, because without you I would not be here. I owe you my life and the opportunity to be with my loved ones." Peter reached his hand out. Jon ignored Peter's hand and instead came to him and embraced him as a brother might do.

"Thank you brother," Jon replied. With that, Jon turned and proceeded back to his bedroom.

Betsy arrived later in the day and came into the bedroom followed by Alfonso who was carrying so many packages he could hardly be seen. "Oh thank you so much Alfonso. Let's just put them here on the bed and I will take care of them."

"Yes, ma'am," Alfonso replied glad to be shed of the load and eager to get about his regular chores.

Jon who was sitting in an English rocker by window put down his reading and looked up with a smile at his bride to be.

"Oh Jon we had the most marvelous time." Jon sat patiently as Betsy threw herself at him, smothering him with kisses and then sinking to the floor at his feet as she proceeded to tell him all the details of where they went to eat, what they shopped for, what they bought. "And Jon, I am sure you know by now, but what a wonderful thing to do of throwing a party for us with all of Peter's friends."

After listening to Betsy, Jon decided against telling her about the intended motive of the party to get Jon close to government decision makers who might be instrumental in decisions which could affect the human race.

"And just what are you reading sweetheart that has you closeted up here all alone?" Betsy said as she saw the paperwork Jon was going through.

"These honey, are some of the decision makers I may have to meet. Peter was good enough to put together a dossier on each of them for me to study."

Betsy stood up and put her fingers to her chin as if to ponder a meaning of what Jon had just shared. "These decision makers wouldn't by any chance be coming to the party would they?"

Jon couldn't help but laugh. "Yes, my dear, they will."

Betsy laughed with Jon. Then she threw her arms around him and whispered in his ear. "As long as we are together, I couldn't care less. Now I am going to take a shower and lay down to rest. Would you like to join me?" Then she giggled and tilted her head to see his expression. He looked up with a grin. "I'll bring the soap."

As they lay on the bed together after making love, Jon leaned over and whispered in Betsy's ear. "Have you thought about where you would like to go for our honeymoon?"

"Yes," came her reply, "but I hesitate to tell you."

"Say what?" came Jon's surprised response. "Why do you hesitate? Wherever it is will be okay with me darling."

"You will think me silly Jon."

Jon laughed. "I know you are silly. That's not the point." Betsy punched Jon lovingly in the arm. "No, really, I would like to know."

Betsy moved as close to Jon as she could. "Jon I want to go home. I want to resume our lives. I understand there will be times you need to travel and speak and do whatever we can do to change the course of things. I accept that. It's just that I want you to myself at home for a little while. Does that sound selfish?"

"Hmm" Jon mused as he pretended he was thinking about it. Betsy gave him another loving whack. Then Jon turned and swallowed Betsy up in his strong arms and whispered to her "That sounds delicious, let's do it."

Betsy enveloped herself in his arms and they made love again.

That night at dinner, the wedding planner was invited. Julie and Betsy and the planner entertained everyone with the details of their shopping. Occasionally Max would offer a comment but the girls pretty much monopolized the conversation.

It was a magnificent dinner. The white table covered in embroidered garden designs with flowers and birds, Waterford crystal glasses, flowers vases, wine glasses and gorgeous handmade china embraced the wide assortment of wine, and food they shared. Max told some funny stories about Betsy as a child who as a grandchild would visit her now deceased grandparents and at 1 year and 5 months greet them when she entered their house with, "Did ya have a good day nana? Did you have a good day poppa?" Jon beamed a smile and approving eye as Betsy blushed and tried to get her Dad to hush with the baby stories. Even Julie chimed in with how strong her mom had been during some really rough times. Everyone had a great time. The house was filled with laughter and pleasantries for the first time in a long time.

As the meal was finished and after desert was enjoyed, the wedding planner as if on cue got up and excused herself as she had to be home. Everyone exchanged good-byes and

Betsy couldn't say enough about how helpful she had been and what a great afternoon they had.

Soon after the wedding planner left, Peter began tapping his wine glass to get everyone to come to attention. Betsy thinking that was the traditional signal for an engaged couple to kiss, leaned over to kiss Jon. Everyone laughed and raised their wine glasses to say "hear, hear" a phrase originated in the British parliament in the eighteenth century as a contraction of "hear him, hear him," and used in an agreement to a toast or in this case a kiss.

Peter laughed. "Okay folks, now that I have your attention, I have an announcement." Again the table raised their glasses and said, "Hear, hear." Everyone laughed. Suddenly everyone got silent as Alfonso approached the table and put down two beautifully wrapped gifts, one in front of Jon and one in front of Betsy. Just then Peter's two boys appeared briefly, acknowledged everyone, and sat down at the table close to their Dad.

CHAPTER 12

A GIFT OF APPRECIATION

The table became very quiet. "Oh mom, wow, presents," said Julie as she looked over her mom's shoulder glancing at Jon and then her mom.

Peter broke the silence by saying, "I know wedding presents come at the time of the wedding. And… I apologize. But I just couldn't wait. So please excuse the improper sequence of this. But I wanted you both alone with your families when you got this. It comes from the boys and me. We hope it makes you happy for many years."

"If I may," interrupted Max. "Life has given us all some interesting twists and turns. Through it all I have been blessed with an awesome daughter, granddaughter and now I am proud to say an awesome soon to be son-in-law and now awesome friends. Thank you all." With that said, everyone raised their glasses to Jon and Betsy and sipped their wine to toast.

Betsy thanked everyone and giggled. "Can we open the gifts now?" she said looking at Peter like a young school girl getting her very own bike. Everyone laughed.

"Please," Peter waved his hand for them to open their presents. As Jon and Betsy began, Peter said, "Wait… wait." Then as if in a teasing way, Peter pursed his lips and said, "First Jon and then Betsy."

Jon slowly and deliberately opened his present which seemed to be a book or printed material of some sort. Betsy chided him in a girlish way. "Hurry sweetheart, I can't wait."

As Jon opened the package, a bound notebook appeared. It had a picture of Peter's beautiful house they were staying in on the cover. As Jon slowly turned the cover, there was a list of the contents of the notebook. There were seven pages of what were called inventory. Both Jon and Betsy looked confused. Then there were pages and pages of each room with pictures and description of the décor and a little history. The very last page was a Deed of Trust conveying the home and all its contents to Jon and Betsy Sullivan.

Suddenly as Jon stared disbelieving at what he was seeing, Betsy broke into tears realizing what the gift was. "Wow," Max said as if someone had knocked the breath out of him. Betsy had stopped crying but the tears still flowed down her cheeks.

Jon looked up at Peter. "Peter I… we… can't accept this. This is way over the top."

Peter abruptly said, "Oh, okay… Julie do you need a home away from home?" Julie looked flabbergasted. Peter then looked at Jon. "Jon no! Now look, dammit. Other than my sons, you have come to mean everything to me. Without you, I would not have my boys by my side. When I said you are my brother I meant it. Besides where are you both going to stay when you come to Washington to deal with the piranha here that need convincing our way of life must change. The boys and I want you and Betsy to have this house."

Both Robert and Arthur stood up smiling in agreement with their Dad. They moved over behind him and voiced their support for Jon and Betsy to have the house.

"Besides, the taxes will be paid each year through a fund we have set up and Alfonso and Marie have agreed to stay on and look after the place while you are away and be here for you when you come to town either permanently or occasionally as the situation requires. That is if you want them to."

Again all Max could say was "Wow."

"Now, Betsy," Peter directed "You open your gift."

Betsy still in tears slowly opened the smaller package in front of her. Inside she found a bunch of keys. Three were for the home, one was for the garage. Then she started crying again. There were three sets of keys for three cars in the garage; a new Lexus SUV, a new Mercedes convertible: and the Bentley in which they had ridden.

Betsy struggled to get her breath. She was overwhelmed. Everyone was now hugging everyone else. Max was still sitting there almost in a stupor going "Wow... Wow!"

Things began to quiet down and the boys excused themselves. As Alfonso started to pick up the dishes, Peter announced Jon and he needed to retire to the den to discuss some information they were reviewing. With that, Jon kissed Betsy and excused himself off to the den with Peter.

Betsy stood up and began to help Alfonso with clearing the dishes. Alfonso looked shocked. "Oh, ma'am, no need of that, please I can do it."

"Alfonso," Betsy said with a sharp tone. "Yes, ma'am," he replied. "I like you a lot. I hope you will decide to stay here as long as you want. But you need to understand, I am just a country girl and you need to let me help whenever I want to. Is that a deal?"

Now Betsy was smiling. Alfonso had never met anyone like her before. "Uh, yes, ma'am… Ah, that's a deal."

With that Alfonso turned to go into the kitchen. He was wearing a big smile on his face. "I knew I was gonna like these people," he muttered to himself.

- - -

Sitting down in his favorite leather chair, Peter picked a copy of the dossiers similar to the ones Jon had read. Jon sat down across from Peter in a burgundy ladder-back chair. He crossed his legs and waited for Peter to begin.

"Jon, the party will be on Wednesday night from 8:00 p.m. till midnight. There will be secret service agents here Tuesday to inspect the grounds and get an inventory of who will be at the party not already on their list. An agent will be at the door greeting guests and checking names." He paused and waited for Jon to comment.

"Peter, will there be a problem with Betsy or I because of the ATFa investigation?"

"No, you are both on the good guy list." Peter laughed. "See it pays to have connections."

Jon did not see the humor in the comment and he looked sternly at Peter.

Peter cleared his throat several times and carried on. "The attendees we should take note of are General Russert who runs the NSA; Senator Carville, speaker of the house; Senator Farmor Minority leader of the Senate and cochairman of the Appropriations Committee. The president's chief of staff, Andy Card, should be here. In addition, I don't know if she will be in town to attend but Senator Margaret Rheinwald is a possibility. Margaret is the chair person for the committee on Energy and Water Development and soon to be announced as head of the State, Foreign Operations and Related Programs. She is a mover, smart as a whip with an IQ that would choke a horse and a mouth that would embarrass a sailor. If you know what I mean. She is not formerly on the National Security Council yet but she will be."

"I am quite interested in Russert," Jon replied. "I want to know how much he knows of the alien intrusion in his operation as well as the ATFa unit which sought to track Betsy and me down."

"Well, ah yes, I can understand that. But aren't we after the decision makers who can steer the country back on track so to speak?"

"Absolutely Peter. There is no doubt about that. But it is hard to clear the woodshed if the vipers are still crawling around."

"The woodshed Jon?"

"Yes, the woodshed, the country and its overall indulgence in crime, greed and war like aggression."

"Okay, Brother. Like I said before, I owe you everything and am willing to follow."

"No." Said Jon as he stood up. I don't want you to just follow. I want you to understand where we are headed if we can't get things turned around. It is not just you and I and

Betsy. It is your sons and their children. The game we are playing in this world has no good ending."

Peter didn't know what to say. Jon could see how Peter felt confused and at odds. He was a merchant; a man who had used his wits and his intelligence and his ability to read people to build an empire around the world wide market of electronics. Jon came over to Peter and put his hand on Peter's arm. "Yes, Peter, we are brothers in a very special way. And I need your help and your guidance to walk through the mine field of greed that permeates the great halls of this country."

Peter bowed his head. Tears began to flow ever so slightly. "Jon I am not that smart. I don't have the innate intelligence that you and people like Rheinwald do. I can follow your direction but I am not sure I can guide anything. I am an old man. An old man with a renewed body but yes an old man."

Jon pursed his lips. Then a wry smile came upon him. "Peter, allow me to share some of the knowledge I have with you." With that said, small wisps of light flowed around and through Peter. Peter closed his eyes. It was like he was in a trance.

CHAPTER 13

THE PARTY

The night of the party started off exactly as planned. The guests started coming in around 8:00 p.m. Maria and Alfonso were at their best. A caterer had been hired and the rooms abounded with food displays and lovely music. A Secret Service agent checked invitations at the door.

Peter was the perfect host. He took Jon and Betsy around and introduced them as friends from North Carolina. When asked what line of work he was in, Jon simply said he was in construction. When asked what type of construction, Jon said he was a builder of high end residential. This subject among the Who's Who of Washington was almost like telling someone you were a surgeon. But instead of medical questions, everyone wanted to know how to build something, or how to fix something, or Jon's view of the real estate market.

While in conversation with the Mayor of Washington, DC, Peter came over and stood beside Jon. As he saw an opportunity to break into the conversation, Peter acknowledged the Mayor, briefly asked about his son currently at George Washington University and then apologized because he had to drag Jon away.

"Jon," Peter said softly, as soon as they were out of hearing range, Senator Margaret Rheinwald has just arrived. I want to introduce you and Betsy. Then I will have Alfonso to fetch Betsy away so you can get to talk to her and get a feeling as to whether she will be friend or foe."

Jon nodded his head. As they moved toward Senator Margaret Rheinwald, she had just had her wrap taken and was now being served a drink. As she walked into the living room, Peter and Jon picked up Betsy and moved toward the senator. "Senator," Peter spoke out. Rheinwald turned around and greeted Peter with a warm smile. Peter kissed her on each cheek and proceeded to introduce his friends from North Carolina.

"Charmed to meet you, I am sure," Rheinwald uttered through a smile which would melt an iceberg. Rheinwald was an attractive woman in her mid-fifties. She had been thru three husbands, the last of whom had been senator of New York. When he died, Margaret was chosen as his replacement. After doing an outstanding job and with the support of the Republican Party the members of which owed her late husband many political favors, on which she was still collecting, she was re-elected for a full term. She is known for her wit and her extensive knowledge. As the senior senator from New York, she is the chair person for the committee on Energy and Water Development and soon to be announced as head of the State Dept.

Shortly after being introduced, Alfonso appeared and after begging apologies requested Betsy's presence in the kitchen.

"Well, Mr. Sullivan," Rheinwald said as Betsy was spirited away, "I understand you are a transplant from Boston and now ply your skills as an engineer catering to the building trade of our lovely state of North Carolina."

Jon could not help but observe how the senator made sure she was aware of who was who.

"Yes, ma'am," Jon replied, "but please, call me Jon."

"Yes, yes, of course Jon," she replied and please call me Peggy."

"Thank you Peggy. Yes, we love it in North Carolina."

"Well, good. My heritage has me related to the man known as 'the War Governor of the South.' I am much proud of that since I am known as the War Senator of the United States Senate." With that she paused to take in Jon's response.

"Yes, ma'am, uh, Peggy, Zebulon Vance was a fierce North Carolina advocate and a powerful governor."

Rheinwald was duly impressed and her manner showed it. "I must say. You take me by surprise. Jon I am impressed you are so knowledgeable about your adopted state. Do you by any chance know why he was so labeled?"

Rheinwald had majored in American History and when it came to the constitution or history she was unmatched. Now she was set upon making sure Jon knew his place in such subjects.

"Well, Peggy, I believe young Vance was so labeled not because he was a war hawk although he did command the Twenty-Sixth North Carolina Infantry, but rather because of his ability to manage the state even during its most tumultuous time."

Rheinwald couldn't have been more excited. Finally she had met a man who might be her equal in knowledge about this country she loved. "Yes, Jon, yes. North Carolina was a most difficult state to manage during the Civil War." She beamed at Jon as an excited school teacher would at a student who had it all together and with whom she could have at length discussions few could appreciate.

"Yes, Peggy, "As you undoubtedly know, of all the Eastern states, North Carolina has the greatest length and the greatest width of any state in what was the confederacy. This vast distance of 560 miles made defending the state during the Civil war, from the Atlantic Ocean and adjoining rivers to the rugged Appalachian Mountains a very difficult task."

"Oh yes, Jon but those Tarheels as they were called made the state proud."

"Yes, there was much pride, but when bacon goes from $.33 per pound to $7.70, there is also much poverty."

"Yes, Jon," Rheinwald agreed solemnly. "But we have come a long way since then on the backs of a constitution that will stand forever as the greatest."

"It could, Senator," replied Jon in a serious tone. "But unless this country gets back to fiscal responsibility and ensuring its people are led by morally strong and vigilant leaders who show by their leadership the need to abandon war spirited on by greed and power, the country, even the world could be in great jeopardy."

"Well, that is a hell of a turn of events," Rheinwald quipped. "One minute you are impressing the hell out of me with your knowledge of North Carolina history and the next you are forecasting doom and gloom on a courtry's financial status when in fact we are the leaders of the world."

"With China, Russia, Japan, Germany, France and Saudi Arabia meeting in secret without the Unites States to discuss abandoning the dollar for a one world currency, bacon could once again reach seven dollars a pound," Jon replied with a look that told Rheinwald he knew what he was talking about.

Rheinwald looked around furtively to see who might be listening to their conversation. Seeing none but in fear of being overheard, she put her hand on Jon's arm. "Please Jon come with me." They both moved through the guests with Peggy leading, smiling and nodding to everyone they passed.

With that said she led Jon to the first room she could find that was empty. When they were both inside, she slammed the door. She faced Jon getting up in his face. "Where did you hear that shit?"

Jon stepped back a pace. "Peggy politicians aren't the only ones who have access to information critical to their country."

"Jon, that information is of a critical need to know basis. How in the hell would you have access to such information?" She paused, hoping Jon would share where and how he could know such things. Seeing Jon was remaining quiet and feeling an urgent need to get this subject under her control, she pushed onward.

"Jon, are you familiar with Standard and Poor's?"

"Yes, ma'am, I certainly am. It is a credit agency."

"Jon, it is the world's best credit watchdog. It is an independent, unbiased company that takes a hard look at all kinds of corporate, mortgage and government debt around the world. They give the United States the highest credit rating possible; A triple-A! Do you think if the United States didn't have its act together; it could achieve such a rating? Answer that."

Jon had already sensed Peggy was indeed a good person at least as she viewed herself. She knew how to work people and how to manipulate others to her advantage. But as smart as she was, she was lonely and compensated for that by being a driver. However, she also had deep respect for those who would hold their ground and resist letting her get the best of an argument. She deeply respected knowledgeable people and her sense was that Jon was one of those.

After pausing to reflect on Peggy's response, Jon commented. "Peggy S&P is one of those watchdogs who are placing a pristine triple-A rating on a load of fraudulent mortgage bonds. It does a bad job because it has no incentive to do a good job. It is not a group of investors. It just publishes credit ratings. It has nothing at stake. I predict that in less than a decade, the United States will have a major financial crisis. I apologize for being so blunt. But there it is."

Jon continued noting he had the complete and undivided attention of the senator. "Aside from the Federal Reserve, China is the largest holder of US securities. Their Dagong Credit Agency has already begun talks about lowering the credit rating of the US from double A to A+. When the US prints money to pay its debts, it undervalues its own currency. This lowers the value of the loans China is making. China is now finding allies interested in creating a worldwide currency and abolishing the dollar as the standard. If this comes about bacon may very well cost seven dollars per pound."

Rheinwald now sensing this was no average shmuck she was talking to, knew she needed to establish a relationship and use such intelligence and foresight for her own ends.

"Jon, I have no problem telling you, you are a most amazing fellow. You are far more intelligent than I gave you credit for and I want you to join me in seeking ways to remedy this situation you so clearly articulate."

Jon smiled and chuckled.

"Jon I am serious. I am about to be named to head a most important cabinet position. I need people like you around me. Would you give such an invitation some thought?"

The senator stuck out her hand inviting Jon to shake hers.

Jon gave her a big smile and took her hand. "I will give that invitation some thought."

"Good," she replied. "Now let's get back to the party before your wife to be sends out a search party."

As the senator and Jon begin to mingle again with the crowd, a distinguished man in uniform confronted the senator. Rather than begin a conversation, the senator introduced Jon to General Russert and excused herself to attend to lady things.

"Well, Jon how do you like Washington?"

"General, I feel like this is a bee hive and the Queen Bee has just left us." The General laughed. "Well, I am delighted to meet you." He added.

"Yes, Washington is a strange place all right; not at all like North Carolina country. Do you have problems with aliens here, General, or is that not in the purview of the NSA?"

The general gave Jon a hard look as he coughed. "Excuse me, my drink must have gone down the wrong way." Recovering himself after some more coughs but still looking hard at Jon, "I assume you mean, sir, illegals?" The general took a long drink, awaiting Jon's response.

"Well, General, of course illegal immigrants are a major concern. However, I was actually thinking of UFO types. Is that an area NSA finds itself involved with?"

The general shook his head as if to say no. "No, sir, I don't believe in such things. Do you?"

"Yes, I believe I do, General. Do you think if they were a reality they would appear in Washington?"

"Not if they had any sense Jon." The general forced a laugh. He was trying to play down the subject but the directness of Jon's approach had caught him off guard and he needed to re-direct the conversation. "I have all I can do to manage the operation of our data centers. That is our prime responsibility you know? It takes a lot of money to safe guard our country by being able to analyze data which may detect some terrorist activity."

"I am sure it does and then there is the need to collect data on any possible alien presence." Jon watched and sensed the general squirming as Jon insisted in bringing up this subject the general wanted to avoid talking about. Of course Congress has to authorize such expenditures don't they?"

"Oh yes, sir, we can't do anything without Congress allocating the needed money." The general seemed relieved Jon was getting away from the discussion of aliens.

"Yes, Jon and thank God for the Patriot Act, don't you think?" Now the general took the offensive and tried to put Jon on the spot regarding where he stood on this noble act designed to further protect the United States from terrorism both foreign and domestic. "Are you familiar with that legislation?"

"Yes, General, I am. Actually the title of the act is the USA Patriot Act which is an acronym standing for Uniting and Strengthening America by Providing Appropriate Tools Required to Intercept and Obstruct Terrorism Act."

"Yes, Jon that is it exactly." The general nodded to acknowledge Jon's astuteness. "Probably very few people know that." The general was smiling and enjoying the change of direction of the conversation. As a waiter passed by with drinks, the general placed his empty glass on his platter and took another. He started to sip his drink and then almost choked when Jon made his next comment.

"Do you think that the NSA would set up a secret black ops group to go after aliens from other planets?"

"Wh… Wh… Why that would be ridiculous. Congress would never allow that."

"Well, I am sure that NSA could take money under the pretense of the Patriot Act and spend it any way they wanted. Who would know?"

Now the general was becoming a bit annoyed and his body language showed it. "Jon this is probably not a discussion we should have here. Peter Slavak, I am sure, would feel annoyed if he felt we were too serious and not enjoying the party."

"Yes, of course, of course, General. Please allow me to let you circulate with the other guests. I have enjoyed speaking with you."

"Yes, same here Jon." With that said both men shook hands and gave each other a cordial smile. "By the way," Jon added as the general was about to move away, "how is Sarah Connors doing?"

The general stopped in his tracks. Sarah is the general's mistress, a former secretary the general hooked up with, and the general's face almost turned blue at the mention of her name.

"Oh, ah, fine, I guess. I haven't seen her in ages. She used to be a secretary of mine, don'tcha know."

"Yes, General, I know. Good speaking with you. Look forward to talking with you again."

The general stood looking at Jon as he moved away and began to chat with others. The general was fuming now. His eyes followed Jon as he moved across the room. His dark beady eyes showed the anger he felt toward Jon. He called over an aide who had come with him. "Get a hold of whoever is now running the ATFa group and give me a status report? Find out what the hell is going on. I want a detail report by early tomorrow."

"Yes, General," the aide responded and then left to do as he was instructed.

As Jon was talking to a neighborhood couple who had heard he and Betsy would now be neighbors, Peter got his eye and called him away.

"Jesus Jon," Peter chuckled "You are having quite a night. Rheinwald thinks you are one of the smartest men she has ever met and wants you on her team. The general has left looking like someone gave him a wedgie. Are you having fun?"

"Well, it is a very informative night." Then Jon paused musing over what Peter had said. "You mean Rheinwald said I was just 'one' of the most intelligent?" They both laughed. Betsy saddled up to them. "Hi guys. What a wonderful party Peter. The folks are wonderful. Jon, I have met both Senator Carville, Senator Farmor, and Chief of Staff Mr. Spade. They are all very friendly gentlemen and all offered to escort me around the Whitehouse."

"Sounds like a winner Honey. How about taking me over and introducing me?"

"Can do, sweetheart. Peter will you excuse us?" Peter gave Jon a wink. "Yes, ma'am. Jon we will have to pick this back up tomorrow."

"You betcha," said Jon over his shoulder as Betsy took Jon by the arm and hauled him away.

Later that evening, when all had left the party and Jon sat alone in his bedroom, Betsy came to him realizing something was wrong.

"Sweetheart," she said as she sat beside him on the bed, "is something wrong?" Jon looked despondent. He didn't speak. Betsy continued. "The party seemed to go very well. Did something happen? Tell me darling. Let me help."

Jon lifted his head, turned slightly and looked at Betsy. She was wearing a blue sequined dress with a low cut that was striking. Her hair was beautifully done and she looked like a million dollars. He put his head back down.

Again Betsy sought to find out what was wrong. Finally Jon turned to her and softly told her.

"Betsy I am afraid of the powers unleashed in me. Without David to guide me, I am fearful."

"Why Jon? So far everything has been wonderful. Have we had our ups and downs? Yes. But look at how things have turned out. David would be proud of the way you have handled it all." She paused, hoping her words would comfort him. She had never seen Jon despondent before and it was beginning to scare her.

"Betsy, I am part alien."

"Yes," Betsy replied with laughter hoping to get Jon to see how she understood. "And you are the man I am ever so deeply in love with. My Dad thinks the world of you. Peter loves you like a brother. Julie is so happy for me. We are very fortunate."

"Are we Betsy? Look!" With that Jon held out his right arm. Slowly it changed into a strange looking appendage from his shoulder down to his fingertips which were now growing grayish nails almost 5 inches long. The arm was snarly and twisted with muscles popping out of the length of the arm. It was the arm of a monster.

"Whoa." Betsy exclaimed as she jumped back from what she was seeing.

Slowly the arm returned to the way it was before the transformation.

"You see Betsy. Now I can, almost at will, transform any or all of me into whatever monstrous shape I desire."

Betsy swallowed hard. Then she came close to Jon and put her arms around him.

"Jon as long as you control it, perhaps it is but another way for you to get others to understand the calamity they face if the world does not change."

"It doesn't scare you?"

"Yes, Jon it is pretty scary. But what scares me more is to be without you. What scares me more is to be in a world destined to collapse and what that means for our children."

"Yes, this is for Julie and the younger generation isn't it?"

"Yes, Jon. But..." Betsy paused and then took Jon's hand into hers. "It is also for our child."

Jon looked over and into Betsy's eyes. "What... Our child?"

"Yes, Jon." She beamed at Jon with a loving smile. "I am pregnant."

"What? How can that be?" Betsy began to laugh as Jon lifted her up from the bed. "Ah, sweetheart," she chuckled, "I think I can tell you how that happens."

Jon put his arms around her and held her close. "Oh baby... I mean we are going to have a baby?"

Now Jon was smiling and laughing. "Wait till Peter hears he is going to be an uncle." They both laughed and kissed and flopped down on the bed in a warm embrace.

After a while as they lay there together, Betsy whispered into Jon's ear. "Darling, perhaps this new power you have found will scare the daylights out of the politicians and get them to take notice and to take action."

"Yes," said Jon as he enjoyed the feelings of once more being a father, "Perhaps it will."

CHAPTER 14

THE WEDDING

It was now Saturday 7:00 a.m.

Betsy woke up first. She rolled over and smiled as she stared at Jon. He looked so content. Betsy had difficulty understanding at times why Jon would want to stay with her. He was so good looking and now with the powers he possessed, able to convince anyone of anything, if he put his mind to it.

Almost as if he could feel the power of Betsy's gaze, Jon turned and looked at her. He smiled and wrapped her in his right arm.

"Surely I am the luckiest man alive this morning Darling. To be here with you is what life is all about."

"I don't know Jon."

"What's that?" he answered as he looked at her demure face and her lips pursed as if she was pouting?"

"Oh Jon. You could have anyone you want. I am just a plain country gal. I don't see what you see in me."

Jon now turned over on his side to completely face Betsy. "Hmm. Well, obviously you don't see what I see. I see the most wonderful woman I have ever known; someone who is loving and caring beyond description." Then after a brief pause Jon's mischievous smile crossed his face. "Of course the fact you are beautiful with the prettiest legs I have ever seen doesn't hurt."

Betsy playfully pushed Jon. She smiled that smile that only comes from being with someone you truly love to the depths of your being.

"Now is the mother of our child trying to tell me it is time to get up on this very special day?" With that Jon swallowed her in his arms and they lay embraced sharing kisses.

Suddenly Betsy threw off the covers.

Jon reached over and moved closer to Betsy in an amorous way. Betsy turned. "Jon don't you realize I am to be married today? She uttered a low chuckle. Jon pulled back and looked at her with a surprised look.

"Wha?" he started to protest.

Betsy pushed Jon away. "Please I am to be married today. What would he do if my husband to be found you here?"

As Betsy continued, Jon started to laugh. "Okay, okay. What would you have me do?"

"Well, leave of course. Get dressed and get out of here so I can prepare for my wonderful husband to be."

As Jon slipped out of bed, he smiled at Betsy's frivolity. "Okay. I'll leave. But don't forget me after you get hitched."

"Oh sweetie, don't you worry. I will be having you back often."

They both laughed. Jon got dressed and left to go to the kitchen and find something to eat. Betsy went in to take a shower.

As Jon entered the kitchen, Marie was preparing food.
"Good morning Marie."

"Good morning Mr. Sullivan. I hope you slept well"

"Yes, thank you Marie."

"Mr. Sullivan, I will have breakfast ready in a few minutes. Mr. Slavak is awaiting you on the outside patio."

"Thank you," replied Jon as he proceeded out to see Peter.

"Well, good morning Jon," Peter greeted him as Jon came into view.

"Yes, good morning Peter."

"I hope you and Betsy slept well."

"Yes. Very well, thank you."

"Please join me. May I pour you a cup of coffee or perhaps some juice?"

Jon sat down. "Coffee will be wonderful. Did you know that despite the negative comments about drinking coffee, five to six cups a day actually helps the prostate avoid cancer?"

"I didn't know that Jon. But then with your alien presence, you probably don't have to worry about that."

"Yes," Jon chuckled. "That is a blessing."

Then after a slight pause, Jon thanked Peter for the party.

"Oh that was my pleasure Jon. Since you brought that up, what did you say to get the general so riled up?"

"Hmm," Jon countered, "did I?"

"Oh you definitely did. In fact, it is probably important we talk about that since he may very well be at the National Security Council meeting you will be attending."

"How so?" Jon inquired.

"Well, first, although he didn't say so, I am relatively sure he knew you are the suspected alien the NSA's ATFa group had been pursuing. And if he didn't put it all together the night of the party, I am sure he probably knows now."

As Jon sipped his coffee, he looked out over the beautifully landscaped yard where a worker was already at work pruning trees on the boundary of the property. "Peter, I would be surprised if he didn't."

"In addition," Peter continued, "he was really hot over the content of your conversation."

"How so Peter?"

"Apparently…" Marie interrupted them with her presence. "Mr. Slavak is it okay to bring breakfast out here?"

"Jon?" Peter looked at Jon for his approval. "Should we have breakfast here?"

"Works for me Peter," Jon replied as he smiled approvingly at Marie.

"That's it then Marie, thank you."

Marie disappeared.

"I am sure Betsy will approve also Peter."

"Oh no, Jon. You will not see your bride to be until later today."

Jon looked surprised. Marie reappeared carrying a large tray, followed by Alfonso who carried a second tray. They set the food down; a plate of scrambled eggs, a plate of link and patty sausages, bacon, homemade biscuits, blueberry crepe suzettes, grapefruit and fresh strawberries. They had even prepared some grits which Marie had felt Jon might enjoy being from the South. Marie and Alfonso stood there awaiting any further requests.

"Thank you Marie and Alfonso. This is wonderful," Peter said. Both Jon and Peter nodded approvingly. Seeing their prepared meal was satisfactory, Marie and Alfonso went back into the home.

"Wow," Jon commented. "There is enough here for four people."

"Yes, well, my sons will be here shortly so nothing will go to waste," Peter said as he chuckled.

As Jon began to put food on his plate starting with the berries and grapefruit, he returned to their previous conversation.

"So, you think the general left in a huff?"

Marie returned briefly to renew their coffee cups. "Thank you Marie," Jon commented in appreciation for her service. "My pleasure, sir," Marie responded.

As Marie returned to the house again, Peter spoke. "Yes, Jon. I think that is a good description. He did leave in a huff. And I might add, he may be a dangerous adversary."

"Dangerous?" Jon inquired as he as he buttered a biscuit and put some egg and bacon on his plate.

"Yes, Jon, dangerous. You must remember people like him have much pride. They do not like to be confronted especially when you have shown his organization to not only be a bunch of bumbling idiots but to have in their midst aliens, the very creature they are seeking."

Peter stopped for a moment to take a bite to eat, and then continued. "They have a short focus and they are so caught up with their own importance and their own power they lose the big picture. Facts become inconsequential and only their perception real or not is what governs."

"Yes," Jon agreed. "Everything is a matter of context and perspective."

"I do wish you had left your brief meeting with him on a better footing. I fear he will try to sabotage your mission."

"Well, he may try. However, he will not be successful. They may not accept my message but they will not sabotage my intent to deliver it as well as to impress them with the force they may have to contend with." Jon paused. Then softly he said, "I hope for the future of our children, the world will take heed and change. There is much to be gained if we listen and let them guide us; and much to lose if we don't."

Peter was quiet as he thought about his boys and their future. As if on cue, they both entered the patio. "Hey, folks," Arthur said. Robert chimed in, "Good morning all."

Peter and Jon greeted the boys. Marie brought out two plates and silverware. She picked up the eggs and replaced the plate with fresh hot scrambled eggs. "Oh great," said Robert with a wide smile. "Thanks Marie." Marie smiled at the boys who sat down and began to dig into the food.

About that time, the wedding planner appeared to announce she was taking Betsy away for some last minute shopping and preparation for the big event.

After she left, Robert looked over at Jon. "Jon will you be joining us for some golf this morning?" Jon looked over at Peter. "Yes, Jon, I am going. These two pups think they can take us in a game of golf."

"Well, Dad, if you think it will be fairer we can pair each of you old folks with one of us." The two boys laughed as they gobbled up the last of the eggs and bacon.

Peter looked at Jon. "I'm sorry Jon. I never asked you if you played golf."

"Yes, Peter. Some years ago I do remember swinging at that little ball. My idea of a good game was if I ended up with as many balls as I started with."

Peter and the boys laughed. "Yes," said Arthur, "Perhaps we should pair you up with one of us so as to avoid a slaughter. Dad's not that good, what is your handicap Jon?"

"My swing," Jon quipped. They all laughed again. "Well," Jon chimed in, "Actually, I think you boys will have a hard time with us. We will use psychology on you."

Both boys bent over in laughter. "Wow," said Arthur, "Robert do you think they dare wager a dollar on the outcome?"

Jon smiled. "Well, make it easy on yourselves," Jon quietly said trying to hold back a smirk.

"Well, okay," Both boys said almost at the same time. "We love a little competition," laughed Robert.

So, it was agreed. They would get dressed and play some golf to while away the morning.

"Oops," laughed Jon. "I am afraid I don't have sneakers never mind golf shoes."

They all laughed. "Not to worry Jon. By the time we get it all together, you will have the shoes, clubs and clothes you need," Peter said.

"Course that won't help you," laughed Robert. They all laughed.

After getting properly clothed, they all piled into the car and proceeded to Sunset Golf Course, an Arnold Palmer designed course. On the way they agreed Robert and Arthur would hit from the expert tees and Peter and

Jon would hit from the regular men's tee. They also agreed on a bet. The losers would pay for the golf and the lunch at the club. "We are trying to make it easy on you old folks," Robert added. Jon and Peter laughed. They also agreed they would save some time by playing best ball. That meant that each team would use the ball position of their choice after each had hit their ball. After arriving at the club, getting properly equipped and getting a cart, Arthur couldn't help but notice Jon was only taking a 3 wood, a 3 iron and a putter. "Jon it doesn't look like you are taking advantage of the wide selection of clubs available. You aren't conceding already are you?" Again the comment sparked a bit of laughter among the group.

"Well, Arthur, with as little as I have played, I am going with the odds of consistency rather than the spectrum of variation."

"Hmm," commented Peter thinking over his partner's strategy. "Besides," Jon piped, "if I need another club, I am sure my partner will let me use his. Right partner?"

"Right you are partner," chuckled Peter.

At the first tee, a par 4 hole that dog legged to the right approximately 150 yards down the fairway, with a bunker waiting if you hit the ball too long and straight, they flipped to determine the order. Robert and Arthur won the toss and decided to let their Dad and Jon hit first.

"Get up there and whack it," Peter directed Jon.

They all stood back waiting to see what Jon would do. Jon teed up his ball. After a few practice swings, he addressed his ball and swung. They all watched as the ball sailed nicely straight down the fairway approximately 150 yards, sitting nicely at the turn for a good approach shot to the green.

"Hmm, nice shot Jon," said Peter. Robert nudged Arthur with his elbow and they winked at each other.

Peter turned to Jon. "You have us set up well partner. If it is okay I am going to take a shortcut." Jon nodded his approval. Peter stroked the ball well but he tried to cut the ball to slice it around the corner of the turn toward the green. It was too much and the ball landed in the brush at the far edge of the turn.

"Whoops, Dad," said Robert. "That is a lot of pressure on your partner."

"That's right," Peter replied, "see if your trash talking will get you anywhere."

The boys laughed. Arthur was the first of his team to swing. He took the unorthodox strategy to go straight over the corner of the turn and gain a positional advantage. "Beautiful shot brother, just beautiful," Robert said as the ball sailed over the corner putting their team closer to the green. "Nice shot," both Peter and Jon chimed in. Since they were playing best ball, Robert didn't need to hit. But on the chance Arthur's shot hadn't cleared the corner, Robert hit his ball straight down the fairway to emulate Jon's hit. The ball sailed too far and ended up in the bunker. Robert growled. "No worry Bro, I am sure we are okay," Arthur said consolingly.

As it turned out, Arthur's shot was a beauty and put them within a chip shot away from the green. Peter's next shot was the better of his team's and both teams were on the green in two. Arthur followed up his great drive with a birdie putt while Jon and Peter two putted. That put Robert and Arthur one up on their Dad and Jon.

"Okay," chimed Arthur with some more smack talk, "You old folks have got seventeen more holes to play. Let us know if you need a breather."

Suddenly Jon realized that his eyes not only were able to refocus on the position of the ball although it may be one hundred to three hundred yards away, but that a sight symbol appeared in his sight when he concentrated on a spot regardless of how far away it was. He was intrigued with this new addition to his already expanding power and he decided to test how it might work. However, concerned as to how ostentatious it would appear if his shots were too outlandishly good, he decided to hold back. Only using it when Peter got into trouble by hitting the ball out of bounds or in a bunker, both he and Peter stayed tied to Arthur and Robert right up through the nineteenth hole.

"Well, old men, we have to give you credit. You have held up well," Arthur continued with his smack.

"Oh give us a break," laughed Peter. "These two old men have given you guys a real competition. Now it is time for us to show you what experience can produce."

"Really," chimed in Robert. "Are you offering to double the bet?"

"Works for me Peter," Jon added. "Good," responded Peter. "Okay boys, you're on."

The eighteenth hole was speckled with bunkers on either side. It was 580 yards long and was one of those holes even professionals would find a challenge.

Robert was up first. He hit a beautiful drive straight down the fairway, avoiding all the bunkers and landing 312 yards away.

"Wow," brother Arthur exclaimed. "What a beauty. I think that is the longest I have ever seen you drive."

"Not bad son but we are not conceding anything, right Jon?"

"Right," said Jon as Peter winked at him. Peter couldn't help but be proud of the way his boys were playing but he was also feeling good about the way he and Jon had kept up. His competitive nature had kicked in and he was determined to outdo his boys.

Arthur got up next and hit another beautiful shot although not quite as far as Roberts' but a good 260 yards down the fairway.

Peter swung next. He tried to put too much muscle into it and paid the price. His ball curved into a bunker on the right 225 yards down.

"Sorry partner" lamented Peter," as he walked away from the tee.

"Not to worry," Jon replied, "perhaps we can get lucky."

Robert and Arthur were elbowing each other, smiling and winking as if they knew it was just about all over. They felt really good when Jon walked over to Peter's bag for the first time and pulled out Peter's oversized driver. It was a club even Peter didn't use because it was so sensitive. It had a small sweet spot. If you didn't hit it square, there was no telling where the ball would go.

Peter shared this with his partner and suggested he just stay with the regular driver or the 3 wood and hope the boys would stumble. The brothers laughed so hard they could hardly stand straight as Peter and Jon openly discussed strategy.

"Humph…" Jon grunted as he looked at the boys laughing. Solemnly he picked up the monster driver and strutted up to the green pretending the driver was so heavy he could hardly hold it. They all laughed.

Jon turned serious as he gauged the distance he wanted to reach which was 10 yards in front of Robert's ball. Addressing the ball, Jon used his visual sight icon to position it in front of Robert's ball. Suddenly he felt his body feel the flow of adrenalin as he asked it to accomplish this feat.

All three watched in awe as Jon drew the monster driver away from the ball back over his head. Peter had expected Jon was just kidding around and would turn after he had addressed the ball and come back and get a more reasonable club rather than this most difficult club, and one he had never swung before.

Suddenly the smirks on the boy's faces disappeared and were replaced with disbelief as Jon brought the driver's head into the ball in form that would make any professional envious. They heard the "crack" the sweet spot makes as a driver hits a ball just the way it is supposed to. They all watched the drive as the ball flew straight and true and landed 330 yards down the fairway.

The brothers were speechless. Peter was jumping and yelling. "That's what I'm talking about. That's what I'm talking about. Way to go partner." Peter laughed. "It's a good thing for you boys we are so old. Otherwise, we might be on the green."

He was laughing ecstatically. The boys were looking at each other shaking their heads in disbelief.

Jon walked back to Peter handed him the club and said, "It has a great feel to it. I was lucky I guess."

"Ya right," Peter was still laughing. "What a lucky shot. Right boys?" he said turning to his sons. "It was a lucky shot. Don't you agree?"

The boys said nothing and walked to their golf carts and left Peter and Jon standing there. "Hmm… are they implying I don't need to try my driver?" Peter was still laughing as he and Jon got in their cart and followed the boys.

After Arthur and Robert hit out, it was Robert's ball which was closer. Robert had landed in a bunker in front of the green. It was a closer shot however, even though it was in the bunker only 50 yards from the flag. Arthur had chosen his two iron. Arthur's ball landed 80 yards shy of the green, just avoiding the front edge of a bunker. It was the better shot actually since playing from a bunker is difficult even for the most seasoned player. Now it was Peter and Jon's turn. Peter took his swing first from the position of Jon's ball. His shot only went 150 yards as he under hit the ball somewhat. Peter's ball lie 100 yards from the flag on his second shot, a strong 9 iron away. Jon was luckier, as his 3 wood with the special use of his visual sighting and adrenalin rush put the ball on the green 10 yards from the flag. Both Robert and Arthur took their swings with no verbal smack offered. Robert's ball came up out of the bunker and landed 3 yards from the flag. It was an awesome shot. Both Peter and Jon complimented Robert. Unfortunately Arthur's shot landed over the green and was out of play. Peter lined up to stroke the ball Jon had put down at 10 yards from the hole. The golf ball came to rest at the lip of the hole.

"Awesome putt," Jon offered his partner. "Great shot, Dad," the boys both agreed.

"Damn," said Peter, appreciative of the compliments but frustrated the ball should hang on the lip. Still a birdie was guaranteed despite missing what would have been an eagle on a hole hardly ever pared by most golfers.

"That's a gimmee Dad," both boys agreed acknowledging the shot was guaranteed to give Peter and Jon the birdie. Jon lined up the thirty-foot putt and sank it for an eagle. Peter was ecstatic. The boys groaned.

Arthur birdied the hole with a nice stroke so they all ended up in a tie. "Wow Dad, you old guys are awesome," Robert said acknowledging how close they came to losing. "Yes," Arthur agreed, "absolutely awesome. You showed us some fine strokes. Dad you should give your fat Bertha," the name they had given to the big driver," to Jon.

Jon laughed. "No. That was just a lucky shot."

They all laughed and headed back to the club house where despite the tie, the boys bought the meal.

As they sat there enjoying the fellowship, Peter suddenly looked very concerned. "What's up Dad?" asked Robert. "Don't look now," Peter replied, "but I had noticed a fellow out on the course who seemed to be following us. I didn't think much of it. Yet here he is over at the bar looking at us."

Without thinking Robert turned quickly and as his eyes met the fellow at the bar, the fellow turned abruptly back to the bar now watching them through the mirror hung over the bar wall.

Jon excused himself and got up. Without looking at the man, Jon walked straight into the men's room just to the side of the bar. After a few seconds, Jon came out and as he did he bumped into the man. "Oh excuse me," Jon said. Then he asked the gal behind the bar for another round of beers. Turning to the man, Jon said. "Please excuse me, I didn't mean to bump you."

"No problem," the man said tersely. "Thanks man." Jon said, and put his hand on the man's shoulder as he turned away and went back to the table.

Jon sat down. As Peter and his sons looked at Jon and waited for Jon to tell them there was no problem, Jon took a pen out of his pocket and wrote, "General's spy."

Instantly, Peter changed the discussion to the golf they played, and the boys played along knowing they should not let the man at the bar think they were aware of anything. The rounds of beers were delivered and Jon asked the girl to get the man he had bumped into a drink and put it on their tab since he had accidently bumped into him. The man acknowledged the drink by smiling and nodding at them and then turned away.

Peter turned the conversation to the wedding planned for the evening. Soon it was time for them to leave. As they drove back to the house, they noticed a dark colored Buick following them.

"Well, Jon," Peter said, "I told you the general was concerned about you. Now he has his hooligans trailing you."

Jon sat like in a trance. Arthur spoke up. "Jon? Are you okay?"

Peter answered, "Son, Jon is focusing on other things. He will be all right."

Jon was focusing on the man in the Buick behind them. He turned the visor mirror so he could see the man who was now talking on his cell phone. No one would understand but Jon was able to, between his vision reading the man's lips, and actually turning his hearing to the point where he could tune out all noise except the man's voice, he could understand what was being said.

Jon finally turned to Peter. "The general is planning to take me hostage at some point. He is determined to deprive me of the opportunity to speak to the president and the National Security Council."

"My god," sighed Peter.

"He can't do that," volunteered Arthur.

"Dad?" Robert said.

There was relative silence on the trip back to the house. The Buick kept a distance but stayed on their path. Only as they turned into the driveway at the house did the Buick disappear.

There was now four hours until the wedding was scheduled to take place. Peter made several calls to secure greater security at the home. Jon retired to rest. Betsy was not at the home and was presumably at a location picked by the wedding planner to stay until the special hour. The wedding would be small. Betsy's Dad, her daughter, Lance, two friends of the daughter, the wedding planner, Peter and his two boys, Jon's old boss Gilbert, and of course Mikki and Nicholas would be the wedding guests. Marie and Alfonso and a hired caterer would be doing the food and drinks. Lance would be Jon's best man and Julie would be

Betsy's maid of honor. Peter had engaged the services of a Baptist minister friend to do the service and the house was already decorated and ready to receive guests. Everything was in place. Jon felt surprised at how special and excited he was feeling about joining with Betsy. It was a new and exciting chapter in their lives.

Jon lay down and closed his eyes. Thoughts of David flooded his mind. Jon wished he could see David and have him there with him during this special time.

Soon it was time to prepare for the ceremony. Alfonso had laid out Jon's tuxedo, cummerbund and all the apparel fixings brought in by the wedding planner. Jon was not into getting so fancy but he knew what a special occasion this was for Betsy. Also he was thrilled their family would all be there.

As Jon was getting his final look in the mirror, Peter appeared.

"My you look great Mr. Bride groom. Anything I can help with?"

"No," said Jon with a smile.

"Well, your best man is here to check you out." In came Lance who went running to his Dad. He threw his arms around him. Lance looked great also with his Tux. "Thank you for coming Son."

"Oh Dad, I am so happy to be here. Wow what a house. And the people are all so nice here."

Then Lance stood back. "Dad?"

"Yes, Son."

"I was afraid you might not invite me because of my story about the Holly Bush." Lance looked up at Jon.

Jon sat down on the bed and pulled Lance over to him. He looked down at the floor and tried to think about how to explain the Holly Bush. Peter had left the two alone. Jon looked around the room.

"Son, when we have some longer time together we need to share about the Holly Bush. Let me just say you were right. I was wrong. I apologize for questioning you. Can you forgive me?"

"Of course Dad, I just wanted you to know I would never lie to either you or Mom."

"Yes, Lance, you are right." He paused. "Wow," he said as he pushed Lance out from him to take a good look. "You look fantastic."

"Thank you Dad. Betsy arranged for me to come and got these clothes for me especially for your marriage to her. And Dad… ?"

"Yes, Son."

"I am so happy you are marrying Betsy. She is such a great gal."

Jon began to chuckle. "I am glad you approve, I am so delighted you are here, and you are right. She is a great gal."

They both laughed and hugged each other.

Peter stuck his head in the door again. "Okay, guys it's time to go. Lance as best man you need to get your Dad town stairs and in place. People are here. Follow Alfonso. He will get you down the back way so you don't have to get involved with the guests. There will be time for that later."

Jon and Lance followed Alfonso down stairs. Going through a passage way, Jon and Lance came out at the back of the family room. Looking around, Jon spotted Gilbert who was smiling and giving him a "thumbs up" sign. Jon nodded and smiled.

The minister came to where Jon stood, shook his hand and had brief conversation with him. The minister took his place and suddenly the room was filled with music. A beautiful country love song set the tone. Suddenly the music stopped, and "Here Comes the Bride" music was played.

Jon's breath was taken away as he saw Betsy enter the room. She wore a beautiful strapless wedding gown made from luxurious matte duchess bridal satin. Adorned with apple, cream, and clear-cut crystal beading with a wrap-like waist and corset back, Betsy was the picture of beauty.

The entire evening went smoothly. Everyone cried and wooed and ahhed appropriately. After the ceremony everyone sat down to a luscious dinner. Betsy had insisted that Marie and Alfonso sit and be treated as guests and that they all be waited on by hired staff. This decision endeared her to Marie and Alfonso as very special people.

Later as everyone left or went to their assigned bedroom, Jon picked up his bride and carried her over the threshold of their bedroom. It was a wonderful first night together, and they would always cherish this occasion made so special by Peter.

Betsy was resigned to the fact their honeymoon would have to be at another time. She understood better than most how important Jon's mission was. The next several days were delightful.

After breakfast on the third morning, Betsy pulled Jon aside. "Sweetheart, there is something I must tell you."

"Oh no," Jon kiddingly replied. "Don't tell me you want an annulment."

"It is too late for that Jon," she said with a bright smile on her face. "Oh good," said Jon. "What's the good news?"

"Oh, I am so glad you asked that way." She held Jon's hand and pulled him close. "You told me you felt great about being a Daddy?" Jon pulled away as he tried to understand what Betsy was getting at. "Well, we are going to have a child together, right?" he said as he beamed at her.

"Ahh, sweetheart," Betsy smiled as she spoke. "I am afraid it may be a big family."

"Huh… ?" Jon struggled to understand what Betsy was saying.

"Sweetheart, how do you feel about twins?"

"Wow. Twins?" Jon enthusiastically replied, "This is awesome. I couldn't be happier. They squeezed each other and kissed passionately. "The Irish love big families." Jon quipped. They both laughed and squeezed each other.

Downstairs, Peter walked out the front door to casually stroll the grounds. As he walked down the driveway, he noticed a black Buick sitting off to the side of the road in front of a large black SUV. No one seemed to be in the SUV but there were several men in the Buick. Peter sought out one of the security men he had brought onto the grounds. "Circle around behind the two vehicles just to the left of the driveway. I want pictures and the license plate numbers on both vehicles," Peter commanded. The man nodded to acknowledge Peter's instructions and moved to get what was requested done.

CHAPTER 15

THE NATIONAL SECURITY COUNCIL

On Wednesday morning at around 5:00 a.m., Jon stirred. This was to be the day he would meet with the NSC. The plan was that Jon would hopefully convince them to change their ways in exchange for continued existence on the planet. He reached over for the alarm clock which was set for 5:30 a.m. and turned it off so Betsy would not be awakened. He turned and looked at her snuggled into her pillow with a contented look. She stirred slightly but seemed to still be in a deep sleep. For fear of awakening her, he quietly slipped out of the bed. He went into the next bedroom where he had arranged his clothes the night before. Using that bathroom rather than the one in their Master Bedroom, he hoped to leave quietly while Betsy slept.

After dressing, Jon quietly went down to the kitchen. Marie was already there and had coffee ready.

"Marie what are you doing up so early?"

"Oh Mr. Jon, Mr. Slavak told me you would both be up early so I wanted to make sure you got a good breakfast before you left for the day."

"Well, Marie, you didn't have to do that but thank you."

"You are welcome. If you will go into the study, Mr. Slavak is already there and I will bring you your coffee before breakfast is ready."

"Thank you Marie."

Walking into the study, Jon said good morning to Peter. "My you are the early bird Peter."

Peter looked up from the paper he was reading. He looked serious.

"Jon, good morning." Jon sat down in the oversized recliner.

"Jon?" Peter paused and put down the paper. "I don't want today to be the end of our relationship."

"Yes?" queried Jon interested in where this was going.

"I know how important you feel your meeting with the NSC is today Jon. However there is an issue we should perhaps discuss."

"Yes?" Again Jon waited for Peter's clarification.

"The Whitehouse is purportedly going to send a car for you. In light of your feeling the general is going to attempt to keep you from the meeting or at worse cause you significant harm, I want you to let me have my men escort you to this meeting."

Jon looked down and a smile crossed his face. "Thank you Peter, you are a true friend."

Peter's face became tense and angry and he corrected Jon. "No dammit I am your brother."

Jon looked up at Peter. "Yes. Thank you. You are my brother. I have come to love you as a brother; a dear brother."

After a slight pause Jon continued. "But my brother, it is important I do this my way. I need to disclose the General for who he really is."

"And who might that be," Peter asked with a puzzled look on his face.

"The general is an alien, Peter."

"What? How do you know that?" Peter had come to the edge of his seat as Jon revealed this. Peter could hardly believe what he was hearing.

"I knew the night of the party. I have the ability to scan life forms. I know very well the scan configuration of this particular alien."

"Wha… wha… how can that be. The general has a long history of patriotic representation in the military. He just didn't just appear out of thin air," Peter stammered.

"Well, Peter, I don't have any indications I am alien. And I just didn't appear out of thin air. Yet here I am. I am part alien with alien powers."

"This is so hard to believe Jon."

"Yes, Peter it is. That is why I must let the general make his moves before I confront him directly."

Peter sat back in his chair with a loud sigh. "Wow I don't know what to say. I… I… I," Peter stammered, "just don't know what to say." Then after some moments of silence, Peter looked directly at Jon. "You know best. Tell me what I need to do in order to support you."

"Thank you, Peter. You being here and protecting Betsy is what I need you to do. I will be fine. When I meet with the National Security Council, it will be they who will have to make some major decisions; decisions which will affect the world as we know it."

"Okay. We will be here waiting… and praying."

Suddenly there was a knock on the den door frame. Alfonso stood there. "Yes, Alfonso?"

"May I bring coffee and biscuits to you gentlemen?"

"Um… Jon?"

"Just coffee for me would be fine."

Peter turned to Alfonso. "Just coffee then Alfonso, thank you." Looking over at Jon, Peter slowly smiled. "You know, I doubt many people in this country really understand what the NSC is all about. Will you be meeting at the Whitehouse?"

"No, the meeting will take place at what is called the Eisenhower Executive Building."

"You mean that monstrosity next to the Whitehouse?" asked Peter.

Jon laughed. "That monstrosity has a very unique position in both our national history and architectural history."

"I knew it as the State, War and Navy building," Peter quipped.

"Yes, Peter, it was originally known as that. It originally housed the three Executive Branch Departments and was used as the place wherein the nation's foreign policy was conducted. It is the largest office building in Washington, with nearly two miles of corridors."

"And you feel this meeting with the National Security Council is important to the outcome you seek?"

"Yes, Peter it is of utmost importance… to the world… perhaps to the universe that this meeting be held."

"Well, shouldn't such a meeting be held with all the world's leaders not just the United States?"

Jon laughed. "Well, that position is what the science fiction writers who would weave such a story would have you believe. However, the United States National Security Council has within its members those who have an abiding interest and influence in the world not just the United States?'

"We do?" Peter asked surprisingly.

"Have you ever heard of a group called the Trilateral Commission?"

"Well, I have heard rumors of such a group. Isn't it part of some leftwing conspiracy thing?"

Jon sat back in his chair and sighed. "Peter, it is very real. It is a group of members from around the globe; world leaders if you will."

"Yes, yes, it espouses a one world theory doesn't it'" Peter's face scrunched up as he was trying to remember what little he had heard about such a group.

"The Trilateral Commission is an international group who seek to be the vehicle for a multinational consolidation of the world's commercial and banking interests. They seek to do this by seizing control of the political government of the United States. They represent a skillful and a coordinated effort with other world powers to seize control and consolidate the four centers of power—political, monetary, intellectual and ecclesiastical." Jon paused, waiting for the effect of this description to be absorbed by Peter.

"So you are saying follow the money; follow the power?"

"Yes, Peter. As you know, unfortunately, that is the way our world works."

"Wow. So Jon you feel influencing the National Security Council will have a bearing on world politics?"

"Yes, Peter, exactly."

"But how does the National Security Council affect what this Trilateral Commission does?"

"Between 1980 and today, every administration since Jimmy Carter has had top level Trilateral Commission representation either through the president or vice president or both. They then have appointed their fellow Trilateral Commission members to top administrative positions. As an example of this world collection of influence, seven World Bank presidents have been members. Eight out of ten United States Trade representatives have been members. Every United States Secretary of State has been a member. The list of Commission members abounds with the names of worldwide powerful figures. It also includes key members of the US Congress and highly placed offices in the US executive branch. And if that infiltration was not enough, one of the two key founders of the Commission has been active within American politics and sits on the National Security Council today."

"Who is that Jon?'

"The man named Zbignew Crezinskew who today is a key presidential advisor to the president of the United States."

"Wow Jon you will be running into a hornet's nest."

"Hmm, interesting analogy."

"That is possible Peter. I hope not. There is much to be gained for the world if they will listen and act."

Suddenly there was a knock again on the door frame. "Please excuse me," offered Alfonso. "A car has come to pick up Mr. Sullivan."

Both men stood up. Peter walked over and to Jon's surprise embraced him. "We will be praying for you Jon," Peter said.

"Thank you Peter," Jon returned the embrace and then walked to the door.

"You aren't leaving without giving me a kiss." Betsy flew into Jon's arms. "Please be careful sweetheart. Come back to me safely."

"I will Betsy. We have so much to share." He kissed his new wife good-bye and went out to the car where the driver of the limousine was holding the back passenger door open for him. The dark black limousine pulled out of the driveway and disappeared.

Peter and Betsy each with their arm around each other watched the car disappear.

As the car approached the city, it suddenly turned into a large warehouse. A large steel door closed behind the car. Jon's doors were locked so he could not get out. The driver quickly exited the car and disappeared around several stacks of pallets. A group of men, six all together came out in the open. They stood in a line, twenty feet in front of the limousine. They were laughing at how easy it was going to be to take this man down. One of the men held a trigger device. "Gentlemen, be careful as I light this up." They all laughed. The man flipped the trigger and the limousine burst into flame. Quickly the men went around a steel barrier as the car burned with an intense heat and then exploded.

"Well, that was easy," said one of the men. They all laughed and cheered.

Suddenly from in back of them they heard; "Gentlemen, do you feel better now?"

The men almost simultaneously spun around weapons drawn. "Wait a minute" the leader of the assassins said to them "Don't shoot yet." Then he ordered two of the men who had electrical shock sticks to approach Jon and subdue him. They carefully walked over to Jon and began to zap him with 500,000 watts in each stick. It was enough to drop any man to the floor either dead or close to dead. Jon just smiled and looked at the men as an adult might have looked at a child who had spilled water on him. Then Jon methodically grasped the end of each stick as they continued to pour electricity into him with no apparent effect. As he did he looked directly into each of their eyes. The two men stopped and turned toward the others who were now five, as the driver had joined the group. "We shouldn't be doing this," they both said to their comrades. Jon walked around them.

The men in the group began to fire their weapons at Jon who had now surrounded himself with an energy shield which stopped and melted the bullets as they hit the shield.

The two men who had advanced on Jon with the electrical shock sticks did not move. The rest threw down their weapons and turned to flee. Suddenly an electrical lariat surrounded them. It knocked them all to the floor. They were stunned and unable to move. Jon went over and touched each of them for a few seconds.

Just as quickly as the five had dropped to the ground, they all got up and stood there as if waiting for instructions as to what to do.

Jon turned and walked out of the building's door followed quietly by each of the men walking in an orderly file. Around the side of the building he found the two black SUVs where the assassins had planned to use them for what would have been the men's get away.

- - -

As the two black SUVs approached the White House complex, the lead vehicle turned into the entrance to the reserve parking at the Eisenhower Executive Office building. Stopping at the gate, a Marine Sentry approached the vehicle and asked what business they had in the building. Jon handed the Marine a blank piece of paper and as the Marine took it Jon touched his hand and mentally transferred the information that he, Jon Sullivan, had been invited to attend a meeting of the National Security Council. The Marine quietly turned and disappeared into the guard shack. In seconds he returned and advised Jon the building administrator had been told plans had changed and that Jon was not coming. The Marine said if he could verify Jon's identity and that of his entourage, he would get them the badges they would need to have in order to gain access to where the NSC was meeting. Upon request Jon collected all the IDs from the seven men and handed those along with his own to the Marine. Again the Marine disappeared into the guard shack only to return with access badges and everyone's IDs'. "Sir," the Marine said to Jon, "your contingent are already members of NSA so there is no problem. Thank you, sir." He stepped back and the gate was opened for them to pass.

"Imagine that," Jon said out of the side of his mouth. "All you guys are NSA folks. Who would have imagined?"

Then with a smile on his face, Jon drove the lead black SUV into the secure parking area. After the second SUV parked beside them, they all, with Jon at the head, proceeded to enter the building and go to the Indian Treaty Room. This room was originally the Navy's library and a reception area. Because of its rich marble wall panels, elaborate marbled floors and gold leaf ornamentation, this room cost more per square foot than any other room in the building. Two Marines stood guard at the entrance of the room. Upon seeing the badges worn by Jon and the others, they opened the doors for everyone to enter.

Everyone sitting at the unusually long conference table turned to look at who was entering. The general had shared with the group just moments before that Jon would not be attending because of another situation taking priority. The general, in particular, turned as white as a ghost when Jon entered the room with the very men who were sent out to deal with him.

"Mr. President," Jon politely said as he returned the President's nod. "Good to have you here Mr. Sullivan," returned President Foster as he greeted Jon. The President glared at the general. "We were told you would not be able to meet with us. I am glad things have changed to allow you to come."

Smiling at the group Jon said, "Thank you Mr. President, fortunately I was able to overcome the obstacles that threatened to prevent me from attending." Jon and his six companions sat along the side wall, quietly to await his opportunity to speak. Each one of Jon's new companions sat at attention staring straight ahead.

Sitting at the unusually long mahogany table were those attending the NSC meeting. They were the following:

President: George Foster
Vice President: Dick Cleaver
Secretary of State: Hillary Burns
Secretary of Defense: Robert Osterline
Assistant to the President for National Security Matters: Elliot Jules
Chairmen of Joint Chief of Staff: General Richard Kline
Director of the NSA: General James Russert
Chief of Staff: Andy Spade
Counsel to the President: Alberto Morendez
Assistant to the President for Economic Affairs: Lawrence Davis
Special Assistant for the President: Zbignew Crezinskew

No one was more surprised at the entourage entering with Jon than General Russert. Jon could not help but be amused at the general's reaction. Jon had not let on to anyone except Peter as Jon was leaving about his scans of those who had come to the party at the Slovaks and that they had revealed the general was, in fact, an alien. Jon settled into his seat as the National Security Council finished their opening comments.

The president turned slowly to Jon as he addressed the members of the council." Fellow members of the council, it is time for us to address a most important subject." Everyone was focused on the president as he revealed what was to become a most Earth-shaking event and one which would change the course of history one way or the other.

The president turned to General Russert. "General, I know and appreciate the time and resources the NSA has put forth in trying to detect and protect the United States from alien intrusion." The general nodded in the affirmative nervously, as every eye in the room was now focused on the general and with excited anticipation as to what this direction of conversation would take.

"Thank you, Mr. President," the general replied again glancing furtively at Jon, his staff of assassins sitting obediently alongside Jon and then back at the president and his colleagues'.

"Yes, General, yes," the president continued. "We are at a time of great unrest around the world. The last thing we need is to have a foreign intrusive alien presence determined to make the worst of our own self caused inflictions."

Now everyone was focused on what the president was saying.

"Mr. Jon Sullivan has been given permission to come here as a representative of an alien race whose presence is already here among us."

The council members turned to one another, looking around the room and at Jon and his entourage. "What… ?" some were blurting out. "How could that be?" others were asking. "Is this a joke… ?" one member uttered. Shock and even outrage filled the council chambers. For several minutes the verbal and body language disbelief raged on. Some stood up and began to pack up their papers when the president quietly said, "Gentlemen and Madam Burns." However, his initial attempt to re-establish decorum failed. Speaking louder, and louder trying to get attention over the mumbling disbelief of his colleagues, the president suddenly began to beat on the table with his fists. Finally as the council members began to quiet down and members began to return to their seats, silence prevailed. "Gentlemen and Madam Burns," the president again began. "The proof of the pudding is in the eating."

Suddenly General Russert rose from his seat. "Mr. President, I must protest this most unusual and out of order procedure. To bring some nobody into the council and attempt to pass him off as some alien representative when in fact I am aware that this man Jon Sullivan is nothing but an unemployed carpenter, is an insult to the intelligence of everyone on this council. I move that this meeting be adjourned and you allow the NSA to properly interview Mr. Sullivan so that my fellow council members do not have to waste their time in such a charade."

"Yes, yes," several council members chimed in. Others sat in their seats wondering if their president had just gone off the deep end and could he survive such a ridiculous claim.

"General, sit down," the president directed the general. The entire table turned silent waiting on which direction this discussion was going to take.

The president turned to Jon. "Mr. Sullivan, would you care to clarify matters here?"

Jon stood up and slowly approached the council table between General Russert and the Chairman of the Joint

Chief of Staff General Kline. Looking across the table and then around it to catch everyone's eye, Jon began.

"Gentleman and Madam Burns I do understand your alarm and disbelief of the likelihood an alien or an alien representative could be standing in your presence. Yet you should understand. Certainly you are aware of the billions of dollars your country alone, not including the rest of your world has spent seeking contact with alien worlds. You bombard the air space throughout the universe seeking contact. Can you be so appalled to find aliens contacting you? You in effect open the front doors of your homes and invite the outside to come in. Then when they do you act surprised and alarmed."

Jon moved slowly around the council table brushing gently up against everyone in the council. "There is an old adage. "Be careful who you seek lest they find you! In addition, when they come they may not be so polite as to introduce themselves until they are good and ready."

Suddenly the Secretary of State spoke up. "Mr. President, do we have to sit here and listen to this man's rhetoric?"

"Yes, Mr. President?" joined in secretary of defense Osterline. "If all this is about is to hear some whacko I am appalled it got this far."

Everyone seemed on the edge of their seat, that is everyone except Zbignew Crezinskew. He had remained seated quietly even when the rest of the council was going crazy over the president's suggestion Jon represented an alien race.

Suddenly Mr. Zbignew Crezinskew stood up and spoke. "Fellow council members, I have great regard for the intelligence of our president. I do not believe this gentleman was allowed in here only because of his words."

Respect for Mr. Crezinskew was great. He had a long sterling reputation with many previous administrations and his words were often noted as being able to cut through chaff and expose the wheat.

Mr. Crezinskew continued. "General Russert, you claim that, for some reason we are not yet aware of, NSA knows of this man. Then you try to demean him by referring to him as an unemployed carpenter." Then slowly as he spoke, Crezinskew stared at the general. "I believe we all here know of a man who once was an unemployed carpenter; one who many believe was the Son of God!"

Suddenly the council room was again silent.

Crezinskew then turned toward Jon, smiled and gave him a nod to continue. "Mr. Sullivan. I guess you could say we, or at least most of us are doubting Thomas's. To use an analogy can you show us your nail pierced hands?" With that said Crezinskew sat down. Everyone was now focusing on Jon.

Jon smiled. "Yes, of course. That is a reasonable request. However despite what powers I show you I am not a Messiah." Then he added, "Neither am I the Devil." Jon was now standing between the Chief of Staff and the counsel to the president. As he squeezed between them, he said, "Excuse me." He just kept walking straight out into the middle of the table. The members of the council were aghast.

"Oh my god."

"What the… ?" Similar expressions of disbelief filled the room as Jon stood in the middle of the table half of his body above the tabletop and half below it. Several council members had to peek under the table to see what had happened to Jon's lower body.

As the council members sat there clutching their paperwork or their brief cases in disbelief, Jon spoke. "It is important for you to hear my message and to be engaged with it. To do otherwise is to cause an end to your species. My ability to manipulate molecular structure is only a benign ability compared to what else I can do."

"This is nothing but parlor magic," shouted General Russert as he stood up. "I will not sit here and listen to this garbage." With that said the general stood up and pushed back his seat. He turned to leave. The men who had accompanied Jon into the room, at Jon's mental command, had already moved toward the general and formed a barricade preventing him from leaving. The general addressed several of his men by name. "Gary, Alan, what in the hell do you think you are doing."

Rather than speaking, the men forced the general back down in his seat.

Then when the General was back in his seat one of the group, the one called Alan spoke. "You sent us out this morning to stop and if necessary to kill this man. That was wrong"

The General blustered and raving shouted out they would all be court marshaled. Stunned by this sudden turn of events, the rest of the council sat shocked over the accusation made by his own men against the general.

The General blustered some more and then declared, "This is nothing but parlor magic tricks and you fools are being taken in by it."

"Parlor tricks?" responded Jon as his body moved upward without any assistance as if it was pulled straight up on the table until he was actually standing on top of the solid council tabletop looking down at the council members. "Is that what you think, General? General, who are you really?"

The council room was so quiet you could have heard a pin drop. Suddenly Jon's body began a transformation. "Do not move from your seats," Jon said as his body began an evil looking transformation. The grey grotesque arm that Betsy had witnessed was now becoming a monstrous looking foreign thing. He spun around looking at all the council members many of whom wet themselves at the horrific sight before them. A gray hideous thing with a head that resembled a vicious creature out of some evil science fiction story with teeth as long as they were hideous replaced Jon. It spoke with a deep growl. "Do not move from your seats," it said, repeating Jon's command but now in a sinister, deep evil growl.

Now moving closer to the general, it spoke again. "You are now the one undergoing an attack alien."

The members of the council sat in fear for their lives and looking at each other as they heard the monster accuse one of their members, General Russert, of being some alien.

Then before their unbelieving eyes, they watched the general's flesh fall away, and a green-looking thing with an axe-shaped head begin to appear. It turned. It growled as it stood to face its adversary. Then as quickly as Jon had transformed into a monster, he turned back to his original self as the green alien was stepping out of the human flesh it had dressed in. The alien was now in a deep growl and

Jon knew what was coming next. Before the green alien could expectorate, Jon shot a green light into what was the outward appearance of the general as well as the green alien thing. The green alien creature began to crystallize as the green ray began to remove all heat from its being. It froze where it stood and continued to crystallize until this frozen concoction couldn't stand under its own weight and crumbled to the floor.

Jon disappeared for a second and reappeared standing off to the side of the table beside the assistant to the president for national security matters Elliot Jules. The council members whipped their heads around as Jon reappeared. "I have the ability to scan for human as well as alien presence. There is no other human here who is an alien to the human race except that part of me which has been given certain powers.

"Now gentleman and Lady Burns, you need to understand why I am here as well as what you must decide. For your decision may very well determine the fate of the world."

Suddenly the president's chief of staff clutched his chest. "Andy," Alberto Morendez, counsel to the president, called out to him. Quickly everyone turned to look at Andy who had now fallen over face down on the table. Those around him stood up. Someone shouted to call for help. Another council member said he knew CPR.

"Quiet," ordered Jon. "Sit down." Everyone did as they were told. Suddenly Jon had moved without even trying to Andy's side. Jon put his hand on Andy's back. The blue-white rays began to encircle Andy. It was but brief seconds and Andy sat back up. He looked around him with an expression that asked what happened.

"Mr. Spade, you were having a heart attack. Your system is now functioning in a more optimal way and you will not need to follow up on the treadmill test you are scheduled to take on Doctors' orders although I understand you will anyway. Just don't share what happened here or the Doctor may be forced to commit you." Jon smiled slightly as he resumed his previous position in the blink of an eye.

With that said, Andy now looking refreshed and healthy. Andy looked at Jon. "Thank you."

Jon continued. "Getting back to the issue at hand, you all here as well as a handful of NSA agents are now aware there are aliens on planet Earth. Please also beware, that fact has no bearing on why I am here representing another alien species except as it may impact the well-being on the planet from which the aliens I represent live."

After a slight pause, and after looking around the council table and seeing he had everyone's apt attention, Jon continued. "Why do the aliens which I represent care about what happens on Earth? "Because," Jon continued, answering his own rhetorical question, "they have the same fears about you that you do about terrorists."

Again Jon paused to see if what he was sharing was sinking in. The Chairman of the Joint Chief of Staff General Richard Kline raised his hand as if asking permission to speak.

"Yes, General?" Jon asked encouraging the general.

"Ah, well, ah," the general stammered, "we are not terrorists so how could that be a concern?"

"You, I guess you mean the United States general?"

"Well, yes, of course," the general responded.

"Hmm," uttered Jon. "So you do not think another world should look upon the United States as a terrorist organization?"

"Well, of course not," offered Secretary of Defense Robert Osterline. "We don't invade countries to change their way of life. We don't bomb innocent women and children. Throughout our history the United States of America has been the deliverer of progress to those such as Japan, and Germany, as an example, even though the United States was viciously attacked and lost many lives to overcome such aggressors." Around the table council members were nodding in agreement to what the Secretary said.

"So, Mr. Secretary acknowledging you make a valid point and perhaps that is why I am here talking to you rather than other governments, what are you doing in the Middle East?"

"We are trying to save millions of people from death and worse imposed on them by dictators who care nothing about the value of human life and care only about their own wealth and power," the Secretary offered this time with more confidence in his voice given support by the body language of his fellow council members.

"So, you saw a threat by others which you unilaterally decided to take action against to protect the citizens of other countries? Do I understand you correctly?"

"Well, yes, that is correct. As well we were taking action against those who threatened our way of life and via terrorism posed a threat to our country and everything for which we stand."

"Yes, that is it. That is it exactly," chimed in other council members.

"Well, good," responded Jon with a smile. "Then you should be able to understand why I am here representing another way of life!"

"Wha… ?" uttered Hillary Burns, Secretary of State. "I ahh we don't follow your reasoning."

"Well, Secretary Burns, the life form I represent views you as terrorists."

Jon gave the council time to let that sink in. The council members talked to each other in rapid succession in disbelief anyone could think of The United States as a terrorist country.

"Mr. Sullivan, how can that be? On what basis do you accuse the United States of being a terrorist country?" Vice President Cleaver asked.

Turning to the secretary of state, "Secretary Burns, would you not agree," Jon asked, "that terrorism is the calculated use of violence, or the threat of violence, against civilians in order to attain goals that are political or religious or ideological in nature? And that this is done through intimidation or coercion or instilling fear?"

"Well, yes of course, I agree but how does that apply to the United States?"

Jon paused for a period of time so that his response would not be lost in the murmuring and chit chat at the council table as members attempted to understand the point Jon was making.

"You represent a country of cartels that intimidate abuse and exploit your own citizens."

The assistant to the president for economic affairs spoke up. "That is a ridiculous comment." Suddenly and after the harsh looks of his fellow council members hoping not to incite Jon to another demonstration of his power or worse, Lawrence Davis shrank back in his seat, looked out apologetically at the others and weakly said, "Ahh, I mean I was just thinking."

Jon could not help but laugh. "Really Mr. Davis. Would you be so kind as to give us the definition of a cartel?"

Now everyone was shooting daggers at Davis with their eyes.

Davis now regretting he had opened his mouth stumbled to answer the question put to him. "Well, Ahh a cartel is a trust or a collusive international association of independent enterprises formed to monopolize production and distribution of a product or service, and control prices."

Satisfied with his answer, Davis smiled weakly at his colleagues.

Looking directly at Davis, Jon asked, "Mr. Davis, does the association have to be necessarily international in scope?"

"Well, ahh um, I guess it wouldn't have to be as long as it meet the other premise formed to monopolize production and distribution of a product or service, and control prices."

"Hmm," Jon thought out loud, "so you would agree then a cartel could be defined as any combination of independent business organizations formed to regulate production, pricing, and marketing of goods by its members?"

"Yes," Davis said as he thought about it, "that would be a good definition."

"That is a good definition defining the drug trade then Mr. Davis, is it not?"

"Ahh well ahh yes," Davis said hoping Jon would stop this dialogue with him.

Jon spun around to face Morendez. "Well, then Mr. Morendez is there a drug cartel?"

"Yes," Alberto Morendez, counsel to the president succinctly responded.

"Okay," agreed Jon as he shook his head in agreement. "Well, how about pharmaceuticals Mr. Morendez, is there a pharmaceutical cartel?"

"What?" "No the pharmaceutical industry provides the new medicines that allow us longer lives and cures and the ability to live with otherwise horrendous conditions." Counsel Morendez quickly retorted.

"I see," said Jon softly. "Mr. Morendez was not your mother told recently that there was no cure for the arthritis she has?"

"Yes," responded Morendez surprised Jon would know such a fact.

"Yet for fifty-four years she had been told by at least thirteen arthritis specialists—all recommended by the Arthritis Foundation—to take various drugs for the pain and go home and live with it. "Fifty four years of thousands of dollars and doctor's bills for medication that did not work. Is that not true Mr. Morendez?"

"Well, yes," Morendez weakly responded wondering how this person would know this. "But it was the best we knew to do."

"Was it?" questioned Jon. "Who does the drug studies to determine their value Mr. Morendez?"

"Ahh, usually the drug companies."

Jon spoke. "Not only is the pharmaceutical industry able to control consumer markets, they also control political leadership through campaign contributions; and also control the so-called regulatory agencies of government. Tight control of government by this cartel is its ability to have legislation drafted and passed that gives a government mandate for products."

"You know, or should know, products are on the market that may be unsafe and ineffective, due to inadequate testing or regulation."

"On what basis do you say that Mr. Sullivan?" challenged the vice president.

"The answer Mr. Vice President is your own FDA whose standard for approval is only 30 percent effectiveness. Under such circumstances, what confidence should there be that the government "of, by, and for the people" is doing its job of protecting citizens against the "profits at any cost?"

"Tell me please," Jon asked the council, "what evidence contradicts the charge that the pharmaceutical industry is a cartel?'

The council was silent.

"So also, I would challenge you to show me how the insurance industry is not a cartel. The United States' medical insurance cartel is the prime reason healthcare cost for the people of this country is twice that of other industrialized countries while the overall quality is half. Your lack of action as governing politicians of this country you claim to love so much is bankrupting the country.

"Wait just a minute," said Vice President Cleaver in an aggressive tone. "We have some of the best medical practices and Doctors in the world. People from other countries flock here to get specialized treatments from the best."

Looking directly at the vice president, Jon said, "Yes the United States has some of the best, the very best. Please tell me who has access to the best? The Saudi Sheiks, the multimillionaires? What about the common citizen who has trouble affording the most basic of medicines and is fought tooth and nail over treatment or procedures needed to save a dying child?"

Jon waited for a response. There was none and he continued. "According to the World Health Organization, the US ranks fifteenth in infant mortality and fifty-fourth overall. Since 1947, when President Harry Truman tried to implement universal healthcare, the AMA and now the Medical insurance industry have selfishly destroyed any real competition in the medical industry. If the United States is truly a moral and religious country, cost effective and high quality healthcare should be a right for every citizen."

After a slight pause and no response, Jon continued again. "Did you not say here that terrorism is done through intimidation or coercion or instilling fear?"

The council members all turned their heads away from Jon and stared at the table in front of them.

"Gentleman and lady Burns, you all have a right to your own opinions but you do not have a right to your own facts."

Finally Secretary of State Hillary Burns looked up at Jon. "So you are saying we condone acts of terrorism on our own people when it comes from within?"

Jon looked directly at her with a warm smile, hoping at least one person is getting it. "Yes, condoning it so long as you all get a slice of the rewards to the detriment of your fellow citizens."

"What?" the vice president said, responding to the Secretary of State's apparent agreement with what Jon said. "Look Mr. Sullivan or whoever you are, we may not have a perfect form of government but it is the best in town."

"Well, Mr. Vice President, like I said, you are welcomed to your opinion but not your own facts. You promote incestuous relationships within your political legal and business entities that threatened the viable existence of what you call democracy. The fact is the alien world I come from wants no part of it. They do not want to see your brand of terrorism permeating where they live."

General Kline raised his hand again. "Yes, General," acknowledged Jon.

"I am not suggesting we want this kind of action you accuse us of, but what can we do to prevent you, the aliens you represent from destroying us?"

The heads of council members quickly turned to the general not believing what he was saying.

"That is a good question, General. The fact is although they are many evolutions away from where you are now, they feel we, you and I, are more alike than we are different. While destruction of your world is up to you and independent of any commonness they feel, the one prime directive is that you not be allowed to invade their society with your terrorist ways.

"Look," spoke up the vice president, "I don't care if you are all powerful, you have no right to call us terrorists.

For the most part we are law abiding, religiously faithful people."

"Are you?" Jon questioned. "You allow the cartels: drug, pharmaceutical, insurance, legal and on and on to take advantage of others and for whose benefit. It is for your benefit Mr. Vice President. Is it common knowledge you have accepted drug cartel money? How many know you have worked behind the scenes to massacre good solid health benefits for the people you represent in trade for, most recently, $150,000 dollars. Should I go on?"

The vice president shriveled down in his seat as the president and others glowered at him.

"Oh don't look so accusingly," Jon berated the council. "You all have done similarly in the same or different ways."

The council looked like a group of elementary students who had just been scolded for doing things behind the teacher's back, thinking they could get away with it.

"You promote sex, violence in language and deed on your televisions. You tiptoe around providing good sound education and promote videos and TV shows that glorify gangs, drugs, larceny, and all sorts of violence. You tacitly allow sex trades, children pornography, and gang violence by not addressing such things directly. You pass laws—laws to protect the wealthy to protect you from the actions of the poor or less fortunate. You make your decisions under the veil of doing what is right, but underneath the veil is money and power, which is the essence of what drives you. Please understand, the alien race I represent, while willing to help, will not allow you to expand your terrorism into the universe."

"Willing to help?" asked the president.

"Yes, they are willing to help you to dismantle your tools of war, assist you through my presence and demonstration of power to convince otherwise unwilling nations to change more into a world of common goals designed for the peace and betterment of all. They are willing to share medical miracles and a variety of innovations to create a better life. But"—Jon paused and looked at each of the council members—"not without a willingness on your part to give up your selfish ways and look for the common good."

Suddenly a voice yet heard from for a while spoke out. "Mr. Sullivan what is time frame for our world to become an acceptable partner in the universe?"

"Mr. Crezinskew, providing Earth agrees to several mandates, such a decision would be made after twenty years from this date as to whether Earth should be destroyed of the human species or has achieved a level of existence no longer posing a threat."

"And those mandates, sir?" Crezinskew further inquired.

"First, that all technology designed to solve the problem of interplanetary travel be immediately stopped. Second that this council unanimously agrees to go after and dismantle the cartels not in the best interests of the people, and third, Mr. Crezinskew, one I believe you will embrace, that this council embraces the concept of a one world order."

Jon stopped and stared at Crezinskew, waiting for his response.

"Well, there are some who do believe in the concept of one world order as voiced by a group called the Trilateral Commission."

"Yes, Mr. Crezinskew. However, there are many who believe every major crisis we face today is directly attributable to policies put forth and executed by members of this Trilateral Commission: Banking/lending/mortgage crisis, energy/gas price crisis, food/shortage/price crisis. Is that a possibility?"

"Well, certainly, Mr. Sullivan there are naysayers about any new approach to world problems."

"Just so long as it is very clear, Mr. Crezinskew, the hierarchy of what a Trilateral Commission or any other organization established tries to do is, people first, then the industry or organization, and last, the government entity running things."

Then Jon turned to the president. "Mr. President, thank you for allowing me to be here today. I will leave how I can be contacted with your secretary, and I expect I will hear from you as to the council's decision within thirty days. At that time, assuming there is agreement, I will schedule to meet once again with the council to work out the details of a plan. At such a meeting, I may bring some other alien representatives to help."

"What if we can't come to an agreement within thirty days?" asked vice president Cleaver.

"Then, Vice President Cleaver, those who cannot agree and/or will not work vigorously to do as I have laid out for you will be destroyed. It is just that simple."

The president quickly stood up and shook Jon's hand. He pumped it enthusiastically. "Thank you Jon. We are, as can be understood, quite bedazzled by your presentation. We will be in touch, and I look forward to working with you."

"Thank you Mr. President." With that said, Jon turned and left the council room. The seven men who had followed him in followed him out.

THE EPILOGUE

"Wow, Jon this has been one incredible summer." Jon looked over from the driver's seat of the Mercedes convertible they were driving back to North Carolina. "Yes, sweetheart, it would have been hard to imagine another one like this."

The top was down, and Jon and Betsy were enjoying the warm day and the air blowing through their hair.

Jon had filled both Betsy and Peter in on the details of his meeting with the council after he had gotten back to what was now their Washington home from his meeting. The next morning they wasted no time in packing up and saying good-bye to everyone in order to get back as soon as they could to Carthage. After all the hugs, tears, best wishes, and a promise to be back in Washington within a month, they had headed out in the Mercedes convertible.

"Jon," Betsy asked, "do you think the council will agree to your terms?"

"Betsy, I believe so. I certainly hope so. Not doing so would be suicide."

"Jon?" Betsy asked as she laid her head back on the seat's head rest and let the wind flow through her hair.

"Yes, sweetheart?"

"Well, Jon it is sad David could not be with us to share this time."

Suddenly catching movement in the rearview mirror, Jon looked over at Betsy with a huge grin. Looking back at the road, he said, "Well, I have an idea. David will once again be playing an active part in our lives."

"Oh, I hope so, darling," Betsy said with her eyes closed and enjoying the ambiance of the ride and the wind in her hair.

Looking back at the rearview mirror, Jon said, "Yes, I am sure we will be seeing David again.

As the car proceeded down the road, there was David sitting in the backseat with his arms outstretched across the seat, his eyes closed and a big smile on his face.

ABOUT THE AUTHOR

David Lawrence is a retired engineer who lives in the country community of Mocksville, North Carolina. He lives there with his wife, Nancy. They have four adult children and seven grandchildren. This book is the result of years of fascination with Earth's efforts to send communications into outer space, inviting whomever to communicate back. In *Alien Brother*, David writes about how one alien race has been monitoring Earth's technological developments and how it handles their increasing fear that the way Earth handles its political and social problems may soon invade the universe with a chaos that they are not willing to accept.

AUTHOR REVIEWS - ALIEN BROTHER

"Lawrence's voice is unlike any I've read in years—wholly original, but echoing with emotional registers reminiscent of Woolf, Lispector, and Baldwin. Alien Brother walks the tightrope between metaphor and clarity, crafting a narrative that feels both intensely personal and quietly universal. There's a rhythmic quality to the writing that lulled me in, and the way the story treats death—not as a clean.

Julien Hart

*****

"There's no question Lawrence is a gifted writer. Some of his sentences are stunning, and the atmosphere he builds is thick with emotion. That said, I found the structure a bit loose. At times, the narrative meanders, and I had to reorient myself more than once. Still, there are sections—especially toward the middle—that are breathtaking. With a tighter form, this could be a literary knockout."

Christine Yeats

*****

"What makes Alien Brother exceptional is not just its poetic prose, but its emotional integrity. Lawrence doesn't reach for easy answers or grand resolutions. Instead, he lets the rawness of absence, the mystery of identity, and the strangeness of memory unravel at their own pace. There's a rare kind of grace in that. I was deeply moved."

Anjali Mehra

"From the first paragraph, Lawrence's prose hums with the kind of intimate emotional weight that feels lived-in and real. Alien Brother isn't just a story—it's an experience, one that pulls you through love, alienation, death, and rediscovery with a deft hand. Every scene was textured, dreamlike, yet never indulgent. This novel shook me."

Mira Delaney

*****

"There's a tender emotional thread running through this novel that I appreciated. The grief is real, the existential questioning relatable. I did find myself wishing for a firmer sense of plot—some chapters felt like fragments rather than part of a whole. That said, Lawrence's ability to express emotional dislocation is impressive, and I'm curious to see what he writes next."

Diana Nkomo

*****

"What Lawrence has achieved in Alien Brother is a balancing act between the speculative and the achingly human. He writes like a poet channeling a mystic—sharp turns of phrase, piercing insight, and surreal juxtapositions that still make sense emotionally. I was particularly taken by the emotional honesty of the narrator, and how the surreal events served not as spectacle but as metaphor. This book deserves attention."

Leena Zhao

"This book is a slow burn in the best way—moody, atmospheric, and brimming with strange beauty. There's a hallucinatory quality to the story, as if you're watching someone else's memories in real time. Lawrence explores grief with a kind of patience that's rare. He allows confusion to exist in the narrative, not as a flaw, but as a reflection of lived trauma. Just brilliant."

Sofia Reyes

*****

"Lawrence invites the reader into a deeply internal landscape, and once inside, you don't want to leave. His writing has that rare ability to disarm you—no grand declarations, just clean, resonant truth. The metaphor of alienation is worked so subtly into the bones of the narrative that it feels both literal and symbolic in every moment."

Noah Wells

*****

"Lawrence's style is distinctively literary, and that's both refreshing and challenging. The novel leans into abstraction in a way that may lose readers looking for clarity or resolution. But for those willing to sit with ambiguity, there's emotional payoff. I appreciated the thematic ambition, even if I didn't connect with every moment."

Theo Martinez

"It's rare to read a novel that feels handcrafted—not just written, but carved out of thought, memory, and sorrow. Lawrence's Alien Brother is like that. The tone is mournful without being morbid, playful in just the right moments, and piercingly sincere. It doesn't explain itself too much—it trusts you, the reader, to feel your way through. And I loved it for that."

Isaac Greenfield

*****